MAGICAL MIDLIFE
BATTLE

ALSO BY K.F. BREENE

MAGICAL MIDLIFE BATTLE

BY K.F. BREENE

CHAPTER 1
JESSIE

L ARGE WHITE VANS waited by the curb as I jogged down the steps of Ivy House. Trunks sat on the front lawn, waiting to be packed inside the vehicles by the gathered shifters and gargoyles. I stopped beside one of them, taking in the flurry of activity.

Sebastian wandered within the hustle and bustle, his head tilted down toward the electronic notebook in his hands. Every so often he'd stop at one of the trunks and peer inside, double-checking the contents. After giving a satisfied nod, he'd make a note and continue on.

"Ready?" Austin asked as he came up to me.

Wary expectation radiated through our bonds but didn't show on his face or interrupt the confidence in his bearing. If a person couldn't feel it, they would have no idea he was keyed up about our fast-approaching trip to his former pack.

"Yeah." But I still took a moment to survey the goings-on.

I wasn't worried about meeting Austin's family or his old pack—his grandma had told me not to waste my brain space on it, and given all we'd had to do, I'd gladly taken her advice—but we were heading toward a massive battle. We'd been up late and awake early these last few weeks, hard at work preparing for a full-on battle. It felt like I'd been constantly training.

There had only been a couple breaks, one for Edgar's flower show, where he'd showcased killer, poisonous flowers to non-magical people (he was now on flower show probation) and a date I'd taken Austin on to repay him for the fantastic dates he'd always planned for me. Other than that, it had all been fighting or magic, and I still felt like we were sorely underprepared.

At least we had something to show for our late-night magical work. The trunks of those cars were about to be stuffed full of potions, and Sebastian and I planned on making more once we got there. We needed to close the gap in magical resources between us and the enemy.

It was a very large gap.

Sebastian and Nessa had shared some numbers with us, harvested from their network. Momar was planning for annihilation. He had ground troops trained by his people, hired mercenaries, and an absolute crapload of mages. Some wouldn't be all that powerful, sure, but others were just shy of Sebastian's level.

We were magically outgunned—badly—and Sebastian wasn't even sure those were the most recent numbers.

Trepidation filled me, but I made sure none of it dripped through my various bonds and connections to my people. Now was the time for leadership to show strength. To show confidence, like Austin was doing. We had to hold up our heads and make it seem like we had zero reservations that we'd come out the victors.

Learning how to put on a front hadn't been easy for me. Thank God for Mimi's coaching.

And yes, Austin's grandmother had said I could call her Mimi. Well...more like demanded, then stared hostilely at me until I did so.

"Right. Okay," I said to myself, doing a quick mental checklist of what still needed to get loaded. I turned to Austin with a nod. "Ready."

We needed to check out Edgar's special project.

He put out his hand for me to go first, and I led the way around the house to the backyard. In addition to Edgar's project, I wanted to check out the grounds and make sure nothing was too terribly out of place. Dare to dream. The gnomes had become absolute terrors. Edgar really had stuck his foot in it when he'd allowed these little buggers to infest the place. It had become a real struggle not to lose my temper.

"Three waves, right?" I asked Austin, the grounds so far clear. "We're still traveling in three waves, starting tomorrow? We've changed the plans so many times, I'm not sure I remember the latest."

"Two waves, one day apart, four groups of people."

I took a deep breath. "Right. Groups one and two will leave from the Clinton Metropolitan Airport on a commercial flight, and groups three and four will leave from the magical landing strip in a jet, since it's too far to travel quickly on foot and we can't take the basajaunak through a Dick and Jane airport."

"Correct. Luggage—normal suitcases—will go with groups one and two, and trunks and the battle supplies will go in the private jets."

"Starting tomorrow," I said, my heart speeding up.

A flurry of anxiousness came through our bonds. "Starting tomorrow," he repeated.

I meant to reach back and take his hand, reassuring him that we'd face his past together, but blotches of red caught my eye as we turned the corner. Paper hearts attached to sticks had been embedded in the decorative gravel along the side of the house, the items all different sizes and heights. Tightly grouped together, they created a red sea of cardboard, the path to get through it winding and convoluted. Treacherous, if you knew what awaited you somewhere in the little voids that had absolutely been built into the otherwise densely packed Valentine's decorations.

"Dang it," I grumbled, coming to a stop and bracing my hands on my hips. "I don't have time for this. Edgar!" I yelled, feeling him on the back lawn. I amplified my voice with magic and tried again. "Edgar!"

I felt him sprint in my direction.

"I'm coming!" I heard faintly as he drew closer. "Coming, Jessie! Coming!"

"I mean..." I kicked at the first line of hearts, knocking them off-kilter. An evil little laugh came from somewhere in the sea of red. "This is nightmare-inducing. I thought the dolls were bad, but they at least aren't vindictive. They don't create booby traps and surprise attacks!"

"They probably would if you couldn't feel them," Austin said as Edgar came into view with his weird, loping sort of run. "You need to circumvent Ivy House's magic and expose the whereabouts of the gnomes on the property."

"I know. Hiding them from me is her funny little joke. She has dark humor, obviously. Sebastian suggested there might be something in the library that can help us figure it out, but we haven't had time lately. Dealing with the gnomes isn't as dire as preparing for the battle."

"Normally I would agree. Now that I'm standing in front of a sea of reinforced cardboard hearts, knowing murderous gnomes are lying in wait to chop something off as we pass through it, I'm waffling on what exactly is more important."

I couldn't help laughing as Edgar caught sight of the problem and slowed to take it all in.

"Oh, Jessie. This is not ideal," he said, on the edge of the heart forest. "No, indeed. I see now why you called me. Don't worry, I can handle this! I'll distract them so you can get across." He trudged into the fray, working hard to stomp down the sticks holding the hearts. "Here we go."

Knives and tiny swords rose above the hearts in three different locations. The hearts bumped forward as the little bodies pushed through them. Occasionally a pointed red hat appeared in an empty space. They beelined for Edgar, now trudging to the northeast corner with a determined expression, allowing us plenty of room to cross.

"Come on," I told Austin, not waiting to see if he'd follow as I kicked and stomped into the heart forest.

A high-pitched laugh rose from my right side. I

barely caught a glimpse of the red hat before the white of a beard came into view. A tiny machete swung above two paper hearts, cutting through the air at me.

"Crap!" I reacted without thinking, spraying it with the spell for elemental fire.

Unfortunately, that spell took a lot of concentration—concentration I didn't have at that moment. Something like magical acid manifested instead. It glopped down on top of the creature and the hearts around it.

Its laugh turned into a horrible wail. Paper hearts waved and shook as the creature ran for the edge, exploding out and then running for the back of the house. Up ahead, dolls jumped out of seemingly nowhere and the chase was on.

Sighing, I said, "Kingsley's territory is going to be a nice reprieve from the absolute weird that has become this house—"

I cut off as Austin grabbed me and swung me up over his shoulder in a fireman's hold. He started jogging through the hearts.

"That has *become* this house?" he asked incredulously, kicking at a little body that popped up. His toe connected with its bearded face. The gnome made a little *weeeee* sound as it flew five feet and crashed into a few of the hearts. "The house has always been weird.

This is downright insanity. How the hell are they hiding in the densely packed heart stick...things? It's like they have some sort of magical space-shifting ability..."

Edgar made an "aaiiiiiii" sound as Austin reached the other side of the maze, breathing harder than a tough alpha shifter really should have after a spat with gnomes. I couldn't help laughing as he put me down, out of breath as well, turning to check on Edgar.

"No, no, no," he said as he picked up a miniature weapon that one of the gnomes had clearly dropped. He had blood dripping down from a cut on his thigh. "That is no way to treat Uncle Edgar."

"Uncle Edgar?" Austin whispered.

Edgar turned into a swarm of insects and hovered across a patch of hearts before materializing again and slashing. His blade clanged into one of the gnomes, eliciting another little howl. Edgar chopped down at it a second time, turned, and chopped at another one that was trying to crowd him from behind.

"Looks like he's figured out how to deal with the gnomes," Austin said, his firm pressure on the small of my back a cue to get moving.

"So then why hasn't he gotten *rid* of the gnomes?"

"Likely the same reason none of you have—he's had a big job to do. Let's hope he at least saw that through."

"None of...*you* have?" I crinkled my nose at him as

we walked. "You're not planning to help with the gnomes?"

"Absolutely not, no."

I laughed and shook my head. "He did manage his tasks, though," I said. "The non-gnome ones."

"We shall see," he said darkly.

Since the flower show incident, which he'd had to help clean up along with the rest of us, Austin didn't have much faith in poor Edgar. And while I saw his point, he also hadn't seen what Edgar had come up with in these last few weeks. I, however, had been monitoring his operation closely.

"The new healer has been a godsend," I said as we crossed the grass and I ignored the doll sentries. I might not like them, but they fulfilled an important duty in ensuring the gnomes didn't make it to the back door. Now if they could just watch the side yard as well... "She and the basajaunak have really helped Edgar with those flowers. I think it's one of the main reasons she agreed to stay."

The new healer, who called herself Indigo because she didn't like her birth name Skye, had answered the accidental summons I'd placed in the basajaunak lands. She'd been understandably hesitant about joining our strange team of mythical creatures.

In the beginning, she'd bonded most with the

basajaunak, walking through the wood with them and discussing the plants used in natural remedies and salves. Then she'd surprised us all by glomming on to Edgar. She was enraptured with his magical flowers, and I suspected she'd only agreed to go to Kingsley's territory with us because she wanted to see them at work.

The path through the flower display at the edge of the grass was wider than usual, and gaping holes now existed in what had been a stranglehold of flora. Edgar was letting the basajaunak eat at will so they could eventually redo this area. The yard was not at its finest.

At the moment, none of us cared, not even Edgar.

"I'm coming, Jessie. Here I come!"

Speaking of, he ran up behind us, bleeding out of a few gashes and missing half a pant leg.

"Don't bother healing me." He waved at me as he loped by. "Indigo can handle that. Save your strength."

"Save my strength for what?" I asked in a wispy voice.

After walking through the trees a ways, we emerged into a decently large clearing. Black plastic tubs covered the space. In each grew a seedling, the bright green stalks anywhere from six inches to two feet tall, with leaves and little branches starting to emerge from the sides. None of them swayed like killer plants 2.0

through 2.5 had. They didn't grow diagonally, either, like 2.6 through 2.8. In fact, they didn't seem to move at all, despite the soft breeze blowing through the clearing.

Edgar stood in the very middle of the group with his hands clasped in front of him. Indigo stood a little behind him, her hand on his shoulder, looking at us quietly. She needed touch as a means to heal, using plants and natural remedies to sometimes aid her magical process.

Basajaunak drifted toward us within the wood. Those closest stopped at the tree line to watch and listen.

I started the same way I always did. "What've we got?"

Edgar gave the same reply he always delivered out of the gate. "Yes, Jessie, thanks for coming." He then bowed. "Alpha Steele, lovely to have you." He spread out his hand, accidentally bumping Indigo. "Meet the Violator."

I lifted my eyebrows. "What?"

"This is the new generation of assault flower," he replied. "Attack flower 3.0, so perfect I want to weep at the mastery of it. I am calling it the Violator."

"They each have names, though," Indigo said, her voice high and childlike, matching her small frame and somewhat mousy appearance. A smattering of freckles dusted her button nose, on which sat large, black-framed, rectangular glasses. Thick bangs covered her forehead, and her brown hair was loosely pulled up into a messy bun. "They aren't all called the Violator. That's just their group name."

"Oh yes, correct." Edgar nodded dramatically. "Indigo is correct—how silly of me to forget. We have given each flower a name, as befits a friend. So here is…" He hesitated as he hovered over the seedling near his blood-crusted leg.

"Ethel," Indigo helped.

"Yes, right. Ethel. And we have Florence the Flower over here—"

"Alliteration was necessary with that one," Indigo said with a little smile.

"Ton, over there. Jan, Cathy-Jane, Marsha-Marsha-Marsha… Let's see. Wayne and Garth—"

"Party on." Indigo lifted a fist.

"Yes. They *are* rambunctious. Dean and Billie-Jo. Jolene—"

"'*Jolene, Jo*-lene,'" Indigo sang, the tune from Dolly Parton's song.

"Very musical, that flower," Edgar responded. "She really likes singing."

Austin had gone still, his automatic defense against the strangeness of this house and its crew.

"Let's move on," I said firmly. More basajaunak gathered around, silently watching. "I notice that they are still. Too still. They aren't reacting to the breeze."

"Oh yes," Edgar said, now walking through the stalks. "That is because they are dormant at the moment. They are just *taking it in*, as it were. Learning how to coexist. They interact, sure, but only when prompted. Once they age up and are settled in one location, they'll act like normal flowers until they're either among friends or enemies."

"How long do we have until they settle in?" Austin asked.

"If stable, about a week. Meaning, if we take them to Alpha Kingsley's tomorrow and quickly find them a new home, they'll be active adolescents within a week. If we do not find them a home quickly, then it will take longer."

I put a hand on Austin's arm. "These aren't like the other attack flowers, which only tolerated the people they imprinted on in their youth. Obviously that wouldn't work if we had them around Kingsley's territory."

"Correct. Yes, thank you, Jessie." Edgar bowed slightly. "I have learned from my mistakes, Sir Alpha. Have no fear—with help from the basajaunak and Indigo, I have baked a sort of safety system into these flowers. If anyone they know vouches for a stranger, then they will treat that stranger as a friend. Until the stranger tries to do them harm, of course, and then they will attempt to kill that stranger in the bloodiest way possible. They are not very forgiving to bullies or enemies, these flowers."

Austin's eyebrows climbed.

"And!" Edgar lifted a spindly finger. "*And* their transportation pots"—he bent down to pat the plastic tub of one of the seedlings—"will allow us to take them home if Alpha Kingsman doesn't want to keep them. They will allow us to dig them up as long as they feel their pots near them."

"Kings*ley,*" Indigo corrected him softly.

"Yes." Edgar inclined his head.

"You see…" Indigo stepped forward. Her toe hit a pot, though, which made her stumble. She reached out to brace herself but must've realized she'd likely crush a flower that way. Instead, she completed the fall, flopping down between two flowers and flailing a little.

"Whoopsie." Edgar hurried to help her up. "That pot jumped out in front of you! I saw it. Silly flower."

Indigo's face turned red, and she smiled in embarrassment. "I'm a little clumsy. My mommy always said, 'Thank the Lord you got the gift of healing, child, or you'd be in a bad way from those two left feet.'"

"What doesn't kill us, as they say," Edgar told her.

"You see," she started again, "the flowers in this batch and the one before it really love people. They love attention and fun. They love children and laughter. We've brought a couple into town and coaxed them out of their stupor. They had the best time! As long as the shifters in Kingsley's pack make an effort to visit the flowers, even just once, they will become friends. If the flowers are treated as part of the community, they'll lovingly guard the perimeter or—what they'd like more than anything—the parks or nurseries. They're designed to protect the community spaces of the pack. The town. The homes. The gardens. The vulnerable."

Edgar's grin was sly. "And the Annihilator was created for the wilds. For the first line of defense. For *destruction.*"

I stilled. "The Annihilator?"

"It's our secret project. Those flowers can be a little...temperamental, but we've put in a couple fail-safes that should work. They really should. Don't worry, Jessie, you're going to love it."

It seemed I hadn't been keeping as close of an eye on the situation as I'd previously thought.

CHAPTER 2

JESSIE

THE NEXT MORNING, I was still stewing about the Annihilator flowers as I stood on the porch, watching the final preparations for our departure. To my utter shock, Austin had agreed to take them with us. He figured it was safe enough if they were kept out in the wilds, where only the shifters' sentries ventured. The flowers would imprint on them, wreak havoc on any intruders, and all would be well.

I'd reminded him that he was operating on the assumption that the flowers wouldn't grow legs and terrorize the community. He'd assumed I was joking.

I most certainly was not joking.

This was his show, though. I'd take lead with the gargoyles, and he would take lead with the shifters—including his interactions with his brother. So now psycho-killer flowers were being transported in their plastic pots to unsuspecting shifters who didn't deal in fantastical and volatile magic. Super.

"Jessie, we've got a problem," a familiar voice said from my left.

I barely stopped myself from sighing as I turned to look at Nathanial.

"What's up?" I said.

"It's the basajaunak."

Terror froze up my middle. "Please don't tell me they've changed their minds about helping."

He minutely shook his head as Ulric jogged up, his dyed hair combed flat to his head. Clearly he was trying to look a little subdued for Kingsley's shifters. It wasn't working.

"The opposite," Nathanial said. "More have shown up. We no longer have room for them on the chartered flights."

We'd made space for two dozen basajaunak and our various cargo.

"How many more showed up?"

"A dozen, all parents. They're watching out for their kids. The lead basandere is one of them. She said she's not operating in a leadership role here, but she wants to keep an eye on things. They have all agreed to fight."

Austin walked up wearing a white T-shirt and faded blue jeans. We'd all be changing into nicer clothes after we landed.

I relayed what Nathanial had told me.

Nothing about Austin's expression or bearing changed. He'd completely done away with the looser persona he'd adopted for Ivy House soil, and even the mildly thawed persona he now displayed in the territory at large. He was back to being a tough, blank-faced alpha shifter, something that would be expected of him in Kingsley's territory.

"We can add on a third wave and charter another jet," he said crisply. "It's too late to change the current setup."

"Not to mention we need to get those flowers set up as quickly as possible," I murmured.

"Tell Mr. Tom to arrange it," Austin commanded. "He can do it from the road. Let's load up. Time to go."

Nathanial nodded and turned, striding away, and Austin pushed forward to bark orders.

Nessa bounded up a moment later with a ponytail and a bright smile.

"Going to meet the in-laws, huh?" she asked me, and then winked. "Nervous?"

"Of course she isn't nervous," Mimi said as she strode past us toward one of the waiting cars. "What would be the point?"

"Of course I'm not nervous," I whispered, mimicking Mimi.

Nessa laughed and turned to stand beside me. Ulric was on my other side, all of us surveying the shifters heading for the cars.

"But seriously, are you nervous?" Ulric asked. "I'm nervous, and the thought of my mom potentially embarrassing me in front of a bunch of new shifters isn't a big deal compared with your deal. Meeting the in-laws is big."

I shook my head as I watched Cyra and Hollace duck into the wrong van.

"Dang it." I started forward, but the new leader of my gargoyle forces, Tristan, beat me to it.

He stopped by the opened door, said a few words, and backed away. Laughing, Cyra climbed out, Hollace after her. Tristan pointed to where they should be.

As if feeling me looking at him, he turned to catch my gaze. A subtle nod and he was walking away again.

"Very efficient, our resident gargoyle," Mr. Tom said, stopping beside us with a basket. "Now. How about some blueberry pancakes for the road? I have some lovely green tea here, should you want it, or even a decaf coffee in case you want something stronger that won't enhance any travel jitters."

"I'm fine, Mr. Tom, thanks."

"If she wanted a bit ta eat, she'd ask fer it," Niamh drawled as she passed by with her cooler.

"Why are you taking a cooler?" Mr. Tom asked her. "We are going on a commercial flight. We cannot take our liquor cabinet. Do you know nothing of the modern ways of traveling?"

"Of course I know about traveling, ye oul goat. Ye stuck me in coach," she said, turning back. "Do ye know how slow they are to dole out drinks in coach? What do ye think 'slowcoach' means?"

"What do *you* think slowcoach means, because you're clearly mistaken."

"Don't worry yer head," Niamh told him. She lifted the cooler so she could pat it. "I've got it all squared away. Ye can bring liquid so long as it is in a small enough bottle. I've got the clear ones. They'll have no idea what's even in it. It's good."

She winked at us and used a finger to tap the side of her nose.

"You cannot bring a cooler full of booze, I don't care what you say," Mr. Tom replied.

"And ye think ye can bring a couple of metal canisters filled with shite tea and useless coffee, do ya?"

"This is for the car ride, I'll have you know," Mr. Tom said pompously.

"Fine. This is also for the car ride. Now mind yer business."

She continued toward the van reserved for my crew.

"I should medicate before I consent to traveling as a team from now on," I muttered as Mr. Tom took off after her. At least he'd stopped harassing me about eating.

Austin looked our way, scanning the people who still hadn't boarded the vans.

"I better skedaddle," Nessa said. "The alpha is all keyed up. I'd rather not be in the line of fire."

She hurried forward, giving Tristan a vulgar hand sign as she passed that made him huff out a laugh and shake his head. Half the time they didn't seem to get along—or *she* didn't get along with him—but their chemistry was a little insane. I didn't envy them the aggravation of trying to figure that out.

Nessa appeared not to be trying. She slipped into the van where Sebastian had already found his place, looking through a spell book.

"I think I better do likewise." Ulric put his hand on my shoulder. "We've got this. All of this—the in-laws, the new shifters and their rules, the coming mage attack… We can handle it."

I took a deep breath as he headed for his place. We didn't have much choice. It was either handle it or die. The mage attack, at any rate. The rest? Well…I still wasn't allowing myself to process any of that.

Austin stood on the sidewalk with Broken Sue,

who'd be leading Wave Two, and Kace, who would stay behind as acting alpha, protector of the territory. I was sure they were going over last-minute plans and directives. Given I had nothing to add, I stopped by the lead van in which I'd be riding and turned to face Ivy House.

"I'm off," I told her. *"Hopefully you won't need a new heir soon."*

"You are the greatest heir I have found so far, and you've summoned and built the most powerful team. In a physical battle, with all your shifters and gargoyles, you will not lose."

"Right. But it won't just be a physical battle. It'll be a magical battle."

"Yes. That part is worrying. You're still somehow pretty terrible at magic. Let's hope you figure it out. I'd hate to have the new interior design stop before it is finished."

I gave her an annoyed stare and then contemplated fire-blasting the establishment.

"Ready?" Austin stopped beside me before glancing the way I was looking. "You good?"

"I'm ready, yeah. Ivy House—Never mind. Doesn't matter. I hope the gnomes find their way in and terrorize her."

Broken Sue and Kace watched our vans pull away,

and through my connection with them, I could feel Broken Sue's uncertainty. It was a sentiment I'd felt on and off from a great many shifters. I couldn't tell if it was trepidation about the coming battle or entering another territory led by another alpha with a different set of rules. The gargoyles shared no such concerns. For better or worse, they seemed to be taking all of this in stride, the coming battle included.

"Have you heard from Gerard?" Austin asked, his hand resting possessively on my thigh.

Gerard was the gargoyle leader of Khaavalor. He'd given me a Porsche for the connection request and kept in contact after he'd left. He'd been the youngest of the leaders I'd met, the most open-minded, and he had jumped at the opportunity to help us in Kingsley's time of need.

"Mr. Porsche?" I leaned against his arm. "I have, yes. He confirmed that he planned to fly in with some of his people at the end of the week. After I warned him about the number of people we'd probably be facing, he offered to bring more guardians. He wasn't worried about the danger in the slightest."

"And you said…?"

"Sure. More the merrier, just like with the extra basajaunak."

He didn't show any sign that he had heard me, staring straight ahead. I could feel his edginess through the bonds.

"Sebastian and I also talked down in the crystal room this morning."

"He's nervous," Austin said.

"Yes."

"I went over the numbers. We have the people to combat this threat. We have the power at our disposal." He paused, now looking out the window. "But we don't have the magic. Gargoyles have a natural ability to withstand a certain amount of spell work, and the potions you guys created should help our shifters do the same thing. But a more advanced mage, a mage high on the power scale, will still be able to break through it. And they can just try and try again. Sebastian hasn't been able to come up with any answers."

He'd obviously spoken to Sebastian as well. I'd never seen the weird mage so worried.

I took a deep breath. "We've encountered dismal odds before. Sebastian and I have been training. There may only be two of us, but we're strong, and we'll concentrate our efforts on the highest-caliber mages. We'll have the home team advantage. Hell, we'll have *fliers*! Fliers are incredibly advantageous in a battle like this. We've seen the proof."

"Those mages will be spread out all over the territo-

ry, and it's a big territory. Kingsley has a lot of land."
His voice was hard enough to cut granite. "Momar
hasn't spent this much time sussing out my brother's
territory and defenses with his mini, harmless attacks
just to shoot himself in the foot by putting their most
valuable players within easy reach. No, each powerful
mage will be protected by a team of lesser mages, just
you watch."

"Okay, fine, but we also know mages are cowards.
Gargoyles, Cyra, and Hollace can fly into those groups,
and some of them will flee. That'll cut down their
numbers enough to give us a chance."

He ran his thumb back and forth along my thigh. "I
hope so. Otherwise, we'll need a miracle."

Austin didn't say much after that. We arrived at the
airport in silence, and even then he only spoke to direct
our people. I took over where I could, especially when it
was my crew that was causing the holdup. And, surprise, surprise, my crew caused plenty of problems in
the security line.

"What is going on?" I asked through my teeth.
Niamh had insisted on bringing her cooler. She'd been
stopped by the TSA, to no one's shock, and was now
arguing with the agent.

"This gobshite won't let me through," she said, her
hands braced on her hips.

"You cannot carry this onto the airplane," the agent said semi-patiently.

"Can't I, me arse." She gestured at the battered blue cooler. "Those are all travel-sized bottles, aren't they? No more than 3.5 ounces each. The cooler is me luggage. It's all above board."

"Take her to prison," Mr. Tom said as he took a carry-on from the conveyer. "It'll be the best place for her."

"Ma'am…" the agent said, ignoring Mr. Tom. He took out a small, clear plastic bottle designed for storing shampoo or conditioner when traveling. Brown liquid sloshed around inside. "This is the right size, yes—"

"See?" Niamh said.

"But you are limited to one quart-size container housing the liquids, gels, and aerosols. This is"—he looked first inside, and then at the outside of the cooler—"significantly more than that."

"Is that whole thing full?" I asked incredulously.

"Not full," Niamh said.

"Mostly full," the man responded.

I sighed in exasperation. "Reduce it to the amount that is allowed and let's go, Niamh."

"Why would I need a cooler if I'm only allowed what I can carry in my pocket?" she demanded.

"Get it done," I told her, my tone brooking no argument.

She glowered at the TSA agent before reaching for the cooler.

"Ma'am, is this your bag?" I heard someone else ask.

Cyra raised her hand with a smile. "That's mine!"

"Oh no," I said softly, waiting for her to take her place next to Niamh in the security area.

Grim-faced, the man looked at her over the suitcase. "Do you have any weapons in this suitcase, ma'am?"

"Yes," she answered jovially.

Hollace, waiting for his bag, glanced over with a grin.

The agent gave her a long, dangerous sort of look that went right over her head before he unzipped the pack and gingerly reached inside.

"Oops. Be careful there." Cyra put out a hand to steady him. "It is very sharp."

"What'd you bring?" I asked, peering in as Niamh started throwing bottles in the trash, grumbling under her breath.

"Just a large, serrated knife," she said, peering into the bag. She affected a strange sort of accent. "That's not a knife… *This* is a knife."

Hollace started laughing. I continued to stare.

"Ulric was watching *Crocodile Dundee* the other day," Hollace explained, stopping behind us. "She thought that was a good joke."

"Yes. I wanted to do that to one of the shifters in this new territory. Sort of like breaking the ice, you know?"

"No—Cyra…" I opened my mouth. Closed it. Collected myself. "No. Take—Get it out. You can't bring weapons on an airplane, Cyra! Are you nuts?"

"You can't?" She poked her finger through the lensless frame of her glasses to rub her eye. The deep scowl in the agent's face bent a little toward confusion. "Why not?"

"I explained that, remember?" Hollace said. "Just get rid of it. The shifters wouldn't have thought that joke was very funny anyway. Most of them probably haven't even seen the movie or wouldn't remember it. It's old."

"Fine," she said, as put out as Niamh.

She reached for the suitcase only to have the agent stop her. "No. I will handle the weapon."

"Can't I at least stash it in the airport and get it when I come back?" she asked.

The agent gave her a hard stare. "No."

It was a miracle he didn't arrest her.

The next issue happened when we were trying to get everyone onto the plane. My boarding zone had already been called, but I stayed back to make sure everyone else got on. Good thing.

"I beg your pardon, madam?" Mr. Tom said indignantly to the ticket agent. He pulled his ticket back, not allowing her to grab it and scan him through.

She paused in a moment of confusion.

"No, this is not a costume party," he said, "and no, we are not cost-playing, whatever that is, a legion of Batmans. An ordinary man with enhanced technology running around the night dressed as a bat with fake muscles is, quite frankly, ludicrous. Little Dicks need to put their faith in something better than mentally unstable vigilantes."

The woman gasped.

Niamh let out a loud guffaw. "Now who's going to prison, ya cheeky bastard," she drawled.

"That kind of language is highly inappropriate, sir," the woman said, her body bristling.

It took me a moment to realize she was reacting to the phrase "little Dicks," which for us meant non-magical kids.

"Right, okay." I rushed forward, bumping into Niamh so that I could get to Mr. Tom.

"Shite," Niamh grumbled, pulling the travel bottle away from her body and looking down at the spreading stain on her shirt. I hadn't even noticed she'd been drinking from her stash—something I was pretty sure wasn't allowed.

"Sorry, ma'am," I told the agent, now trying to angle my body so she couldn't see Niamh. "He didn't mean— He, himself, is a little off-kilter."

"How *dare* you," Mr. Tom said, stepping away a little.

I yanked his ticket free and handed it to the agent. "His age has caught up with him. We're getting him treatment."

"This is an outrage," he said, his hands on his hips and his wings fluttering.

The other agent, standing beside the first, noticed. Her eyes rounded.

"They're mechanized. Here we go." I scanned the ticket myself, something half the agents had people do anyway. I handed it back to him and magically shoved him toward the tunnel to the plane. "All is well."

Next I turned to Niamh and reached for her ticket.

"Get rid of that!" I whispered at her, my gaze dropping to the little bottle that she hadn't stowed away.

"Yer such a spoilsport," she grumbled, and, with very impressive sleight of hand, the bottle disappeared somewhere into her clothes. "I'll scan it. Good heavens, Jessie, cut the apron strings."

She pushed ahead of me and scanned her own ticket.

"Don't worry about that muppet," Niamh told the

agent. "He insists on that ratty old cape. The oul codger thinks Batman stole his identity. Never got over it. Sure, our friends dress up in capes just to make him happy. Too much trouble, if ye ask me."

"Right, okay." I stepped in again to hurry this along. "People are waiting. No need to embellish the story."

Despite the fact that he had a first-class ticket and should've gotten on the plane with the first boarding group, Tristan was the very last person, besides me.

"Hey," I said, stepping in beside him with my ticket finally out and ready to be scanned.

"Hey," he replied, gesturing for me to go in front of him.

"Why were you way back here? Did you decide that joining this territory was a terrible idea and, as Niamh would say, you were about to pull a runner?"

He gave me a lopsided grin, then broke down into chuckles. "No, but I decided I better take up the rear in case someone got ejected or hauled off to prison or…who knew what."

Tristan had taken lead during Edgar's flower show fiasco. He'd had a few moments of *what the hell have I gotten myself into*, followed by some hardcore self-reflection that Austin had had to walk him through. The poor guy had been thrown for a loop.

"I appreciate it," I told him honestly, waiting for

him. "Maybe you can take over my role as babysitter."

The agent's eyes widened as she looked up at him, taking in his height and width. Her throat bobbed with a hard swallow, and then an appreciative flush crept into her cheeks as she noticed his handsome face.

"Wingman does me just fine, thanks," he told me, nodding his thanks to her before walking with me toward the tunnel. "I don't have enough patience to manage that crew. It's like herding cats toward a bathtub."

I laughed with the analogy. "At least I've earned the free champagne, huh? That's a plus."

"You have, no question. Jessie…if I may…" He slowed as we neared the open passenger door. "What are we walking into with this new shifter territory? I've heard that Austin's brother is a lot more intense. Is that going to be a problem for our people?"

I stopped next to him and half turned, looking back the way we'd come. "Honestly, Tristan, I don't know. Some of the shifters are nervous, which makes *me* a bit nervous. I suspect there isn't a lot of joking around in their pack, and showing any levity might make them think you're weak. They'll want to prove their dominance over the merged pack. That might mean a lot of challenges. I just don't know."

"You're saying that if my gargoyles laugh and act

like normal people, they'll get heat from these other shifters?"

I briefly hesitated in answering. "I expect so. I was warned that they'd challenge me, and that I should go hard when they do. 'Nearly kill them' sort of hard. I think we're about to walk into a turbulent situation, although I can't say for sure. It certainly defies my logic that they'd want to challenge us, since we're showing up to help them. And what is with shifters thinking they need to have the emotional range of a stone to look tough? It's so dumb. But..." I shrugged. "That's the culture as I understand it. A culture Austin has slowly started to change in our pack. Other than that, I know as little as you do."

He studied me for a long moment, his eyes sharp and wings still. A smile slowly soaked up his expression.

"A little turbulence might help pass the time," he finally said. "Go hard or go home, right, Jessie?"

CHAPTER 3

SEBASTIAN

T HEY'D JUST ARRIVED at a motel about a half-hour away from Kingsley's territory. Austin had booked a collection of rooms so they'd have somewhere to get freshened up and wait for the basajaunak and extra supplies on the chartered flight. Once all the species in the first wave were collected and presentable, they'd travel the last leg of the journey to their new home for the foreseeable future.

Sebastian wandered a little way from the people pulling their carry-ons from the van. The Rocky Mountains rose in the distance, huge and jagged with snow-capped mountains and formidable peaks. The sky stretched overhead, the puffy clouds seemingly right over top of them, lower than in O'Briens, given the elevation change. Trees bordered the little town, and streetlights ran the length on either side of the street.

Kingsley's territory was due north, nestled in the

rolling hills between mountain ranges, straddling a river. In all the traveling he'd done for mage dinners or conventions, he'd never been to Wyoming. It might've been too rural for the mages he often meddled with, but wow, it sure was beautiful.

Regardless, he knew that if he saw any mages in this area, especially right outside of Kingsley's territory, they were enemies. That was just logic.

He watched an old Toyota slowly roll by, the man in the driver's seat staring out the passenger window at the vans and their group of misfits. A woman walking her bulldog down the way stopped as the dog lifted its leg to a bush. She raised her hand against the glare of the sun, checking out the strangers. News of their arrival would spread fast. With any luck, they could keep their adversaries in the dark about how many mages they had.

They'd left survivors after their battle with Momar's people in the basajaunak lands, wanting the story to get back to other mages. But it had developed and changed in ways Sebastian hadn't anticipated, possibly because they'd hit the surviving mage with a nightmare spell and sent him home in a coffin—not the kind of thing conducive to good mental health. It was like the story had gone through a few rounds of the game "Telephone" in a loud bar full of drunks. It had been twisted and morphed, becoming something *other*. Something dark, about an intensely powerful magical monster.

Jessie.

Based on what Sebastian had heard through the pipeline, Momar still didn't know the infamous Elliot Graves was helping Jessie. Sebastian would like to make sure that stayed an open question for as long as possible. The less their enemies knew, the less powerful they'd be.

"Okay everyone, listen up," a shifter shouted, putting up his hands to get everyone's attention.

Sebastian vaguely recalled that he was one of the shifters who'd grown up in Kingsley's pack and joined Austin's pack with Kingsley's blessing.

"We've got six rooms booked," the shifter went on, "which is nearly half of this motel. You'll need to get in, get dressed and/or showered, and get out. While you're waiting for your turn, or waiting for everyone to finish, feel free to explore the town. It is mostly comprised of Dicks, but they are aware of shifters. The Dicks are like those in Alpha Steele's territory—either okay with magic, or very good at turning a blind eye. However, they have likely never seen a gargoyle. Don't mind them staring. There is a strict no-challenge policy outside of Alpha Kingsley's pack. You can use posturing to stop someone from staring, but no violence. Not unless they start it, and they rarely do."

"We're not so fragile that we get up in arms whenever someone looks at us," one of the gargoyles muttered.

"Maybe that's because no one notices you," said a shifter with short platinum-blonde hair—Isabelle, her name was. She smirked, and the gargoyle glowered.

Austin nodded to the announcer before hefting a couple of bags out of one of the vans and murmuring something to Jessie. She glanced out over the crowd, a little crease between her brows, before nodding and heading toward the motel.

"John, get them a key," the announcer said, motioning to someone in the crowd.

"Jessie's going to hang back to make sure her team follows protocol," Nessa whispered, walking up to stand beside him. "Betcha anything."

"Well if it weren't for her, I doubt a couple of them would've even been allowed on the plane."

"Niamh's on shaky ground after what happened in the air." Nessa grinned. She'd been caught with her alcohol stash but had refused to relinquish it.

Sebastian started chuckling helplessly, remembering Mr. Tom shaking his head and muttering, "You should never try to take a puca's alcohol. That's a sure way to get killed."

"But you do it all the time," Ulric had replied to him.

"I tell her to stop drinking, or not to start drinking, or to get rid of that insufferable cooler, but I never try to actually take her beverage. There are some lines that a body just should not cross, especially with foul-tempered, miserable old lushes."

Sebastian sighed. "I'm surprised Cyra didn't get arrested for what she did with that fireball."

He hadn't witnessed it, but apparently she'd started rolling fire across her knuckles out of boredom. When the flight attendant hurried over to take away her lighter, Cyra had taken it upon herself to prove she didn't have one by creating a fireball.

The flight attendant had, quite rightly, freaked out, and the onboard marshal had been forced to frisk her.

"Yeah," Nessa added. "Thank God for Jessie keeping her head and calming things down."

"She didn't find it as funny as everyone else did," he said. "Cyra is a nut. I love her antics."

"Me too. I was laughing so hard I had tears running down my face."

"Hey, Weird Mage." The shifter who'd been shouting directions walked over to them with a hard expression and no-nonsense vibe. He held out a key. The scratched red plastic attached to it read *3*. "You and your gal pal are in the first batch to get showers. Get freshened up." The shifter paused with a slight sneer. "Dress shirt, slacks, combed hair... You do have a comb, don't you?"

In their territory, only the newest shifters tended to show signs of animosity toward Sebastian. He'd proven himself in the pack multiple times over by now.

Apparently old habits died hard. Now that these shifters were heading into battle with mages, they were letting old misgivings resurface. Sebastian had wondered how he'd be received in Kingsley's pack. He'd probably just gotten his answer. He hoped it wouldn't escalate.

"He doesn't, actually," Nessa quipped, always quick to come to Sebastian's defense. "Not since you borrowed it to comb out your bush." She looked down at his crotch pointedly. "You might try to trim that down, by the way. I've heard it helps make things look bigger, though I doubt there's much of a point with you."

Fire kindled in the shifter's eyes. Nessa always knew how to cut to the quick of a person.

"And what about you, Gal Pal?" The shifter leaned into her a little, dominating her with his size. "You always walk around looking like a little rat. Did you have to raid the lost-and-found bin for this trip?"

"The lost-and-found?" she asked innocently. "No. I

needed something nicer. I grabbed the date-night clothes you use on your sex doll. I was surprised you had so many outfits. Never felt the touch of a real woman, huh?"

His body bristled, and his arms flared away from his body, the dominating posturing turning aggressive.

"What did you just say to me, mage—"

"Cam!" Tristan's voice was a whip crack. The shifter leaning into Nessa jerked away. "What's the delay? Get moving."

Tristan wasn't in charge of the shifters, but it didn't seem to matter. Cam straightened up quickly, pulling back on the aggression. Without a word, he turned and headed back toward the vans.

Tristan stood a little removed from the others, his blank gaze on Nessa. In a moment, he went back to scanning the goings-on of everyone else.

"How gross would that be?" Sebastian asked as he grabbed his carry-on. "His sex doll? Ew."

She grabbed her bag, and they walked toward the motel. "I know, but he's a dimwitted grunt. I knew he'd miss the details. I would've had a field day if someone had said that to me."

"I'm still stuck on *ew*."

She laughed as they entered the shabby room that hadn't seen an update since it was probably built in nineteen-too-long-ago.

"See anything?" she asked, jerking her head in the direction of the street.

"Only looky-loos so far. Our outfit is turning heads."

"Of course it is. There's a bunch of hard-eyed stacks of muscle standing around outside of luxury vans. Half of them have *capes*, for goodness' sake. Everyone in this tiny town is going to know within the hour." She affected an older man's voice. "Hey, Ethel, there's a bunch of guys dressed up as Batman at that motel on the strip. Damndest thing I ever did see."

"Yeah, true. None of these people have probably seen gargoyles before. Even the Dicks who are used to turning a blind eye will talk about that. If Momar has people monitoring the towns bordering Kingsley's territory, and he'd be a fool not to, they'll know we're here in no time at all."

"I'll shower first," Nessa said, putting her suitcase on the double bed nearest the little table in the corner. "I need to do hair and makeup and all that. It'll take forever."

When she'd finished showering, he quickly rinsed off the airport cooties and dressed in smart attire. He'd asked around to find out what everyone else planned on wearing before picking out his threads. No flashy dressing this time around. He needed to fit in.

"Which watch—" Nessa pulled the curler away from her hair, cocking her head to look at his bare wrist. "No watch at all?"

"A watch on me would be a dead giveaway. It'd be like a fan in the hands of a debutante. I'll unconsciously give subtle cues without meaning to, and any mage even remotely worth the air they breathe would clue in. No, I'll bring it with me and slip it on right before we meet Austin's brother."

"And which watch will you be slipping on, pray tell?"

He reached into his case and brought it out, a classic diamond-studded Rolex, a brand everyone knew with the added bling to make a statement. It was a watch meant to wow people who knew nothing about watches.

Nessa's eyebrows climbed. "A bit much, no?"

"Naomi told me to dress like I was going to a mage function and I was the most important mage there. In shifter terms, the alpha. I can't very well change my clothes in the car—that would be too awkward—and not even Tristan is planning on wearing designer attire, so I figured I'd add the bling with the watch."

"So you're going to strap on the Elliot Graves persona for the shifters?"

"Yes."

A knock sounded at the door. Sebastian opened it to find a gargoyle with a thick chest and unruly hair.

"Shower free?" he asked in a collection of grunts. "I won't interrupt you banging your girl. We just have a lot of people—"

"It's free, it's free." Sebastian stepped away, waving the gargoyle in. "She's just getting ready. Both of us are."

The gargoyle grunted again as he headed into the bathroom, not bothering to shut the bathroom door behind him.

"I swear." Sebastian closed it for him. "These guys are so blasé about sex and nudity."

"Yeah. It's nice. I like how open they are. Anyway, Sabby, I know Naomi isn't trying to steer you wrong, but she doesn't really know you, either. Donning that persona will make you a target."

"That's what I told her. I was going to wear something simpler, but then Niamh, who was eavesdropping, told me that I'd stand out regardless, being the dirty mage, and this way they'd know it didn't bother me."

"Did she mention that you'd be inviting trouble?"

"No. I think Niamh hopes it'll catch me by surprise and plans to laugh at the fallout."

Nessa sighed. "You willingly went along with this plan?"

"When those two women gang up on you, you do what they say."

She smiled as a lock of hair slid from the curling iron. "I'm just making sure you know what you're getting into. If you play high-level mage with those shifters, you need to be Elliot Graves down to your core, something you've had trouble with around powerful shifters. You can't let them see your weaknesses if you present yourself as having none. They'll rip you apart."

He looked in the somewhat crooked mirror hanging on the outside of the bathroom door, working on a magical face that was entirely new. It was the blandest one he could construct. It would hopefully ensure eyes slid right by him, especially since he wasn't particularly tall or muscular.

Just as he was finishing, the bathroom door swung open, revealing cut muscles, shimmering wings, and way too much skin.

"Pardon me," Sebastian muttered, peeling away from the mirror.

The gargoyle stepped out after him. "You've got a different face. How the hell—"

"Magic," Nessa said drolly.

The gargoyle blinked a few times. "Why wouldn't you make yourself better looking instead of worse?"

"Beauty is in the eye of the beholder," Nessa said in

the same tone.

"Not with that face." The gargoyle shook his head.

Sebastian prevented the frown that was budding about the quality of his new face. He'd been going for boring, not "monster on the hill." Too late now—he didn't have time to dream up and magically work out another.

"Anyway," the gargoyle said, apparently air-drying, "I heard your conversation through the door. Don't worry about those shifters. You do you. Walk the walk. Show them clowns *all* the swagger. If they try to push back, me and my boys got your back. Ain't no shifter going to be messing with you, we'll make sure of it. I don't care whose territory it is."

"Thanks, bro," Sebastian said awkwardly, grateful and relieved, and wondered if he should offer to tap knuckles or something.

"Just don't say 'bro,'" the gargoyle said, turning back for the bathroom. "Stick with what you're good at."

"Solid advice," Nessa said.

"All right. I think that's me leaving." Sebastian grabbed his suitcase. "I'll be out by the vans, looking bored and trying to fit in."

"Good luck, brother," the gargoyle said within the steamy space. He was pulling on some briefs. "Won't be too easy with that face."

Sebastian closed the door behind him, still able to hear Nessa's laughter as she finished with makeup and hair.

Niamh waited beside the van Sebastian had ridden in. She wore a black pantsuit with a sparkly bumblebee broach on her lapel, simple yet *chic*, and held a swatch of black fabric under one arm.

"Um." He pointed at the van, then swung his finger to the one behind. "Did you want to switch rides, or…"

"Don't be daft. C'mere." She shook out the fabric, a thick, shiny black cape. "Put this on."

"Wh-what?" He pushed her away as delicately as he could.

She shoved his hands to the side, swung him around, and fastened the cape around his neck. Grabbing his shoulders, she jerked him until he was facing her again and then tightened it.

"Why is this happening?" he asked as Edgar walked up.

"Now." She stepped back to survey him. "Presto-change-o, you're a gargoyle. How d'ye like—"

"Them apples," Edgar said. He had on the same pantsuit as Niamh, but with a sparkly ladybug broach. The twinning would have been weird regardless, but the pants had not been designed to accommodate an appendage. They were much too tight, showing an outline of something no one wanted to see. "You look nice, Sebastian," he said. "Except for the face, of course. But you must know that, since you put it on."

"Why are you wearing…" Sebastian cleared this throat. "Who dressed you?"

"Oh." He looked down at himself. "Mr. Tom accidentally ordered the wrong type of suit for me. It's okay, though. I fit in!" He scooted a little closer to Niamh, looking between them.

"Back off," she growled.

He smiled at her, the prominence of his canines reduced and his teeth ten shades whiter than usual, before taking a large step away.

"Better," she responded. "Well?" Niamh lifted her brow at Sebastian. "What're we waitin' for, lads? Let's get moving."

"W-wait. Wait, wait." He held up his hand as he backed away from them and then veered to the side, nearly falling into the opened van. "I'm not going anywhere with this cape on. I look ridiculous!"

"Yes, you do," Edgar said solemnly. "Maybe taking off the face will help."

He shook his head at the vampire. "This is obviously a cape, not wings." He pointed at the clasp against his throat. "It won't fool anyone."

Maybe Sebastian should rethink the watch and persona he'd planned for later. Nessa might have a point. If he couldn't keep his composure with people he actually knew, how would he ever keep up the big-shot mage schtick with scary shifters?

Tristan walked up wearing clothes similar to Sebastian's—a trendy sport jacket over a button-up with a popped collar and slacks. The difference was, Tristan had a lot more to show off.

A few buttons at his neckline had been left undone, revealing his man cleavage, as Nessa would call it—a slice of each popping pec showing through the V of the shirt. A curve of tattoo peeked out, its shape still covered. His slacks hugged his large, powerful thighs and his hair was relaxed, slight curls around his ears and falling across his forehead. It made the gargoyle look that much more dangerous, though for the life of him, Sebastian couldn't put a finger on why. Tristan had shaved as well, but it didn't detract from his rugged handsomeness and certainly didn't diminish his powerful aura.

"We were just about to leave without ya," Niamh told Tristan.

"No, we weren't," Sebastian said, grabbing for the clasp of the cape.

"Stop that, you." Niamh slapped at his fingers.

"Okay, let's go," Tristan said, holding out his hand to indicate they should start moving.

"Wait—slow down, *what*?" Sebastian was too dumbfounded to stop Niamh from pushing him along. "Tristan, I'm wearing a cape. Are you in on this? What would Mr. Tom say about me disguising myself as a mighty gargoyle?"

"He would not appreciate it," Edgar replied.

"That's why we didn't tell him, like," Niamh said. "He'd bluster and blow and hullabaloo, and who needs to hear it? He's off waiting for Jessie to need him, so we're in the clear. She'll be a while. Austin always likes to work out his anxiety in the bedroom."

"People in this area have never seen gargoyles," Tristan said, scanning the sides of the street. "They'll think my cape is nicer than yours, and we're both a little touched in the head. This way, no one will know what you truly are. No mage would ever dare look that ridiculous."

"Especially a mage as ugly as you are now," Edgar added.

"Seriously, what is wrong with this face?" Sebastian hunched as he walked, resigned that he wasn't getting out of wearing the cape. "I was going for boring. I don't want anyone to notice me for long."

"Oh, well, that will work, then," Edgar said. "Hideous and boring really amount to the same thing when it comes to people not wanting to look at you twice."

"Oh my God, please stop," Sebastian begged.

"You got it, bestie!" Edgar gave him a thumbs-up, and while he'd clearly put time and effort into his teeth, his nails looked like he'd been digging graves for the last hundred years…by hand.

"Fine," Sebastian said. "Where are we going and why?"

"To the bar, obviously." Niamh motioned for them to hurry up. "Tristan can see through invisibility spells, so he'll see if anyone is spyin'. If they are, ye'll help neutralize them so we can grab them. If not, I'll chat up the bartender and see what I can find out about the goings-on this close to the territory. The bartender is bound to know or have heard somethin'. If we're lucky, we'll get some information we can use."

It was a good plan, Sebastian just wished it hadn't been sprung on him. He surely could've been a lot more useful if he'd had even a day to do a little planning.

Edgar, giving Niamh a lot of space but still in front of Sebastian, looked over his shoulder with a goofy grin. The vampire squeezed his eyes shut for a moment, opened them again, and re-faced front.

Whatever silent communication that was supposed to be, it was utterly lost on Sebastian. Which was probably a good thing. Understanding Edgar was surely a one-way ticket to the Land of No Return.

"I see you're wearing a similar ensemble to what you had on at the cairn leader dinner," Tristan observed. He was walking beside Sebastian, something Sebastian was embarrassed to admit he hadn't noticed until that moment. "No watch?"

"I didn't want to stand out," he replied. "That was before I knew I'd be wearing a cape. Not even a long cape, either. A flimsy, cheap cape only down to my knees. I'm not only posing as a gargoyle, but a weak gargoyle at that. This is not doing wonders for my ego, I'll say that much."

Tristan ignored his complaint. "Natasha seems to have a fascination with watches. I figured I'd better learn about them for when I take her out."

Sebastian frowned, something that would distort his current face a little. He immediately smoothed his expression again.

"You're taking her out?" Sebastian asked. "From what she's said, I didn't think that was a possibility."

"I am taking her out, yes. Just as soon as she realizes it *is* a possibility."

"Ah." Sebastian scanned the sidewalk across the street. "Is this a 'no means yes' situation? Because that's a really good way to get you dead."

Tristan tilted his head back and laughed, a joyous sound so unlike the intense vibe he so often gave off.

"I'm not so stupid, no," Tristan said, his smile gleaming in the pale afternoon sun. "She won't admit it, but she's looking for a fairytale. She wants a knight to sweep her off her feet. She just doesn't think knights can be anything other than good, moral people. I aim to prove her wrong."

"And save her?"

"If she'd like to be saved, sure. Or I'll jump down into the trenches with her, and we can live like the world is on fire. We complement each other, she and I. I know what she likes even if she hasn't quite realized it herself yet. Once she has had me, she won't remember anyone else's name."

Niamh looked back with raised eyebrows. "Fulla yerself, aren't ya? Gotta be tough, lugging' that ego around wit'ya everywhere."

"I know what I'm good at," he said in a low whiskey voice, "and I know how to coax a thrill out of even the most buttoned-up individuals. Which she most certainly is not. I'll give her the ride of her life, and I don't mind the slow game we're playing leading up to it. It increases the anticipation until the inevitable explosion."

Sebastian had to hand it to the guy—he did seem in

tune with Nessa's vibe. He was dark and wicked and dangerous, all the things she loved, while still being good-humored and fun, both things she enjoyed. Sebastian guessed that Tristan, unlike anyone else they'd met, had the ability to sweep her away to a place she wouldn't want to come back from. A place where she might expose all the things that haunted and hurt her. But that would give him the ability to rip her apart, and Sebastian suspected she would never take that risk. She was already so damaged.

Broken Sue was safer for her. He was focused more on himself than on her, reaching for a branch to pull himself out of his turmoil. She was that branch, happily so. It was easier to help someone else than to let someone see your demons. At least, he knew that she thought so. And when Broken Sue was mended, he'd realize the darkest parts of her life were too dark, and she would be free. She would walk away unscathed.

With Tristan, she might never want to walk away at all. And Tristan didn't seem like the sort of guy who ever planned to settle down. He had too many secrets...and possibly a past that still chased him.

Or maybe Sebastian was just reading too far into things. He was great at judging people, but who knew— he could have it all wrong.

"My shadow needs a good leader to keep her safe,"

Edgar said, pulling Sebastian out of his reverie. "I won't be around forever, you know. Sooner rather than later, I think Jessie is going to retire me."

"She should, for those gnomes," Niamh grumbled. "Ye've really stepped in it there, boyo."

"Yes," Edgar replied.

Tristan pointed ahead at a rusty sign down the strip that might've started as bright blue but had slowly lost its coloring to the elements. "That bar, there. The guys originating from Kingsley's pack said it's the best, though I've heard it's not the nicest. I wouldn't mind a bar with seats I didn't stick to."

"Would ye *schtop*?" Niamh said. "Had fancy bars in the Forgotten Wood, did they? Swank clubs and cheese and wine?"

Tristan had only joined the world of the gargoyles some fifteen years ago. Before that, his origins were mostly a mystery. Their only clues were his knowledge about dark places and seedy creatures and his strange orange blood. Old-world blood, containing magic of its own.

"We all know *you* don't care about seats," Tristan replied, "so long as you have a drink in front of you."

"Right ye are," she responded.

"So on the off chance that one of Momar's people is in that bar right when we come in, we will…" Sebastian let the sentence linger.

"Grab him," Niamh said.

"In front of a bunch of witnesses?"

"Sure, why not?"

"Because they might tell the enemy agent who comes looking for their missing guy?"

"Kid, yer not connecting the dots." Niamh slowed a little, probably to chastise him before they got to the bar. "This is a shifter town. They get the shifters who want a little fun away from Kingsley's uptight rules. To keep their welcome, they don't cause trouble and they don't raise a fuss. The people here will be loyal to the pack. Their livelihood depends on it. If we tell them we're helping the pack, they'll hold their tongues."

"I agree," Tristan said.

Sebastian just sighed. He'd been outvoted, so he'd go along with it, but there was one thing he was sure of—everyone had their price, and Momar's mages had the money to pay.

CHAPTER 4

NIAMH

"**I**S THERE A signal, at least, if you see someone with an invisibility potion?" Sebastian asked Tristan.

The weird mage was too worried about plans and setups and the like. He needed to learn to go with the flow. Tristan had proven excellent at that. Niamh had told him the plan after she'd had her shower, and his only question had been "Where'd you get the cape?"

"Say something," Tristan replied. "Or nod, maybe. Jerk my head? You'll get the idea."

"That's if Edgar doesn't accidentally find them first," Niamh said. "Always count on Edgar's extreme creepiness. He wanders into corners and then gets a *baytin* by whatever is there."

"Yes. I did seem to be pretty good at finding the invisible people in the tests," Edgar said. "I got a few lumps on my *poor wee noggin* for my efforts, though."

Niamh glowered. "Are ye tryin' to mimic my accent? Do I sound Scottish?"

"Ah." Edgar clasped his hands in front of him innocently. "I see what I did there."

"But do ye?" Niamh pushed.

His simpering smile could make a glutton give up
food. "Not really."

"If yer not careful, I'll retire ye meself."

"Yes."

"Here we go." Tristan worked his way to the front of
their group. "I know this is a stretch, but try to act
normal."

"I'm impersonating a gargoyle by wearing a cape,"
Sebastian muttered. "How normal did you anticipate
this going?"

The bar wasn't nearly as dingy as Niamh had expected from the exterior. Light streamed in through the
door, left open despite the chill in the air, with two large
windows embedded on either side. Though the bar's
varnish was rubbed away in many spots, the stools were
newer and the booths looked recently refurbished.
Business must've been good despite the small size of the
town. They clearly relied heavily on the shifters' patron-
age.

Only a few people graced the seats, two large-bellied
men up in their years and a red-cheeked middle-aged
guy with greasy hair.

Tristan stood in the empty space in front of the door, between the bar and a table positioned against the wall. He surveyed the surroundings for a moment, looking for any invisible lurkers, before taking a seat at the table, facing the door.

"Sebastian." Tristan pointed at the seat opposite him. "Wings go outside of your chair."

"I thought my life might go many ways," Sebastian murmured, clearly to himself, "some of them truly terrible, but I never imagined getting lessons on how to be a gargoyle."

"Oh, quit yer grumblin'," Niamh said, taking a seat at the bar. She wasn't a low table sorta person in a place like this. Too much effort to get up and down. "It could be worse."

"Like lessons on how to be a puca," Edgar said.

Niamh stopped before sitting and stared at the vampire for a moment. "Did someone wind ye up? What's makin' ya so unbearably chatty all of a sudden?"

Edgar made like he was pulling a zipper across his mouth. He was worse than usual, lately. He was probably excited to unleash his plants on the unsuspecting.

"Sit here," she told Edgar, pointing to the stool beside hers as she lowered. "I think I'd better keep me eye on ye. We don't need ye spookin' the customers and getting us kicked out before we have what we need."

A tanned bartender came out of an opening at the back, what looked to be an entrance to a kitchen or backroom. She noticed the new people, her light brown eyes darting between Niamh and Sebastian. It was clear she was about to turn toward the bar but slowed when she noticed Tristan's back. Her gaze took in the wings pooling on the ground in a way capes didn't, and then the massive shoulders supporting them.

With a little crease between her brows, she started that way. Not even Sebastian's new mug could put her off checking out that great big gargoyle-monster.

"Hey, boys." The bartender stopped where she could see them both, and then her body jolted as if she'd just gripped a bolt of lightning. Niamh watched as the younger woman soaked in Tristan, taking in his face, chest, and then his glowing eyes. This time her words came out breathy. "Hi. What, ah…" She cleared her throat. "What can I—What *are* you?"

Tristan looked up at her slowly, not at all reacting to her sudden flush and flustered demeanor. He was used to it, Niamh knew. The amount of women who fawned all over him in O'Briens was joke-worthy.

"Thirsty," he said, his deep, dangerous tone making her visibly shiver. She backed up a pace, and Niamh wondered if he was releasing a bit of his special magic, a nightmare-inducing sort of emotional terror. Jessie could replicate it in spell form, but not nearly so controlled. They'd felt it for the first time at Edgar's shite flower show a few weeks back. Niamh had meant to research which creatures were known for such magic, but she hadn't had a chance leading up to this trip.

Regardless, the effect would ensure the bartender stayed behind the bar, probably close to Niamh—a position that would allow her to admire his face and body without getting the scare factor. Perfect. It was starting to seem like Tristan and Niamh might work incredibly well together.

"Sure," the bartender said, popping her hip. "What can I getchya?"

"Hennessy, neat." He looked at Sebastian.

"Do you have Four Roses, single barrel?" Sebastian asked.

Her gaze was slow to find him. "Yup."

"I'll have that please, one ice cube."

"Sure thing, coming right up." She looked down Tristan's back in passing, checking out his wings. She had definitely never seen a gargoyle before.

Behind the bar, already working on Tristan's drink, she glanced over at Niamh and did a double take at Edgar, who was awkwardly sitting on the stool beside her.

"Hello," the bartender said slowly.

"Don't mind him." Niamh waved Edgar away. "He's not dangerous, just senile. Everyone finds him off-putting, not just ye."

Her eyebrows climbed. "Oh-kay."

"What kind of ciders do ye have?" Niamh asked, trying to get the show on the road. She was feeling good about this outing. This woman was obviously used to shifters and townies, so anything abnormal would definitely have stuck out to her. Momar's guys would definitely qualify as abnormal.

The bartender rattled off the options as she finished the lads' drinks. Two weren't actually ciders and the other two were crap.

"I'll have a whiskey," Niamh said once the woman had delivered the drinks to the lads and returned.

"And how about…you?" The bartender gave Edgar a side-eye, clearly not wanting to look directly at him.

"Oh, I'm content just to sit here and watch all the patrons in a non-creepy way." He did that weird, simpering smile again.

"He'll have a whiskey, same as me," Niamh said.

"So, what's the occasion?" the bartender said conversationally as she got to work, glancing at Tristan again. "Costume party?"

"Yeah," Niamh replied. "Where's your clown suit?"

The woman huffed out a laugh before turning and

putting their drinks on the bar. "What are you really here for, if you don't mind my asking?"

Niamh could see the wariness hidden beneath her bartending bravado. That was *very* good news. It meant she paid attention to the clientele instead of just going about her job like a drone.

"Business transaction," Niamh said with a heap of boredom. "Maybe. I shouldn't speak out of turn. We haven't gotten the job yet. We're headed to the Barazza territory."

"Oh yeah?" The woman leaned against the bar, glancing out the door and then at Tristan for a moment. "Been to that territory before?"

"No. First time. They're expecting us later today. What do ye know of it? Seems like the alpha's got a right stick up his arse."

She grimaced before glancing down the bar at the other patrons. One was low on beer, so she headed that way, grabbing him another. He muttered a thanks and went back to watching the TV showing sports highlights.

The bartender wandered back and said in a low voice, "You probably shouldn't say that too loudly..." She spared another glance at Tristan, clearly admiring the view, before finishing, "He's very well respected."

"Well, sure. But that doesn't mean he's not got a

right stick up his arse."

Her expression was half smile, half grimace as she pushed back to lean against the back edge of the bar. "I've never met him, so I don't know, but you should be fine. The guys who come in here from that pack are almost all gentleman. They cut down trouble to almost zero."

Niamh grunted, sipping her drink. A body had to be careful when getting information off people. Slow and steady, a little yank at the thread of information each time.

The bartender wandered down to check on the others, and Niamh downed her shot and passed the empty off to Edgar.

"My, that was tasty." Edgar rubbed his belly.

She took his. "I'm not Jessie. Ye don't have to pretend with me, like."

"Oh, I like to. It helps me fit in."

"Trust me, it doesn't."

"What's going on with that pack, anyway?" the bartender asked after moseying back, not in a rush.

"I don't know whatch'ye mean," Niamh answered.

The bartender crossed her arms over her chest, leaning back again. "All the regulars from that pack have been pretty close-lipped about it, but it seems like they've got some trouble going on."

K . F . B R E E N E

Niamh looked at her for a moment before glancing over her shoulder, as though about to impart some juicy gossip.

"Now, I don't know fer sure like, so don't go quotin' me, but it looks like he's in the market for some extra padding in the defense department." She lifted her eyebrows in a serious way before leaning back, only to lean forward again and give a little more. There was an art to this sorta thing. "Seems like someone is tryin'ta take over his pack or something, I don't know. Or attack it. He's looking for help, from what I'm gathering. That's why we're headed there, at any rate—to see what's what."

Niamh shrugged, glancing over her shoulder again before sipping her whiskey.

"And that guy with the cape just there," the bartender whisper-murmured so Tristan wouldn't overhear—a futile effort given his enhanced hearing— "he's with you?"

"Yeah. He's the head of our outfit. It's weird, though. He got a counteroffer *not* to help the pack. When does that happen? Really strange setup, all of it. I don't quite know what to make of the whole thing. Something doesn't feel right." Niamh shrugged. "But I just go where I'm told. I don't have any credentials for anything else, and I'm too old to start over."

The bartender snagged her lip with her teeth, looking at Tristan thoughtfully.

"I've seen some strangeness," she finally said, quietly. "I mean…not as strange as…" Edgar got a side-eye again, met with a smile.

"Would ye stop smilin' at people?" Niamh told him, elbowing his bony frame. "It gives them the fright, so it does."

"It's fine," the woman said quickly, putting up that bartender bravado again. "But I've seen more out-of-towners come through in these last bunch of months than I ever have, that's for sure. And they're all a little…"

She made a face like she wasn't quite clear how to explain it.

Finally she put her hand to her chest and leaned toward Niamh just a little. "I'm a Jane, as shifters call me, so I don't really know the details about…" She waggled her finger between Edgar and the guys. "These strangers I've been getting aren't shifters, but I can tell they're not Dicks and Janes either. They're just a bit…"

"Off?" Niamh surmised. "Magical people can be. I've dealt with all kinds. Some I just want to throttle, like the senile vampire sitting beside me."

"Oh wow, he's a vampire?" The bartender looked at Edgar more closely now. He frowned at her, probably to prevent a smile. "I wondered if they existed."

"He's very old," Niamh said.

"Very old," Edgar repeated. Then mimicked zipping his lips again.

"Steer clear of the younger ones," Niamh went on. "They are incredibly dangerous. Don't get mixed up with them. But ye'd know it if they were in yer bar, trust me. Yer skin would crawl, for one, and ye'd assume death was imminent. They wouldn't have any reason to come here, though."

"Yeah, no, nothing that extreme," the bartender said, voice still low. "More like… The guys I'm talking about are just odd, you know? Like their clothes don't really fit right. They have this casual, almost messy look, but they sound super arrogant and uptight when they speak. *Very* condescending. And I'm like—who do you think you are? And why would you spend all that money on a fancy watch when you dress like a goober-hobo?"

Bingo.

"Sure, plenty of Dicks are weird, though, aren't they?" Niamh said, shrugging. "Or maybe it just seems that way to me because I don't understand them."

"Well, I *do* understand them, and sure, I could understand if one guy was like that. *Maybe* two if it was some social media fad for middle-aged guys or something, but"—the bartender leaned in, wanting to prove her point—"they all kinda act and dress the same."

"Is there some commune around here for middle-aged guys who can't dress for shite and think fancy watches are the next midlife crisis must-have?" Niamh asked, chuckling a little, making light of it. "They're probably all friends. How long have they been around?"

"See? That's just it!" The bartender grinned in a knowing way. "When they come in, they don't talk to each other." She pushed up to standing and lifted her eyebrows at Niamh, driving the point home. "There could be two at the bar, three stools apart, nursing their watery American beers, and they'll never once look at each other. But it's obvious they knew each other."

"How do ye know that?" Niamh asked.

"Oh, you can always tell," Edgar said, nodding. "Always. Right, Mistress Bartending?"

Niamh was about to knock him off his stool when the bartender said, "I can. See? Vampires know. There's this energy those guys put out—they pretend not to notice each other's presence, as if the other person doesn't exist. I usually see that attitude in guys who want to fight each other. These guys, though, have no animosity. They just sit there quietly, two semi-identical antisocial guys a few feet apart, staring at virtually nothing. It's *weird,* man. It's not right." She leaned against the bar now. The floodgates had opened. "And you know what else is weird?" She glanced up when someone walked in through the door. Confusion knotted her brow. "Okay, seriously, what's up with the capes?"

"Hey." Ulric sat kitty-corner to Niamh. "What's going on?"

Jasper took the seat next to him. "We got tired of waiting around."

"Bugger off, will ya?" Niamh groused. "I was just talkin' with…" She waited for the bartender to provide her name.

"Tammy. The regulars call me Tam-tam." She was turning on the charm for the new additions, her smile sweet and a little spicy. "What *are* you guys? Or is it a secret?"

Both gave her a delighted look—someone new to enchant with gargoyle charm.

"You've never seen a gargoyle before?" Ulric asked.

"If not, I am happy to let you inspect me physically," Jasper said. "Just say the word."

"Fer feck's sake," Niamh muttered.

The bartender's eyes lit up. "Gargoyles? *Really?*" She put her hand to her chest. "I'm a Jane. But I know all about…" She made a circle in the air with her finger. "What can I get you? You know, before that *very close* inspection…"

The boys preened at her flirtatiousness and placed their orders.

Niamh stayed in character, since the bartender was within hearing distance, and gave a gossipy account of the conversation. She knew Ulric would pick up the baton. He was great in these situations.

"Oh yeah, something is definitely off," Ulric said quietly, leaning in. He put a well-timed glance over his shoulder at the door, then down the bar. "There's no shifters in here, are there? Or the…weird people, whoever they are?"

"Do ye think we'd be talkin' about it if there were?" Niamh shot back.

"Right, right." Ulric glanced at the door again. "I'm a little anxious to find out what's going on, aren't you?"

The bartender set the guys' drinks down in front of them and then got another round of whiskey for Niamh and Edgar before leaning in again. She seemed to have totally forgotten about the two at the table.

"Okay," she said, "tell me if this is weird. Everyone else thinks I'm nuts, but they're all Dicks or shifters trying to get laid, so…" She gave a long-suffering look. "The oddly dressed out-of-towners come in in shifts, it seems like. I don't mean shifts measured by hours or days, either. We're talking weeks. There'll be three guys who're suddenly regulars for a week or two at a time. Those three will come in almost every day, when the place gets lively, and nurse their beers. Right? So three guys for a week or two. Then the *next* week, three different guys. Same schedule. Same weird kinda dress code. Same not talking to each other. Then the next week…"

"It's always three?" Jasper asked in confusion.

"And it's always guys?" Ulric asked. "Do they hit on anyone?"

"Yes, always three," Tim-tam or whatever her name was said. "Always guys. Rarely talk to anyone. If a drunk shifter tries to engage in conversation, they don't say much but don't shrug off the conversation, either."

Plying for information without asking for it. It made people trust you more, and drunk people just kept talking and talking, their filter entirely gone.

Still, Tim-tam obviously didn't know what was going on with the pack, so the shifters mustn't have given away *too* much in her presence. Then again, the mages could have used a privacy spell of some sort, keeping others from shushing the drunk guy into silence.

"Do ye ever see them again?" Niamh asked. "Once they switch out for the week or what have ye, do they ever come back?"

Tim-tam pointed animatedly at Niamh. "Yes! One

of the groups I have seen *three* times! The whole group, back from the abyss."

"And the same groups are always together?" Niamh asked. "They don't choose a new friend from their commune to go with them to the bar and make everyone uncomfortable?"

"Same groups, cycling through." Tim-tam flared her hands in an incredulous sort of way. "It's weird, right? I've never seen anything like it, and I've bartended in a few different places."

"You need to stop with all those conspiracy theories," one of the Dicks said from down the way. "It's a fun hobby, but when it starts to grab hold, it's best to walk away."

Tim-tam rolled her eyes. "See?" she murmured to Ulric and Jasper. "What did I tell you? The shifters have the same attitude, mostly. They don't notice anything strange, but I don't think any of them care enough to listen, you know? Too busy wanting to talk about themselves." She quirked an eyebrow at Jasper.

He pressed a palm to his chest. "I will be glad to listen. My mouth will be too busy for me to speak."

"Oh my God." She laughed, but the flush was creeping back, probably because it was obvious he was entirely genuine. This was why he didn't have to dress up or even shower to get the ladies. Once they got a good ride, they didn't care about the trivial things, like matching socks.

Tim-tam shook her head and wandered down to the guys at the other end of the bar. "*They* think it's weird," she told the Dick who'd spoken up, the one with nothing else to do but make the bar his business.

"They're just humoring you," the Dick said. "They wear capes, for Christ's sake. They'll humor any pretty girl who speaks to them."

"Not everyone can be Superman," Ulric called down. "But some of us can try!"

"So...that's interesting information," Jasper said under Ulric's shouting, his gaze zeroed in on Niamh. "Kingsley shouldn't let his people come here to get drunk. Who knows the sorts of things they've been saying?"

"Agreed," Niamh replied.

"Real quick," Ulric whispered as Tim-tam headed around to Tristan and Sebastian, sitting as quiet as ye please. "The strongest shifters back at the hotel thought they sensed a magical presence, but it was too far away for them to draw any more information. They checked out the area, but I guess whoever it was got away very quickly."

"Someone is checking things out but keeping their distance," Niamh murmured, switching her empty glass for Edgar's full one. She ignored Edgar's "Yum."

"That's what they figured," Jasper said. "They went to interrupt the alphas to let them know, and we came down here to tell you guys and see if you noticed anything."

"Don't think so." Niamh looked around Ulric to the two guys, Tristan staring out the door and Sebastian messing with his phone. "Tristan would've done something."

"Yeah, most likely," Jasper said as Ulric bent toward them to join the hushed conversation.

"Maybe it was one of the mages who hangs out in here," Ulric said. "Doesn't sound like they come in until it gets busy. If one of them shows up, Tristan can grab him and Sebastian can magically subdue him."

"Why is it all guys, like?" Niamh wondered idly. "As I'm getting up to speed with mage politics, I see that there are just as many female mages as male. Why is Momar using only male mages out here?"

"They're expendable?" Ulric asked.

"Sexist bastard?" Jasper suggested.

Ulric frowned at him. "I was talking about the guys being expendable."

"Whoa, bud"—Jasper put out his hand—"cool your tits. I was talking about the mage organization."

Now Niamh wanted to push those two off their

stools. She blew out a breath, turning around to check the light. "Austin won't put off going to his brother's today. As soon as the basajaunak get here, he'll be rarin' to go."

"We still have some time," Ulric said. "I'm guessing the presence, we'll call it, will come down here eventually."

"Yes, but as she just *said*"—Jasper pointed at Niamh—"we might not have the time. It's getting late, and the alphas want the whole pack showing up to Kingsley's as a unit."

Tim-tam had stopped to talk to the guy at the very end of the bar but was now coming back in their direction with the empty glasses from Tristan and Sebastian.

"We have until the basajaunak arrive until—"

Ulric cut himself off as glasses shattered, Tim-tam having dropped what was in her hands. She started screaming, joined by both Dick patrons, who scraped back on their bar stools. Ulric, Jasper, and Niamh all looked around in confusion.

"That is no way to greet a paying customer," a deep voice said by the door.

The basajaun secretly called Phil stood in the doorway in his kilt, hard hat, and reflector construction vest.

"It's okay, folks." Ulric stood and raised his hands.

"It's fine. He's with us. A real nice guy once you get to know him."

"Is that a Bigfoot?" asked someone down the bar.

"I find that offensive," Phil said, making his way into the bar to stand behind Edgar. "But I will happily forgive you if someone pours me a drink. I'm parched."

"Thank you for coming," Edgar told Phil, standing. "Here, have my stool. I will now happily stand just behind you in the corner. That would suit us both well."

"See?" Jasper said. "We're out of time."

"The shifters in charge said we all need to head back," Phil said. "I'll just have a really quick one while they get organized to leave. Oh, and there seemed to be some sort of presence at the motel. *Her* felt it the best, and so she chased after it, but she forgot to look both ways. We keep trying to tell her, but she never listens. Don't worry, she's fine, but someone will need to work out insurance for the dent and cracked windshield. Needless to say, by the time she started running after the scent, it had gone. Smelled magical, she said. Probably a mage that tucked into a car and away they went."

So they'd missed another of them.

Probably for the best. There were too many pack members loitering around for Niamh to make an easy snatch and run. Someone would get in the way, they'd probably miss their target, and then the mages would know their invisibility spells weren't so invisible.

This way, the mages only knew to stay away from the basajaunak, something they likely would've done anyway. Niamh's little crew could make a return trip and grab the three odd dressers in this town, no problem—they just needed to come at the right time.

And the other towns bordering the territory? They'd probably all hosted some of these bad-dressing mages. They could round them all up. It would just be a matter of getting to them before word got out that some of their brethren had gone missing.

No problem. Niamh had gone up against tighter deadlines with a lot more dangerous creatures.

This detail was gearing up for an epic bar hop.

CHAPTER 5
JESSIE

I STOOD BESIDE one of the vans that would transport the basajaunak as the people who'd gone to the bar returned to the parking lot. It took a moment for me to realize Sebastian had a cape on, and I spent another moment blatantly staring.

"It wasn't my idea," he said.

"But why…" I turned as he passed a grinning Nessa and climbed into his van.

"I think it really suits you," she told him, leaning against the edge of the door. "Can you flutter it?"

"Shut up," he said from within.

"Nice and slow," Dave said as he tried to help *Her* fit into the interior. They were nine-foot-tall creatures with a lot of girth. We hadn't really thought the transportation angle through. "Pull that leg—"

"Do y'all need some help?" a man called.

I turned to find a man in his late forties or early fifties at the edge of the parking lot, a plastic bag in his hand from the quickie mart down the street. He wore a thick flannel coat and dirty blue jeans with work boots and a beat-up old trucker's hat.

"Only, I saw you strugglin'." He half turned to point down the sidewalk at a pickup truck parked by the curb. "They're awful big creatures for that little bitty van. Where y'all headed?"

I hesitated for a moment, not sure if I should answer. There was almost zero chance this character could be a mage, not in that outfit, but I didn't know how the pack was perceived in the border towns. I didn't want to spark any animosity.

Dave didn't have any such qualms. "We are going to the shifter pack a half-hour away," he called.

"Oh yeah?" the man replied. "Well, I got a camper that would probably help. It'd give y'all a little more legroom, at least. How many are ya?"

The basajaunak gathered next to the motel, standing near trees or within bushes, suddenly became visible. They'd been told to stay out of sight until they boarded in case another invisible mage happened by. If we could grab one before heading to Kingsley's, we'd have one less to worry about later. Plus, it kept the basajaunak out of the way.

"Didn't see them over there." The man looked

around for a moment, maybe counting them up. "Lemme give my buddy a call. We can at least transport some of 'em."

"He seems like a do-gooder," Dave said as Phil stopped next to us and put his hands on his hips. "He seems like he wants to help," he continued, giving me a hopeful look.

"The vans are pretty tight," Phil said.

Austin glanced over, in the middle of directing people into the vans in the order he wanted them to arrive at his brother's territory. I knew he wanted to make a flashy entrance. A bunch of camping trailers would not fit the image he wanted to project.

Her paused to hear the verdict, her position— halfway in and halfway out—looking incredibly uncomfortable.

I sighed and looked back at the man. "I'll pay you for your time," I told him. "You'd really be helping us out."

"No problem." He put his hand up in a wave that turned into a thumbs-up. "I'll be back right quick. You just wait there."

He half jogged back the way he'd come, wasting no time.

My heart swelled, and I motioned *Her* out of the van. It always made me a little gushy when perfect strangers went out of their way to help me. I hadn't experienced any of that growing up in L.A.

As I left them, making my way to the cargo vans at the back to check on the killer flowers, I noticed Mimi sitting on a bench in front of the motel. She made a point of nodding her approval. Given the importance of image to shifters, I was suddenly nervous that Austin wouldn't agree.

Putting that out of my mind, because what was done was done, I rounded an open cargo door and stared into the sleek black van. Even the killer flowers had been given top-of-the-line transportation.

Indigo sat amongst them, reading. These were the calmer flowers, the ones they called the Violators, which I would absolutely be changing to the Protectors, because Violators sounded seriously icky.

"How are we doing?" I asked her.

She looked up, blinked a couple times, and then glanced around at the flowers. They stood stock-still, waiting for permanent placement before they started interacting with their surroundings.

"Doing well, I think," she said. "They didn't seem to like the airplane much. I think it was the pressure change. But being in the car? I think they like it just fine. Don't you, Violators?" Her voice changed, as though she were talking to a pet. "Don't you just *wuuv* car rides? You're going to be at your new home soon, isn't that exciting? Yes it is, huh? Yes it is!"

"Okay, then." I gave her a thumbs-up. "Looking great. We're just waiting on some transportation help, and then we should be on our way."

"Okie-dokie." She smiled at me, adjusted her glasses, and went back to reading.

The second van, transporting the other half of the Protectors, held Hollace, also reading a book. Out loud. To the flowers.

"Hey," I said as I looked in at him. "How's it going?"

He paused for a moment, lowering the book. "Fine. Edgar had to go do that thing with Niamh, so I said I'd take a turn watching the seedlings."

"Okay great. We're—"

"I heard. Campers, basajaunak, waiting. What do you think the accommodations are going to be like there? A tent in the woods, kinda like the basajaunak lands, or more like O'Briens?"

"I think more like O'Briens, though I'm not sure how much space they actually have for guests and strangers."

He nodded and looked back at his book. "Life has never been dull since I joined this outfit."

I grimaced. "Regrets?"

He lowered the book again to meet my eyes. "Not

even a little. I've had enough dull for a while. That's why I answered the summons. I'm right where I want to be. We all like that you keep life interesting. The gargoyles included. They're happier than pigs in shit since they signed up. I don't think they realized how dull their lives really were with all those pseudo-battles and pretend fighting they did. We were made for this. You're letting us do what we're made for. It's a damn good time."

"He says as he reads to flowers." I grinned.

He lifted the book again before turning a page. "Attack flowers. Big difference."

The last two vans held the violent flowers. There was a metal grate sectioning off the driver from the flora, and the van doors had been kept closed. The only person they would chill out for right now was Edgar, and even that was hit or miss. Apparently, they didn't much like traveling and wanted everyone to know it. How the hell we were going to unload the things was anyone's guess. We'd barely gotten them into the vans.

"What's the ETA?" Austin asked as he met me, checking his watch.

"Careful, people will think you're a mage." My smile had zero effect on his hard, expressionless face. His eyes didn't even soften. "We're just waiting for some help from the locals. The basajaunak were having a helluva time fitting into the vans. I know you wanted to look ultra sleek and—"

"It's fine. Just hurry up if you can. We're wasting time." He glanced me over before about-facing and walking away, his emotions frustrated and annoyed.

I twisted my mouth to the side, watching him with trepidation. I'd never seen him like this, hard and unyielding. Rigid, almost. At the same time, I understood. He was going home after nearly sixteen years to a pack he'd left in tatters. It would be his first time seeing or talking to his mother in all that time, and I knew he was worried she wouldn't want anything to do with him. He'd also have to face childhood enemies and people who'd told him he'd never amount to anything. Who'd predicted, when he hadn't even been a teen, that he'd pick a fight with the wrong person and get stuffed into an early grave. Or, worse, that he'd turn into his father.

He'd wanted to prove to those people that he'd changed. That he had done something with himself. Not only that, but he was using his resources to come to their aid.

Old me would've crumbled. I would've forced the basajaunak into the vans and told the guy thanks but no thanks. I would've tried to please Austin.

Magical me realized, however, that it did not matter

K.F. BREENE

one bit how the basajaunak showed up. They could be riding tricycles or wearing tutus, in some beater camper or stuffed in a luxury van too small for them. In whatever manner they arrived, they would bring the wow factor, more so than any other creature. Just having them on our team was incredible, something Austin was currently forgetting.

So I didn't go after him. I didn't try to smooth things over. I let him be grumpy and gruff and unyielding, and when I proved him wrong, I would absolutely expect groveling.

After ten or so minutes, a line of trucks ambled down the street. There must've been ten campers in all, from spruced up and shiny to a million years old but still running. Our new friend had called in favors to help us out.

Tears actually clouded my vision this time. I was such a sap about this stuff.

They parked on the side of the street, still taking up part of the road and not worrying about it. The guy from earlier stepped down from his truck and met me on the sidewalk.

"Thank you so much!" I gave him a hug. "This is really amazing. I can't thank you enough. All of you."

I stepped back and waved down the line. Beeps sounded back, their acknowledgement.

I stuck out my hand to him. "I'm Jessie."

"Howdy, ma'am. Hank." He shook it before looking at the motel. "Okay, then. Let's get 'em all loaded up."

It didn't take long, all the basajaunak organizing quickly and stowing away with plenty of head- and legroom.

"What are they? Bigfoots?" Hank asked after he closed the door to his camper.

"Basajaunak, actually. Don't call them Bigfoots. They hate that, and if you piss them off, they are about the meanest, most violent creatures you'll ever encounter. Grizzly bears might as well be teddy bears in comparison."

"That right? Huh." He flared his eyebrows and shook his head. "You see summin' new every day. All right then, what should we do, just follow y'all?"

"Yeah, that would be amazing. How much—What can I pay you for all this?"

"Ah now." He waved that away. "We're just bein' neighborly. Happy to help."

Austin met me at the first van, waiting beside the open door. Everyone else had been tucked in, with doors closed and motors running.

He stopped me before I took my place, his eyes so open now.

"I'm sorry," he said softly. "I wasn't thinking back

there. You were right—the basajaunak deserved better than traveling like a bunch of sardines in a can. Forgive me?"

I threaded my arms around his neck. "I had it all planned out—I was going to prove to you that I was right, then give you the cold shoulder until you owned up to it. But now here you are, taking away all my self-righteousness."

"Please kiss her in an area that won't ruin her makeup," Mr. Tom called out from the van behind us, having to lean over the gargoyle in the front passenger seat to do it. "I won't be able to fix her from way back here. I'm not *Go-Go-Gadget!*"

I held my breath for a moment. "He's amazing at ruining a moment."

Austin smiled down at me. "Yes, he is. And he apparently thinks you don't know how to do your own makeup even though you just did it, without his help, an hour ago."

"I think he's trying to forget that, actually. He's tucking it into his blind spot and hoping he still gets to do it in the future."

Austin kissed me on the forehead, and then the tip of my nose. His eyes lingered on my lips, and I felt the heat of his body pressed against me, the gravity of our mating bond within me.

"Don't do it, sir," Mr. Tom called. "You don't have the makeup in that car to fix her up."

Austin laughed just a little before hugging me tightly. "If he wasn't trying to help me by helping you, I'd probably go back there and pull his arms off."

"He'll never know how close he came."

Austin handed me into the van and stepped in after me. He pulled the door closed and gave the order to get going. Tristan sat in the front passenger seat, with Sebastian and Nessa in the far back. Mimi shared the seat with them.

"You moved the mages up to the front van, huh?" I asked, seeing Sebastian turn around to access his suitcase.

"I want my brother's pack to know that I value these mages," Austin replied, clasping his hands in his lap as he looked ahead. "That they have a place of importance in our setup. There is going to be some animosity toward them because of the situation. This is my effort to negate that as much as possible."

"They'll be glad for these mages before it's all through," Mimi said.

"It might not be a fun ride getting to the finish line," Sebastian murmured as he pulled a watch from his carry-on. "Especially since I'm strapping on my arrogance."

"That's the very thing that will keep them at bay," Mimi told him. "At least long enough for Nessa to sneak up behind them and stick one of her knives in their throats."

"You know me too well," Nessa replied with a laugh.

"Does Kingsley allow his people to terrorize guests?" I asked Mimi. "I know his patrols can't be everywhere at once, and there are always going to be skirmishes, but from the way you're talking, his territory sounds lawless."

"Austin has a unique situation," she told me as the land spread out around us. We'd passed the town, and farms dotted the way. "He's dealing with a variety of magical creatures in a new and quickly growing territory that's faced several attacks already. There are a lot of moving parts, so he has to keep a firm handle on any aggression."

"Safety, at the moment, comes from having control," Austin said.

"Exactly." Mimi nodded. "Kingsley, however, has mostly known peace. He was handed an established pack in a smooth transition from mother to son. He's had virtually no challenges to his authority." Austin's arms flexed and his emotions went turbulent, but he didn't comment. I knew he was thinking about his past.

"Furthermore, his pack is solidly organized, with almost everyone knowing where they stand in the hierarchy. He can allow random challenges and posturing between pack members without it unsettling the overall pack structure. Everyone in his pack knows where the line is and what'll happen when they cross it. But you're bringing in an influx of foreign creatures, some incredibly aggressive. There's no telling how things will go if aggression starts to boil."

"We'll watch out for our own," Tristan said from the front, supremely confident. "Gargoyle cairns are more tightly controlled. I'm used to stomping out even microaggressions—brutally—and I'll use that ability if the situation calls for it."

"Don't cut down on our fun." Nessa laughed. "I'd love nothing more than to sneak up on a shifter and stab him while yelling *surprise!* That would be a good time. I bet they wouldn't expect it."

"That is usually what surprise means, yes," Sebastian said. "And for the record, I'm more than fine with your cutting down on our fun, Tristan. I've never been fond of angry shifters."

"I don't think they'll be overly fond of angry mages," Mimi replied.

The farms gradually ceased until there wasn't much but flat land covered in trees and brown grasses with the mountain ranges rising on either side. The bumpy, two-lane road wrapped around a curve with the softly rolling hills, cutting out our view for what was to come. When it finally opened up, though, I couldn't help sucking in a breath. I hadn't known what to expect, but I definitely hadn't expected *this*.

A sprawling town glittered in the dying sun, windows sparkling and light dancing on metal. Whereas our territory had three very small towns that we were working on merging together, this was a large, cohesive area with what looked like a couple of big stores, a tall sign for an inn, and even a building a dozen or so stories high.

In short, it was *much* bigger than what Austin and I were working with, and the empty space around it, closed in by mountains, was an enormous tract of land that I had no idea how a couple mages could possibly defend against what was sure to be a spread-out attack.

"We should've brought more killer flowers," I murmured.

CHAPTER 6

AUSTIN

THE VAN CLOSED the distance between Austin's current life and the home of his youth. He'd forgotten what a large, spread-out territory Kingsley reigned over, isolated from the Dick and Jane towns. The population was just shy of ten thousand people encased in a huge tract of land. It had to be the reason Momar was taking his sweet time. Taking down this mammoth of a territory would seem like no small feat.

Austin knew better, though.

Most of the shifters living here desired a peaceful life. They might sprout fur and claws, but that didn't mean they knew how to fight. When Momar attacked, only a portion of Kingsley's people would take up arms. Most of the fighting would be done by the police force, a small unit in comparison to the whole.

Austin and Jess's territory had less than half as many people, but they had twice as many fighters,

K . F .   B R E E N E

maybe more. They essentially ran a battle unit instead of a town.

Until this moment, he'd completely forgotten how chill his upbringing had been, and how turbulent he'd made things.

He'd known leaving this place was the best thing for Kingsley's pack. For his family. But until right this moment, it hadn't dawned on him that maybe leaving had always been the best thing for *him*, too. Not just because he'd found Jess, but because he wasn't built to sit back, idle. He was built for turbulence—and he was damn good at navigating it.

He looked over at his mate, sweet and serene and beautiful. He should feel bad for dragging her into a life like this, full of danger and uncertainty, but he knew she was built for this sort of life, too.

He hadn't even set foot on Kingsley's soil, and he already knew he'd be happy to leave and get back to his own territory. He was excited for what would come after their victory here, because he had to believe it would be a victory. He loved his life. His mate. The promise of the future. Life couldn't end just when it was finally getting good.

His goals weren't humble. He wanted to bring the shifters together, to fight the mages on their home turf, to rip out Momar's spleen and topple the corrupt

Mages' Guild for good. He was anxious to see what he could do with production cairns and if they could ascend to the upper tiers of gargoyle society. Hell, he was even anxious to meet Jess's ex and see how that all played out, something in the works now that he'd gotten engaged and then threatened to drag Jessie back into his life to "celebrate."

But in order for all of that to happen, they'd have to make it through—

"You okay?"

Jess's voice cut through his reverie. He smiled down at her, taking her hand and stroking his thumb across her skin. He meant to say, "Yes," but instead said, "I love you."

She smiled at him before bumping her shoulder against his. "You probably won't be so quick to say that after I embarrass you a handful of times."

Sebastian huffed out a laugh.

"He's embarrassed himself plenty," Mimi said. "He might like for someone else to do it for a change."

Truer words had never been spoken.

They arrived at the alpha headquarters, the tallest building in the territory, a few blocks away from downtown. The parking lot was large and empty, Kingsley having obviously cleared the way for Austin's arrival. An adjoining park had lush green grass with chalk lines forming a soccer field, a play structure on the other side with a couple of kids swinging, and a skate park alive with activity.

"We need to put in more parks," Jess said as the driver pulled into the parking lot. "More kids are moving into the town, and they need a place to play."

The front door to the building opened. As Austin gave instructions on where the van should park, Kingsley filed out with a line of his top shifters. They followed him down the walkway and to the concrete pathway in front of the building, their formation crisp and lineup perfect.

Austin's gut pinched. He recognized every single face, most of them having wished him good riddance all those years ago. A few of them had always hated him. In the end, they'd all been on Kingsley's side, not wanting Austin to challenge Kingsley's authority even when Kingsley had offered to step down for the good of the pack. And that was how it should've been. Austin hadn't faulted them for their stance. He'd been glad his brother had backup. But man, they'd been the worst, and he doubted they'd forgotten the past or gotten over their hatred of him. Dealing with them would be a rocky affair.

"I'm right here," Jess whispered, squeezing his hand. "We're better together. Stronger. I've got your back, baby. I'm here to support you in any way you need."

She'd clearly felt his turmoil through the bond.

He gave her a soft kiss, letting it linger, before backing off and reaching for the door.

"I saw that, sir," Mr. Tom said as Austin climbed from the van, the old butler waiting in his new tux with a straight back and an air of importance. "You might wipe off the lipstick unless you are hoping to start a new trend in which only half of the mouth is covered."

Austin ignored him as the trucks and campers pulled into the parking lot. Kingsley didn't show any of the confusion he must feel.

"I'll just go sort that out," Jess told him, hurrying to the first truck and lifting her hand for the driver to stop.

As practiced, Austin's shifters lined up along the walkway, their line as perfectly crisp and uniform as Kingsley's. The gargoyles did the same with Tristan standing at the head, his face uncustomarily hard and unreadable, easily the largest person in the parking lot.

As an introduction, it was perfect. His shifters had immaculate form, and the gargoyles fit right in with them. If it had been left at that, they would all have immediately felt like they were on a level playing field, ready to get down to business.

But then Jess's crew exited their vans in a disorganized huddle. Even though Austin had wanted to impress his brother and show his dissenters he'd come a long way, he could barely contain his smile.

"What do we do?" Cyra asked Hollace, much too loud for a whisper. "We didn't practice with the basajaunak in campers. Should we get in a line and wait for Jessie?"

"As opposed to waiting in a blob?" Niamh asked before walking up in front of the shifters. "How're'ya doin', Kingsley? Are ye well? Shite. I'm meant to call ye alpha. Sorry about that."

"Find your place," Mr. Tom told Cyra and Hollace as Nathanial walked to his position, Ulric and Jasper right behind him. "It shouldn't be this difficult."

"Said the guy *not* in his place," Ulric murmured.

Indigo, the healer, hastened up with her luggage, having apparently forgotten they were supposed to deal with that later. Nearly to her position, she tripped and, because she didn't let go of the stuff in her hands, crashed down onto her face. Her glasses skittered along the pavement, hopped the tiny curb to the walkway, and stopped against one of Kingsley's shifters' shoes. The shifter in question, Bruce, had a square face, flat top, and zero sense of humor.

He looked down at them, and then at her, making no move to either get the glasses or step forward to help in any way.

"Oh no, Indigo!" Cyra jostled into Hollace, trying to get to her. Ulric and Nathanial were already there, though, hauling her up and trying to separate her from her luggage.

"We'll get it later," Ulric murmured furiously. "Just let go—*we'll get it later.*"

"I can't see," Indigo told them, waving her hands. "Everything's blurry. I need my glasses."

"Here, use mine." Cyra stepped forward and stripped her glasses from her face.

"Yours don't have any lenses in them," Hollace reminded her.

"Oh yeah. Well, where are hers—"

Cyra cut off as she spied Tristan. He'd stepped out of his line and walked over to Bruce with the grace and confidence born of a natural fighter. He stopped in front of the other man, his stare hard and direct.

"Excuse me," Tristan said, and the viciousness in his tone was clear. He bent, his gaze slipping from Bruce, his head bending, exposing the back of his neck. He was making a statement—he didn't think Bruce posed a threat. One could argue it was a challenge, something Austin knew Tristan would be happy to face.

Butterflies fluttered through Austin's stomach, but he didn't move. Kingsley's gaze zipped over to him as Bruce tensed up, unable to hide his response.

Tristan straightened as though uncoiling. He held up the glasses to the other man, standing just a fraction too close. His eye contact was definitely too hostile.

"You must've missed these hitting your shoe," Tristan said in a dangerous tone. "Luckily, they didn't break. I know you must've been concerned."

The gargoyle paused for a long beat, tension curling through the air as Bruce flexed his muscles. A moment before the posturing slid into an actual challenge, Tristan pulled his gaze and stepped back. He clearly had shifter protocol down to a science. He might be a gargoyle, but that didn't mean he couldn't play the game with shifters.

Well done.

Indigo was finally separated from her possessions and placed in her spot, behind the official members of Ivy House. Edgar came next, smiling, the suit he wore matching Niamh's and not fitting at all.

Kingsley took in the vampire, looked at Niamh, went back to the vampire. When his gaze met Austin's this time, he wasn't able to hide his bewilderment. He'd met them before, sure, but time had clearly dulled his memories.

The vampire hit the spot where Indigo had tumbled and let out a cry of alarm. He pitched forward, his hands waving. "Whoa!" he said as he crashed down onto his shoulder and then rolled dramatically.

"What are ye at?" Niamh said, sidestepping so as not to get hit by his kicking legs.

"What are they tripping over?" Ulric asked, looking at the offending spot. "I don't see anything."

"Thanks so much!" Jess called, pulling Austin's focus away from the train wreck that was the Ivy House crew.

She came around the first truck, her hair catching the late-afternoon sun and a smile gracing her face. She walked with poise and confidence, her arms swinging, not at all concerned about drawing challenge with her animation.

He'd been worried this would happen. He'd been worried she'd call attention to her differences. To the ways she didn't fit in.

Seeing her now, though, followed by a dozen basajaunak who probably made the small hairs on these shifters stand on end...he couldn't have been prouder. She was unequivocally herself and wouldn't sacrifice that for anyone. She was incredible, and he was glad they all got to see it.

"There isn't anything there," Edgar murmured. "I just didn't want Indigo to be embarrassed."

"*Eejit,*" Niamh said.

"That's actually very sweet, Edgar," Cyra said.

K . F . B R E E N E

"He needs to work on his falling," Hollace replied. "It wasn't at all believable."

"It is if you eternally think of him as a vaudeville character," Ulric said. Clearly none of them remembered that they were supposed to stand quietly, waiting for the formal greeting.

Jess reached Austin and Kingsley, still beaming.

"Oops." She frowned, pulling her lips down. "Oh wait, no." Her expression smoothed out as she stopped beside Austin.

It was only then that Austin realized two of Jess's crew hadn't yet taken their places.

Sebastian walked forward with all the swagger and arrogance of a man who literally owned the world. One hand was tucked into his pocket and the other was a little bent, showing off his gleaming watch as though it was his ticket in.

Nessa walked beside and a little behind him, her curls bouncing, her cleavage displayed, and her hips dramatically swaying from side to side. Her black dress had a sheen, and her makeup gave her the vibe of an "evil temptress" in a Bond movie.

They stopped just behind Jess, each of them looking out to the sides as though supremely bored of the situation and the people they were meeting. Austin wasn't sure the show was wise, but it was certainly

100

effective. They had the attention of every one of Kingsley's shifters.

Mimi walked up behind them, a little gleam in her eyes saying she'd enjoyed the greeting, which had gone on longer than anyone could've anticipated. She'd clearly been the reason behind the mages coming last instead of first. Austin wasn't sure what angle she was going for with that. He'd need to speak with her about it.

"Austin, welcome home," Kingsley finally said.

"Alpha, it's good to be home. It's good to see you again." Austin stepped forward, taking Kingsley's hand and then turning it into a one-armed hug.

"You remember my beta, James." Kingsley jerked his head at the guy next to him, a stocky dude with a layer of fat over a stack of muscle and gray at his temples.

"Beta," Austin said in greeting, inclining his head.

Kingsley announced the names of the other guys and gals in his line. "If you or your people need anything and I'm not available, any of my team would be happy to help. Just say the word."

"Thank you." Austin put his arm around Jess, his hand resting on the small of her back. "You remember my mate and co-leader, Jessie."

"Hello, Kingsley, nice to see you again!" She beamed

at him, stepping forward with her hand outstretched. "Crap, sorry." She struggled to contain her smile. "Alpha. It's nice to see you again."

"My people have been briefed on your situation," Kingsley said, taking her hand, his eyes twinkling. "You can let slip a smile or two. Okay, no, the laughing is taking it too far."

She laughed harder and stepped back, covering her mouth with her hand. "Epic fail on my attempt to have no expression."

"Epic fail," he agreed.

Austin went about introducing the important people, making note that his shifter beta wouldn't be in until the second wave arrived tomorrow. He wanted to see their reactions when they first laid eyes on Brochan.

"One thing, alpha," he said once he'd finished, "before I let Jess introduce her people. Some of the basajaunak showed up at the last minute. We'll be adding them to our group. We're also not entirely sure how many more gargoyles will be coming in from a cairn we're friendly with."

"Not a problem," Kingsley said easily. "We have plenty of room. Now, Jessie, if you wouldn't mind, can you give us a rundown of the creatures there?"

"Yeah, of course."

She turned and did just that, having to stop a couple

times for James to ask for more details, like what kind of magic a thunderbird did, or how Niamh chose between her two forms. At the end of her account, seriousness stole over her. "This is very important," she said. "As a female gargoyle, I have the ability to form a connection with the people I fight beside. It's like a blood bond. If you accept, we will feel each other's whereabouts, I'll be able to gauge your general emotional state, and so on. I believe it's supposed to help me keep everyone organized and safe in battle. The offer is almost always unconscious. If you feel it, you are more than welcome to accept it, but know that I'm not sure how to undo it. Yet. Don't carelessly accept."

"And if we don't want this connection?" Kingsley asked, his voice wary.

"Then deny the offering. It doesn't seem to be hard."

"It isn't," Sebastian said.

"Regarding those mages…" James said. "I beg your pardon, but how do we know they won't turn on us? I've never met a mage who has liked shifters."

"Have you met any mages at all?" Nessa asked him, lowering her gaze after a moment, clearly so he wouldn't take it as a challenge.

James paused, and then answered with mild disdain, "No, I don't expect I have."

"Most mages haven't met any shifters," Sebastian told him, his gaze still bored. He didn't lower it. "Not properly, at any rate. I'll spare you the details of the work I've done with Alphas Steele and Ironheart. The bottom line is, if the enemy captures me, they'll torture and then kill me. It would behoove me to help you to win, because that's the only way I don't die. Not that I'll likely be much help, so it probably doesn't matter."

"How so?" Kingsley asked.

Sebastian lifted his hands and looked around. "This is a sprawling, isolated territory with very little cover outside of the township—from what I've seen so far, at any rate. Given the numbers that Momar is sending, there is no possible way Jessie and myself will be able to protect you all from their magic, not even if I'm flown overhead. Basically we're taking knives to a gunfight."

Jess had turned to look at him, and fear soaked into her expression. "Are you being serious right now or are you playing up that persona? I can't tell."

"Note to self: don't take Jessie on an undercover mission," Ulric murmured.

Sebastian met her eyes. "I got the schematics of this place, but"—he shook his head in frustration—"it's more spread-out than I was envisioning. Much more isolated. Obviously I've only seen a portion of the territory, but what I have seen is a nightmare. If they have off-road vehicles, they can likely move faster than our shifters. Maybe our fliers in some places." He pointed at Nessa without breaking his gaze away from Jessie. "See if you can get any info on their gear. We only know about their magical guns so far. Let's see if they're planning anything else."

"Got it." She pulled her phone out from her cleavage and started tapping the screen.

"We have the fliers to combat the mages, though," Jessie said, bracing her hands on her hips. "With Gerard's guardians, we should have about as many gargoyles as they have mages. Gargoyles can withstand a degree of magic."

"Gargoyles can withstand a *degree* of magic, yes, but they aren't impenetrable. The higher-powered mages will punch through their tough hides, and they'll have plenty of time to do it because it's grassland and dirt out there, only dotted with trees. They'll throw spell after spell before the gargoyles can reach them. This isn't like what we faced in the basajaunak lands, Jessie, or in your territory. This is the big leagues. These will be power players with power approaching mine. A few of them working together? Stronger than you. They have the upper hand here, and we haven't a hope of—"

"Okay, okay, okay." Jess held up her hands. "Let's take a breath. Look, mages are cowards and their mercenaries are no match for shifters. We know this. The gargoyles can dodge the magic while still applying pressure to keep those mages running scared. After the shifters handle the mercenaries, we'll apply pressure to the mages. You and I can strike them down one at a time if we have to. Or create more nasty potions for the gargoyles to throw at them. This is possible. We *can* do this. We just have to think it through, right? Think it through, Sebastian."

He took a deep breath, his gaze going inward. "Okay," he said softly.

"Sebastian, Nessa, Niamh," Austin said, "we need more information. We need to know exactly what Momar's group is thinking. We felt the presence of at least one mage in town. We need to grab a couple—"

"We leave the Dick and Jane towns out of our affairs," Kingsley said, his tone hard. "Our business is none of theirs, and theirs is none of ours. It's our truce with the Dick world. It's how our ecosystem continues to work, or don't you remember?"

"Beggin' yer pardon, alpha," Niamh said, "but ye've got yer shifters running into town, drinkin' a bunch and flappin' their gums to the mages hanging around there. Those mages are tellin' everything they hear to their bosses. Yer basically injecting yer business into that town, and it's keepin' the mages lurking. Yer not exactly practicing what ye preach, if ye get me."

"It's cool, though," Nessa said. "We're not going to bother the Dicks and Janes. We're just going to remove some vermin without anyone knowing. They won't miss them—"

"This is not up for debate," Kingsley barked, his tone brooking no argument. "We will not hunt those towns for our enemies. We can hunt our lands, but not theirs. Even though my shifters know better than to talk about our business outside of the pack, I'll keep them from leaving until the attack. That'll end any information leaks you assume have happened."

Austin stared at his brother, his power swelling and his frustration paramount. His brother's willful ignorance about the supposed divide between his people and the border towns was incredible. Maybe Dicks and Janes didn't cross pack lines often, but plenty of shifters did. They had girlfriends and boyfriends in the border towns, hookups and friends, businesses, sometimes even mates they left the pack each night to stay with. It was complete neglect to leave them to the mages.

Austin held his tongue, however. They were in front of their subordinates. He couldn't challenge Kingsley's authority in front of everyone.

Damned if he could make himself break eye contact, though. Damned if he could stop his power from surging or dampen the energy that crackled between them. They were heading into dangerous waters right now, a challenge for dominance imminent. One they'd both follow through with because neither of them knew how to back down, their pasts be damned.

"Okay, okay, okay." Jessie ran her hand up Austin's arm and over his shoulder. "We're tired, tensions are running high, and we've got a big puzzle to work out. We're all a little wound up."

She brushed her fingers across his neck and pressed her body to him, drawing his focus to her like a moth to flame. He bent down to give her the kiss she was tilting her head back to receive. Her smile was disarming and easy, and her fingers slipped between his, further anchoring him.

"So. Protocol." She winked at him before turning her attention back to Kingsley, who'd shifted his gaze to her as well. "We've done the introductions, we've raised the alarm as to the magnitude of threat we're soon to face, and now we all...break up for naps, right? Or a rest and a read?"

"I trust my house is still in working order?" Mimi stepped up between her grandsons. "No parties in it, I hope."

"Mimi," Kingsley said, his voice gruff. "Did you enjoy your holiday?"

"Greatly. It's going to become my permanent residence, or didn't your mate sing it from the rooftops?"

He grunted. "Dinner is at eight." He spoke to Austin, still keyed up. "Mom looked after your house. It's ready for you. The beta will show the rest of your people to their accommodations. They'll be spread out across a couple of hotels and inns, except for the mages, who will be in a bungalow near downtown where they will be under constant surveillance. I realize he's been with you awhile, but my people need to know we're watching him. The basajaunak will be in the park nearest your house. There should be plenty of space for them. The rest of the territory knows to leave it alone. Earnessa invited you and Jessie to our place for dinner tonight. See you then."

He didn't spare anyone a glance as he turned and walked back into the building. His people followed him, clearly uneasy, except for James, who stayed behind with a guarded expression.

"I have my car around back," he said, looking everyone over. "When you're ready to move out, I'll show you the way."

"Go grab it," Austin said, not doing enough to temper the command in his tone. "We'll load up now."

When James jogged away, Austin gave Niamh a poignant stare he knew she'd understand. She'd have to slip away with a small team to extract some of those mages from town. All of them, if possible. That town needed to be cleared of vermin, and given the mages were only there because of the shifters, the shifters had to take care of it. How Kingsley couldn't see at least that, Austin couldn't fathom.

"He can't know we defied his orders," Austin told Niamh softly, walking her to the van she'd ridden in. "It'll lead to a challenge, and that would...complicate matters."

"I'd planned to use one of his cars..."

"Do not plan to use one of his cars. I'll make one available to you. Tell Sebastian and Nessa to get me a list of the gear the enemy will be using, and anything else they can scrape together. Sebastian's fears are incredibly valid. The way he chose to share them wasn't ideal, but it probably helped put everything in perspective. We have work to do."

"Yes, alpha." Niamh got into the van.

Austin turned—and then immediately jerked backward—not having noticed Edgar sneak up on him, which was worrying, since Austin should've felt the vampire's proximity in a few different ways.

"Hello, ma'am," Edgar said with a smile.

Austin just waited. There really was no point in reacting to the vampire's antics. At least he'd cleaned up his teeth.

"What about the flowers?" Edgar asked. "The sooner we get them into the ground, the better."

"That's on the schedule for our meeting with the alpha, Edgar, as you know. Please go put on some pants that fit."

"Yes, sir!"

Suddenly Austin wasn't so sure Kingsley was going to go for the flowers. It was easy to see the merit in something like lethal flora once the absurdity no longer registered. Austin had been worked in gradually, though. Kingsley's people weren't used to the level of weird that Ivy House could conjure up. They'd probably have a hard enough time adjusting to the gargoyles.

Austin hadn't thought the situation with Momar could get any more challenging. He'd just been proven wrong. Possibly very wrong. And this town was much too big to evacuate.

CHAPTER 7

JESSIE

"YOU HANDLED THAT situation beautifully," Mimi said as we followed James in the van to the first of the hotels our people would be staying in. The passengers were the same as coming to the territory. I felt a touch on my shoulder.

"Which?" I asked, taking in their downtown as we passed through. The square had benches, vibrant grass, and a really cute gazebo with small businesses all around. People loitered, chatting or just sitting there and taking in the closing of the day.

"With the two alphas." I heard her lean back. "It was perfectly done, backing them both down without making either of them feel lesser for it."

"She backed me down," Austin said. "He followed suit."

"You shouldn't have needed her to," Mimi replied.

"I know. I didn't realize we'd see things so differently right off the bat. It's…concerning."

"You two have always seen things differently."

"We were younger then."

"But no less thickheaded."

Austin shook his head a little but didn't comment. I had a feeling he wanted to roll his eyes.

"We need to get those mages out of those towns," I said. "It's insane, allowing them to lurk right at the border. What is Kingsley thinking? It's a miracle no one's gone missing."

"Or have they?" Nessa asked. "It's not like he'd volunteer that information when he was trying to make an ill-conceived point."

"He's thinking like a man who's never faced a situation like this before," Mimi replied. "Until recently, he's only dealt with shifters, and while our kind can certainly be cunning, none of the hostile packs have ever been powerful enough to pose a problem for him. He's unprepared for this fight. I always suspected, but it took getting to know your territory and how mages think to be sure. You're going to have to push him, Austin."

"He is not the type to accept being pushed," Austin replied. "It'll result in a challenge."

"Then you meet that challenge diplomatically, assume control of this situation, and make sure we all survive. The family won't like it, but the family would like seeing their pack and their loved ones die far less. Desperate times, as they say."

"It was my fault," Sebastian said, rubbing his chin. "I should've handled that situation differently. I created a tense environment."

"Wouldn't have mattered if you had," Tristan said. "The fact is, we're not going to comfortably coexist. We need to focus on getting the job done and protecting our own. Begging your pardon, alphas, but there is no way in hell I am allowing Natasha to be separated from our group and put under *their* surveillance. I doubt you want the weird mage in that sort of situation, either. These people are scared, and they don't trust or even like mages. We can't risk that one of them will do the ill-informed and stupid thing of trying to kill the mages in their sleep."

"Impossible," Sebastian said. "I have a lot of spells to prevent that. They'd die long before I would."

"Also a bad situation," Tristan replied. "And what about when you aren't there? Natasha doesn't have that kind of power."

"They can stay with Jess and me," Austin said. "I have plenty of room."

"That's probably best, anyway," I said, "because we need to figure out what we can do magically to level out the playing field."

"We've been trying that for weeks," Sebastian said wistfully.

"One question," Nessa said. "If Kingsley likes to keep the Dick towns and his pack separated, did we just make a huge blunder with bringing in a bunch of townies with campers to deliver the basajaunak? Maybe that's what got him riled up."

"Bah." Mimi batted the air with her hand. "We get food and products from Dicks all the time. They come in to deliver and sometimes stay for lunch or what have you. We get Jane and Dick visitors, and the various mayors and their offices come by from time to time, or the police chiefs when something big is going on. Kingsley just likes to pretend our people don't go seeking fun in the border towns, and now he has a reason to put a stop to it."

"Why would he care?" Sebastian asked.

"Shifters didn't used to be welcomed," Mimi replied. "When the pack was taken over from my late mate, they created a lot of turbulence for Dicks. Not to mention it was a couple of generations ago, and people were close-minded about what goes bump in the night. It was a rough time. When I regained the pack, I worked to mend those fences, so to speak, but we were quite separated by then. Denise, Austin's mom, followed in my footsteps, trying to repair bridges and establish trade and goodwill. Kingsley maintains the semblance of a divide, and he's in the position that he can turn a blind eye to the Dicks without it being a problem."

"Until now," Nessa said.

"Until now," Mimi confirmed.

✧　✧　✧

KINGSLEY

THE LIGHT FALLING through the windows dimmed as the day slid into night. Kingsley sat forward in his office chair, his elbows planted on top of his desk and his gaze far away, thinking about the meeting he'd just had with Austin.

Well, not *just.* It had been over an hour since he'd turned from his brother and shut the door behind him. Over an hour stewing in the anger and frustration that meeting had caused. Over an hour of growing uncertainty about the fate of this pack and his family.

His phone clamored across the wood. Earnessa's picture popped onto the screen. He should be home by now, getting everything set up for dinner. This was the big reveal of Austin's mate. Everyone was curious to learn more about the woman who'd finally pinned his wild younger brother down. They wanted to know if

Jessie could handle him or if their relationship was as doomed as Kingsley's parents' had been.

Mother and son would also need to reconcile. Kingsley had no idea how that would go. His mom kept her emotional cards close to her chest at all times, not even confiding in Kingsley. He did know, however, that the reunion between his daughter and his brother would likely be fraught. Aurora was not quick to forgive, and she'd been devastated when Austin left without saying goodbye.

All that lay before Kingsley, and usually he'd be eager to get to it. It was about time for their family to get together, whole once again, easy and friendly but with the little arguments family always seemed to have at these things. Aurora's new man-friend was a source of contention, for one. Kingsley's son Mac having zero interest in the future of the pack or a role as alpha was another issue.

But those seemed like trivial nothings compared to what had happened at that meeting earlier.

A knock sounded at the door.

"Come," Kingsley barked, ignoring the phone and sitting back in his chair.

His beta entered with tight eyes and tighter shoulders. This wouldn't be good news.

"Did you get them all settled?" Kingsley asked.

117

James took a seat in one of the plush leather chairs facing the desk, a remnant from when his mother had ruled from this office.

"Yes, with a couple of housing changes." James leaned back and crossed an ankle over his knee, getting comfortable.

"Which are?"

"Most notably, the mages won't be taking that house after all."

Kingsley planted his elbows on the arms of the chair and steepled his fingers. "Where will they be staying?"

"With Austin and his mate."

Now Kingsley's eyebrows lifted. Austin was breaking protocol there. Usually an alpha stayed solely with family.

"Did he give a reason?" Kingsley asked.

"They worried about the mages being separated from the others in case any of the pack decides to try to…cut out the threat."

"Meaning he thinks my people won't know friend from foe?"

"Yes, and I didn't push, because when it comes to mages, I'm not sure we *do* know friend from foe. Most of the pack won't easily tolerate mages within our borders." James hesitated for a moment. "Not to mention that Austin's mate—"

"Jessie. Use her name. She might not be a shifter like us, but she is his forever. She's good for him. You saw it yourself. She has a wild side, but her personality balances it. I saw it firsthand."

James held Kingsley's gaze for a moment before looking away. "I did," he admitted. "I didn't think anyone could back that polar bear down. You remember how his old girlfriend, Destiny, used to incite him against me, trying to get him to kill me and take the beta position. It almost worked on a few occasions."

"I remember. Jessie isn't like that, and Austin is firmly in control of that beast."

Firmly in control, in a way their dad had never been his whole life. Kingsley had seen his brother's beast earlier, looking out of his fiery cobalt eyes, ready to be let off leash. But Austin's cool logic had reigned supreme—he'd used the beast instead of letting it use him. His control would make him ten times more dangerous. Ten times more effective.

"Not to mention," James started again, "that Jessie explained a mage's countermeasures to break-ins. They happen in the mage community a lot, it seems. For those that are higher-powered, at least. We can't let him accidentally or purposely kill any of ours."

A weight formed in Kingsley's middle, but he simply nodded. He needed time to work through his misgivings regarding the mages—and also what that one mage had said to them. He needed more information.

"The other housing changes?" he prompted.

"Only some of the basajaunak stayed in the park we'd chosen."

"Where did the others go?"

James shook his head. "They just wandered away. Austin's—Jessie apologized about it. She said she'd figure out a compromise with you once they have some idea what might work. The landscape here is much different than what they're used to, I guess." He paused. "They don't seem…entirely in her control."

Kingsley dropped his hands to his lap, allowing his fatigue to come through. They'd only just arrived and already the headaches were piling up. He would've liked to say this was all a mistake and to hurry Austin's people out of here, but the growing ball of unease in his gut said that would be a mistake.

"Only one of them is under her influence, I guess," Kingsley said, "and as you saw from the meeting earlier, with her people wandering every which way, that influence is nothing like what we're used to."

"Noted. I'm inclined to compromise in this case, alpha. Those creatures are massive, and I've heard basajaunak are incredibly effective in battle. They'll give us an edge."

"Agreed," Kingsley said. No other pack in history, as far as he knew, had ever had aid from the basajaunak. It was promising and exciting, as long as everything went smoothly, but Kingsley wasn't entirely sure it would. Not after earlier. "That it?"

"No." James pulled a piece of paper out of his back pocket. "Edgar—the vampire—has requested a shack. He'd like it put on Austin's premises so he can watch them from a safe and nonthreatening distance. Austin and Jessie denied the request, but the vampire then asked me in an aside if I would build him a secret shack." James lowered the paper, his mannerisms showing his befuddlement. "I denied the request. The old gargoyle, who calls himself a butler, requested to stay with Austin and Jessie, which Austin also denied. He then requested a shack, as well, because if he was going to be cast aside like a peasant, he'd live like one. That request"—James looked over the top of the paper at Kingsley—"was also denied, and prompted a razzing by the puca."

James's eyes were sparkling. He clearly thought the whole thing was asinine but hilarious.

"Oh, and…" He cleared his throat. "The phoenix doesn't think the trend of wearing underwear should continue. Especially bras."

"They're...an eccentric bunch," Kingsley said, not sure what else could be said to explain that sort of behavior. The pack would think them mad. And maybe they were. But they were effective in battle, something he'd seen a bit of firsthand. He didn't have much knowledge about gargoyles, but he suspected that lead enforcer, as Austin called him, could handle a great many enemies without batting an eye. He also seemed to have a very firm handle on the rest of the gargoyles, all as big or bigger than shifters, all muscular, all hard-eyed and keyed up, ready for battle.

"Also..." James went back to his slip of paper, turning it over to retrieve more notes. "When the vampire cornered me after Austin and Jessie had gotten into the van, he talked about planting flowers in the territory." His eyes dulled. "Weaponized magical flowers, to be precise."

Kingsley pushed to standing. He couldn't handle any more of this right now. This territory was a home to ten thousand people, most of whom wanted to live peaceful lives, untouched by the darker, stranger parts of the magical world. He wanted to keep it that way—a goal that had seemed doable with Austin's help. The magical attacks on the edge of the territory thus far had been mostly manageable, with few losses. If there *were* mages in the border towns, they hadn't caused any trouble.

It had led Kingsley to re-evaluate the nature of the threat he'd once perceived. Honestly, since the attacks hadn't escalated, it didn't seem like mages would risk waging a full-scale attack on them after all. It made Kingsley wonder—and his top shifters with him—if the enemy actually had the resources to take on a pack of Kingsley's size. It didn't seem so from the last grouping of months.

Except that mage earlier had been telling the absolute truth as he knew it. His body language had made that perfectly clear. Jessie had been obviously worried, as well, no better at hiding her feelings.

Kingsley needed to think. He needed a second.

He excused himself from James and made his way home, his mind still in turmoil as he parked and then made his way to the front door, letting himself in.

"I've been calling you—where have you been?" Earnessa said, walking into the foyer with her hair in curlers and wearing a robe. "The pizza oven needs to be started, and you promised to help set up the food stations. I don't know what sort of things your brother's mate would like, and I never seem to get it right when it comes to your grandma."

He shook his head as he pushed past her. "I had a run-in with Austin."

She followed him into the kitchen, where he pulled

his wallet and keys out of his pocket and dropped them on the edge of the counter. She whisked them away immediately, opening the drawer in front of her and depositing them inside.

"What sort of run-in?" she asked, an edge to her voice. "I thought you said he's changed."

"He has. He's more confident now. He's grown into the leader he always had the potential to be."

She popped out a hip, leaning heavily on the counter. "What does that mean? You don't think he's going to challenge for placement and remove you, do you?"

He could hear the worry in her voice. She'd never trusted Austin, not before he'd challenged and almost killed Kingsley, and certainly not after. The fear that Austin would take over the pack and displace Kingsley and his family had haunted her. Haunted all of them, maybe.

Now, here he was again, stronger and better than ever, ready to lead a large pack.

"I don't know," Kingsley said, peeling off his suit jacket and putting it on a nearby chair. "If he challenges me, he'll win. There is no question. His gargoyle beta—lead enforcer—would even be a hard battle for me. That gargoyle would dominate James, no problem. And I hear Austin has a shifter beta who used to be an alpha. As small as Austin's outfit is, it's stacked."

"But I thought you said he had his own territory," Earnessa pushed as she started taking things out of the fridge. "I thought you said he was happy where he was and wouldn't want this territory."

"I'd thought that, yes. I still think it. But the way he pushed back on me today..." Kingsley gripped the edges of the counter. "I don't get the feeling he's going to play submissive even though I'm the alpha of this territory. He's going to fight me on each decision, and Jessie isn't always going to be there to calm him down."

"You were submissive to him when you visited him, though, weren't you? You followed protocol?"

"Yes. And I'm realizing now that it wasn't hard. What *is* hard, however, is puffing myself up as more dominant when we both know I am not."

Earnessa was quiet for a moment. "If he challenges...he'll stop before he kills you, right? He won't get so mad he can't stop?"

Kingsley let out a breath, turned, and pulled her into a hug. "I'll be okay. I don't think he'd kill me." Kingsley hoped it wouldn't come to that. Not again. "I just worry about his taking over for the coming attack. My job as alpha is to keep life as normal as possible for everyone. I don't want our pack to become a war zone if it doesn't need to be. I'm worried he'll finish the job he started when he left and tear our territory apart."

CHAPTER 8

JESSIE

I DID A quick last check in the mirror and then changed my mind about the necklace.

Austin had said to look semi-dressy but casual and have some bling but not go overboard. Which was all well and good, but without the Ivy House crew around, I had to dress myself, something I'd never excelled at. My ex would constantly tell me that I was too formal, or too casual, or wearing black to this particular luncheon was *all wrong*. I'd always had to go "run and put something a little more appropriate on."

Except Austin would be happy with anything I chose because he was a little too supportive about my terrible fashion sense. Could the guy not have given me a picture or something?

After trying on everything in my suitcase, I'd decided on a black halter turtleneck gown that showed off my shoulders and had a slit up to my mid-thigh, but otherwise the bottom reached down to my lower calves. To make sure I wasn't too dressy, I wrapped a wide leather belt with a stylish buckle around my waist. To complete the ensemble, I'd chosen a gold strappy sandal with a three-inch heel, a gold and diamond bracelet, matching dangly earrings, and a necklace that did not work at all.

Hence the decision to lose the necklace.

After grabbing a clutch that only had lipstick in it, I headed downstairs, ten minutes late.

"No, no!" I heard Nessa shout. "Get out of here! This is not your dinner."

She and Austin were in the kitchen, both at the large island that took up a bit too much space. Austin stood near the double sink by the oven—I'd never seen both of those things built into an island—and Nessa held her hands out over a cutting board, keeping him from peering too closely at the contents.

"All I'm saying is—" he started.

"I hear what you're saying," she replied, "and all *I'm* saying is it's not your dinner. Mind your own business." Nessa lifted her eyebrows at him, stared a moment longer, and slowly dropped her hands to continue chopping an onion.

"You're gonna ruin it," Austin said, shaking his head but not wandering away. He wore a pink dress shirt tucked into slim-fitting navy slacks, ending in brown leather shoes that matched his brown leather belt. His five o'clock shadow and messy-styled hair, teamed with the fancy watch I'd gifted him, made him look modern and sophisticated, a little trendy, and a polished sort of rugged.

The man could do *posh* in his sleep. It was really annoying.

"And if I were making *your* dinner, maybe I'd be worried about what you thought." Nessa stuck her tongue out at him.

I heard footfalls and turned to see Sebastian coming down the hall to join us.

He smiled at me. "You look really nice, Jessie."

Austin glanced over his shoulder and then did a double take, his gaze sweeping down my body and then lingering on my face. His shoulders came around slowly, as if some other force were turning him.

"You look beautiful, baby," he said softly, taking the few steps toward me.

"Yeah good, go bother her," Nessa said before pointing at his back with the knife and catching my eye. "How can you stand him? He's a know-it-all in the kitchen. It's smothering."

"Maybe take a lesson—you might learn something," he replied, full of bravado. Nessa rolled her eyes.

"This is a strange setup for a kitchen." Sebastian stood next to the windows lining the wall. Below them was a bench seat topped with pillows and a cushion. "Is this bench seat in case the cook wants an audience or something?"

"Probably, and I'm sure he made plenty of use of it," Nessa replied. "His head is big enough to think he's some sort of celebrity chef."

Austin's grin was cocky, his demeanor uncommonly loose around them right now. "I didn't design this house, nor did I remodel it. I decorated the interior and went with it."

"Which is the only reason I'm saying anything." Sebastian turned around and sat down. "I don't even have a great view of what you're doing, Nessa. I'd rather sit at the island."

"Except you can't because of how it's positioned in the kitchen." Austin's gaze drifted back to Nessa's cutting board. "The design is not well thought out, something I didn't care about at the time. I was more interested in the size of the house."

"No surprise there," Nessa said, "your being a guy and all."

"Okay, we're going to head out." Austin opened the pantry and grabbed out a bottle of red. He looked at the bottle, frowned, and then looked at another. Then a

K . F .   B R E E N E

third.

"What is it?" I asked, debating on putting something in my clutch. It wasn't like I'd need money or anything, though.

"Nothing." He hefted the first bottle. "Ready?"

A wave of butterflies washed through my stomach. I was about to meet the in-laws, who had a bunch of shifter rules I was still learning. Hopefully Mimi would help me keep out of trouble.

"Yup." I stepped in close to him so he'd drape his arm around me.

He steered us toward the hall leading to the front door but paused at the edge of the kitchen. He turned back to face the mages.

"Don't burn my house down."

"Hah!" Nessa pointed a knife at him. "You and I are going to have a cookoff, bub, and I am going to rock your world."

"What amazing delusions of grandeur you have." He started forward again.

"You look great, by the way, Jessie," Nessa called. "Knock 'em dead!"

"Not literally," Sebastian added.

"She's fun." Austin opened the front door for me, waiting for me to go first. "If you didn't notice it, the garage is just on the side of the house."

We'd sent back all the rented luxury vans, and Kingsley had said he'd get the team some transportation in the meantime.

He paused after opening the detached garage, staring at a white Ford Taurus that had to be ten years old or more. It had a dirty windshield, iodized paint in some places, and a small dent in the driver's door.

His look my way was bewildered before he led me to the passenger side and pulled open the door. Before stepping away, though, he bent in to inspect the seats.

"Doesn't look like you'll stick to anything," he murmured, before heading to the other side and peering in there as well. He grabbed a set of keys off the hook near the back before climbing in.

"You guys just keep your keys in the garage where anyone could steal your car?" I asked as he gingerly threaded the key into the ignition and turned it.

With a cough, the car roared to life, much louder than it had any right to be. The radio blasted Bruce Springsteen's "Glory Days" from a cassette tape deck.

Austin tilted his head to the side as a smile crossed his face. He rested his hands on the steering wheel for a moment, looking through the windshield at nothing.

"Not when I had my Bugatti," Austin finally said, putting the car into gear. "I abandoned it years ago on the road when I decided to cut across the mountain. I asked him to get me something to drive around while I was here. He clearly thinks this is funny. And given his scent is all over that garage, no shifter in their right mind would touch it."

He drove in silence for a moment as the tape played.

"I should've backed down earlier," he finally said. "The last thing I want is to cause trouble in this territory. I've done enough of that for a lifetime. I want to reconcile with my family. I want to be on good terms with them again."

"I know," I said, patting his thigh. He grabbed my hand and held it. "But you also have to remember that if we don't hold up our end of the bargain and do all we can to help secure this territory, then you won't have a family. None of us are going to survive. Mimi made a good point. I mean, if something as logical as clearing out Momar's spies affronts him, we're butting up against some real problems."

Austin sighed and shook his head. "I'm not sure what I thought this homecoming was going to be like, but it hasn't started out great."

"It's going to be fine. Let's stay happy and fun and easy at this dinner and not talk about work. It'll be good."

He squeezed my hand. "I should warn you, Mimi and Earnessa don't really get along."

"I'd already gotten that impression."

"And my mom likes to tell my brother how to do his job. It creates tension, especially when too much wine has been poured."

"I'm happy to stay out of it."

"And Kingsley likes to enjoy a cigar and a brandy in his study." Austin paused for a brief moment. "Men only. You'll be left on your own for a bit."

"I told you before, Austin, I'm well versed in handling all sorts of family drama, including the kind that's directed at me. I'm a pro at being neutral. It'll be great."

He squeezed my hand again before pulling it away to turn onto a long driveway leading up an incline and to a large house. The entranceway had a wood trellis over it, flanked by windows with white shutters. A few cars were parked around the side, all of them fancy and newish, including a sporty BMW, a Lexus SUV, and a Mercedes sedan. It was like arriving at my ex-mother-in-law's house.

Another wave of butterflies invaded my stomach. At least Mimi was here. I had to keep reminding myself that I had her. And Kingsley, if he didn't run away to the men-only part of the house. The two of us had always gotten along.

"Here we go." Austin left the keys in the ignition and climbed from the car, his own nervousness coming through the bonds.

He met me on my side and took my hand, walking me toward the entrance.

"I used to think this house was massive," he said, his walk slow. "It's six bedrooms, over seven thousand square feet."

"That's a lot to heat. What changed?"

He huffed out a laugh. "Ivy House."

"Well…yeah, but Ivy House comes with dolls and now gnomes, so…"

His hand stalled in reaching for the door handle. Instead, he slowly swung it to the side and pushed the doorbell instead.

"Things will start feeling normal again," I said softly, wrapping an arm around his. "You'll see."

"We should've brought a cooler and some clam dip."

My bark of laughter was entirely unintentional and very ill-timed, because Kingsley opened the door to a face full of my spit.

"Oh my God, I'm so sorry." I reached forward to do damage control, immediately tugged back by Austin. "Right, no touching. But seriously, I'm so sorry. He made a joke, and I didn't expect it, and…"

Kingsley stared at me as he wiped his hand across his cheek. "Yes, I can see how a joke of his might catch you by surprise."

"Sorry." I curled my lips under in an effort to rein myself in, but his reaction was just so comical—and it felt so good to laugh after all the tension Austin and I had both been feeling—that I devolved into a fit of giggles. "Sorry!" Now I laughed harder because I couldn't stop, holding my stomach and bending over. "Oh my God, what a freaking life we've landed in, huh?" I let a few more chuckles pop out. "Phew." I wiped under my eye to dislodge a tear of glee. "So, anyway, what's for dinner?"

"Hopefully whatever drugs you took." Kingsley stepped back from the door. "Welcome. I think."

"Nice car, jackass." Austin lightly punched Kingsley as we passed him, entering the house. "I can't believe you didn't find one with an eight-track."

"Like that? I figured as your mate keeps you flush with the sports cars, I would get you a Common Dick vehicle. The cassette deck was an added bonus."

Austin curled his arm around me, bracing it on my hip and pulling me in close. Kingsley looked between the two of us for a moment, and I worried he'd mention what had happened earlier.

"Do you need a tour, or can we just skip to the food?" he asked, his face still deadpan and his tone droll, as though having dinner parties was like pulling teeth.

This time I tried to get a hand up to stop the spit flying at him, the laughter taking over again.

"Maybe...I should...step...outside," I said through giggles, wiping the other eye now.

"Jesus." Kingsley shook his head and walked into the house.

My laughter turned to wheezing as I tried to keep it in. Austin just waited patiently, a crooked smile on his face.

"Sorry," I whispered, really trying to get myself under control. "Sorry." I straightened up and cleared my throat. "Okay, I think I have it all out now. Hopefully they are in the other part of the house and couldn't hear me."

Of course, I wasn't that lucky—we'd just walked into a cavernous area that held a family room, an open kitchen, and a glass dining table across from huge picture windows. The floors were all beautifully polished wood, with echoing rooms and an abundance of open space, nothing to really catch sound.

"Oh no," I whispered as Austin walked us toward the kitchen, crowded with people looking our way. I cleared my throat again, the fit of humor now a distant memory.

"Hello!" A woman about my height walked forward

without a smile. She had deeply bronzed skin with high, rounded cheekbones and lush red lips. Straight black hair fell to her lower back, and a sleek red dress was cinched around her waist. Her deep brown eyes held a hint of wariness, and her posture tensed up a bit when she zeroed in on Austin, but she was no less stunning because of it. "Welcome! It's been so long."

She stopped about three feet away, usually the distance a person would put out their arms for a hug.

"Earnessa, hello. Thank you for having us," Austin said formally.

Neither of them moved toward each other, and I remembered Kingsley asking Austin's permission to hug me once.

"Oh." I pointed my finger between them. "You guys can hug if you want. Or high-five, or whatever you want to do. I don't mind." They didn't move any closer. "Or just stare awkwardly, I don't know. Whatever you think is best."

All movement stopped. Eyes came my way, and the silence rang in my ears.

My mouth fell open at what I'd just nervously babbled. I didn't know how to backtrack, though. This time I didn't have Mr. Tom's weirdness, or Niamh's crass outbursts, or Edgar's creepiness to break my fall. I was the odd one out in this room.

"Never mind," I mumbled. Earnessa now studied me quietly.

"Earnessa, everyone," Austin said, "may I introduce my mate, Jessie Ironheart, co-creator and co-leader of the Dusky Ridge Convocation, mistress of Ivy House, and the only female gargoyle in existence. Jess, meet Earnessa, mate of the Gossamer Falls pack alpha of the Barazza line."

"Hello," I said warmly despite the cool way she continued to study me. I gingerly lifted my hand, seeing if she'd go for the handshake.

"Jessie, welcome." She didn't reach forward, so I dropped my hand immediately. "It's good to have you. Please, let me introduce you around."

She gestured. I expected Austin to release me so that I could walk wherever she wanted to stick me. Instead, he stepped forward with me, his hold around me tight, keeping me firmly pressed to his side.

We stopped in front of an older woman who had Kingsley's look about her, with a square face and somewhat rounded nose. What once might've been sandy-blonde hair was now light gray, cut just below her chin. Her bearing was regal and her style of dress was similar to Mimi, elegant with flowing silks in pastels.

"Please meet Denise, the former alpha of the Gossamer Falls pack and mother to the current alpha."

I smiled even though no one else in this house did. It was supposed to be allowed among family.

"It's really great to meet you," I said, bowing stupidly without meaning to. I clasped my hands tightly in front of me to prevent myself from forcing a hug or trying to initiate that high five I'd mentioned earlier.

"Hello, Jessie," Denise said, her voice warm even though it didn't reach her eyes. "You were a past Jane, is that correct?"

Austin just barely tensed.

"Yes," I said without reservation. It wasn't something I considered embarrassing, even if her intention had been to shame me. It was who I was. "A magical house chose me to be its heir, a mage manipulated me into taking the house's magic, and I learned to fly by being tossed off cliffs. It's been a really wild year. I've forgotten what normal looks like, hence...you know." I gestured at myself. "The way I began this dinner party."

"That's not how you found your wings, though," Austin said, his fingers digging into my hip and the bonds all kinds of emotionally turbulent. "You had to learn to fly when we were trapped in a cage above a cave full of spikes."

"Oh yeah." I nodded and hooked a thumb toward Austin's chest. "He jumped onto the cage through a

searing magical spell, somehow didn't black out from
the pain, and basically told me that if I didn't figure out
how to fly and consequently save him, we'd both die
there together. This all had to be done before the
basajaun, who was guarding me at the time, finished
pretending to have a sprained ankle." I leaned into him
a little harder. "It's probably hard to believe any of that
really happened, but there you go. That's my life now."

Denise studied me for a moment. "It is hard to believe, yes, but you are clearly telling the truth."

She meant that I was advertising my every thought
with my body. It wasn't something I could help.

"Being a past Jane, you are a hugger?" Denise asked,
her hard stare a little off-putting.

"Usually, yes," I replied. "Sometimes hugs can be a
bit awkward. Like with strangers who randomly guffaw
at the beginning of dinner parties. Me, I mean. Which
you probably knew. Because you must have heard…"

Oh my God, why couldn't I stop babbling!

"You all probably have the right way of it," I finished up, and then promptly wanted to die.

"Yes, I see. Maybe when we are better acquainted,
then."

I bobbed my head, because that was nice of her,
even though it sounded like she'd rather hug an angry
crocodile.

Her light brown gaze moved to Austin, and I could tell his heart rate increased.

"Austin, you've returned home," she said, zero emotion showing in her tone or expression.

"I shouldn't have waited so long. Can we..." He paused for a moment, half glancing at me.

"Jessie, come sit near me and we can finish the introductions." Mimi held up her hand from somewhere behind two younger people. A stool scraped, and the younger people pushed forward in confusion, glancing behind them. Mimi was sitting at the kitchen island. So was Kingsley. "Then maybe we can eat," she continued. "I'm starved. I had nothing in my fridge when I got home. *Someone* cleaned it out and didn't refill it."

"Will you be okay?" Austin asked me quietly, his head bent toward me.

"Of course." I slipped out of his grasp. "Don't worry about me—I have some party jokes saved up."

His mood didn't lighten, but he nodded before stepping away with his mother, hopefully to reconcile and heal.

Head kinda down, feeling incredibly uncomfortable and probably advertising that fact, I walked around the gawking kids, ignored the staring hostess, and sat between Kingsley and Mimi. She slid a glass of wine my way, bless her.

"You need that more than me," she said. "Drink up. I'm looking forward to those jokes. Now, Earnessa, where were you in the introductions, or would you like me to take over?"

"No, Grandma Naomi, I'm sure I can handle it, thank you." Earnessa's tone could cut glass. She appeared behind the older teen boy, about Jimmy's age if I had to guess. He had a slightly lighter complexion than her, with wide-spread eyes, a narrow nose, and hair that flopped down onto his forehead. "May I introduce Cormac."

"Mac," the boy said, putting out his hand. "Put 'er there."

His eyes glimmered, and my smile grew as I shook his hand.

"And *this* is Aurora," Earnessa said, pride ringing in her voice. Maybe you weren't supposed to pretend you didn't have a favorite child in the shifter world?

The young lady was a stunner. Her stare was surly, but given both of her parents had the same resting look, there'd probably been no escape. She had wavy dirty-blonde hair down past her shoulders, with lighter blonde highlights, high eyebrows, and almond-shaped hazel eyes that were more than a little cool as they beheld me. She had her mom's cheekbones and full lips and her dad's strong jaw and defined chin.

She was older than I'd expected. They both were. Kingsley had described them as being college age, but Aurora looked to be in her mid-twenties. She must've been really little when she'd saved her daddy from Austin, because I remembered that Austin had stayed around the territory for five years after that, learning from Kingsley. He'd been in O'Briens for just under sixteen years. So yeah, mid-twenties sounded about right. She would've been an impressionable age when he'd left, ten or so if the math checked out.

One thing about her drew me in. Her intensity. That must've come from her grandfather, because it was the same as Austin's, rough and raw and volatile.

"Is it rude to ask extended family what they shift into?" I murmured to Mimi out the side of my mouth.

"Still a yes," she responded, just as quietly, even though everyone could obviously hear us with their bionic sensory abilities.

"You know what I am," Kingsley said before taking a sip of wine. "You almost got me into a fight with a phoenix, remember?"

"Contrary to your beliefs, dear sir"—I lifted my glass in a salute—"we are not always talking about you."

"That's the problem—you should be," he replied.

"I apologize." I smiled and bent my head to Aurora. "Hello. It's really nice to meet you."

She studied me for a moment, and I let her, feeling the pulse of her power, unable to help answering it with my own. My gargoyle twisted and swirled within me, liking that intensity.

"You're not what you seem," she said in a low voice, energy vibrating through her.

"Careful there, Aurora," Kingsley warned.

I smiled at her. "It's fine. And actually, I am exactly what I seem. Part Jane, part gargoyle, and part lost. Kinda weird. Happily a follower until I need to be a leader, and happily peaceful until I or my people are threatened. That's the thing about people—we're never just one thing."

"So you do magic?" Mac asked, leaning over his sister to be closer. Both were at the island now.

She popped her shoulder to get him to back off. "How come you don't have wings?" she asked. "I saw some gargoyles in town earlier. They all had wings."

"I do magic, yes," I said to Mac, "and females don't have wings in human form." I shrugged. "My wings are smaller, and I can't fly for as long as the males, but I *can* do magic, like mages."

Aurora looked at me for a moment longer before stepping away. Mac pushed in to take her place.

"I'm a panther, like Mom," he said quietly. "Aurora is a tiger, like Dad." He winked before turning away.

"Just so you can stop wondering."

I chuckled and faced the island again. Too bad Mac seemed like the black sheep of the family, because I could tell I'd get along with him perfectly. Everyone else, however, might be a trial.

CHAPTER 9

AUSTIN

A USTIN SAT ON the couch beside his mom in Kingsley's study. The place had gotten quite a refresh since Austin saw it last. Maybe adjourning to smoke cigars and drink brandy was a thing of the past.

"I don't have words for the apology I owe you," he told her, his stomach in knots. "'I'm sorry' doesn't cut it, and I know that. I should've told you I was leaving. I should've had the guts to explain face to face instead of taking off in the middle of the night."

She studied him for a long moment, showing no emotion, not even in her eyes. That had always been her way. The pain his father had unleashed on her had taught her to hide everything away. That was something she'd admitted to him once, and only the once, after drinking too much gin.

"I understand why you left, Austin," she finally said. "I agreed with it. Maybe I didn't like the way you did it at first, but given the state of the pack after you left, I understood why it was necessary." She took a deep breath. "What I don't understand is why, in all this time, in over fifteen years, you never once called. Or wrote. You never once told me that you were alive."

The air went out of him, and he sagged where he sat.

"I should've called," he said softly. "I know that. But the truth is…I was lost. I didn't know where I was headed or where I wanted to end up. I didn't know if I'd survive the darkness within me, or if it would emerge in the wrong town or with the wrong creature and that would be the end of me. Eventually I found a forgotten corner of nowhere and just…" He shrugged. "I didn't intend to be an alpha. I didn't take the title or claim the territory for a long time. I just…went to sleep, I guess. I didn't want to trouble you with my life. With my directionless existence. I knew it wouldn't sit well, and I didn't intend to change my mind. I figured it was for the best to take a back seat."

After another pause, she said, "What made you change your mind?"

"A woman walked into my bar after starting her life over. She wouldn't be defeated. She wouldn't yield. She entered her first magical battle as a Jane, fearless. She rose to her true potential—*keeps* rising to her true potential against impossible odds. Somewhere along the way…I realized I wanted to join her."

"Love is truly a miracle. But has she seen you? *Really* seen you?"

"She has seen all the parts of me that you've always advised me to hide. She's seen my rage and my twisting darkness. She's seen my ruthless possessiveness. She's allowed me to be open and honest and expressive. I haven't hidden anything from her, and yet she loves all of me anyway."

She looked away, emotion registering in her eyes, but when her gaze returned, they were steely again.

"But is she able to handle all of you?" she asked. "Seeing it…and being forced to temper it for the sake of your young or your family are two different things."

His heart felt heavy, and he understood now why he'd always been so afraid to love after Destiny. Why he'd tried to find a hole in the world and sink into it, comforted by obscurity. It was this language, damning him for the sins of his father. Casting doubt on him because of his genetics. When he was young, he hadn't controlled his inner darkness, that was true, but it was because no one had taught him *how*. No one had helped him find balance with his beast. He'd instead found the opposite, a woman who'd exploited him, further convincing his family he was unstable.

As an adult, though, he'd learned his way. Jess had helped him. And, in turn, he'd helped her. They'd learned from each other.

With sudden clarity came understanding. He would no longer suffer at the hands of his father. He would not live in the past. It was time to look forward. To protect their future.

With confidence, he looked his mom right in the eyes and said, "She cannot only handle all of me, she wants to. You have no idea what her beast is capable of. What *she* is capable of. We're a good match."

She clasped her hands in her lap. "I hope so. She's a pretty, lovely sort of person, I think. Her company is easy to keep despite the colorful babbling she employs when she's nervous. But son, those characteristics will invite challenges. You cannot fight all her battles for her, regardless of how much you might want to."

"She'll invite one challenge everywhere she goes, I have no doubt. But only one. After that, the naysayers will dry up. If you don't believe me, just keep your eyes on this territory."

Mercifully, his mom dropped the poignant line of questioning and moved on to asking for details about O'Briens and Ivy House.

"Well," she said after a short while, pushing to standing. "We better go save poor Jessie from Grandma

K . F .   B R E E N E

Mimi. Mimi didn't bring her book this evening for some reason. She's probably picking on everyone right now, running them ragged."

It seemed Mimi hadn't told them much about her time in O'Briens, and no one knew that she and Jess got along incredibly well. There was strength in an easy-going nature—it helped a person more easily navigate the assholes.

Maybe *that* was why he and Jess got along so well...

"Yes, Naomi, I understand that," Earnessa was saying when they reached the kitchen, using her whole arm to point at the fridge. "But it fits in the hole. Why wouldn't I get an enormous refrigerator if it *fits in the hole*?"

"I cannot fathom why you are going to such lengths to try to convince me that you didn't want a big refrigerator," Mimi replied. "You designed this house. You designed this kitchen. You had the plans drawn up. You *created* the hole that you then had to fill. This isn't rocket science. You wanted a big fridge, you got a big fridge."

"I cannot fathom why you always bring it up," Earnessa shot back.

Everyone but Mac sat at the island or hovered around the kitchen. No pots were bubbling or smells were billowing out, something Austin had noticed when they got there, but he now wondered if they'd been waiting for him to help prepare. Except there weren't any ingredients to chop up or work with.

"Excuse me," he said to his mom, and made a quick detour to the couch, where Mac was bent over his phone. "Hey, bud."

The boy looked up—no, not a boy. A young man now, with a few whiskers and budding muscle tone. Austin had missed so much of his life. Of all their lives.

"Hey Uncle Auzzie." Mac lowered his face a little, looking up from under his lashes. "Or are we calling you Uncle Austin now?"

"You can call me whatever you want. How've you been?"

Mac shrugged. "Same ol', same ol'. I'm learning to be an alpha even though I don't have the right temperament or any interest—"

"You have the perfect temperament and plenty of strength," Kingsley called from the island. "It's the laziness that's the problem."

Mac rolled his eyes. "They think I'll come around. Did Mimi tell you?"

"She filled me in on the hot buttons to avoid."

"Yeah." He lowered his voice so his dad couldn't hear. "I'd rather skip the pack and try my hand at being a Dick engineer. I want to build things and live in a big city. I'm not sure how much longer I'll play the dutiful son, you know? Aurora has the alpha game locked down. Not every alpha's kid needs to follow in the family footsteps."

Austin blew out a breath, half sitting on the back of the couch to look down at his nephew. "I just got back. I'm going to have to stay neutral on this one."

"You're going to be Switzerland?"

He grinned. "Exactly. Good luck. Hopefully having your black sheep uncle around will take some of the pressure off you."

"Maybe," he said grumpily. "Oh yeah…" He pushed up a little more so he could look over the back of the couch toward the island. "Is she really a female gargoyle?"

"Yeah. You should see her form. It's…something else."

He grinned. "That's cool. I might stick with the pack if we can bring in some different creatures."

Austin put up his hands. "Switzerland."

Mac laughed as Austin crossed the distance to the island, stopping beside the end closest to where Aurora sat.

"Hey," he said to her, his heart aching for not having kept in touch. For things having turned out the way they had. She'd been his little buddy back in the day.

She'd blossomed from a preteen, all knees and elbows, into a young woman with a very hard scowl. "How're you?"

Her eyes narrowed just slightly, her stare aggressive. Her power swirled, hitting him in a rush, one hundred percent alpha. The challenge caught him off guard, rattling through his mind and yanking on his beast. A rush of rage immediately flooded him.

Before he could blink or even get his bearings, the air in the kitchen flash-froze, turning solid. Anger boiled up from his bonds with Jessie, quickly replaced by calm, cool understanding. Magic still pounded, though, slicing through the dense air, throwing a wall between Austin and Aurora. He could see it shimmering, knew who put it there, knew the cause.

"Jess," he said, struggling to speak. He could barely see her through the now-throbbing magic, making his eyes sting. "Are you good?"

"I'm having a scary little moment just now. I felt her challenge you, and my gargoyle nearly swept me away. I'm good, though. I've got it. I'm just trying to calm everything down, which is not easy because Kingsley's magic has popped off, and Earnessa's magic is pounding at me and my people felt my stupid magical pulse I didn't mean to send through the connections and are coming here for battle. Lots of big personalities in the mix. I'd really love to step outside and cool down, but if anyone rushes me right now, things might get…messy."

It seemed Austin's mom would have a new member of the family to worry about. At least Austin wouldn't be alone with his title of *unpredictably dangerous.*

"Earnessa, Aurora, stand down," Kingsley commanded, his power crackling through his words.

"I can make them stand down, Kingsley," Jess said through clenched teeth, "but I cannot handle much more of your power smashing into me."

"End the spell, Jessie, and I'll get a handle on this," Mimi said. "Denise, when you can, get Earnessa out of here."

"Let's all find our *chi*," Jess said right before the magic slid from the room.

Austin's mom and grandma moved quickly.

"What *was* that?" Earnessa demanded, pushed from the room by Denise.

"Come on, girl." Mimi practically dragged a stunned and wide-eyed Aurora off her stool. "What sort of a fool are you to challenge a woman's new mate? Are you out of your mind? That is the fastest way to get yourself killed—"

Her voice drifted away as they hurried down the hall.

Another pulse of magic shot out from Jess, calling

off her people.

Kingsley tensed. "What was that one, an all-clear?"

Jess hopped from her stool and hurried to Austin's side, plastering herself to his body. She breathed him in, her eyes closed, tilting her head up for a kiss. He complied quickly, knowing she was acting on her gargoyle's need to ensure her mate was safe. This was purely primal, all of this. Aurora should've been old enough to know better. He said so.

"I'm sorry," Jess started.

"I'm not talking to you, Jacinta," he said firmly, pouring alpha into his tone. Into the magic emanating from his body.

She shuddered against him, badly shaking now that the adrenaline was wearing off.

"Yes, please keep doing that," she murmured. "I am not in my right mind just now. I'm making all of our people nervous. Tristan is coming, even though I sent the magic to call him off."

"That new mate bond hasn't calmed down yet?" Kingsley asked, leaning against the counter on his elbows.

"No," Austin said. "If anything, it's gotten stronger. Did you hear what I said?"

His brother gave a world-weary sigh before standing to grab the bottle of wine and refilling his glass. "Yeah, I did. And yeah, she knows better. She's just at an age right now when she's trying to flex. She's got a lot of power, and she's getting impatient about using it. I'll talk to her." His gaze went to Jess. "Jessie, I apologize about that. Thank you for not...doing the million things you could've done that would've been infinitely worse than what you did."

Jess shook her head and peeled away from Austin. "I still need to get a breath of fresh air. I'll have to talk to Tristan, anyway. He's nearly here."

She headed for the door at the other end of the large room, leading out onto the patio.

Kingsley leaned forward again, rotating his glass and watching the wine swirl within it. "Aurora's been a handful these last few years. She's got a streak of Dad in her." His gaze came up to Austin. "Like you."

Austin glanced toward the door through which Jess had disappeared. Her emotions were still unsettled, but her anger and frustration were completely gone. She was no longer in danger of losing her cool from that challenge.

Austin took a seat at the island. "Is she ready for her own pack?"

"If she were like most budding alphas, yes. A small one to cut her teeth on. But that wild streak of hers is always pushing for more. Bigger. She's not destructive like you were—usually—but she's restless. She's not content to wait for me to hand over the reins like I did with Mom. She needs guidance."

"That you can't give her?"

Kingsley shook his head slowly. "No, not anymore. I don't have that wild streak. I was always the calm, patient—"

"Balanced one, I know. What do you plan to do?"

Kingsley looked away. "I don't know. Watch her around you and Jessie to make sure she doesn't accidentally get herself killed?"

Austin stood to get himself a glass of wine, but then just took Jess's for now. It was easier. "I'd say she won't, but gargoyles aren't known for their soft temperament."

A smile touched Kingsley's lips and his eyes sparkled. "That was something, though, huh? I didn't even know what was happening until I couldn't move. Jessie has come a long way. I remember when she didn't have any control. Now she's strong enough to stop herself from protecting her mate and re-staking her claim."

"The Jane in her wars with the primal needs of the gargoyle, that's why."

"Whatever the reason, it's created a great mix, though Mom probably won't think so. You two will be banned from dinner parties."

Austin laughed. "I was thinking the same thing."

"Though I will say, throwing around a bunch of magic and freaking everyone out is a lot more exciting than arguing about a fridge hole."

"That sounds awfully dirty, Dad," Mac called from the couch.

"Mac, I forgot you were there," Kingsley said before taking a sip of his wine.

"Story of my life," Mac replied, going back to his phone. "Pretty sweet magic, though, I have to say."

"Did you crap your pants like your mom and sister did?" Kingsley asked.

"Nope." Mac stood and came around the couch to the island, placing his phone down before he sat.

"Put it away," Kingsley warned.

Mac rolled his eyes, but he grabbed up the phone again and stuffed it into his pocket. "When her magic kicked off, I just enjoyed the ride. It was a rush. I liked the feel of it. It's spicy, kinda, don't you think?" He was met with blank stares. "Well, it's cool, at any rate." He looked around the empty counters. "No snacks?"

"Mom got distracted by Grandma Mimi," Kingsley answered.

Mimi walked into the kitchen a moment later, catching Mac digging into a bag of chips.

"You're going to spoil your dinner!" she accused him.

He tilted the opening of the bag her way, and she reached in to grab a few for herself.

"Speaking of dinner," Austin ventured. "Is that something we might start preparing, or are we hoping this night will last forever?"

"Mac, go get your mom and Granny," Kingsley said. "I think the introductions are about done."

Mac grinned, dropping the bag onto the counter and walking from the kitchen.

"Where's Jessie?" Mimi asked with a crease in her brow. "You didn't chase her away, did you?"

"She's outside with that enormous gargoyle," Kingsley said, then looked at Austin. "Where do you find these creatures…"

"Yeah, he's something, isn't he?" Austin replied. "Just wait until you see his other form."

"Okay." Earnessa came bustling in like nothing had happened. She tapped the counter in front of Austin and looked around the kitchen, ignoring Mimi. "Where's Jessie?"

Austin's mom walked in gracefully a moment later, her gaze lingering on Austin for a moment before shifting behind the island. Kingsley grinned at Austin, both of them knowing their mom was thinking about the potentially dangerous mate Austin had found. She wouldn't be wondering if Jess could handle him anymore.

The patio door opened and Jess stepped back in, her face a little flushed from the cold and a large shape behind her disappearing into the night.

"All good?" Austin asked her, standing again as Mac re-entered.

"Mostly," Jess said, her hand at her side. A large tear ran the length of her dress, from just under the side of her breast to her hip. "I need some clothespins or something. I nearly shifted earlier, and the dress couldn't handle it."

"Oh my—here, come with me." Earnessa held a hand out. "We can find you something to wear. You're about my size."

"I might need some socks for my bra to fit into your clothes," Jess said, giving Austin a funny look as she passed him.

"Let's head out." Kingsley stood and grabbed his glass. "They probably won't be long changing."

"Aurora?" Austin asked.

"Will keep to her room and get leftovers if there are any," Mimi replied with a slightly raised chin. "She's lost the privilege of our company."

"It was my fault as much as anyone's," Austin replied. "She's angry with me. She has every right to be."

"An alpha can have many emotions," his mom said,

"but she must be conscious about when to show them. She knows this. It was a grave slip in her control, and she needs to reflect."

"The women have spoken. C'mon, Austin, Mac…" Kingsley jerked his head toward the back door, this one leading to the sunroom. "Let's get things underway while they fuss about fridge holes and borrowed clothes."

"Why me?" Mac asked, pausing in reaching for the chips again.

"Because you're a man." Kingsley followed that up by beating on his chest.

"That answer has zero relevance—"

"Just go with your father," Mimi interrupted. "Give us a moment away from your whining."

"Maybe I should challenge Uncle Auzzie so I can go to my room, too," Mac grumbled, trudging after Austin and Kingsley.

"Don't even joke about that," Austin's mom warned.

"Why?" Mimi replied. "He's never going to be an alpha."

"Don't you start," Mom told Mimi. "We've had enough arguing for one day. Go get a book if you need to—"

Kingsley closed the door behind Mac, cutting out

the sound from the kitchen. He paused with a weary sigh.

"Did you miss all the bickering, Uncle Auzzie?" Mac asked, perusing the long table set up with all sort of ingredients. He grabbed a piece of what looked like sausage and popped it into his mouth. "Dinners are always like this now. That, or everyone pretends to be social and the conversation is awkward and forced. It's a real hoot."

"No one asked you," Kingsley said, walking over to the table with Austin to check everything over.

A plethora of shredded cheeses were identified with little signs. Chopped veggies, also labeled, lined one side of the table, and cut meats covered the middle. A couple of different fruits, including pineapple, had been arranged at the end.

The table beside it held balls of dough, large cutting boards, and bins of flour. A third held wooden trays, plates, utensils, and tomato sauce.

Kingsley crossed the room to the far French doors.

"Don't tell me you got a brick oven," Austin said, following him.

Kingsley stopped before reaching for the handle, though. As he looked out, his body tensed and his power swirled, but he didn't push through the door to confront whatever was troubling him.

"One of yours, I believe," he said, turning.

Mr. Tom stood just outside wearing a trench coat, large gold glasses with dark lenses, a checkered scarf, and a fedora hat.

"What *is* that?" Mac asked, coming to see.

"It's a weird gargoyle who can actually blend into stone and buildings but instead chooses to put on these ridiculous, elaborate disguises that paint him as the nutcase he is."

"Sticks and stones, sir," came Mr. Tom's muddled voice through the door. "Sticks and stones."

"Nothing wrong with his hearing," Kingsley said, finally opening the door.

CHAPTER 10

JESSIE

"I'M REALLY SORRY about that, Jessie," Earnessa said as I quickly changed into a navy dress that was a bit loose everywhere but the bust area, which was *very* loose. "She's always had an affection for her uncle despite…the past."

"They have a similar intensity." I stepped out of the large bathroom decked in marble with threads of gold running through it. "No sweat. I get it. I was just surprised, is all. It's hard to be rational where Austin is concerned."

"I get that." Earnessa led me out of the bedroom and down the arched hall with ten-foot ceilings. "It was like that with Kingsley when we first mated. I was love and rage side by side, throwing girls across bars and challenging anything that got near him. But you've been mated awhile, haven't you?"

"Yes. A few months now."

"Does the mating fervor last longer with female gargoyles?"

"Honestly, nobody knows. There's not much information about my beast. We've had to do a lot of guessing."

Mimi and Denise were murmuring quietly in the kitchen together when we walked in.

"Where are the guys?" Earnessa asked. "Getting the fire ready, I hope?"

"Yes." Mimi pushed off from leaning against the counter. "We chased them out so we could have a little peace. Kingsley mopes much too frequently for my taste, always put out when we have these dinners."

"I wonder why," Earnessa murmured, giving me a knowing look before bustling me toward the side of the big room. "Let's go join them. Jessie, I heard the craziest thing today, by the way. Did you get townspeople to transport your Bigfoot? Or...is it Bigfeet when plural?"

I let her coax me out of the door as I explained the various details about the basajaunak, including their names, as I took in what Earnessa had referred to as a sunroom, which held three long tables filled with food items. A hot tub sunk down into the floor at the other end.

"Here we go..." She led us toward two French doors beyond the hot tub, and we stepped out onto a deck that ran the length of this side of the house. Lawn chairs and umbrellas had been folded up and stowed to the side under a canopy. To my right, under a covered area, hunkered a large grill with space for charcoal and gas burners lined up below it. A counter unit with a granite top held what looked like a small refrigerator and other drawers and cabinets. Two round outdoor tables had been arranged next to it, the chairs pushed in, and beyond them stood the three guys, with Kingsley stoking the fire of a big brick pizza oven.

Mr. Tom stood off to the side in a "disguise," the leaves of a nearby tree partially covering his face but nothing else. I'd felt him near but ignored him and, given the others were also ignoring him, figured it couldn't hurt just to leave him at it. It would be far too much effort to shoo him away.

"Very cool space," I said, feeling the overwhelming urge to return to Austin's side and glue myself to his body.

He must've felt it, because he turned, his hand in one pocket and the other holding his glass of wine. His hand left his pocket, reaching for me, an irresistible temptation. I met him halfway, wrapping my arms around his middle and soaking in his heat.

"You look nice," he said, holding me tight. "Feeling a bit better?"

"I'm usually pretty good at this family stuff, but this time I'm a little overwhelmed."

"Understandable. Life within a house of alphas isn't easy to navigate."

"Okay, everyone." Earnessa smiled and clasped her hands in front of her. "As you can see, we will be having brick oven pizza tonight! You have everything you need set up in the sunroom, and when you have the pizza of your dreams, bring it out here and my amazing mate will fire it up for you. He is incredible with that oven, I'm telling you! All our friends rave. Denise, you know, you've had it before." Her smile burned a little brighter, almost at half-mast now. "Okay, let's eat!"

"*Finally,*" Mac said, the first one through the doors.

"She talked you up pretty hard," Austin told Kingsley as we followed the others. "You'd better deliver."

"Usually she nitpicks at me. She's probably trying to compensate for how lovey-dovey you two are. It's making us look bad."

"Sorry you're not as awesome," Austin said, holding the door for me.

"No, you're not." Kingsley shoved Austin and walked in after me. "Thanks for holding the door, chump."

"Kingsley, be nice to your brother," Earnessa admonished him. "He'll think we don't want him here!"

"You don't," Mimi said, and Mac—standing by one of the tables of fixings—spat out a laugh before turning around and starting to cough.

"You'd better eat everything you just spat on," Denise told him.

"Yes, ma'am," Mac said, wrestling with a smile.

"Shall I give you a demonstration?" Austin asked Kingsley at the dough station.

"Oh, what, you're a pizza-making expert now?" Kingsley asked, crossing his arms over his chest with his wine glass tucked below.

"I was single and living on my own for a long time in that backwoods town without a lot to do besides tend bar and work on my hobbies."

"And pizza making was a hobby?"

"Of course. I knew one day you'd get that brick oven you've always wanted, but your mate wouldn't let you get because she was worried you'd burn the house down. You can wear people down like the best of 'em."

"Bullshit," Kingsley said as Austin rolled up his sleeves to reveal his muscular forearms.

"Do you need an apron?" I asked as my body tightened up. He'd actually never made pizza for me, and I was incredibly eager to watch the dough-tossing show.

"Oh! I almost forgot." Earnessa hurried to a little cabinet in the corner I hadn't noticed. "I had these made up."

Her eyes glimmering with excitement, she hurried to us and held out white aprons stenciled with a logo consisting of a half pizza on top of the pack name. To the side and a little behind the logo was a waterfall.

She looped one over Kingsley's neck before turning to Austin, then held two aprons out to the side for me to grab.

"I'll let you put it on him." She lifted her eyebrows at me before taking aprons to the others.

"Mom, no, I'm not wearing a—"

Earnessa swatted Mac's hands. "Cormac, do as your mother says. Put this on."

"Aurora doesn't have to."

"Aurora is secluded in shame and won't be joining us."

"Can't I just grab a pizza and go seclude myself in shame?"

Earnessa shoved the apron at her son, who was acting more like a spoiled teenage boy than a budding young man.

I reached up and looped the apron over Austin's neck, getting a kiss for my efforts. I tied it around his waist, leaning in to him to do it, before pulling on mine and securing it.

"Okay, I'm all set for the show, hot stuff," I told

him.

"You guys make me a little uncomfortable," Kingsley grumbled, taking a step back.

With a grin, Austin grabbed a handful of flour and tossed it onto the cutting board before spreading it around a bit. That done, he worked the dough for a moment with his fingers before dropping it onto the cutting board. He grabbed a rolling pin from the side and flattened it out a bit.

"This is enough dough for a personal-sized pizza, right?" he asked Earnessa.

"Just a little bigger than, yes," she said, standing beside the toppings table and watching us. The glimmer had faded from her eyes.

He picked up the dough again with both hands, then used his right to pull it in toward his chest before tossing it up. He caught it with the same hand and repeated four more times as I watched his bicep pop and release, pop and release.

On the fifth time, when it came down, he caught it with both hands. Making fists underneath the dough, he shimmied it across his knuckles before throwing the pizza up just above his head, spinning perfectly like I'd seen in a great many pizza restaurants. He caught it with the backs of his hands before throwing it up again, his hands getting a little wider and a little wider with each toss, stretching the crust out.

"They weren't really intended for all that," Earnessa muttered. "Just rolling them and sorta…" She put fists in the air like she was pressing something down onto a table. "Just sorta flattening them out would've been fine."

Austin finished by turning the dough on his hand a little before looking around for where it was supposed to go. Kingsley reached under the table and grabbed what looked like a brand-new, shiny pizza tray and laid it on the cutting board. Austin set down the dough, finishing by ensuring there was a good crust.

"Thanks, bro. Good lookin' out." Kingsley stole the pizza-shaped dough and headed to the pizza sauce, leaving Austin back at square one.

Austin smirked, shaking his head, and I laughed, loving seeing them razzing each other.

"Uncle Auzzie, can you show me?" Mac popped a piece of sausage into his mouth and hurried to Austin's side.

I watched with a swelling heart as Austin painstakingly walked Mac through the steps of prepping and throwing the dough, having to start over three times before his nephew got the hang of it. He never once tried to hurry things along or lost his patience, his entire focus on helping the young man succeed.

As Austin loaded the dough onto a fresh pizza pan, a worrying vibration thrummed through me. I turned away quickly, closing my eyes, narrowing in on that feeling. It was from my connection to one of the gargoyles, I knew, but I'd have to concentrate to get more information. Those connections were a science, and my knowledge was still at a remedial level.

The vibration thrummed again and then continued, allowing me to localize the feeling to a gargoyle in the air, due west from here, high up and circling. He'd spotted something, if I had to guess—very likely beyond the town, given the distance, but I didn't have a great frame of reference. I needed to do some flying tomorrow. Suspicion but not worry came through the link. He lowered in the sky a bit, then a bit more, before dawning understanding took over. He must've recognized whatever it was that had initially made him suspicious.

I kept tabs on him as he continued to circle. To watch. In another few minutes, he pulled away, and I let the connection fade into all the rest.

"What is it?" Austin asked, waiting beside me.

Kingsley paused by the French doors with his completed pizza in his hands and looked back.

I quickly told them what I'd felt. "It's nothing. False alarm from one of the gargoyles."

Kingsley didn't turn away, though. "You feel those

connections all the time?"

I toggled my hand as Austin picked up a pizza pan prepped with dough. "Mostly they're in the background. Only certain emotions trigger me. Just now, it was suspicion and caution. Danger, fear, intense anxiety, usually related to an enemy and not something like a spider—it's like the connection knows what's battle related, and everything else is filtered out."

"Huh," Kingsley said, fully facing me now. "And it's permanent?"

"For now. There *has* to be a way to reverse it—I just haven't had time to figure it out. Right now I'm just trying to figure out how to organize it. In battle or training, it can be incredibly overwhelming because I have emotions coming at me from all angles. I don't have time to sit all calm and collected in a field somewhere to sort through them."

"So you can employ a silent warning system?" Kingsley asked. "We've struggled with that. We get trespassers, the ones trying to feel us out, but we can never catch or kill them because a wolf howl immediately alerts them that they've been seen. We've tried telling the sentries to run a distance away so they can call it in, but these mages mask their scent and—"

"No, no, no!" Earnessa walked between us, her hands raised. "No work talk. This is a family dinner, remember?"

Kingsley's jaw clenched, but he nodded and re-sumed his walk toward the brick oven.

I looked at the empty cutting board. "So…" I gingerly reached for a ball of dough.

"Jess, no." Austin chuckled, his free hand on the small of my back. "I've got ours."

I looked between him and the personal-sized pizza dough he had on his pan. "I realize you like sharing, and I'm all for that, but you'll need two of those just to feel moderately full."

"We'll make more later. I'll teach you how."

Looking into his soft eyes and handsome face, I smiled like a dope and let him steer me toward the pizza sauce.

"Okay, let me guess what you love," Austin said, removing his hand from me and reaching for the handle of the ladle. He straightened up and put his head back for a moment. "You like a little spice in your sauce, I seem to remember."

He let the handle go and lightly dipped his finger into the sauce before tasting it.

"Not hygienic," I murmured, watching his lips close around his fingertip.

"Meh. It'll do. We can add more with the ingredients. Okay." He circled the sauce around the dough before leading me to the cheese. "You like your cheese."

"Mr. Tom never gives me enough cheese," I said as I watched Austin sprinkle four of the five available options onto the sauce. "Correct, blue cheese does not belong on pizza."

"My girl is a carnivore," he said, looking over the options. "But does she feel like being a fancy carnivore today?" He glanced down my body, taking in the apron and dress that wasn't mine. "I'm thinking we need a laid-back pizza. How about…"

He spread on pepperoni, sausage, salami, and linguiça.

"What would've been fancy?" I asked as he headed to the veg.

"A little prosciutto, maybe a balsamic drizzle…" He looked over the vegetables.

"Let's do that with the next one."

"As my lady commands." He spread on some yellow onion and green bell pepper before hesitating at the sliced olives. He released a breath, and I grinned as he reached for some.

"I thought we were sharing?" I asked sweetly, knowing he hated the very idea of olives.

"We are," he said, spreading them on half. "I'll be feeding you first, and I have your half all picked out."

I laughed. It was an intimate, often erotic thing for

shifters to feed their mates, a sort of throwback to their primal need to look after loved ones. I didn't share the same primal excitement, but I loved the way Austin responded to it, to *me*.

He sprinkled the pie with salt and pepper and a couple other spices before heading for the door. He stopped, though, noticing Mac standing not far away, holding his uncooked pizza, watching us.

"What's up?" Austin asked, glancing at his nephew's creation. "Do you need help?"

"No. I'm picking up tips on how to woo girls. This is legendary."

Austin started forward again. "I never did any of this with—" He side-eyed me. "Before Jess."

"Nice recovery," I joked.

"But I can see how it would be a good party trick. Wear a stupid apron—"

"Check," I said.

"Toss the pizza dough—"

"Preferably with shirt sleeves rolled up, exposing muscular forearms," I added.

"Okay, back up," Austin said. "Next, Mac, get muscular forearms."

"Har, har," Mac said as we stepped outside. "That's about the only thing I've got going for me—my physique. I have the body of an alpha but not the drive for it."

"There could be worse things." Austin handed our creation to Kingsley, who used his fancy pizza peel to move his cooking pizza over and slide ours into the oven.

"You know Auntie Jessie really well, though—"

"Aww, cute." I smiled brightly at him. "You're calling me Auntie Jessie!"

Mac paused for a moment, not sure what to make of that apparently, and continued. "What about if I'm going for a girl I don't know that well?"

"What are we talking about?" Kingsley asked, suddenly gruff. "What girl?"

"You just watch her body language," Austin said, moving out of the way so Mac could give his pizza to Kingsley. "You stop by things, or suggest things, or randomly talk about things you *might* do, like fancy versus laid-back—"

"Cheating!" I smacked Austin's arm. "Very suave."

Austin laughed. "Just pay attention to her signs. She'll tell you what she wants, even if she doesn't voice it."

We continued talking about idle nothings while the pizza cooked. Once it was ready, Austin sat us away from the others and placed our food down in front of us. One of his hands slid up my shoulder and around the back of my neck, pulling me closer so he could taste my lips. A moment later, he lifted a slice, watching as I pulled a pepperoni from his offering and popped it into my mouth.

"It was a rough start to the night, but I like the direction it's going," Austin murmured, his eyes hooded and his body hard.

"I didn't set up any fondue for afterward," I said after I finished the bite. I'd done that recently after a date I took him on. The chocolate fondue had been an erotic treat, though soon forgotten as we explored each other's bodies.

He smiled as he fed me a bite of pizza, and then accepted one from a slice I held up for him, realizing too late what he'd been offered.

"No! You didn't!" He pulled away from me, laughing and then making a face. "I can *feel* the olives in there. How *dare* you!" The last was said to mimic Mr. Tom's new favorite phrase.

Mr. Tom's eerie voice rose from the darkness. "If that was intended to mock me, I can assure you, I am not wounded."

"Feel the olives?" I took a bite of the slice I'd grabbed for him. "Hmm! I don't know about *feel*, but they sure are delicious."

"They have a weird consistency."

"*You* have a weird consistency." I stuck my tongue out at him and laughed again.

We finished that pizza and went back to make more, Austin teaching me how to catch and throw the dough and laughing at how bad I was at even the simplest things in food preparation.

"If it hadn't been a chore for you, if you'd had passion to learn, you might've picked it up a bit better," he told me, taking over the sauce application.

"Maybe you can teach me?" I sprinkled on the same cheeses he'd used on our first-round pizza. "I'm sure you can make it fun if anyone can."

"I'd love to," he said softly.

We ate our fill and then went back into the kitchen area, where we took seats at the island and drank wine while Austin and I told stories of the Ivy House crew's crazy antics. Dessert was served, a raspberry tart, and the evening ended with small or half-smiles from most of the shifters, a gleaming smile and hug from Mac, and an overall feeling of goodwill.

"My mother has no idea what to make of you," Austin said as we drove home in the Taurus.

"She was certainly staring a good bit. But she didn't belittle me, unlike a past mother-in-law, so I'm cool with that. At least we can be civil."

"It's not a like or dislike situation. It's..." He tried

turning the radio down, but the knob didn't seem to do anything. "Oh-kay." He left it alone. "I was so much trouble in my youth, and ever since I nearly took Kingsley down, I've been labeled as *dangerous*. I've always been the one to watch, the one who might unravel and take everyone with me. I think she worried she'd see herself in you—the survivor of abuse who couldn't get help because she thought it might look weak to the pack. I think she was ready to help you get free, or help you work through the pain she was certain I'd cause."

"Oh Austin, no, that can't be." I put my hand on his thigh. "She clearly loves being in your company. I could tell."

"She loves me, yes, but I'm also a haunting reminder of my father. I was like him in my youth. She's blinded by trauma, I think. But you've shown her that you don't need help. You're happy to sit on my lap and trick me into eating terrible vegetables."

"They're a fruit, actually. The fruit of an olive tree." I gently squeezed his leg, trying to lighten the mood.

"Fine, whatever. The point is, I think she was looking for those little signs of wariness a victim often shows when they're worried they've stepped over the line with their abuser. There weren't any, though, and now she's not sure what to make of us."

"Ah." I nodded. "Got it. Well, in time she'll realize that you've changed your trajectory in life. I truly believe that, Austin. In the meantime, since she's not the alpha anymore, maybe this is a good time for her to finally get some help? Maybe you or Mimi can give her a nudge. It's sad and unfair that she's had to carry that burden for so long."

"I'll talk to Mimi about it. Or maybe Kingsley, find a way to broach the subject."

He parked in the garage and left the keys in the car, probably hoping someone would take it.

"You still need to patch things up with Aurora, huh?" I asked as he opened the front door.

"Yeah. I'm not sure what'll make that better. I really screwed up."

He ducked around the corner of the kitchen, finding the space clean and shiny. On the counter waited a plate covered in plastic wrap with a handwritten note on top of it: *Tell me this isn't better than your wildest dreams!*

He snickered softly, putting the plate in the fridge. "She's going to get a page of fixes for that dish, no matter how good it is."

"You should do that pizza trick with her. I bet she'd be so pissed you guessed her favorites."

"I'll have Tristan do it." We headed down the hall,

and he turned off the lights as we went. The others were clearly tucked away in their beds or out wandering around town. Either way they'd be fine, since I doubted Sebastian would let Nessa out of his sight. "He drives her nuts for some reason."

"Probably because he is so confident he's going to claim her, and she wants Broken Sue."

"What a tangled web." He opened the bedroom door for me before hesitating at the hall light. "I don't have a nightlight, and the mages can't see in the dark if something happens."

"They have hands, though. They can turn on the light if they need to…"

A grin worked at his lips. "Valid point. C'mere."

He entered the room after me, whisking me up and closing the door, and I squealed in surprise. He flicked off the light to our room and carried me to bed, holding me tightly.

"I had a really good night, all things considered," he murmured against my lips. "I don't want to lose my family again."

"You won't."

I fell into his kiss and we slowly shed our clothes, savoring the glow of a night deepening our bond and extending our family. I had a feeling Jimmy would really like Mac despite the difference in magic, and I already had a fondness for Mimi. Earnessa would hopefully grow on me, and even if she didn't, I felt like with time we could become friends. And as far as mothers-in-law went, I'd had a lot worse.

We crawled between the sheets, and I cuddled up against Austin's heated skin. My body fit against his sensuously, and my heart beat slow and sure.

"I think Kingsley really likes you," he told me. We still lay on our sides, our hands roaming.

"I think Kingsley really likes *you*," I replied, feeling up his broad back, tracing the muscles there.

"My relationship with him is probably going to get complicated before long."

He kissed down my neck. "It got complicated earlier today, and you two still had easy camaraderie."

"I barely pushed back earlier today. We didn't do much more than almost challenge each other." He sucked in the peak of my breast, and I let my eyes flutter shut.

"I think it's good that family time and work time is separated." I moaned softly as he moved to the other before wrapping my legs around his middle as he worked back up to my lips. "If you two fight about work, at least you can spend quality time together and remember you're brothers."

"Eventually, fighting about work is going to be

fighting about his choices as alpha, which is as good as insulting his entire way of being. It'll bleed into family time."

I captured his lips, opening them with my own and swiping my tongue through. "Not if we figure out a way to keep it from devolving."

I angled my hips up to his hard length as I wrapped my arms around his neck.

He groaned softly. "Always the problem solver, hmm?"

I smiled through his kiss. "Not totally. I had to tell my parents that I was in a cult to explain my current situation. We can make this work. Even if things get rocky, you'll have time to mend them. If we pull through with Momar."

"*When* we pull through," he growled, and a shiver arrested me.

"Yes, alpha," I said in a silky voice, clutching his shoulders as he plunged into my depths and filled up my world. "I love you so much, Austin," I murmured, tilting my head back to soak in the exquisite feelings. "I love that we complement each other so effortlessly, and that you like public displays of affection."

He moved faster, and heat blistered through me, so delicious and heartfelt. Consuming.

"I love you, too," he said, reaching between us to

work what I needed.

I fell into his touch. Into the emotion coursing through our bonds. I felt limitless with him, like anything was possible. Nothing would stand in our way.

An explosion of pleasure tore me apart. I cried out, digging my fingers into his back as he shuddered out his release. Our breathing was harried and my heart knocked against my chest as a lovely euphoria set in.

I smiled, my eyes growing heavy, sighing softly at the welcome feeling of his weight on me.

"That better have been good to compensate for how loud it was," we heard through the wall.

Clearly Nessa had stayed in this evening.

"I forgot how thin these walls are here," Austin whispered, the bed shaking with his laughter.

"Why are the sheets fresh?" I asked. "This place doesn't seem like it was shut up for fifteen years."

"They said my mom was looking after it, but I wonder if my niece or nephew used it from time to time. When I left, I said in my note that they could."

"Hmm." I kissed his cheek and snuggled a little deeper into the mattress, tightening my arms to keep him put.

"One more time," he murmured, lifting to kiss me again, already hardening. He was never sated for long.

"No way. We can't do a marathon tonight. For one,

Ulric and Jasper always embarrass me about it, two, we have a lot of stuff to do tomorrow, and while I can heal, that doesn't totally compensate for zero sleep, and three, when you really get going, there's no way I'm going to keep the volume down, and the whole house will be up all night."

"Okay, okay. Just one more, though." He started moving slowly. "I'll stop at the one, I promise."

I laughed because I could never say no to him. Then I kissed him again, loving the feel of his lips. It was my favorite thing about us, our kiss. It felt like we poured our souls into each and every one. If it was the last thing I did on this earth, it would be enough. And a small, scared part of me wondered if the end would be soon.

CHAPTER 11

JESSIE

"OKAY, WHAT'S THE status?" I walked through the grass in the square downtown. My purple muumuu flowed around my legs and my flip-flops clapped against my heels. Nessa kept pace with a walkie-talkie, a little behind me, and Tristan waited in front of us on the sidewalk at the edge of the grass.

"The plants are—"

"No, Edgar." I put out my finger to stop him. He was loping beside me to keep up even though walking should've been perfectly fine. "We still need to ask Kingsley about the flowers. We'll get to that after the gargoyles do some mapping of the territory, okay?"

"Yes, Jessie." He fell away again.

We wouldn't need him right now. We weren't doing any training until the rest of our team arrived later in the day, and we couldn't come up with a strategy until we had a full rundown on Kingsley's defense capabilities while looking at a big, 3D map of the territory. Right now, we were getting our bearings in the sky, looking for any interlopers. I was done with letting the enemy sneak around the perimeter and getting away with it. We had to cut off Momar's information.

"The potion of those at the perimeter has been consumed, and we're just waiting for them to disappear," Nessa said.

I nodded and stopped in front of Tristan, noticing the walkie-talkie in his hand and the purple muumuu plastered to his body.

"That doesn't exactly fit you," I told him, trying to contain my humor. Non-battle-hardened shifters waited all around, watching our operation. I didn't need any challenges at the moment, and smiling tended to give people here the green light if they felt so inclined.

With our crew, we had a feeling they'd definitely feel so inclined. It was just a matter of time.

"Cyra supplied it, thinking she was helping me out," he replied, his grin saying he dared someone to make his day. "I didn't want to be rude."

"No one in their right mind is going to challenge you, you know," Nessa said.

"They will." He stepped away a little so that I could sit on a little bench, facing the grass. "Someone will convince themselves that gargoyles are lesser and aim for the largest one they can find to prove how big their balls are."

"Just don't chop those balls off. Jessie is strictly against that," Nessa said.

"We're trying to get along here, guys," I said. "This is Austin's family."

"They're not his family," Tristan growled, his eyes sparking. "At least not the people I've heard talking about him around town. A great many have poor things to say about him, and not much better things to say about the shifters who left here to live in our territory."

"He just needs a chance to show them that he's changed." I looked up at the sky, blocking the sun with my hand. Various colored specks dotted the frigid blue. "If the mages look up, they'll see us. If they have binoculars, they'll be able to sketch us." I puffed out a breath, putting my hand back down. "We need potions for everyone, not just the gargoyles on the perimeter trying to catch sneaky mages."

"Except remember what Sebastian said?" Nessa lifted her eyebrows at me. "We don't have nearly enough potion, we don't have the resources to make nearly enough, and you two in no way have the energy to *make* nearly enough. We need to ration."

"They probably already know you have gargoyles," Tristan said as the walk-talkie he held crackled. He didn't hold it up to his ear. "They'd be dense if they didn't. Gargoyles fly. That's pretty logical. What they don't know is how effective we are."

"Why would they approach the territory if they thought they could be seen?" I asked.

"They have invisibility potions, too, remember," Nessa said. "Besides, they might be more cautious, but they'll still come. They have to. Momar's people do not fail to complete their orders unless they want to be killed. They'll come, we'll snatch 'em up, and we'll crack them open and learn all their secrets."

"Very confident," I muttered, sitting down on the bench. "Maybe a little overconfident."

"Well, you know what they say—dress for the job you want, am I right?" Nessa winked at me as Tristan's walk-talkie crackled again. "Do you plan on doing your job, or are you just going to wait around all day for the challenge you're sure will come?"

His eyes sparked as he beheld her. "Are you picking a fight with me for a purpose, or just because you're bored?"

She tilted her head and grinned at him. "Bored. Say naughty things to me, Daddy."

I could feel my eyebrows lift. When she wanted to provoke him, she really went for it.

"Gargoyles are a go," a voice said through the walkie.

"Aww, shoot." Nessa snapped her fingers. "Too bad. I guess now we'll have to wait until *never* to get back to that conversation."

Gaze rooted to her, Tristan held out his walkie slowly. She took it with a devilish grin before he gingerly stripped off the muumuu. His skin shone in the morning sun, cut muscle and swirling ink. His carefully tended man garden was standing proud, her words obviously affecting him erotically. I yanked my gaze away quickly.

I was the only one, though. Nessa's eyes dipped low and then lingered before she pulled them back up.

"That's it?" she said, but the flush in her face betrayed her.

"Sometimes too much, depending on where I put it," he said smoothly before walking out to the center of the square with swinging shoulders, a cocky grin, and oh so much swagger.

He bent into a crouch, and then his gargoyle emerged, as large as a basajaun with a hair more width. His hide shone like liquid metal as his claws elongated, glistening black on his hands and feet. His wings extended down his back.

He straightened now, looking at the gathering crowd and letting them gawk. And then he glanced back at Nessa and held out his hand.

"What does—" She looked down at the two walkies in her hands. "Damn him. He planned that. Well, if he thinks I'm going to jog out there like his magical assistant or something…"

She stepped forward and threw one of them, her aim perfect. The walkie arched through the sky before nearing him. He reached for it lazily and snatched it out of the sky as his mighty wings snapped open with a *crack*. Several people in the growing audience flinched. His knees bent, and then he catapulted into the sky, ascending at a speed that elicited *oohs* from the crowd.

"He can certainly put on a show, I'll say that much," Nessa murmured, tilting her head back to watch him. "I always wonder if one day his brain will crack, and he'll kill me before I even get a chance to flinch." She sat down next to me. "Do you ever wonder that?"

I stared at her mutely for a moment. "No, but if I did, I wouldn't continue taunting him."

"Meh." She shrugged. "The fun is in not knowing. Okay." She held her walkie out. "We're just waiting on our big monster to let us know when everyone is in position, and then we'll be rolling. Do you need anything?"

I shook my head, closing my eyes. A sea of connections lit in my mind's eye, and I started organizing them by proximity, altitude, and other categories. I'd been painstakingly practicing this for weeks. Eventually it would be muscle memory, but I'd have to put in a lot of hard work to get to that point. I certainly wasn't there yet.

"Okay," I said softly. Things were about as organized as they were going to get. My gargoyle pulsed within me, sending out a shock wave. *Get ready.*

A voice came from close by. A man. "What are two pretty little—"

"Not now, bruh," Nessa barked. "Can't you see we're working? Get moving before I kick that leer off your face. Isabelle, what are you doing? You should be running interference!"

"Got laid up." I heard jogging as Isabelle ran up. "Some idiot tried to shove me, and I needed to break her arm really quick. These people do not like visitors."

"Or maybe they just don't like our type of visitors," Nessa replied.

"Probably more likely. I'm going to call in some basajaunak. I don't think anyone is dumb enough to mess with them."

"We shall see."

I wanted to tell them to *shhh*, but I repressed the urge. I'd need to do this in the middle of a battle while I was fighting. Quiet wouldn't be an option. I needed to start learning that now.

"Let's get going," I said, focusing in on the various groupings I'd made.

Nessa radioed up to Tristan, who was hovering right above us about a hundred yards in the air. His wings went from long, slow flaps to thrumming in a certain pitch. I sent a pulse of power up to ride the sound, carrying it way out, and added a distinctive flare that essentially meant *push northeast*. The goal was for the gargoyles to commit my various directives to muscle memory, so I could silently give orders during a battle.

When the gargoyles stopped, I noted their location. Northeast. Good. The next group followed their directive too. On and on we went, my surroundings falling away as I worked the connections. I could do this. I could create Kingsley an invisible (presuming we had enough potion), silent patrol.

"Okay." I opened my eyes to find a ring of basajaunak closing me in. Nessa still sat beside me, somewhat placidly, and Isabelle was nowhere to be found. I asked after her.

"Oh, well, a dude sauntered up to her, all bravado, just as the basajaunak were closing in. I guess the guy didn't see them, because he said something that wasn't very nice. Then he flew over the crowd in a very impressive display of acrobatics. Dave likes Isabelle. He showed it by grabbing the guy by the head and flinging him."

"By the head?" I gasped. I hadn't heard any of that. I'd had no idea my concentration could get so ironclad when I was working on the connections. That would probably be a bad thing in battle.

Nessa grimaced for my benefit. "Yeah. It probably didn't work out too well for that guy. But in all fairness, he started it. So anyway, after that, the onlookers decided that they had somewhere else to be."

"Crap," I said, pushing up to standing. "I need to be able to do that connection thing *and* pay attention to my surroundings. Kingsley is going to lose his mind when he hears about this."

"Okay, but mention the guy starting it. I saw the whole thing. I was right here."

"Dave, please don't kill people," I said as I squeezed between *Her* and *Him*. Hopefully soon they'd all decide they needed secret nicknames like Phil. Or just join our team and get non-secret nicknames. "We're supposed to just maim."

"Sure thing, Jessie," he replied from the other side of the circle. "I have learned my lesson."

I turned to quirk an eyebrow at him, but then decided to let it go for now. I'd need to gather all the basajaunak around this evening and explain the rules in detail. Again.

"I'm going up." I shed my muumuu and shifted, taking flight quickly and joining Tristan. Together we headed north, looking down at the shifter town and memorizing the layout from the air. People stopped near cars or on sidewalks and stared up, shielding their eyes from the sun to watch us fly by. We were an anomaly in this place.

Just outside of town on the northern side, Austin waited in polar bear form with a handful of our shifters. He reared up when I flew overhead and issued a fierce roar that seemed to concuss the air and reverberate off the surrounding mountains, pushed in close on the eastern and northern sides. Those areas wouldn't be so hard for us to defend, I was thankful to note. If the mages had vehicles, they'd find it nearly impossible to get over the almost desert-like shelves of rock and jagged peaks. If they had flying transportation, like a helicopter, my gargoyles would ruin their day.

Then again, they could always erect magical defenses. Sebastian was currently creating a list of what that might look like based on what his network had heard of Momar's plans. Unfortunately, they were bringing in less and less information as the battle drew closer. Momar had a lot of information on Kingsley's territory, but we had very little to go on in comparison. It was less than ideal.

I felt a gush of readiness and warmth through my bonds with Austin, felt his anticipation building and his adrenaline pumping. He was preparing his mindset for battle, thinking on how we'd lock this place down and confront the enemy.

I accidentally answered him with a pulse of magic. It blasted love and devotion across the sky and also tumbled downward, rolling across the ground and over all of our and Kingsley's people. Traces of it vibrated along each of my connections, flowing into the creatures on the other end. It was like sending a steamy text meant for your loved one that instead wound up on your grandmother's phone. How awkward.

In my mind's eye, a thick, solid connection lit up between Austin and me, like an unbreakable axis, and the other connections flared in response. It seemed like a huge, 3D, colorful spider web intricately connecting us all in our preparation for battle.

Then it dawned on me. The mate protector's magic, the magic Ivy House had reserved for Austin, would not only give him enhanced fighting prowess—it would also allow him to help me direct our army. With my magic, he'd be able to see them, feel them, and maybe even communicate directives to them if we could figure out how. Our situation couldn't be better suited for it—him on the ground and me in the sky.

Too bad that same magic tended to twist the mate protectors' minds. Past protectors had killed their mates in a fit of jealousy and greed. It was one of the reasons Austin hadn't taken the power, the other being that he wanted to meet the shifters on an equal playing field, with no extra legendary gargoyle magic passed down from a magical house.

Both of those reasons were why I hadn't pushed him. But man, would it be useful right now.

He led a group of shifters north to the border and then turned west, running along the territory line. Kingsley had been adamant that we stick to the pack land, only fighting when the mages and mercs breached the boundary. I didn't understand it, but there was so much space between the pack border and the surrounding towns that it didn't seem worth arguing the point.

I felt the gargoyles who'd taken the potions that would make them invisible and immune to others' invisibility potions. They were right over the boundary line, able to see for miles and miles, unless Momar had come up with a new potion that ours couldn't penetrate. It was always a possibility.

Austin picked up speed, covering the ground quickly and shedding shifters as they headed to their new posts. To the south, I could see two cars taking the small road leading away from the pack. None coming in. We'd need to set up some sort of checks to make sure we knew who was coming and going.

Toward the east, the terrain transformed into a rocky incline, too steep to be of much good to anyone. When we circled back to where we'd started, more shifters were waiting for Austin, and this time they accompanied him back toward town. As he hit the outer streets, cutting through the middle, they flared out until he had someone posted in every section.

I met him at the southern edge of the town, landing next to Tristan and shifting into human form. Not long after, the whining of three SUV motors could be heard coming closer.

Austin shifted into his human form, his eyes on me. "Tristan, watch her. Let me handle what comes."

Confusion dragged down my brow as Tristan partially stepped in front of me, his wings ruffling.

"Why, what's coming?" I asked, putting my hand on Tristan's arm to push him out of the way. I should've known he wasn't going to budge without magic.

An old Bronco, a beat-up Chevy pickup, and some sort of off-road, adult-sized go-kart-looking thing sped down the street, passing the last two houses. The Bronco pulled up in front of us, the Chevy to the side, and the go-kart thing with big tires jumped the curb onto the weeds and natural landscaping. They were trying to block us in for some reason.

My power started to pump, fanned higher by the possibility of my mate being in danger. The invisible gargoyles stationed in the air lowered, on hand in case there was a problem.

Austin put his hand out. "Hang on, Jess."

James, Kingsley's beta, stepped from the Bronco, leaving the door open behind him. His bearing was tense and authoritative. Behind us, Bruce climbed from the go-kart thing with his shoe laces untied and a hostile demeanor. A guy I didn't know came around the pickup, equally grumpy, ready for a possible problem.

"Beta," Austin said by way of greeting, his voice a growl.

"Austin," James replied, his gaze direct and dominating. "We've gotten word that you're spreading your people around our territory."

He'd gotten word? Did he not have eyes? It wasn't like we were trying to hide it.

"Correct," Austin replied.

"There are concerns that your operations are heavily militarized and that you seem less like a pack friend and more like a hostile takeover."

"I'm here to help fortify and defend this pack," Austin said, his gaze not dropping. "How did you anticipate

I'd do that, by sequestering my people to the town square to sing 'Kumbaya' while braiding each other's ass hair?"

He'd totally stolen that from Niamh, and it was epic. I barely hid my snicker. Tristan didn't stop himself from chuckling softly.

"You did not clear this *fortification* with the alpha," James said, and Bruce took a step closer.

Tristan changed position, his hand finding my back and nudging me between Austin and himself. He apparently thought I was breakable.

Annoyance and frustration ate away at Austin, felt through our bonds.

"The sole point of my people being here is to help protect the pack, James, as you well know. Otherwise I would've just brought my mate to meet my family. My people are learning the layout, defining the territory, and creating an invisible patrol"—he pointed up at the invisible gargoyle fanning us with his wings—"that the alpha expressed a desire in creating. If my people seem militarized, it's because we've dealt with smaller-scale versions of the sort of attack you're about to face. If I were you, I'd be damn glad someone experienced is taking over the job you are ineffectively handling. Now, if we're through, I have some things to discuss with my team before we meet with the alpha tomorrow to go over a *unified* defensive setup."

"I don't like your tone, Austin," James said, stepping a little closer. "I don't like your coming back here and treating this place like your own. You left this pack. You threw in the towel and walked away. You don't get to come back and start throwing your weight around, making decisions, taking over the alpha's right to lead."

Austin's power started to pump now, his aggression rising with James's obvious posturing.

"I came back here *to* protect my brother's right to lead. Momar wants to take that away, and his people *will* kill you if given the chance. You'd better get your head on straight. I'd thought you cowboys knew the stakes, but it seems you've deluded yourselves. I can work around you or work through you, but get one thing clear…" Austin took another step forward, his brawn and power easily showing his dominance in this situation. The other man couldn't help but flinch. "I will make any decisions necessary to ensure this territory survives. I have a house here, family. I will protect them by any means necessary."

I'd thought Austin was done, his bearing hostile now, his anger flaring. The other man was clearly having a hard time keeping eye contact, his body bowing under the pressure.

Instead, Austin moved up until he was right in

James's face.

"One more thing," he growled. "If you ever have your man push up on my mate again, I will rip your throat out and choke that man with it, do I make myself clear?"

Tristan moved so fast I startled. He turned around and rushed Bruce, picking him up above his head and readying to throw. He didn't toss him outward, though—he tossed him *upward*.

The invisible gargoyle caught the flailing shifter easily, flew farther into the air, spun, and then let go. The shifter somersaulted in the air before landing fifty feet away. Dust puffed up on impact and a feeble moan escaped him.

"I look forward to my meeting with the alpha tomorrow morning," Austin finished. "In the meantime, my people, including the one above you, will stay put."

He burned his glare into James for a moment, making the man visibly melt where he stood, before turning and putting out his hand for me. I took it and allowed him to walk us around the Bronco and down the street a ways.

"Jess, I'm going to shift. I want you to climb on my back, okay?" His eyes were ruthless and emotions almost frenzied. "You will stay on until I fall to my belly to let you off. Got it?"

"O-okay," I said hesitantly, confused but feeling his urgency.

"Tristan," he said, his gaze darting to the guys now conferring near their vehicles. "Excellent work back there. You read the situation perfectly. I want you to lie low for the rest of the day unless something happens in town with the gargoyles or on the perimeter. Keep them to their positions but don't allow them to engage with the locals if at all possible. I'll send word when Brochan arrives with the second wave. We'll meet them then and discuss matters further. Fly above us on the way back until I drop her off."

"Yes, sir." Tristan took a step back. "Oh, and alpha, in case Jessie forgets to tell you, Dave broke a belligerent local's neck. He was about to challenge Isabelle. The locals were upset but didn't push the issue with the basajaunak. I assume they will push back in other ways."

Austin sighed, bowing just slightly. "Got it. I'm sure it'll get brought up in the meeting tomorrow."

He took a few steps away and shifted into his polar bear form.

"Stay safe, Jessie," Tristan said softly, leaning toward me just a bit. "That big alpha will burn down the world if something happens to you. While that would be a damn fun time, I'd rather not lose you all the same."

I stared in confusion as he shifted into his gargoyle form and took to the sky.

What the hell had I missed back there? How did this relate to me specifically?

"STAY HERE AND play with magic for the rest of the day, okay?" Austin stood with me in the doorway of his house, having walked me through town on his back with Tristan flying slowly right overhead. It almost seemed like some sort of armored guard.

He'd changed into jeans and a white T-shirt, his usual uniform in our territory, and was ready to head out again.

"What am I missing?" I asked, dressed in a similar outfit. "Are the townspeople going to revolt or something?"

"I'm not a favorite around here. I was respected before I left, to a point, but I also kept my head down a lot. Now I'm back with a crew, and my head is most certainly *not* down. That show of strength by the beta and that clown Bruce proves that they don't like my being here with a force behind me. They're clearly going to make an issue of it whenever they can. Until we can talk to Kingsley, I'd prefer if you guys lie low."

"But you had a bunch of supporters before you left, I thought. You must've had friends. Kingsley brought a bunch to our territory when he helped us out. He even left them with you. Aren't they speaking up?"

He suddenly looked drained. "And that's just it. I created a divide when I left. I've heard that a bunch of people took off after I did, seeking out other packs. Kingsley weeded out a few others whose loyalty he questioned. Now, here I am, back again, the guy who walked away with his middle finger in the air—or so they think—and bled the territory of good shifters. Not everyone thinks that way, sure, but some of these people hate that they need my help. *Hate* it. They'll listen to their alpha, but they won't like working with me. They'll be watching me closely, making sure I don't step out of line. You just saw the first little ripple."

"Okay, I get that. And I get them being...annoyed about our people suddenly playing G.I. Joe in their territory. I'm sure that must be jarring. But I'm the co-leader. Why did you carry me back to the house to be sequestered here?"

He cupped my cheek. "James was sending me a message earlier. He knows that the most important thing in my life...is you. And the way to hurt me the most would be to hurt you."

Shivers ran through my body. Then fire lit up my middle.

"I will—"

He put his thumb over my lips to stop me from speaking, shaking his head. "This isn't about you, Jess. I will always let you fight your own battles. But this isn't your battle to fight. This is mine. Threatening you is an act of war. *Against me.* They think their threat will cull me. Fifteen years has dulled their memories, I think. You are *mine*. Mine to protect at all costs. I made my own statement by bringing you back here personally, and now I will make another."

He paused, not elaborating.

"Just do me a favor, Jess, please," he said after a moment. "Watch yourself. Respect my wishes. You know I would never put Baby in a corner unless I had to."

I huffed out a laugh, moving in to hug him. "I know. I had no notions of rebelling against my house arrest. I just wanted to understand."

He pulled back so that he could look down at me. His breath dusted my face.

"I'm going to get a little possessive from here on out." He tilted his head back and forth. "Maybe a lot possessive. Maybe not totally rational. My beast feels the threat to you, and I don't have the power to freeze air to stop myself. I hope your gargoyle enjoys the ride."

He winked at me before turning and walking down the steps.

Butterflies filled my stomach. I had a feeling my gargoyle would greatly enjoy that ride, yes. I just worried how crazy this was going to get.

CHAPTER 12

JESSIE

I GLANCED UP from my magical theory book as the doorbell rang. Sebastian wanted me to start learning the principles in addition to doing spell work. Given we were both exhausted from making potions all afternoon, this was supposed to be my break for the evening.

"I'll get it," Nessa called from the kitchen before exiting, wiping her hands on a dishtowel. "I hope it's an angry local come to pick on Austin's woman, because I'm going to get dibs on shooting them with the crossbow I found."

"Where'd you find a crossbow?" I called after her, sitting forward. "And don't kill anyone! It might just be someone selling magazines."

Her footfalls stopped. Then started again, coming toward me this time.

She poked her head around the corner. "Did you just reference selling *magazines*? Did I hear that right?"

I felt my face flush. "I just aged myself, didn't I?"

"Yes, you did, Jessie. Yes, you certainly did." She laughed and turned away as the doorbell rang again. "Just hold yer horses, pardner," she said like a cowboy.

I hurried in her direction, in time to see her pick up the crossbow from the little table beside the door.

"Did you bring that in your luggage?" I asked, mystified.

"Nope." She loaded it as a knock landed on the door. "I was nosing through Austin's things, and I found it in the hall closet. Cool, right? I'm going to steal it. Don't tell him."

She flipped the lock and swung the door open while stepping back and lowering the crossbow, all in one smooth motion. An arm jetted forward, followed by a large body, the hand grabbing the end of the crossbow and jerking it upward. Nessa squeezed the trigger as another hand reached for her throat. The arrow lodged in the ceiling above the door as Tristan forced her back to the wall behind her and pinned her, leaning in to trap her there.

"What are you doing, little monster?" he asked in a silky voice that would probably give me nightmares. "Why are you trying to shoot me with a crossbow?"

"Damn it, you're fast," she said through a constricted throat, breathing heavily. "I wasn't trying to shoot you. I was armed in case someone was coming for Jessie."

He didn't let her up, his lips close to her ear. "Yet you pulled the trigger."

"Because you rushed me, dipshit. What'd you expect me to do, stand there and get my throat grabbed and then pinned to the wall while Jessie just watched?"

"And yet…that is exactly what happened…"

"Right. But this way I got to shoot a hole in Austin's house. I think he'll be fine with it. That sort of thing probably won't faze him, right?"

He shook his head a little before backing off, his face inches from hers as he retreated. Their eyes locked for a moment, her body loose and pliant within his proximity despite the apparent danger. Her lips fell open, drawing his notice, and he licked his.

"Should I do something?" I asked with a grimace. "I kinda fell asleep at the wheel there for a moment."

Tristan blinked a couple of times, as though waking from a dream, before smoothly stepping back, his eyes glowing brightly. Nessa's face was flushed.

"No, I think the little monster and I know where we stand," he said.

"Yeah, I need to get way faster. Next time I'll get you, pretty boy." She waggled her finger at him before putting the crossbow back. "Now that I have you"—she pointed at Tristan—"c'mere and taste this."

"You haven't had me." His voice was whiskey and fire. "I'm eager to rectify that."

"Heh. Nice volley." She motioned him on.

"Brochan and the second wave are en route," Tristan said as he passed me. "Alpha Steele requests that you meet him dressed exactly as you are. I'll escort you there. Natasha, we don't have much time," he called as he followed her.

Tristan wore trendy jeans and a T-shirt that had been specially made for gargoyles to account for the wings. And, for him, the shoulders.

"What happened to dressing nicely?" I asked as I followed them into the kitchen.

"I don't know. I didn't ask," Tristan replied, stopping at the island and looking down at the lasagna Nessa had made. "Where's the weird mage?"

"He's out in the backyard working on a particularly nasty spell," Nessa said, scooping some of the lasagna onto a plate. "You look like a guy who eats a lot. What do you think of this?" She handed the plate to Tristan before turning for a fork. "Austin seems to think he's the best cook in the world, so before I challenge him, I want to make sure this lasagna is up to snuff."

"All the things you could be doing and you're challenging the alpha to a cookoff?" Tristan said, before taking the fork and dutifully sampling a bite.

"I need to take breaks, and what better way to enjoy myself than rubbing the alpha's face in my superiority?" She smiled at him, watching his mouth as he chewed.

"And you didn't have Jessie taste it because…" Tristan glanced at me before taking another bite.

"She doesn't have a refined palate."

"Dude." I spread my arms wide. "I can hear you."

"Jessie, my love, that shouldn't come as a shock." Nessa laughed as Tristan went for yet another bite, eating faster now. "Well?" she asked.

"You and the weird mage are supposed to stay in tonight," he said, continuing to eat. "You'll have gargoyles watching the house in case something should happen."

"Fine, fine, but how is it?" She leaned closer to him, her eyebrows raised.

He finished the plate in record time, now eyeing the dish that contained the rest.

"I'll be back for more after I take Jessie into town," he said. "I'd prefer it if you served it to me wearing a lacy teddy, but I'll take it however you want to dish it." He set the plate down and motioned me out of the kitchen. "After you, alpha."

"It's good, right?" Nessa followed us toward the door. "Think it'll wow Austin?"

K . F .   B R E E N E

When we got to the door, he reached up and yanked the arrow out of the ceiling. "It's the best lasagna I have ever tasted, and yes, I'm a man who likes to eat. As far as wowing him, I couldn't say. He seems confident in his cooking, and he's not known for his false bravado."

"Huh." Nessa cocked a hip, chewing her lip. "Yeah, good point. I better get him to cook something similar before I offer mine up. I haven't really analyzed the stuff I've tasted that he's made."

She closed the door behind us, nearly bumping me with it as she did so.

"Nothing seems to rattle that woman," I said as I glanced around the front yard, looking for his ride. "She's been in touch with their underground network off and on all day, and even though she swore a couple times, I've noticed no other signs of stress. Did you come by car?"

"I flew. What'd she swear about?" He bent to grab a satchel he'd stowed just behind a decorative rock.

"She didn't say. I guess she and Sebastian are planning to share some information with us at the meeting tomorrow morning."

Tristan stopped at the mouth of the garage. "What is this?"

"Kingsley's prank on his brother."

"I'll say," he muttered, heading to the passenger seat

and opening the door. I started toward the driver's side. "No, Jessie," he said, still standing beside the door. "I'm opening the door for you. I know where we're going. I'll drive."

I shrugged and changed direction.

"Are you being a gentleman or a bodyguard?" I asked as I sat in the passenger seat.

He closed the door and crossed to his side, adjusting his wings so he could sit more comfortably.

"Both. You probably don't need a bodyguard around here, but Alpha Steele feels better if someone is watching your six, and I enjoy doing nice things for ladies. It makes them glow most of the time. Except for you, because you're used to it with your mate."

"So why keep it up?"

"Because I like when ladies do what I tell them." His grin was wicked, but his eyes sparkled with mischief.

I couldn't help smiling as I shook my head. This gargoyle was dark and complex, and I had a feeling he did like telling ladies what to do, behind closed doors, in sheets of satin. Nessa had better be careful with this one. His was the sort of passion you probably had to be prepared for, or at least compliant with. He battled in life, and he battled in the sheets. I knew something about that. I was a gargoyle, too.

Speaking of...

I leaned forward so I could look up through the windshield. None of the gargoyles dotted the sky, not that I was surprised—I'd felt them all land at about noon. I hadn't called Austin to ask about it, not wanting to bug him. I asked Tristan now.

"Kingsley requested it," Tristan said, no emotion in his voice. "It was upsetting some of the locals, I guess."

"Those guys from earlier?"

"Probably. Might have been other people too."

"I don't understand what's happening in this town. Kingsley asked for our help, but now they're fighting us. Or they're threatening me, of all things. It's like they don't understand the seriousness of the situation."

"Honestly, they might not. While Momar's taken out plenty of packs, none of them have been this big. They might not realize how far up shit creek they are. Maybe they don't want to know. Ignorance can be a crutch. We'll have to convince them of the gravity of the situation tomorrow morning when we go over every-thing."

"Okay, sure, I can understand that. But why is Kingsley allowing his pack to threaten Austin through me? Or challenge our people or just be genuinely crappy? It's counterproductive."

Tristan let out a breath. "I doubt Kingsley knows how deep the animosity runs. His people have a lot of respect for him, so they're not going to treat his brother like that in front of him. Even if they are jealous."

"Jealous?"

"Yeah. Alpha Steele is wealthy, he's handsome, and he's got a lot of power. More than that, he's privileged. He's been allowed to create all sorts of turbulence in this pack and suffer no consequences because he's the brother of the alpha. I'm sure that galls. On the surface, it looks like Austin is allowed to do whatever he likes. Come and go as he pleases. Be an ass but never get punished for it. And now he's returned with what looks like a militarized force that's disrupting their way of life. People don't like disruptions in general, and they're even less pleased because it's coming from him."

"And you think Kingsley is blind to all of this?"

"Sometimes it's a lot easier to see a problem as an outsider looking in. Kingsley hasn't had to run a tight ship before now, but he must know that Austin Steele could take this pack out from under him at any time."

"He knows Austin wouldn't do that."

"Wouldn't he?"

I squinted at him. "You think he'd leave everything we're creating in O'Briens?"

He gave me a sidelong glance. "They aren't yet seeing eye to eye about how to face the coming attack, and unless they get on the same page, it's going to lead to a standoff. Austin Steele will win that standoff."

I scoffed. "This is so annoying. All of it, including my having to play a damsel in distress when I am plenty capable of knocking out the threat on my own."

Tristan laughed softly as he pulled into a parking space facing the square. Austin waited near the gazebo with our gargoyles and shifters lined up in front of him. My crew were nowhere to be seen, and I heaved a little sigh of relief. We hadn't gotten an opportunity to talk to Kingsley about Edgar's flowers, and I knew he'd ask about it. And probably look dejected or mope. I wasn't in the mood to deal with him, especially since the fate of the flowers was out of my control at the moment.

"Sometimes role playing can add a little spice to a relationship." Tristan's wicked grin was back. "You play damsel, and he plays the big protector. Tarzan and Jane."

We cut through the grass, beelining for Austin as a line of black vans showed up, carrying the second wave of our people from the motel in the border town. Buses had been acquired for the basajaunak.

Austin's gaze roamed over me as I neared him. Then he reached out a hand and drew me close.

"How was the rest of your day?" he asked as the vans came to a stop and doors swung or slid open.

"Fine. Uneventful. Yours?"

He didn't respond and I didn't push, instead watching as Broken Sue walked around the front of the leading van. His eyes were hard, his bearing straight and tall, and his movements graceful. He scanned the square and took note of each person, a silverback gorilla sizing up his new surroundings. People around the square slowed in their walks and turned in their chairs, spying him.

The shifters and gargoyles lined up around him, and then the basajaunak crowded in behind them, all of them cutting across the grass to meet Austin.

"Where's Kingsley?" I asked. "I'd thought he might want to meet the rest of your team."

"He's meeting with his people and hammering out some defensive measures. He saw our preliminary defensive setup and wanted to get with his people to discuss it."

"Was he pissed?"

"No. He was proud of my ability to structure and lead a team. He taught me, after all. It's a reflection of his abilities as well as my own."

"And yet his people were pissed about it."

He squeezed me a little. "Luckily, their respect for him outweighs their dislike of me. Hopefully it'll be enough for a solid working relationship."

He didn't sound so sure.

"Did you mention the flowers when you saw him?" I asked as Broken Sue neared us.

"Yes, and he tensed up. I decided not to push the issue today. We'll address it tomorrow morning when we go over everything. I let Edgar know so that he wouldn't bug you."

I smiled and leaned harder into him. "That is the nicest present you could give me."

"I know." He didn't smile at me—he wouldn't, not here—but I felt it through our links. "His questions about why Kingsley didn't immediately see the genius of those flowers started to warp my brain. His logic goes in odd loop-de-loops. Thankfully, Indigo was there to distract him."

"Where are they all, anyway?" I asked. "I haven't been in contact with any of them. I'm sure Mr. Tom is beside himself with annoyance. It didn't even occur to me to ask, though, I'm embarrassed to say."

"They're all lying low, most of them sticking to their hotel rooms. Edgar and Indigo are babysitting the flowers, and Niamh and Phil are drinking in the bar. I was going to tell them they couldn't, but…it's Niamh. I didn't feel like arguing."

"Sir." Broken Sue stopped in front of us wearing jeans and a T-shirt. He'd gotten the memo not to dress up. "Jessie."

"How was your trip?" Austin asked him. "Any problems?"

"All was quiet until the motel in the border town. We had a lurker. Invisible, but I could still feel him or her. We tried to wander closer, but they stayed out of reach. I didn't want to push the issue until I'd spoken with you."

"We had one, as well. A basandere went after it but collided with a car and lost the mark. The territory's alpha told me in no uncertain terms that we are not to hunt the mages in the border towns. He has drawn a firm line that the pack is to stay separate from the Dick towns."

"Except the border towns are not the alpha's jurisdiction."

"That thought had crossed my mind. I'd be going against his wishes if I ignored him, though, and we've already had a...difference of opinion. I'd like to keep the peace. I have a rough history here, and a few people have not forgotten."

Broken Sue studied Austin for a moment, his face the customary blank that would fit in really well here. "If you send your people in secret, and someone sees them, you'll look like an alpha who doesn't have control over his people. A weak alpha, in other words. Or that you'd intentionally disobeyed the territory's alpha."

"Correct."

I raised my hand. "It would be easy to say I had no control of my people and I couldn't care less how people perceive me. Send my people. Besides, the mages aren't technically on our team. They don't count. Neither do the basajaunak, except for Dave."

"That thought had crossed my mind," Austin said, looking out at the square as the light dimmed. More townspeople had shown up, scoping out the newcomers or the crew as a whole. They were giving us a wide berth, though, not that they'd probably know or care what Broken Sue and Austin were talking about. These were average Joes, not part of the pack's defensive unit. It was easy to see the difference in how they held themselves. They also never stared for too long, not wanting to incite a challenge.

"Tristan is an issue," Austin said. "He's a beta. Given his abilities, though, he needs to go."

"Would shifters care that you don't have control over me?" I asked. "Because I'm a co-leader and a gargoyle. Tristan can go on my authority. Kingsley can thank us after we save their asses."

"Subtlety isn't your strong suit," Tristan said with a laugh. "I'm fine with facing public punishment, if that'll make things easier. Whatever the reason, Kingsley isn't seeing things clearly. Those mages aren't just dangerous to the pack, they're dangerous to the Dicks and Janes around here. It's his duty to minimize that threat."

"Which would be an easier message to sell if the mages had harmed anyone," Austin said, "or if Kingsley weren't so adamant about leaving the Dicks to handle their own problems. We're up against a third-generation pack leader here. This pack has mostly known peace and stability for two of those three generations. We need to keep in mind that disrupting the pack will have drawbacks."

"If there is one thing that will go to hell quickly when those mages move in," Broken Sue said, "it'll be any kind of stability. You need to talk some sense into your brother, or just take over. The alternative is both of you losing your family and your pack. Trust me, a rift as an alpha is a small price to pay for your loved ones making it out of this alive."

It was clear that Broken Sue was facing down his demons in being here. It was also clear that he was right. We needed to push past Kingsley's comfort zone if we were going to make it out of this thing.

CHAPTER 13

AUSTIN

AUSTIN NODDED AT Brochan before taking a quiet beat and looking out over the square. He felt more comfortable now, with this former alpha turned beta here. Tristan was excellent at his job and even better at reading between the lines, but he wasn't a shifter. He didn't know enough about pack life and the politics of being an alpha. Austin really wanted to keep this situation from turning more volatile. To smooth everything out with himself and this pack.

Part of that, though, was to show strength and make it entirely clear that he would not bend to intimidation tactics, especially any involving his mate. He was an alpha in his own right now, and it was time for the dissenters in this territory to look at him in a new light. They didn't have to like him, or even respect him, but they damn well better get out of his way. Brochan could help brainstorm the best ways to carve out that tricky path, pushing back on the pack but not directly on Kingsley.

"What do you think, babe?" he asked, looking down at Jess. "Want to go for dinner and a couple of drinks after?"

"Oh." She gave him a confused look. "I'm not a target anymore? Did you sort everything out with Kingsley?"

Brochan tensed, his gaze snapping up from her to Austin, a question in his eyes. He did not tolerate threats directed at mates—his wounds were still bleeding from horrifically losing his own.

From Austin's talk with Kingsley, it was clear he hadn't known anything about James and Bruce's antagonism. If he had, he would've mentioned something. For that reason, Austin had kept his brother out of it, at least for now. He was just fine handling this himself, presuming it didn't get too destructive.

"It'll be fine. I've got you," Austin told her, his hand on her hip. "Brochan, Tristan will help you all get settled. We've got a meeting with Kingsley and the top tier of his pack tomorrow morning to go over this whole situation. We don't need you until then."

"I'll get my stuff stowed and meet you at the bar, sir," Brochan said, correctly assuming he'd head to the bar for drinks instead of staying in the restaurant.

Murder sparkled in his eyes. "Text me the location."

Austin didn't argue. A little backup from a shifter of Brochan's caliber would send the right message.

"I'll head back to check on the mages once I get everyone squared away," Tristan said. "Natasha made one helluva lasagna. She's gunning for your cooking prowess, sir."

"Tell her to keep practicing," Austin told him, starting off toward the car.

Tristan laughed, heading for the vans.

"We didn't have any problems at the house today," Jess said as they walked. "I don't think anyone is going to break in and go after them, do you?"

"Very doubtful, but it gives our people something to do until we can iron out the specifics with Kingsley. At least he agreed to keep the invisible patrol on the perimeter. We've got some eyes out there that they won't see. Now we just need those enemy mages to check the perimeter so we can grab one or two of them. We need more information."

He tucked her into the car and drove them to a spot on the outskirts of town. It was a hole in the wall with a few shabby tables outside, badly listing to one side or the other. The sign flickered, half of it out, and the front door had red paint peeling off to show dingy brown beneath. For all that, the food was out of this world. Or it used to be, back in the day.

"I'm glad to see this place is still running," Austin said, finding a parking spot two doors down from the restaurant.

The interior was nothing special. The wood tables had carvings on them, various initials and a couple of phallic symbols. Pictures decorated the walls in old frames, and the counter had a rusty metal bell. Five out of the six tables were occupied by young shifters Austin thankfully didn't know. The couples sat close, feeding each other bits of meat and looking longingly into each other's eyes.

Wrapping an arm tightly around Jess to show his claim, Austin stopped with her at the counter and softly struck the bell. It clanged, having lost the ability to ring somewhere along the way.

"Yeah, yeah, I'll be there in a minute," a familiar voice called from behind a hanging blue cloth. It separated the kitchen from the front area.

"This was my favorite restaurant," he told Jess, leaning against the counter and pulling her closer. "It's the best barbecue I've ever tasted."

"Better than yours?" she asked.

"Hands down—"

"No!" The owner stepped through the curtain. Angelica was way up in years, with white-gray hair cut

K.F. BREENE

short and deep lines etching her face. She stooped a bit, her spine no longer arrow straight, but her eyes were no less kind than he remembered. "Austin Barazza! I heard you were in town. Come here, boy."

She walked slowly around the counter with her arms out, a small smile on her round face. Knowing Jess wouldn't bat an eye at the greeting, he wrapped Angelica in a tight hug and rocked her a little before rubbing her back and stepping away.

"I'm glad to see you're still up and running," he said, slinging his arm around Jess's shoulders.

"Well, of course. What else would I get up to? My, my." She looked him over, her eyes twinkling. "You look great, Austin. It does me good to see you again. We've missed you around these parts."

"I don't think that's a sentiment widely shared."

"Bah." She batted her hand through the air. "Anyone who matters missed you. Now, who have you got there?"

"Angelica, allow me to introduce my mate, Jacinta Ironheart. Most people call her Jessie." He looked down at her. "Jess, this is Angelica, the woman who ruined barbecue for me."

"Oh now, don't say that." Angelica laughed and shuffled a little closer, putting out her hand for Jess. "I'm sure yours is even better, Jessie. Good to meet you.

I'm glad this sweet boy finally found someone special. If you treat him nice, he'll treat you like a queen. And if you treat him mean, he'll *still* treat you like a queen, so you can be as moody as you want."

Jess laughed and took her hand before being pulled into a hug. Angelica finally stepped back and patted their arms, looking between them.

"Yes, what a lovely couple. Lovely! Now, Austin my boy, what'll ya have? The usual, or a dinner for two?" She retreated back to the other side of the counter.

Austin ordered his favorites and a few things Jess might like to try, then spent some time chatting with Angelica about his new setup in O'Briens and the crazy that was Ivy House. When the food came, he retreated to one of the open tables and pulled Jess's chair close. They fed each other from their plates like the other couples were doing.

"Yes, this is amazing," Jess said after trying the brisket and licking her lips. "Absolutely amazing. Holy crap."

He slid his thumb beside her lips, smearing away a little sauce before sucking it off his finger. "It'll ruin you for other types of barbecue."

"Probably, yes." She laughed. "Barazza." She finished chewing and took a sip of water. "I like that name. Remind me again why you changed it to Steele? I mean…why Kingsley got to keep his name but you lost yours?"

"The name stays with the pack. If I'd taken over for Kingsley, I would have kept my family name, since I'm of the same line. It denotes the generational pack leadership. I started a new pack, though, so I go by a different name. The name the town chose for me."

"Right, right. But your name on the deed for your house in O'Briens is still Austin Barazza?"

"That's my legal last name, so yes. Just like yours is Evans. I need to legally change it to Steele; I just haven't gotten around to it. It's not exactly important, since I can't have kids. It can't be a generational pack, I mean."

"I need to get rid of Evans," she murmured. "It belongs to my ex."

"You can always change it to Ironheart. Or…if you really like Barazza that much, I can keep it as my legal name…if you want to share it with me," he said quietly, his heart full. It wouldn't affect his alpha standing, since the world would still know him as Steele. He'd made that name for himself before he ever became alpha. It was his blessing and his curse—by virtue of who and what he was, he was always in trouble, always tumbling with the biggest and baddest around. At least now he had a purpose for it.

Her eyes were so soft when they met his. Her smile,

and then her nod, sent fireworks racing through him.

"We'd need to get married for that to apply in the Dick world, though," she said, and her face flushed crimson. "Since…you know…you built the house when it was primarily a Dick town—"

He kissed her, long and slow. "I'm looking forward to it."

Her beaming smile tightened him up in all the right places.

"She's your perfect fit," Angelica said, coming over with a chocolate brownie and putting it on the table between them. "It's nice to see you so happy for once, Austin. Really nice."

"There's just one problem." Jess grabbed a corner of the brownie plate. "There is no *we* in chocolate. So…"

She pulled the plate toward her, sending Angelica into a fit of laughter.

"Yes, oh yes, I like this one!" She put her finger in the air. "No 'we' in chocolate. Yes."

Jess pushed it back, laughing. "Maybe I'll share just this once."

After they finished their dessert and headed on their way, Austin brought her to the bar where Niamh and Phil were already drinking. Despite his need to show people he wasn't afraid of their threats, he didn't want his mate uncomfortable or his warm glow diminishing.

Unfortunately, he had a feeling he'd need to make a stand. It was the shifter way. Better to do it around friends.

"So Nessa is hellbent on proving she's the better cook, huh?" Jess asked as he drove. "What brought that on?"

He grinned. "She probably needs a distraction—or an outlet. I'm happy to oblige. I'll make her rue the day."

"And you're not even doing it as a distraction—you're just a horribly competitive jerk."

He laughed at that, parking in the back lot of the bar. "Correct."

Back in the day, he would've entered the back way, keeping his head down and slipping into a spot in the corner. Now, though, he didn't want anyone thinking he was getting preferential treatment as the alpha's brother. Even as a visiting alpha.

He wrapped his arm around her shoulders, the possessiveness in him pumping up in intensity. She veered toward him a little, demurely, tucking into him like it was the only place she'd ever think of being. His power pulsed at that.

Two guys stood outside the door, off to the side. One held a vape, the smoke earthy and sweet, and the other had a traditional cigarette. They both looked his way, one giving him a stare while the other did a double take.

Austin vaguely recognized them, though both carried more weight than when he'd last seen them. Back in the day, the guy with the beard had struggled to grow any whiskers at all. Both dropped their gazes immediately and shuffled a little farther out of the way.

"King's Head Tavern," Jess read as they stepped through the door. "Kingsley's bar, then?"

"Yup. He's never been subtle about his purchases."

The interior had a pub-like feel, with worn wooden barstools, side booths, and a long tabletop that acted as a second bar surface, positioned about five feet away from the bar top. Two posts ran up from the long table top on either side, both covered with various stickers people had brought in over the years. The floor was clean and polished but looked worn, just like the cream walls boasting a variety of sports pictures. It had looked this way since the grand opening some eighteen years ago, always giving off a rustic, neighborhood pub feel. Kingsley knew how to run a business. Austin needed to clean his bar up and affect this style. Then maybe Tristan would stop complaining about sticking to the seats.

"I'm still learning things from Kingsley," Austin murmured, spotting Niamh and Phil at the back corner of the bar, each bent over their drink of choice. Brochan sat on Niamh's other side, and Austin was surprised to see some of his people standing or sitting behind them, drinking their beers with hard faces and alert eyes. Brochan had called in more backup, and all but two were shifters. Jasper and Ulric hated missing a night out.

People looked Austin's way as he moved through the bar, many gazes sticking to him, although some flicked to Jess. Postures bent, though, and bodies shuffled to the sides, giving Austin space.

"Destiny doesn't still live in this territory, right?" Jess whispered, still pushed into the shelter of his body. It would make her look weaker while making him appear mighty. He knew her gargoyle must be feeling that. She was making a sacrifice for him.

Unfortunately, she was also making herself bait.

"No, she's long gone," he replied, not mentioning the other women he'd known in this place. He hadn't dated hardly at all, but he also hadn't said no to women sharing his bed. He wasn't a saint.

Most of those women would've moved on by now, thankfully, finding steady partners and many settling down with kids. They wouldn't be out here trying to make trouble.

✧ ✧ ✧

NIAMH

"UH-OH," NIAMH SAID softly as Austin Steele and Jessie made their way toward her.

The barman, who didn't speak much and wouldn't offer his name for some reason, moved away after depositing a drink. Niamh's gaze swept the patrons, catching a few guys near the wall puffing up like muppets, taking offense with Austin Steele for some reason or another. Maybe just because Austin Steele was a big guy who was currently acting like he owned the place. One hard look from him, though, would stop an altercation.

That wasn't what had Niamh's attention.

"What?" Phil bristled. "What is it?"

"Keep yer hair on, would ya?" she replied. "Ye'll ruin all the fun."

"Are you seeing what I'm seeing?" Ulric asked, stepping behind Niamh. "This isn't going to go well."

"Alpha Steele thought Ironheart would be a target," Broken Sue said. "It didn't seem like this was what he had in mind, though."

"Indeed," Niamh said. Several of the young women in the bar had taken notice of Austin. They saw a rich, handsome alpha with a hot body—a Barazza—and they knew his mate was not a shifter. Not a shifter like them, at any rate. That sort of thing mattered in a strictly shifter pack. They didn't get out much.

Then there was Jessie, cowed and middle-aged and needing her strong alpha to protect her in a boring neighborhood bar with limited personality and nothing really going on. These women saw a golden opportunity to have a little fun, hopefully followed by a lot of fun if they could wrangle that alpha.

Jessie would not respond well to them. Not one bit. And Austin Steele seemed completely oblivious to the danger.

"What's the story with that other threat?" Broken Sue asked before sipping his bourbon. "Alpha Steele seemed on edge about it."

"I'll say. Tristan said it came from the beta and a couple of other guys with a decent amount of power. Fools, the lotta them. They'll use Austin Steele's people to fortify their pack, but they want him to grovel while they do it? As if he would ever."

"And they're trying to use Jessie to make him grovel?" Broken Sue asked.

"Apparently so. They clearly don't know anything about female gargoyles."

"Should we take off?" Ulric asked as Jasper sauntered over, his hair mussed and bright pink lipstick streaked along his jaw. "I don't want to get hit in the side of the head by a barstool or anything."

"Would ye relax, like?" Niamh turned to scowl at him. "When has she ever let her people be put in harm's way? It's bound to be a good show. There's an exit right over there. Worst case, we get pushed out by her magic and take off for the bar around the block. It'll be grand."

"Hey, guys." Jessie beamed at them as they got close. She was still holding tightly to her mate, and Niamh wondered just what she was playing at. Was she trying to give the people at the bar a false sense of confidence or what? "How's it going?"

"Oh, fer feck's sake," Niamh groaned, noticing the old-as-sin butler standing just outside the bar window wearing a beanie, black-rimmed glasses he must've stolen from Cyra, and a heavy coat with the collar pulled up around his face. "What is that *eejit* doing here?"

Austin Steele stared at Mr. Tom through the window for a moment before minutely shaking his head and looking away. "He showed up at my brother's house last night, as well."

"He's just watching out for me. It's fine." Jessie's brow was furrowed as she studied him. "I mean...it's weird, we all know that, but it's fine. He thinks this is his job." She hooked her fingers into Austin Steele's pocket and turned to him, tilting her head up. "Are you ordering drinks?"

"Of course," he replied, bending to kiss her before signaling for the bartender.

"Austin," the bartender said when he landed, a man in his early sixties with a full head of hair starting to thin on the top. He wiped his hands on a white towel. "I heard you were back in town. How goes it?"

"Good, Oliver, thanks. Do—"

"And we finally get his name," Niamh interrupted, leaning forward to give Oliver a poignant look. "Thought ye could remain mysterious all night, did ya? Well now, here we are."

His look was bored. "It seemed like you were having too much fun making up names for me. I didn't want to ruin it."

"Ye wouldn't know fun if it bit ye on the arse," she responded, knowing she bugged the holy hell out of him. It was the only distraction to be had in this place. Everyone kept themselves on a very tight leash. "C'mere, give us a smile. It'll make ye prettier."

Another stare before he shook his head and went back to Austin. "What can I get you?"

"Do you have a wine list?" Austin asked.

"A wine list?" Oliver huffed, looking behind him at the two Sutter Home bottles for an individual pour, their tops dusty. "We got two kinds. Red…or white."

"A Coors would be fine, thanks," Jessie responded.

"Bottle or draft?" Oliver asked, eyes dull as he looked at Austin Steele's new squeeze. He wasn't overly impressed with the choice.

"Draft, please, thanks." Her little smile and overly polite demeanor would not help matters.

"And you?" Oliver asked Austin Steele.

"Bourbon, on the rocks, and I'll get a round for the rest of my people." He made a circular motion around Broken Sue, Niamh, Phil, Jasper and Ulric before turning and gesturing to the shifters hanging out behind them.

Their show of togetherness would likely worsen the divide between the two packs. This was all going to get worse before it got better. To Niamh's mind, Austin Steele was the wrong sort for these parts, too powerful, too wild. He was just the type to bring in a bunch of other powerful creatures and upset the balance of this sleepy, entrenched pack. They saw him as a threat regardless of why he was there.

"All of them?" Oliver looked behind Austin Steele, getting the drink list. "Okay."

"I'm just going to run to the restroom really quick," Jessie murmured to Austin Steele, tilting her head up to get another kiss. He complied eagerly, not because of the perceived situation with the beta, but because he clearly couldn't help himself. The two were utterly besotted with each other. It made them volatile.

Niamh liked volatile.

She grinned as Jessie drifted away with her head down. Two of the three interested female parties straightened up and pushed out their boobs. None of them had noticed one another, so focused were they on what they thought was the prize of the bar.

But Niamh had business to handle before the fireworks.

"Austin Steele, c'mere, I got a line on a warehouse," she said, keeping her voice low. "I met a right wanker down the bar a ways there. Real shady, that lad. He was trying to sell me—Well, it doesn't matter. They didn't do a damn thing."

"Drugs," Phil said. "He sells drugs."

Niamh turned to the basajaun with wide eyes. "What are ye, some kind of narc?"

"A what?" Phil asked.

"Yer supposed to keep those types of things to yerself, ya muppet."

"They did not work, those drugs," Phil replied, indignant. "He is the muppet, not me."

She shook her head at him before turning back to Austin Steele. "Anyway, he can get us a warehouse. The people renting it aren't in the area, so we'll need to clean up when we're done, but we've got a place for...an interview should we catch any...magical people."

Austin Steele glanced around the bar, not noticing one of the women start his way, her neckline scooped low and her sparkly dress short. She was probably ten years his junior.

He then glanced in the direction Jessie had gone before pushing in a little closer to Niamh. They all knew Jessie would hesitate at playing dirty with those mages. She'd eventually get there, they'd seen proof of that, but they didn't have time to convince her. They needed to move fast.

For a wonder, after Austin Steele had learned more about the dirty world mages existed in—Niamh didn't keep much back from the alpha—he'd stopped feeling any kind of moral duty to protect them. In fact, he was very much on the "mess with what's mine, and I'll ruin your life" train. Niamh knew he could be coaxed into it. Jessie was the sunshine in that pair, no question.

"This is a very delicate situation, you understand that," Austin Steele told her in an equally low tone. "I'd prefer it if no one knew we gave this command. If you get caught, Jess will have to be the fall guy. Unfortunately, that will make her appear weak, but I'd like to keep in Kingsley's good graces."

"Ah, sure, but Kingsley's people aren't supposed to leave town, right?" Niamh asked. "That's easy. They won't want to get caught any more than we do. It'll be grand. But what about that warehouse? That lad is asking for a few quid to make the deal. More than it's worth, surely, but when I called around today, I couldn't find a better alternative."

"Try to talk him down a bit, but keep him happy. We don't need him talking about this deal."

"Do ye not *get* people or what?" Niamh asked him, leaning away a bit so she could see his face clearly. "I recorded us buying drugs off him. That's called black-mail, Austin Steele. If he starts running his mouth, he'll get Kingsley breathing down his neck. Do ye think he wants that kinda heat? No, he does not."

"Can I go?" Phil asked.

"Now yer gettin' on me last nerve," Niamh told him. "Even if ye could keep your mouth shut, ye'd scare away all the magical people."

"I can hide in the trees."

"What fun is that?"

"I have a flask and you have a way of running people off. When the mages run out of the bar, I'll grab them."

Niamh turned her mouth down in thought as Jasper snickered. He had a point.

"Hey there."

The silky voice pulled at Niamh's focus.

"Austin Barazza, right?" The woman Niamh had noticed moved in closer to Austin Steele, her cleavage on display and her tongue gliding out to wet her bottom lip. "I met you at a party before you left, remember? Cadence."

The utterly blank look on his face said he had no clue, and he didn't really care that she knew it. Ulric ran his fingers across his lips like he was trying to wipe his smile away.

Another interested woman across the way adjusted her hair, stuck out a hip, and started forward as well. She clearly wanted to throw her hat into the ring.

"Move down," Niamh whispered at Phil. "Give them a little room."

"I don't think that's such a good idea," Phil whispered back as Broken Sue got off his seat and cleared out of the way. "I think we should tell that woman to scram. The alpha is obviously—"

"Move down, hurry!"

"I heard you were back in town." Cadence pushed in closer, moving her bust to draw his eyes. "It's so lovely to see you."

She ran her hand up Austin Steele's arm and then over his shoulder, the touch already inappropriate but becoming obscenely so when she let her hand trail down his chest.

"I have a mate," he told her, his voice hard, his body tense.

"Austin." The other woman arrived, and now there was a wide circle around Austin Steele, his people having all pushed back toward the wall. No one in their right mind was getting involved in this.

"I think I'll just get up," Niamh murmured, doing like Broken Sue and clearing out.

"Hi," the other woman said, taking to his other side and gently grabbing his arm. She was younger still, fifteen or more years his junior and not even eighteen when he'd left. "You're the alpha's brother, right?"

"I was just meeting up with my old friend," the first woman said, her gaze hostile.

"I'm okay with three." The newcomer batted her eyelashes at Austin. "The younger generation is a little more fluid about that sort of thing."

"As I said, I have a mate." He looked over their heads, not engaging. He wouldn't strip Jessie of her right to defend her claim on him, though. He apparently did not at all care about this bar. "She's with me tonight. You must've seen her."

"She's a gargoyle, right?" The second woman snickered, pushing into him a little more. One of her hands settled low on his stomach. His unease at the touch was evident and his scowl was a warning. "You should find a *real* mate to help lead your pack. A shifter. I hear you have a—"

Acute rage blistered through the Ivy House link a moment before a wave of power swept the bar. The power didn't sting, though. It didn't hurt. Niamh wondered what Jessie's angle was. She'd better not back down from defending her claim. That would make her into a target the whole territory would try to hit.

CHAPTER 14

JESSIE

T HE ANGER AND power pumping through my body beat in time to my heart. I couldn't think straight. I couldn't claw my way around it.

Two women clung to Austin, their hands moving down his stomach.

A gush of magic escaped me, but I managed to stop it from flaying the skin of everyone in this bar.

I was supposed to be Jane to his Tarzan, letting my big, strong man protect me. I was supposed to lie low and let Austin handle things. I was a non-shifter visitor who shouldn't level this place and cut down everyone in it.

One of the women looked my way and snickered. She leaned her cheek against his shoulder.

She was challenging me.

Another gush of magic rocked my body, feeling like it turned my bones to water. I closed my eyes for a moment, felt myself sway.

Still, I kept it all in, hiding it. Containing it. I wasn't sure who'd be on the receiving end of my rage. Austin hadn't pushed them off. He hadn't stepped away, which obviously meant that he hadn't told them he was taken. But he was so tense. So uncomfortable. I could feel his disgust and impatience through the bonds.

Then I realized why. He was giving me a chance to fight my own battles, to defend my claim. It was the shifter way.

A gush of aching power felt like it was trying to split me in two. Darkness swirled and my gargoyle rose to bask in it. Once I let go, I wasn't sure I could pull myself back from total destruction. Kingsley would be furious.

And then Austin's gaze found mine, sinking into me, sparking hot. *Handle this.*

My resolve cracked. My control fled. Power exploded.

The front door slammed shut, and the side exit wedged closed. Magic dropped over the windows, glimmering green, trapping everyone inside.

"Get. Off. Him," I growled, but I didn't give them a chance to answer. Couldn't.

I was on them in moments, grabbing the first and flinging her. She hit the nearest wall and fell as I snatched the throat of the other one.

"Get Indigo," someone yelled. Niamh, now pushing at Ulric. "Hurry, fly and get Indigo. Jessie, let him out to get her."

I released the back door near him, still holding the woman's throat. I didn't plan to rip it out. Instead, I let my gargoyle push to the surface and take over, replacing fingers with claws as my whole body shifted. I ripped to the side, slitting her throat shallowly like Nessa might've done, enough to maim and severely freak her out, but not enough to kill a shifter. It would send a strong message, something the shifters back home had insisted I do.

She screamed and tumbled away, her clothes ripping like mine had just done as she shifted into her other form. A wolf, and a small one at that.

I was back at the first woman, though, picking her up as she was shifting. The flash of heat and light didn't bother me. I slammed her down as her form grew larger and then turned hairy.

"What the hell...are...you," I said, battering her animal form against the wall. It looked like a huge hamster crossed with a rat. "A rodent...of...unusual...size?"

I dug claws into her midsection and ripped. That wound would really suck for her.

Clearly no longer an idiot, she lay still, putting up the white flag.

I rose slowly, shedding light from my very pretty gargoyle form, which was also splattered with blood. It was probably messing with everyone's minds, especially as I opened my mouth, letting saliva drip down, not so pretty at all, and roared.

People shouted and screamed. Banging sounded on the front door, people trying to get out. More than one person yelled into a cell phone.

No help besides a healer would get into this bar, I'd make sure of it. They'd all see what it meant to disrespect a female gargoyle's claim.

I stalked toward the wolf slowly. She was waiting in a suddenly cleared area between the long tabletop and the booths at the side. Her head was low and her lips were pulled back, revealing her teeth, snarling. She did not intend to put up a white flag, it seemed. She was ready for a challenge.

After cutting out the excess sound in the bar with magic, I stalked closer to my challenger, my toes clicking against the ground. I pumped gushes of magic across the bar, pounding the patrons with it, causing enough pain to induce fear but no more. They hadn't acted up and so they wouldn't be punished. They'd get a warning, that was it.

The wolf bristled and then lunged, snapping her teeth. I let that sound be heard. I let her efforts propel her closer. And then I answered.

I met her lunge and snatched her up before launching into the sky. The ceiling was only about fifteen feet high in this area, but it was enough to get her over the tabletop. Her teeth sank into my shoulder as I situated her body and then ripped into her with the claws on my feet. Her howl of pain didn't slow me down as I turned her and scratched along her sides.

She yelped again, now flailing, trying to get free. I spun and threw her, aiming at a window. She hit it smack in the middle, striking my magic and bouncing off.

The crowd parted around her, hands out, looking down at her landing. I allowed the sound back, panicked screams, shouting. Two people were recording everything.

The wolf lay still. Blood seeped from her side.

I didn't wait for Indigo. I patched the two women up enough to keep them from dying. The second had been on the brink. Then I shifted into my human form.

"Niamh, Jasper, erase all pictures and videos," I barked. "Phil, make sure the bar patrons comply with our request to strip away any recordings. Patty wouldn't want this leaked. Broken Sue, slip out the back and go get that jacket from Mr. Tom so I can wear it. Who knew his disguises might be useful? Have him run back to the house and grab me something else to wear."

The last shreds of my ruined clothes fell away as I turned and walked back to Austin. He waited right where I'd left him, his eyes burning with love and arousal and his hands reaching for me immediately.

"Or next time, you could just tell them you are mated…" I wrapped my arms around his neck and closed my eyes as he squeezed me.

"I did. Twice. I didn't push them away because…I wanted to see the show."

I pulled the back of his neck, bringing his lips closer. "*I* was supposed to witness a show. Kingsley is going to think I'm an absolute menace. At least I didn't hurt his bar. Or kill anyone."

Harried knocking sounded at the side door.

"It's Ulric with Indigo," someone called, and I released the magic from the bar.

The doors flew open. Ulric fought to get through the crowd, dragging Indigo with him. She looked around wide-eyed before pushing her glasses up onto her nose.

"They won't bleed out," I said as Broken Sue struggled through the panicked crowd.

"Oh." Indigo paused, looking between the two shifters still in animal form. "Yeah, it looks like they'll live. Should I not bother to heal them? I'd hate for them not to learn their lesson, whatever the lesson might've been."

"Astute," Ulric said, nodding at her.

"Go ahead and help them if they want it," I said. "The challenge is over."

"You guys want these beers, or..." The bartender, Oliver, leaned on the other side of the bar amid the drinks he'd gotten so far.

"Are...we allowed to stay after having a bar fight?" I asked hesitantly.

"They were at fault, not you," he said, pushing the Coors forward. "You didn't mess up anything in the bar. Except for the floor, but blood comes right up. This isn't the first time we've had a challenge over a mate. This was a lot more entertaining, though, I'll say that. Unique. Still, I coulda done without the painful magic."

"Sorry about that," I said. "It served a purpose."

"Yeah, no doubt. No doubt." He flared his eyebrows and blew out a breath. "Now I see why an alpha of his caliber is messing around with a creature like you. Makes sense."

"Careful how you speak about her," Austin growled, and a shiver of pleasure ran through me.

Oliver put up his hands. "No offense meant. You want a fresh one?" He pushed Austin's bourbon forward. "The ice is a little melted."

Austin took the coat from Broken Sue and draped it around my shoulders before pulling it closed at the front. He started to answer Oliver, but a commotion at the front and side doors had him looking up. His body immediately tensed, and power gushed out of him before he moved me behind him.

Hard-eyed shifters I didn't know entered, their bodies stacked with muscle. I recognized them as part of the pack's defenses, the peacekeepers of the town. There was no telling how many people from this bar had called them, all trapped and desperate to get out.

Broken Sue leisurely walked to the other side of Austin, stepping back even with me. Jasper and Ulric helped box me in, but were then moved aside by Phil, who clearly wanted in on the action no matter what the action was.

"Austin." A woman with her hair pulled back in a tight bun led the team from the side door. "Can't say I'm surprised to see you in the middle of a bar fight over a girl. Looks like you're falling into old habits, huh?"

Our shifters pushed forward from the back wall.

"He has no blame in this," one of them said, "and if you had any sense or trust in this pack, you'd know it."

"Well, looky here," the woman said. "Alpha Kingsley dropped you off at his baby brother's new territory in the middle of a Dick town. You chose to stay, yet you still had the balls to show up here? We all knew you had no pride, you didn't have to try so hard to prove it."

"We showed up here to save your ass, Wanda," another of ours, Cody, said, with the ringlets and cute dimples.

Wanda gave Broken Sue a once-over before her gaze flickered to Phil. She resumed looking at Austin. "The one true alpha is on the way. I assume he's going to bail you out like usual. Family, and all that."

"The one true alpha?" Broken Sue said with power radiating around him and humor in his tone. "What is this, *Lord of the Rings*? One alpha to rule them all? No other alphas can exist in your world. Just the one, and he is god."

"In this territory, yes, you bet your ass he is," Wanda said, stepping closer.

"My goodness, you're easily rattled," Broken Sue replied in a low, aggressive tone, humor still weaving through his voice. "You must be nervous about the power staring you down. You'd hate to make a mistake and challenge someone your one true alpha couldn't handle."

A tense beat passed before Austin put his hand in front of Broken Sue to calm things down. The conflicted emotions through the bonds said he had kinda wanted to turn Broken Sue loose. If they'd been anywhere else but his brother's bar and/or territory, he surely would've.

"My mate received a challenge to her claim on me," he finally said, and then briefly went over the steps leading up to the altercation. If I'd felt any guilt before, I wouldn't have after the explanation. Based on shifter code, I'd had a right to kill them. Not doing so was an act of mercy.

"The challengers rolled the dice," he concluded. "They lost."

"I bear witness," Oliver said, his arms crossed over his chest. "There could be no doubt of their mutual claim. Those girls didn't come over until Ironheart went to the loo. It's as he says. They even brought in a healer to patch the girls up. That's sportsmanship."

"I'm doing it slowly," Indigo called from the front door. "Really slowly. I'm leaving the pain, too. They really did deserve it. Jessie and Austin are very cute together. Who would want to come between that?"

"She's going to fit right in with us," Ulric murmured. "If we'd had any doubt."

"You were taunting, then, huh?" Wanda said, not backing down. "You were taunting the girls so you could cause a problem, just like this big bruiser is trying to taunt me into a challenge? That how you guys played it?"

"Jesus, Wanda, give it a rest," someone said in annoyance. "It's not Austin Steele's fault. Let it go."

"Austin *Steele*?" Wanda said, but a strange twang in my middle grabbed my focus.

I turned quickly and shut my eyes, recognizing the feeling as one of the connections. Broken Sue bumped into my side and Phil's hand covered a shoulder, but my attention was fixed inward.

The twang turned into a vibration, and I felt cautiousness radiate from the connection.

I shoved against a hairy side to get more space, opening my eyes but not seeing anything. The vibration continued, a sense of stealth wiggling into it. The gargoyle was working his way closer to whatever had grabbed his attention in the southeastern part of the territory. There was a cover there, trees in addition to the usual river and brush.

"Alpha," Austin said, drawing my attention.

Kingsley entered the front door of the bar, immediately taking in the scene. His gaze stalled on the drinks at the end of the bar, and then everyone gathered around me. Closer still and he saw the blood where the large rodent shifter had lain. Either Indigo had moved her, or she'd moved herself.

"A claim challenge?" he asked as the vibration in my middle increased in frequency.

I breathed faster, adrenaline starting to pick up.

"Shoot, where's my phone?" I tapped the coat pockets as though it would magically appear there. Then looked along the ground. It would've been in my back pocket or…

I spied it on the edge of the bar, belatedly remembering that I'd set it down before heading off to the bathroom. I always worried about dropping it into the toilet.

"Yes. Two women," Austin said. "She handled them both. I didn't touch either of the women. She managed her control incredibly well, better than you or I would have."

"Yes, I saw her control the other night." Kingsley looked around the bar as I grabbed my phone, my hands shaking. "Witnesses? Oliver?"

"Yes, Tristan," I whispered into the phone after tapping his name. "I'm getting a strong caution and stealth feeling from the southeast border. Could be something. Could be nothing."

"What'd you say?"

I opened my mouth to repeat myself, only to realize that hadn't come from the phone. Austin had turned, exposing me to Kingsley, both of the men looking at me with mirroring hostile stares. I wasn't totally sure which one had asked.

"Do I check it out?" Tristan asked through the phone.

"Yes. Fly high out there. Mind the moonshine. You're hard to see but not impossible. Keep your phone in your hand. Do not engage. Report back with what you find."

Austin stepped closer. "Jess, what's going on?"

I told them quickly, staying attuned to that connection. I couldn't send out a burst of magic to direct any of the other invisible fliers because a mage would feel it. They wouldn't know what it was or what it meant, but they'd be spooked.

"Damn it," I said softly. "We need a better way to communicate with the people on the territory line."

"My gargoyle form is dark, Jessie," Jasper said. "So is Nathanial's. He's still on the roof. He couldn't get in because of the altercation earlier."

"Go," I said without thinking about Austin or Kingsley. "Stay out of sight. See what Tristan needs, if anything. I'd be seen. I don't have any potion."

"Are you sure someone is there?" Kingsley asked as Jasper took off running, shedding clothes as he went. "Wait—" Kingsley reached forward to grab my arm. "Stop giving directions—"

Austin grabbed Kingsley's wrist before his hand reached me, his knuckles white, his body braced.

Kingsley's jaw clenched, but he pulled his hand back quickly. "Stop giving directions until we can think this through," he finished.

"I'm sure that one of the gargoyles is slowly moving up on something in order to check it out," I told him, wanting to step toward the door and put my eyes on the sky. At the same time, I didn't want to trigger Kingsley with my insubordination, something that would in turn trigger Austin. "If the mage is invisible, like him, he's going to have to be damn close to be sure. Tristan is an insanely fast flier, and he'll be able to see through the spell. Hopefully. We should know in a moment—"

"Make sure your people are out of there," Austin told Kingsley, thankfully jogging for the door. "We can't have a visible runner scaring them off."

"I have no way of doing that," Kingsley said, now jogging with him. "They'll know not to engage with any intruders, though."

"Miss, your clothes," Mr. Tom said as we exited the bar. "What is going on?"

A blast of *alert* radiated through the connection. Then surprise and alarm bled through one of my Ivy House links. It took me a moment to realize they were in the same location.

"It's Edgar," I said, now afraid for a different reason. "The patrol has found Edgar. Why the hell is Edgar way out there?"

"He was going to inspect locations for his flowers," Mr. Tom said, catching up to me as the others fell back. "He didn't think anyone would notice."

I could read the Ivy House link so much easier than any of my other connections, feeling a flash of pain, a surge of moping, and then a burst of adrenaline. He was battling—he must be.

Humor came through my connection to the invisible gargoyle, followed by pride, while Edgar gave me more moping and some embarrassment. His pain hadn't totally diminished, but it was a dull ache instead of a life-threatening injury.

"He didn't think anyone would notice?" I rounded on Mr. Tom. "We have a patrol specifically to ensure someone notices! Why wasn't this cleared with me?"

"Well now, miss," Mr. Tom said indignantly. "You've been shut up and whisked away and taken out—when would one of your poor, loyal, *forgotten* servants have the ability to beg you to be included—"

"Okay, okay, okay." I put up my hands to stop him.

"We've had to twiddle our thumbs, hoping you aren't dead or—"

"*Okay*, I said. It's not like we've been here long. It's been *one* day, Mr. Tom. I hardly call that forgotten."

"And last night."

"Twenty-four hours. Let's keep our expectations in check, shall we?" I put my hands on my hips, turning back to the alphas. "Sorry, guys. False alarm. The patrol must've given Edgar a knock. The good news is, the patrol is effective. The bad news is—"

I cut off as another connection pulsed, beaming joy and cunning ruthlessness. It was in the same location as the others. My phone rang, and I stared at Tristan's name for a moment before answering.

"Hello?" I asked, putting it to my ear.

"Edgar got one."

"Wh-what? Got…one what?"

Tristan laughed. "A mage. Our gargoyle patrol felt something strange leaving the territory and followed it toward the river. That must be when you clued in. The presence stopped. Our gargoyle thought whoever it was might feel wind from his wings, so he went a little ways away and landed, then snuck up on foot. The mage mustn't have noticed Edgar. Our patrol certainly didn't. Edgar says he was just minding his own business, picking a nice little area for Clarence the Clubber, when he bumped into something and got a fright. That something was the mage, who tried to hit Edgar with a spell, I guess. He was too close, though, so the mage banged him over the head with a flashlight. Edgar grappled for the flashlight, got a hold of it, and banged the mage with it. The mage fell, our guy hurried toward the commotion, and now we have a knocked-out mage and a vampire asking to be retired because he went against your orders and was creeping around the territory when he shouldn't have been."

Tristan stopped to laugh. Both alphas were staring at me with barely contained impatience.

"I'm going to be honest, Jessie," Tristan continued, "that vampire can definitely try the patience, but when you least expect it, he is useful. Damn useful."

"Yeah." What did you do with all of that? "Okay. Ah...well, fly in that mage. Get him to Austin's house, stat, before he wakes up. Maybe bring Edgar in case the mage needs a bite to keep him knocked out. I'll meet you there. He needs to be magically contained or he'll be dangerous, and that's a job for Sebastian. I'm sure Kingsley—sorry, the alpha—and Austin will want to meet the patrol wherever they are. First, though...are you sure this mage was alone?"

Tristan let go of a breath. "No, Jessie, I'm not. I can see in the dark, but the ground is hard out here. I can't see enough detail for subtle tracks, if they even left any. You can try getting shifters with good noses out here to see if something got through whatever potion they used."

"Yeah, will do. Good work, all of you. You pass that

on to the patrol. He would've gotten the guy if Edgar hadn't gotten in the way, I have no doubt. That was a win for both of them, and you for reacting so quickly."

"I deserve an award. I ate a crapload earlier. I have a cramp, actually. It hurts. That was a good lasagna."

I rolled my eyes and said bye, then hung up and explained everything to the alphas.

When I was finished, Austin turned to head toward the house but stalled when Kingsley didn't budge. I felt his alpha power beating into me, antagonizing my gargoyle.

"We're going to have words, Jessie Ironheart. You need to rein in yourself and your people. This is not how I run my territory, and it is not how I'm going to handle this coming assault. Do I make myself clear?"

Austin's power swirled, his beast now antagonized, but Kingsley wasn't being scary. He was like a parent telling his child how disappointed he was in them, and for some reason it was devastating coming from him.

"Yes, sir," I answered in a small voice, wilting.

He touched my shoulder, gave it a little squeeze, and I felt like crying in gratitude that he'd give me another chance. What a trip.

"And you." Kingsley speared Austin with his hard gaze. His whole demeanor shifted, aggressive now, brimming with frustration. "I don't know what's going

K.F. BREENE

on with you, and I won't ask. But if you're going to handle whatever it is yourself, you better tone it way down, or I will be forced to step in. Do I make myself clear?"

I frowned in confusion, not sure exactly what he was talking about, as Austin said, "Crystal."

Kingsley let out a slow breath. "Whoever would've thought your fruit loops vampire would show up my experienced shifters? I'll never live this down with Mimi. Come on, we have work to do. We need to scout out the territory while Jessie and her people handle that mage. I assume your mighty beta shifter is as good in the field as he is at riling up my people?"

"Better."

"At least that's something. And after this is all over, I'll want to know why that enormous beta gargoyle has eyes that glow. That's not a gargoyle trait. I looked it up to make sure. You've got secrets. I don't like secrets."

"You're just sore that my people have already bagged a mage," Austin said, starting off.

"Yes. I am. I thought I was being obvious about that fact."

I watched them go for a moment, feeling Mr. Tom's presence beside me.

"Well, miss. I assume now you will allow me to see you home, since no one else will have you?"

I sighed. This was my lot in life.

"You can make me a coffee, Mr. Tom. This might be a long night."

CHAPTER 15

SEBASTIAN

"**H**EY! WE MIGHT have activity over here."

Sebastian blinked and straightened up out of a painful stoop. His back popped and his neck felt like it had been glued on wrong.

"Huh?" he said, his voice like cobwebs.

"Hey." Nessa grabbed his shoulder and jerked him upright. "You can't get lost in work and come out of it slowly. This time the threat is all around us. C'mon, come with me. Something might be happening."

She took off at a fast walk toward and then through the back door of Austin's house, leaving the sliding glass door open. That meant he was supposed to come right this second.

He rubbed his eyes, returning his focus to the bubbling brew in the pot in front of him. The acid bomb-like potion needed another five minutes of stable heating before it could be taken off the burner and cooled. Walking away now, after five hours or so of careful work, would ruin the mixture. He couldn't take that risk.

He stirred the mixture counterclockwise for one stroke, then re-checked the potions book he'd found in Ivy House. He stirred one more stroke and closed his eyes, listening to the mixture. Feeling the way forward with his unshakable magical intuition. In times like this, where sleep was mostly nonexistent and stress was dangerously high, he could almost hear the potions talking to him. *Half a stroke. Just another half stroke and you've got it.*

He did as instructed, stopping the spoon at seven o'clock, if the cauldron were a clockface. That oughta do it.

"Sebastian!" Nessa shouted.

Her stress was at a dangerous level, too. There weren't enough lasagnas in the world she could make to calm her down. The closer they got to Momar, the more complex everything became. The more room for error. The chance that they wouldn't all live to see tomorrow. None of them would. Jessie and Austin and all of them. Sebastian had pulled them into the Land of No Return. There was no longer any way out. This battle was just one of many dangerous things to come.

He couldn't think about that now. One thing at a

time.

He straightened up out of his stoop again, watching the liquid bubble merrily.

"Just one more minute," he called.

Or had he just thought it? It was hard to say. He'd been muttering to himself, and thinking out loud, and thinking quietly for so many hours straight that he couldn't quite tell if there was ever someone on the other end of his words. At least Ivy House had flickered her lights or pulsed her crystals or *something*. The plant life in this backyard were horribly inactive.

Something hard hit his head.

"Ow!" He rubbed the offending spot as a shove sent him toppling off his stool. "Dang it, Nessa, this potion is almost done! It's dangerous—don't touch it."

"I wasn't going to touch it. Get up. Tristan's been gone for a while. He might've found something."

"What?" Sebastian closed his eyes for a moment, and then fell down a wormhole.

"Damn it," he heard, right before a foot slammed into his back. "You should've slept when everyone else did. Not now. Get *up!*"

Nessa's hands were rough. Or maybe it just seemed that way because he didn't want to get up.

"Just two more—" *Ding!* "Oh. The timer is done. That was a fast five minutes."

She sighed, hauling him to his feet and then graciously waiting while he moved the happily gurgling mixture off the burner before turning off the gas.

"We must always think of safety," he murmured.

"You can't work like this under these circumstances, Sabby," she said. "It's not working."

"Fantastic wordplay."

"It really wasn't." She directed him toward the open sliding glass door and then shoved him in.

"Jessie drugs me to sleep from time to time. Maybe you should ask Mr. Tom for the formula."

"Or maybe you can be a big boy and look after yourself for once."

He rubbed his eyes again, stopping at the too-big kitchen island. Her face swam into view, circles under her eyes and faint lines etching her tired face. "What's with you?" he asked.

"I've got news. This time it's not our network that's under fire. It's Jessie's people…and *us*. Remember we said to never get personal? That we'd never stay alive if we didn't stay on our island? Well, you've built a bridge from our island to another island, and it's a lovely tropical island, with welcoming inhabitants and warm words, and now our island is under siege—"

"Whoa, whoa, whoa." He held up his hand to stop the barrage of words. "At least when Patty babbles, it somehow makes sense. What?" He looked up at the corner of the room. "Where is Patty, anyway?"

"She's coming with the third wave, I've heard. She wanted to talk to the basajaunak parents."

A knock sounded at the front door. Nessa eyed Sebastian, a warning of some sort, before jogging that way. He still had no clue what was going on. Something to do with Tristan, but—

"Get your face on," she said, jogging by again. "And your wings."

He turned and looked after her, his mind swirling with fatigue now that he'd stepped away from all his projects. A nearly empty casserole dish of lasagna sat on the counter and his stomach grumbled. He couldn't remember the last time he'd eaten. His thoughts were a swampy mess in his head as he drifted over to it, thinking about getting a bowl and then having a notion that that was wrong somehow.

"Hi, bestie." Edgar smiled as he approached the island. "Oh wow, look at this, huh? Delicious." He rubbed his stomach.

"Yes. I was thinking of having some, actually. Would you like some? Nessa is a fantastic cook. A better baker, but that's beside the point."

"Is it?" Edgar asked.

"I'm really not sure."

Edgar nodded as though that all made sense, and panic flared through Sebastian, carrying a nice dose of adrenaline. He seemed to remember it was a bad sign if Edgar thought he made sense. Yes, no question—he had to snap out of it. He couldn't go to sleep yet. Something needed his attention.

With that in mind, he crossed to the fridge and grabbed out an energy drink. Time for his fourth or fifth wind.

"We're on the move," Edgar said, dogging his heels. "I regret to inform you that I will need to ask to be retired very soon."

"Again?"

"I'm afraid so. I *did* leave town when I knew I shouldn't have, and planted about five flowers, which I definitely shouldn't have done, but they were starting to turn surly. I figured I'd better plant them before they dug their heels into the ground and started eating townspeople."

Sebastian paused at the front door. He really needed this Red Bull to work faster, because his mind still wasn't making sense of words. Or maybe that was a good thing in this instance?

"Just this way, I think." Edgar gestured down the stairs and to the right. "I also would like to confess that I brought a few gnomes from Ivy House. I know I shouldn't have, but they really are very good at sneak attacks, and isn't that what we need—"

"Wait…" Sebastian stopped at the closed garage door, his hand up. "Did you say you brought *gnomes*?"

Edgar nodded, one eye blinking slowly and the other staying open, which was both hilarious and terrifying. This dead creature's parts were now starting to malfunction.

"Is that funny?" he asked, and Sebastian realized he was horror-laughing. That was a new one.

"It really shouldn't be. How'd you get gnomes here?"

"Very carefully and with a lot of rope and duct tape. One escaped on the plane. He must've chewed his way out, because half of the blood I brought was spilled on my clothes and there was a hole at the corner of the suitcase and no gnome. I'm sure the airport has anti-gnome strategies in place, though. It should be fine."

Edgar paused for a long moment, looking at Sebastian placidly. Sebastian didn't have the words to stop this madness. He just stared back, hoping for the best.

"I flew here by way of gargoyle," Edgar said pleasantly and with a little smile.

Sebastian started laughing again.

"Hey." Tristan laid a heavy hand on Sebastian's shoulder from behind. Sebastian didn't even startle.

You really couldn't be afraid of anything after having been trapped in mental gymnastics with an ancient vampire. "You okay, bud?"

"No, I don't think so," Sebastian answered. "Edgar has thrown me for a loop. I half wonder if I'm having a nightmare."

"At least we can share the nightmare together," Edgar said with that little smile.

"I need your help." Tristan steered Sebastian around the corner of the garage and to a side door. "The mage woke up. He tried to blast me with magic, but it obviously didn't have much effect on me."

Sebastian pounded the rest of his energy drink, trying to crank his mind back to life, and waited while Tristan opened the door.

"His magic didn't work on you, huh?" he asked the gargoyle with mysterious blood origins.

"Hardly at all, no. Whatever spell it was felt like a gentle slap. He seemed to think a potion had protected me, so he tried again with the same effect. The definition of insanity, I guess, right? Trying the same thing but expecting different results."

"Not…so much in this case. How is he contained?"

"I tied his hands with cable for now. Nessa gave me a potion to feed him to strip away his invisibility spell. He seems to have gotten enough down, so you should be good."

"Sebastian, wait, your wings and face," Nessa called, but Sebastian was already entering the garage, still a little hazy as to what in the world she was talking about.

It wasn't until the tied-up mage looked up from the seat where he'd been confined, in the middle of the mostly empty garage with oil stains on the concrete floor, that Nessa's words finally made sense.

The mage sitting there said, "Elliot Graves," in an accusatory voice.

When said by a mage, so often in that way, the name acted like a trigger. Sebastian's spine straightened of its own accord, his shoulders rolling back and a little smirk taking over his expression. His arm came up, as though he had a watch, and he posed in that humble, dirty garage like he was wearing a three-thousand-dollar suit.

"Oops, you've caught me," he said, his speech a little lilted and his tone filled with sardonic humor. "I'd ask what brings you to this sprawling shifter pack, but we both know the answer, don't we?"

The mage, an unremarkable middle-aged man with brown eyes and thin lips, didn't strain against the ropes. He didn't try to twist his arms to the sides to use his fingers for magic, which meant he probably couldn't pull off the more complex spells that would require such steps. His body was athletic, though, slim and fit. He was a field guy. A spy or a runner. A guy with a decent amount of magic who'd proven he was great at getting himself out of tight spots. A guy with a sixth sense, mages would say, able to detect the unseen.

Well, sixth senses and intuition wouldn't protect anyone from an attack-flower-planting vampire who never did as he was told.

"*You're* the mage backing the female gargoyle?" The mage sneered. "You think a bunch of altruistic shifters and weird magical creatures are going to help you regain your perch as the king of mages? You're going to need a lot more than that to take on Momar."

"Hello, hello." Nessa walked in with black stiletto boots up past her knee, a miniskirt, and fishnet stockings. Black eyeliner had been hastily drawn around her eyes and her hair was pulled up into a sort of messy punk-rock bun. She must've heard Sebastian being outed as Elliot and thus rushed to don her own alter ego. "Sorry I'm late—I was preparing for the info extraction."

"And the Captain." The mage looked her over. "Prettier than I'd heard. Tell me, honey, do you do anything besides blow your boss?"

A swell of power filled the room, and a shadow started to emanate from Tristan, who'd been standing

K . F . B R E E N E

idle in the corner. His form seemed bigger, somehow, broader, more intense, things that weren't necessary, given he was already such a colossal creature. Tendrils curled like claws from his suddenly thick aura, climbing up the wall and across the floor.

Sebastian blinked rapidly, wanting to rub his eyes. Wanting more Red Bull. He couldn't tell if this was a fatigue- and fear-induced hallucination or if this was another layer of Tristan's magic that the large gargoyle-slash-monster hadn't yet exposed.

The mage looked that way nervously, licking his lips. His body started to tremble, probably plagued with the sort of fear his brain hardly understood. A primal fear that said, *Run, get away, you're gonna die!*

"What…" The mage's voice was wispy. "What is it?"

"I bet Momar doesn't have one of *those*, huh?" Nessa laughed. "He's not a cuddly teddy bear inside, either. He's every bit the nightmare he looks." She surveyed the shelves in the garage. "Look at all these rusty…tools and things. We might go old school with this session." She picked up a pair of pliers that had been left to the elements for too long and glanced the mage's way. "Get a little medieval with it, shall we?" She winked. "I don't blow him, no. He's not into that sort of thing. I wish I weren't. It's so often an unwanted distraction. Alas, I do like a little pump and grind some of the time."

She walked toward the mage with a sultry sway of her hips before straddling the ends of his knees and resting the pliers on the his privates.

"I can make it so you won't ever think about that particular distraction ever again." She smirked and leaned toward him, showing him a little cleavage he didn't even glance at. His eyes were still wide, terror making them shine. He knew what the Captain and Elliot Graves were capable of. That knowledge would be playing on his courage, but add in the threat of a foreign monster...*thing*, and this poor mage was suddenly vastly out of his depth.

Sebastian chuckled as Nessa trailed the pliers up the mage's stomach and rested them against his chin.

"My, what pretty teeth you have, grandmother," she said softly, tilting her head as she surveyed him. She skimmed the tool along his cheek. "What pretty eyes you have. I might like them for my collection."

"Should we offer him a deal first, Captain?" Sebastian said as Edgar slunk in, scampering to the corner across from Tristan. "We do love a good mole, don't we?"

"Oh yes we do." She thunked the tool onto the mage's chest, making him flinch, before pushing off his lap. "I don't see how we could, though. If he let slip that

Elliot Graves is mixed up in this shifter's humble territory, it would cause all sorts of changes to our plan, don't you think? Delays"—she picked up a wrench—"spies, assassins. It would be a whole thing."

"I won't mention anything, I swear," the mage said, trembling. "I can get you great intel. I really can. I know some of the higher-ups. They trust me. They trust the information I give them."

"Three-minus T minutes," Edgar announced.

Nessa paused in her perusal of the garage as the mage continued to babble. She was the only one who could understand Edgar's countdowns, probably because she was the one who'd taught him how to incorrectly use them.

"What's happening in five minutes?" she asked him.

"Jessie will be here. Ulric, Jasper, and Nathanial with her. I wasn't sure if...you know." Edgar rolled his finger through the air. "If you needed to hurry up and torture him before she shows up. She is mostly against that sort of thing, if you remember correctly. Except when she loses control and does something awful, but usually she frowns upon medieval-style emasculation or castration. I've seen it done a time or two, though, should you need some help. I just barely escaped from getting my own penis and testicles sliced off. It was a situation of lucky timing. The female in question wanted to kill me herself, you see. Instead, she was killed and I was turned into a vampire." He frowned, looking downward. "Or was the vampire part a different time? I'm losing track—"

"What *is* that?" The mage was looking at Edgar now. "What is that thing? It's not natural!"

"Well now…that hurt my feelings," Edgar said, squinting at the mage. "But you know what they say, sticks and stones might break your bones, and surely get your penis and testicles chopped off…"

Sebastian started laughing again, definitely a defensive reaction.

"Edgar, you go stall her," Nessa said, looking at the shelves in the back of the garage now. "Tristan, you wait here and guard him. I'll put a little duct tape on his mouth… Where is the duct tape? Every garage in the history of the world has a half roll of duct tape lying around."

Edgar took off at a lope.

"Ah-ha! Here." Nessa snatched something from a peg on the wall. "Never been used." She stalked across the garage and slapped it against Tristan's chest. "Put that on him. Elliot, a word?"

She dragged him outside and then around the corner, out of earshot of Tristan. Still, Sebastian applied a sound-deadening cone over them to make sure. Nessa stood at the edge, one eye trained on the side door.

"We're up shit creek if that mage gets back to Momar," she told Sebastian. "This guy isn't sleek enough, suave enough, or arrogant enough to be one of the elite spies. He's a middle-range runner, that's it. When he goes back, he'll get a dose of truth potion. They'll torture him for more information once they realize he was caught here, Sabby. They cannot know we are here. They *cannot* know you're the mage rumored to be helping Kingsley."

"Nessa, I'm not stupid, just tired. I know all of that."

"Really? Because you've just randomly started laughing multiple times tonight and occasionally powered down to drool. I don't think your mind is online. Which leads me to my second point. We need information from this guy, and while I'm pretty sure we could get Jessie and her people to lower their standards enough to get it, I don't think Kingsley is going to allow it. He doesn't even want us cleaning out the border towns, for God's sake. He's a Boy Scout, and Austin is hesitant about pushing him. We can't take the chance of this guy getting away alive, for any reason."

"So what are you thinking?"

"First, you need sleep. A lot of it. I need you fresh. Then, while the powers that be argue about how to peel the information out of this guy, we frame his escape so we have some time to interrogate him properly."

"Where are we going to take him, though?" Sebastian asked, rubbing his face, willing the fog to clear from his mind. "We can't have him screaming in a motel room in a small town, not to mention stealing a car to get there is probably going to be noticed. It's not like there are woods we can run through and hide in."

"I'll figure that out. You get some sleep, then start thinking of ideas for how we can get him out of here without anyone being suspicious. We need to magically hide his scent, too, remember."

"Okay, okay." Sebastian nodded, now squeezing the bridge of his nose. "We should come up with a reason for why we can't interrogate him right now. Just in case Kingsley or Austin have a few questions and our guy gets chatty when he has one of those big alphas in his face."

"I don't think he'll be any worse off with them than with the monster gargoyle and all his party tricks. C'mon. Let's get to Jessie before the alphas come back."

CHAPTER 16
TRISTAN

THE MAGES PAUSED to tear down their ineffective sound-deadening spell, which hadn't done much more than fuzz their voices a little. For him, anyway. Sebastian should've known that. His fatigue was affecting his performance.

While they were occupied, Tristan silently strode along the wall of the garage and stepped back through the door, walking in far enough for his gargoyle magic to fall away. He crossed his arms over his chest a moment before Natasha came into sight, stopping in the doorway.

His heart beat a little faster as she smiled radiantly and gave him a thumbs-up, her eyes shining with cunning intelligence. With laughter, trying to hide her fear.

"You okay to hang?" she asked, her gaze turning just a bit intense. Her pulse sped up to match his—he could feel it inside her. And then came the lightning bugs of energy sparking and zooming between them—something that often happened when they were together. The lights pulsed and danced, ethereally beautiful.

She couldn't see them, which meant she wasn't open to him or to that facet of her magic. Not yet.

That was okay. He liked the hunt. He had limitless patience.

And she liked being prey.

"Am I just supposed to watch him or what?" Tristan asked, purposely sounding a little grumpy.

"Yes, you are. That's what it means to be a gargoyle beta after the shifter beta has arrived. You're expendable."

"I'm not the only one, it seems. Why don't you wrangle me up some dessert while you're standing around with your thumb up your ass, waiting for your almost-brother to create some useful magic?"

She minutely flinched, her brow pulling in just a little, and then her eyes started to sparkle. A high heel clicked as she stepped farther into the garage, her hip swaying, full of sass. The lights frenzied between them.

"Okay, Daddy," she said softly, tightening him up. He hadn't realized he was into that kink, but the way she said it, teasingly, nodding to the inside joke from when they first met—it was like bait he knew would trap him but still couldn't refuse. "I'll make a little chocolate for the left-behind beta, how would that be?"

"Sounds like a good consolation prize for not being the pack favorite."

She tsked at him. "You know better than that," she purred. "It's not a pack, it's a convocation, and you're still an outsider."

He wasn't sure if she was trying to dig a knife in his ribs with that last comment, but it definitely didn't. He'd always been an outsider, in every place he'd ever lived. Every "home" he'd ever dwelled. Cairn, pack, convocation, wandering the wilds—he was the odd one out. There was strength in that, as long as a guy knew his situation and accounted for the foolishness of those around him. She knew that better than anyone.

He watched her silently, watched that radiant smile slip as intensity soaked up her eyes. Watched her body sway, just slightly, her breasts heaving with her breath.

"You best get back in," he murmured, eyes on her mouth. "I'm sure Edgar is asking to be retired, and I doubt Jessie wants to hear it."

She blinked rapidly, sucking in a breath and looking a little lost for a moment. And then she turned and quickly strode from the garage, brought back to reality.

The intoxicating feel of her slid from his body. Their connected energy pulled taut and then stretched apart, nothing anchoring them together to keep it put.

After taking a deep breath of his own, he started in one part of the garage and slowly worked his way around, identifying everything of use in it. The mage breathed quickly whenever Tristan neared, his nostrils flaring, sweat running down his temples. Maybe Tristan wouldn't need any tools. Mages definitely seemed an easily intimidated, breakable sort. When they were trapped or without use of their magic, at any rate.

When the voices caught his ear, he retreated to the corner, arms crossed over his chest again.

"Hey, Tristan." Jessie entered the room with a tight smile. "Thanks for watching him." She looked around the garage quickly and then stopped in front of the mage as Edgar slunk in behind her, finding a corner in the shadows near the door. "Thank God this is not my jurisdiction. This is Austin's gig. I don't have to make the call on what needs to be done with this guy."

"You two co-lead well. It's rare when both parties so effortlessly move into and out of the power role."

"I think it's more of a struggle for him than it is for me."

"I could be wrong, but I don't think it is a struggle for him at all."

She turned to Tristan, taking a quick moment to glance at his arms and down, assessing him for any

K . F .   B R E E N E

injuries. She did it any time one of her people came out of a not-totally-safe situation.

She took in what he'd said with a flush and a little smile. He'd never in his life seen two people so happily matched.

"Well," she said, taking a deep breath. "If you'd like, I can watch him while we wait. Nessa said something about you wanting chocolate."

"If you'd just let me run in and use the restroom really quickly, I'm fine to watch him. Natasha can bring dessert out to me. Unless you don't think Austin would mind if I just used a bush around the side?"

"Oh my—no." Jessie gestured him in. "No, please. The restroom. Use the restroom, where you can wash your hands…"

He grinned and nodded, exiting and now hurrying. With the vampire watching Jessie, he wouldn't be creeping around. Of everyone in her crew, Edgar was probably the easiest to lose track of. He always seemed to turn up when Tristan least expected him.

He headed through the front door, pretending he was doing what he'd said he'd do, and heard Mr. Tom arguing with Natasha in the kitchen about how to properly drug Sebastian. Four people down.

So where was that weird mage?

"Hey."

Tristan kept himself from freezing, barely, as he finished shutting the door. Then he turned to see the droopy-eyed mage.

"Hey," Tristan replied, giving a cursory glance over his shoulder to denote his impatience at leaving Jessie. "You okay?"

"Yeah," Sebastian said, bowing. "I've been up for too long. I'm just waiting for the alphas to get here so we can secure that mage. In the morning we need to go over what we're going to do with him—how we're going to get the information out of him, I mean."

Wow. He *was* tired. His brain had clearly turned to mush. Good news. It would help knock one of the items off Tristan's to-do list.

Pointing toward the backyard, he said, "Why don't I help you quickly get that camping stove and stuff squared away so something doesn't fall over and light the house on fire, and then you can take a catnap before the alphas get here?"

"What about Jessie?"

"I'll send Mr. Tom out to her. Edgar's in the garage, too. She'll be fine for a moment with that mage, won't she?"

Sebastian swayed a little, furrowed his brow, and straightened up. "Crap, I'm tired. Yes, she should be. The worst thing that could happen is if the mage breaks free somehow and tries to attack her. She'll accidentally kill him, most likely, or Edgar will get there first and bite him. I think we're fine on that front. She hasn't yet met a mage at the top of her or her class. His or *his*, I mean. Hers—You know what I meant. The closest she came was in my caves, and they were all preoccupied with me, mostly. Anyway, I'm babbling. Yeah, if you could help, that would be great. I have a potion I've worked really hard on and I don't want to spill it. Especially because if I do, it'll likely blow us all up and spray acid on everything."

Sebastian continued to babble as Tristan quickly stepped into the kitchen to tell them what he was doing and direct Mr. Tom on what he needed to do.

"Yes, great idea. *Go*, Mr. Tom. I've got this." Natasha tried to push the old butler from her space.

"I just hope you don't kill him, that's the thing," Mr. Tom replied, dragging his feet. "There is an art to putting someone to sleep without their knowing. I'm just not sure a woman who deals in poison and killing people should give it a whirl, are you?"

"I bake without killing people, Mr. Tom," she replied. "I'm sure I can handle mixing a drink."

"That remains to be seen. We'll let Master Tristan be the first to try your cake."

Cleaning up the weird mage's station took no time

at all. Tristan helped him carefully stow the potion in a safe place so it couldn't be turned over, then waited until Sebastian's back was turned before he swiped and pocketed three vials of the potion he'd need later on, kept in carefully labeled boxes with all the other magical stores they'd brought.

That done, he left the weird mage with Natasha, said he needed to use the restroom before he got back, and headed that way through the house. When he reached the little-used study, though, he quickly ducked in, heading into the far corner, where an older couch sat in front of a pristine though old-fashioned coffee table. A layer of dust had collected on each.

He lifted the couch with one hand and brought out his bundle, tucked away earlier in the day. He had one of these here, one in the room he'd been stationed in, a third buried outside the grounds at Kingsley's, just off his property and under a rock, and two more in his luggage in case they needed to be stowed away else-where. He'd always been in the habit of being prepared. It had saved his life more times than he could count.

The clear plastic bottles, a tiny bit bigger than the vials he'd taken from the weird mage, weren't labeled. He didn't need the rope or cloth from this bundle, because both things were stocked in the garage. It didn't matter that the cloths out there were ancient—based on smell, they were free of chemicals or oils, and the captured mage would be dying tonight anyway. Details wouldn't matter.

After grabbing what he needed, he closed up his bundle and stowed it back under the couch. Hopefully Austin didn't get the sudden urge to read an old *National Geographic* and head in there, smelling his whereabouts before the scent grew stale.

He did actually use the restroom, making a show of it so the mages would hear.

"Light a match," Natasha called from the kitchen.

She'd clearly paid attention to when he'd left her proximity and how long it had taken him to exit the bathroom. She was always aware of him, whether she admitted that fact to herself or not. She was aware of dangerous things. Alluring things. Things that felt good to be in the proximity of.

He didn't respond, making his unhurried way back out to Jessie.

"There, miss, see?" Mr. Tom gestured at Tristan as he walked into the garage. "It's fine. Tristan is on the case. All will be well."

Edgar emerged from the shadows like a ghoul as Jessie grimaced, wringing her hands. The mage was slumped in his chair.

"What happened?" Tristan asked, having wanted to

linger by the wall so no one—notably the vampire, who had a strangely keen sense for when a person was trying to hide something—would notice the things in his pockets. Instead, he veered, making sure his back pockets, holding the larger items, couldn't be seen by the vampire.

"The miss was doing what anyone would've done and made sure the ropes were tied tightly," Mr. Tom said, his wings fluttering importantly. "When I tried to help, we got our wires crossed, and *whoopsie daisy*, the ropes slipped and the miss slammed him with a spell. Edgar, also wanting to help, quickly rushed in during the slipping rope situation and bit the mage on his arm."

"It takes longer for my serum to work when the bite is way down on the shin like that. But his pants were tight and his arms were flailing, so I thought that was the best spot."

"Yes, thank you, Edgar, though I see limbs confuse you as much as keeping time does. As you see, Tristan, this mage is knocked out. Very weak pulse. Edgar sucked a little too much blood, I think."

"Or it was the spell," Jessie said nervously. "I put a little too much power into it."

"It's okay, Jessie," Edgar replied. "You can blame me. I don't mind. We'll say I didn't know my own suck." His smile slowly spread, revealing his elongated canines, stained red. "Get it?"

"No," Mr. Tom replied. "Anyway, miss, let's get you into the house for a cup of coffee, wouldn't that be nice? We'll leave a very competent Tristan with the hopefully not-dying mage, and we'll prevent a heavy-handed Nessa from accidentally killing Sebastian. All will be well."

"I need a holiday," Jessie muttered as she let them escort her from the garage.

"Yes, miss. Of course you do," Mr. Tom soothed her. Edgar, thankfully, followed them out.

Tristan waited for a moment before checking the mage's pulse. It was definitely weak, but not terminally so. Just enough to shift blame if there was any when the morning came.

He stowed his items up high, where the vampire wouldn't be able to reach, then went around touching and messing with other things under the guise of being bored, but actually to spread his scent around the rest of the garage. After that, he really did look for something to cure his boredom.

It took about an hour for the alphas to show up, hard-eyed and keyed up the way shifters got when protecting their territory. They hadn't seen anything else of note, and it had been too dark to check out what the mage was up to. They'd have to leave all that for tomorrow.

Tristan had been anticipating that Kingsley and Austin would want to ask some questions of the mage. Then they'd talk about, and likely argue about, how to get the information the mage was unwilling to easily give up. The next argument would be about what to do with the mage once they no longer needed him. Tristan one hundred percent agreed with Natasha's assessment on that.

Tristan's solution was to wait until the mage came to before enforcing an additional injury (a precise blow to the head with the right amount of force and in a way that wouldn't bleed or show the bruise).

Given Sebastian was drugged and asleep, everyone else was dead tired, and any hope of an interrogation session was impossible because the mage was currently unconscious, the crew at large having decided to postpone the question-and-answer session until the following day, after the meeting.

"I can take over," Brochan told Tristan after the alphas had left, standing just inside the side door to the garage.

Tristan paused in sitting down in front of his half-formed statue made out of nuts and bolts. He glanced at the statue, then at the slumped mage, and straightened a little.

"Natasha has some dessert for me, anyway, don't you, Natasha?" he called, feeling her walking toward them.

"What's that?" She entered with raised eyebrows, stopping beside Brochan before giving him a sly glance. "Hello, Mr. Sue. Fancy meeting you here."

Brochan's expression didn't change, nor did he react.

A smile lit her face, playful but devious. Her posture changed, slinky and sexy, hips and bust accentuated. A wanton joke, perhaps. She was clearly teasing him.

A small sparkle of energy kindled between them. Shared desire. The energy wasn't dancing and playing, though. It didn't zip between them. They weren't connecting in a way that would allow the spark to grow and flower.

The *why* was obvious...to everyone but the lovely Natasha. Even Brochan knew, Tristan was fully sure.

No matter. He'd let her play her games and dance around her desires, watching the circle get smaller and smaller until she did what she longed to do: beg Tristan to be fully sated. To be pleasured in a way she'd been missing all her life with the ineffective good boys she met in bars.

Treasured in a way that would make even Austin

and Jessie's relationship seem dull.

He finished sitting down by his statue. It was the perfect excuse to send Brochan away, anyway. Them both away, he guessed. She'd want to go with him. At least he could then get things underway.

"I'm good here. I haven't done much today. Get some sleep, Brochan. Alpha Steele is going to need a heavy hitter those shifters understand, and that's you."

Brochan assessed Tristan in that way of his before looking at the mage. "Do you have your crew for backup, or do you need extras?"

Tristan didn't bother looking up. "I don't need a crew—his magic doesn't affect me. But they're here to guard Jessie, just in case. We're all good here. Enjoy my dessert."

Natasha paused with her hand on Brochan's arm, her head snapping to Tristan in confusion. The moment was over in an instant.

"Slap me five." She put up her other hand, always playing the clown for him, to help him find his way out of the darkness. It was noble, what she did, for him and for that weird mage. Why couldn't she see that those were the traits of a hero, not a villain?

Now she had Tristan to play the villain, though. She wouldn't have to get her hands dirty anymore. Not out of necessity.

Starting with tonight.

Brochan didn't engage, and the spark between them fizzled as he left the garage.

Natasha hesitated before following him, her body tense, as though stalling wasn't her choice.

"Do you want me to bring you dessert?" she asked.

Her energy tugged at Tristan, and he closed his eyes to savor it.

"No," he said, letting his eyes drift open again. "I'm good. See you tomorrow."

Still she hesitated for a moment, and then took that step away, stretching their connection until it broke. In a while, all was silent. Not even Edgar crept out in the grass, having been taken home. Mr. Tom, too, had been told to go back to the motel. Jessie and Austin would be entwined and preoccupied, Sebastian drugged out, and Natasha hopefully entering the dream world to thoughts of him.

He stood as the captured mage moaned.

Tristan's gargoyles were spread around the perimeter, all in stone. They would only emerge if Jessie or he willed it.

The mage groaned louder. Tristan collected the supplies he'd need, then set them in a neat row on the ground about five feet away.

First, he took the potion he'd taken from Sebastian,

three vials in all. There was no telling how long this would take. He twisted off the top of the first and tucked the cap into his pocket so he didn't leave any evidence behind. After ripping off the duct tape, he fed the potion to the mage a little at a time. The mage sputtered at first and then took it all as though it were water.

Then he did give the mage a little water while the potion started to work.

The mage's form hazed, followed by his words. The potion was taking effect. No one would be able to see him—a risk, but more importantly, no one would be able to hear his screams.

Tristan applied some of the contents of the little orange bottle onto the cloth before pressing it to the mage's nose. The man tried to hold his breath, like they all did, struggling against his ropes. Finally, though, he gave in, sucking in much-needed air. Then breathed faster, then faster still as his eyes widened and pupils dilated with fear.

Tristan applied his magic to heighten the effect. He let his aura of shadows roam, biting into the mage's middle with cold claws that showed no discernible marks. Wrapping around his heart and softly dragging across the jugular.

His magic teamed with the elixir in that orange bottle would make the nightmares soften his mind. The mage would spit out just about anything the asker wanted to know.

It was old magic. Blood magic. Magic no one in polite society would dare talk about. Black magic, some might say, but to Tristan's kind, just as natural as the mage magic sitting in front of him. Just as pure, or just as corrupt, depending on the eye of the beholder.

Natasha had no idea what a monster really was. No idea how far he would go to protect himself and his own.

"No, no, no, no," the mage whined, over and over, eyes soaked with fear. He would plead next. He'd beg. He wouldn't even know what he was begging for, just that he was so scared he couldn't see his way out of the nightmare.

The truth would set him free.

Free from the terror. Free from living—at least after Tristan applied what was in the clear plastic bottle. Free from his soul if Tristan willed it, but even he never went that far. Not yet. He hadn't had the cause to.

"Now," he said in a rough voice, "I want you to tell me everything you know about Momar and his plans for this territory, and then I want you to tell me every last detail you know about Elliot Graves and his Captain."

CHAPTER 17

AUSTIN

"D ID YOU GET some sleep?" Austin asked as he stopped beside Tristan.

Tristan would be the only gargoyle in this morning's pack defense meeting. It was limited to leaders, essential personnel, and those of Jess's people who'd ignored their commands yesterday and needed a talking to.

"I got enough," Tristan replied. "Indigo said she'd make me feel better." He quirked an eyebrow with a little smirk. "She didn't say how, exactly..."

Austin barely stopped himself from chuckling. He needed to keep with shifter norms right now, and alphas didn't show emotion.

"How about you?" Tristan asked as Jess turned Phil away from the lineup. Of the basajaunak, only Dave would be in attendance. "Did you go back to sleep after I woke you?"

Austin looked out over the parking lot as Kingsley and his people arrived, right on time. His brother was always punctual when it came to official business.

"No. It's okay, though. This morning I let Jess make me feel better." He couldn't help it—he quirked an eyebrow. The big gargoyle laughed.

Tristan had awoken Austin shortly after three in the morning to tell him the prisoner's breathing was dangerously shallow. Austin had witnessed the man's death—his deathly pale skin, his glassed-over eyes, his muttered words. Where he should be in the morning, why, people he would talk to, things he had witnessed.

Austin had scrambled for something to write on, only to have Tristan stop him, saying, "I've got it all." He'd hesitated, like he hadn't wanted to divulge anything else, before saying, "I tell you this out of respect for our working relationship and my pledge of loyalty to Jess and your convocation with her. Being this transparent doesn't come easily to me." He took a deep breath. "I orchestrated this moment. They had spells on him, I think, to hamper the types of things he could share, but my magic broke those barriers. I have all the information he had to offer."

He'd explained his worry that Kingsley wouldn't agree to the means necessary to extract information from the mage. A worry Austin had shared. Given they sorely needed the information, Tristan had known something needed to be done.

That something had presented itself in the midnight hours, it seemed, when the mage had awoken in a sort of fever dream. Since his pulse had beaten strongly, and he hadn't seemed in any danger of dying, Tristan had leaned on him with his nightmare magic. All the information about Momar had come tumbling out, including the reports he'd sent in to his boss. Mutterings, mostly, but coherent enough to be incredibly useful.

In the end, however, Tristan's magic had proven too powerful—he'd pushed too hard, and it had pulled the mage under.

This was all told to Austin with infallible confidence. Tristan's body language corroborated his story perfectly, relaying the facts and omitting nothing.

Kingsley would have believed it easily.

Austin wasn't Kingsley.

Austin had lived a rougher life than his brother. He'd learned not to take things at face value, an education he'd paid for dearly many times over.

Tristan's story had been wrapped up just a little too perfectly. Taking the blame was the nice bow on top. Jess would be absolved of any guilt, Nessa and Sebastian wouldn't have to take matters into their own hands to protect Sebastian's slip-up, and Austin didn't have to go against Kingsley's wishes or admit he'd lost control of his people. All while they gained incredibly necessary information and rid themselves of the source. A perfect end to a flawlessly executed subterfuge.

He hadn't pushed, because the result had been necessary, but he wouldn't forget the little inconsistencies. Like the mage's voice, raw and rough at the end, an effect that usually resulted from intense and consistent screaming. Or the strange smell, like some sort of chemical, that had hovered around the mage's face. Or the fact that Tristan had seemed a little too knowledgeable about how Momar would react to learning Elliot Graves was working with Jess.

Austin also couldn't shake the feeling that something had been omitted regarding Tristan's magic. He struggled to believe so much information had been extracted with nothing but his swirling nightmare power, especially if the mage had been screaming (and, if so, why had no one heard that?).

There had to be more to the story.

That gargoyle had secrets, and he wasn't keen on sharing.

Austin wasn't the type of leader to turn a blind eye.

For now, though, they had the information they needed about that mage's dealings with Momar. Austin trusted Tristan enough to believe in that. Anything else was peripheral at the moment. When the time came, he felt sure Niamh would love to help sort it all out.

"A reminder," he told Tristan, "to keep your expression neutral through this meeting. It's what they expect. Otherwise they might think you're taunting them. We don't need any more tension."

"Yes, sir."

"When the unexpected happens—not if, *when*—roll with it. There's no telling how Kingsley's people are going to react to Jess's people, but I assume it won't be rationally."

"No problem, sir," Tristan said, watching Kingsley's people walk toward them in two orderly rows with Kingsley at the pinnacle. "Having been on the other end of that, it'll be nice to watch the fireworks this time."

"Funny. That's what Niamh always says." Austin walked down his line of people, all shifters, with Brochan at their head.

His beta stood the way he always did, spine straight and shoulders back, head high, gaze just a fraction lower than straight on. His posturing was just shy of *alpha*. Dangerously shy, it seemed, judging by how Kingsley bristled and his people coiled with tension.

Brochan's status had never bothered Austin. They knew where each other stood, and the beta was appropriately respectful. If Kingsley and his enforcers were worried about their inability to challenge Brochan and win, that was their problem. Austin would not cut the legs out from under his people to ensure others stood taller, not even for his brother.

It was a wonder, though, why they hadn't had the same reaction to Tristan, who was just as mighty in battle as Brochan—maybe even more so, depending on those secrets he was hiding. Too different, maybe. Unable to properly size him up. Or maybe it came down to the fact that he always looked like he was wearing a cape.

"Austin." Kingsley stopped in front of him.

"Alpha." Austin bent his head in greeting.

Kingsley's gaze roamed over the people Austin had brought and then over Jess's crew, settling on the cooler at Niamh's feet and the doily-wrapped can in her hand.

"Is that alcohol?" he asked, unable to hide how mystified he was.

"Champagne." Niamh hoisted it up. "I found it in the corner store near the hotel. They didn't have any proper black *tae*, so I figured this would do the trick. Fierce handy, putting it in a can like this."

"It's nine o'clock," Kingsley said.

"Yeah. That's why I'm drinking champagne." She said it like *duh*. "It's a perfectly respectable drink for the morning. Like a mimosa, but without the orange juice."

Kingsley stared at her for a moment, then at Austin. Without a word, he passed into the building, his people following.

"Nice goin'," Ulric murmured.

"What was I supposed to do? I don't drink coffee," she shot back. "I could be drinkin' the moonshine I got off one of the locals last night, but am I? No. I'm drinking a mimosa."

"Except it's not a mimosa, it's straight champagne," Jasper said.

"Better fer ya." She took a swig. "Orange juice is too sugary."

"Off to a great start," Jess murmured, entering the building at Austin's side.

"Could be worse," he replied. "He could've had one of his people try to take it from her."

"I think at this point we know it could always be worse."

On the second floor, they entered a large room with a custom-made table in the middle supporting a 3D map of the pack territory and the town therein. Kingsley had clearly continued updating it through the years, the town having grown since Austin was here last.

"You're expanding the town?" Austin asked, noticing his mom, Mimi, Aurora, and Mac standing at the back. It was customary to invite the former alphas to such meetings for their experience, and the possible future alphas for training.

Kingsley took a stance at the side of the table with his back to the windows. "I buy land whenever the neighboring farmers will sell it to me. The town expands at its own pace."

Austin took the opposite side of the table, looking down on all the little figurines, then the grid of fishing line not too far above it.

"Cute," Jess said, stepping beside Austin. "Look, there are little wolves and—Oh, these are the creatures your people turn into, huh? Neat." She pointed at the fishing line. "Awesome! That's for the gargoyles, right?"

"Yes," Kingsley said. Most alphas Austin had ever met would've given clear signs that she was wasting time. Not Kingsley. He watched her patiently, allowing her to analyze each street and smile at the little animal figurines.

"Very cool." She put her hands behind her back, finally straightening up. "We should do something like this."

Cyra pushed in next to her and pointed to a strip of land on the eastern side. "I found an area here that is a bunch of rock and dirt. No bushes or anything. I could unleash all my firepower on the enemy, and you wouldn't need to sap the heat afterward."

"This map is mostly accurate in the details," Kingsley said, stepping back now to allow Jess to pass by if she was so inclined. "The map indicates that there is vegetation there. Possibly you were in a different location?"

"There was some vegetation, yeah. That's the right place." Cyra nodded as Jess traveled around the table, checking out more details. Cyra trailed her before pointing at another spot. "Right there, too. Your map hasn't been updated since yesterday at about noon. Those areas are all black now."

"You were supposed to keep that to yourself," Hollace said through his teeth. "Remember?"

"Oh, I was?" She glanced over at him. "I thought the secret was about the—"

"Stop her," Ulric tried to interrupt.

"—strange creature that I accidentally-on-purpose killed this morning?"

"No, that was information you were supposed to tell the alphas," Hollace murmured, looking at his feet with his hands behind his back. "Except you were supposed to do it either before or after the meeting, not right at the beginning while everyone was staring at you."

"Especially after Niamh already cast a bad light on our crew by drinking on the job," Jasper muttered.

"*Jaysus*, Mary—it's just a little champagne, like!" Niamh replied. "It gives me less of a kick than that horrible dredge, coffee."

"How dare you!" Mr. Tom said, turning on her.

"Now sucking down the basajaunak brew," she continued, "would be drinking on the job. That stuff'll put hair on yer—"

"Enough," Austin barked, crackling power through the room. Too much power, unfortunately, showing everyone he had more than the reigning alpha. Still. It couldn't be helped. Kingsley was only so patient, and judging by his posture and his crimson hue, his head was about to pop off. "Alpha, I apologize. Some of the people gathered in this room are not used to pack life."

"Not even yours?" Kingsley asked, his direct gaze aggressive.

Austin held on to his beast and lowered his eyes, showing submission. "Not even mine. They are a subset of our convocation, led by Jess, who has a much looser structure. They are more of a peer group than a defined hierarchy."

"That is not how we do things in this pack," Kingsley said, his tone like ice. "If rules are set, like temporarily not leaving the boundaries of the town, I expect those rules to be followed." He raised his voice for the whole room. "*Do I make myself clear?*"

His power rippled through the room, followed by a surge of hostility through the Ivy House bond. Jess straightened up slowly, her eyes suddenly on fire and pointed at Kingsley. Her power pumped, stronger and more volatile than the surge that Kingsley had just sent out. She'd also just unconsciously proved she had stronger magic than the reigning alpha. Not a great start for either of them.

"We're good, Jess," Austin said softly, pushing warmth through their bonds. "That is a standard and justified request. We'd ask the same."

Kingsley noticed her stare and was thankfully slow to turn to meet it, likely because he sensed what Austin did. His people probably wouldn't know that, though, treating her power with the same vague indifference that they did Tristan's.

She blew out a breath, braced her hands on the table, and slowly bent her back. The movement looked like it cost her a great effort. "Sorry." She shook her head. "I mean, yes, you make yourself clear. Or whatever I'm supposed to say."

"Strange creature?" Kingsley asked Cyra, easily navigating away from Jess's borderline disrespect of his position.

"I flew it here before the meeting," Nathanial said, stepping forward. "I knew you'd want to see it, but there wasn't enough time to apprise Jessie and Austin Steele about it before you were due to arrive, so we felt it was better to wait until the standard business was done. We left the basajaunak with it. It'll be safe until you're ready to check it out."

Austin nodded at Nathanial. He'd handled the situation with textbook precision, though Austin wished he'd learned the news before his brother, in case it wasn't something he wanted to deal with as a team.

"And this creature was where?" Kingsley asked Nathanial.

"I picked it up along the river, in pack territory, about a hundred yards away from where the mage was found."

Kingsley's look turned intense, swinging toward Cyra now. "And you were there why?"

She spread her hands helplessly, her gaze flicking to Jess. "I was…wanting to see…the abduction sight of the mage?"

Half of Jess's crew wilted, hanging their heads. They weren't even going to pretend that was a good lie.

"And the real reason?" Kingsley pushed, his face turning crimson again.

"It was me." Edgar stepped forward, his whole body bent and his arms just sort of dangling. "I did it. I am the culprit. She is trying to take the blame for my gross negligee."

"Your gross…what?" Bewilderment bled through Kingsley's expression. Edgar could crack the best of them.

"I think he means negligence," Austin said, realizing what this was about. "Alpha, if I may, this is an order of business I'd hoped to discuss with you later in the meeting. Not the creature—I didn't know about that—but the matter Cyra is likely referring to. I ask that we put off the specifics until a later time. I think we've gotten far enough off track as it is."

"Fine." Kingsley stepped forward again, his movements brusque, his patience at an end. "Let's get down to business."

CHAPTER 18

JESSIE

I LISTENED TO Austin and Kingsley negotiate the various placements of their defenses. It was like watching a chess match. I hoped one day I could be that good at organizing a defense.

In the end, it was determined we'd have a couple of our people in the shifter town, and the rest would be posted along the borders of the territory. That was probably for the best. Our fliers able to cover more area and the townspeople wouldn't need to worry about strangers watching their goings-on.

That topic out of the way, Kingsley moved the conversation on to what we'd do in the event more mages were caught assessing the pack defenses.

"Did you check out the metallic element by the river where the mage was captured?" Austin asked as Kingsley gestured to his shifters. The beta came forward holding a stack of papers balanced on a laptop.

"We did. We'll get to that in a moment." Kingsley set the computer on the edge of the table and handed back the stack of papers.

In the corner of the room, a projector blared to life, flashing a spreadsheet across the wall. The projector guy pulled down a screen to better showcase the image.

"That's a list of all the attacks we've had, where they took place, when, and a summary of each." Kingsley motioned James around the table. "This is a report in paper form of everything you'll see on the slides. Now, as you can see, most of the attacks were made by two or three mages. We usually catch them shortly after they cross the perimeter, except in the cases of deep night. It is rare for there to only be one, so we're thinking one or two probably got away yesterday."

The slide flipped as I took a packet from James.

"This next slide shows the severity of the various attacks. As you can see, most of these mages ran after they were found out. But a few of these instances have resulted in severe altercations where we've had wounded shifters and one death. The worst outcomes were always against three mages."

The next slide flicked onto the screen, and I could feel the impatience from Austin and also a low hum of emotion from a gargoyle connection, nothing dire. I homed in anyway, not incredibly interested in Kingsley's analysis of when the mages had struck and his predictions on when they might come again. The world fell away and that connection came into focus. Tristan. He was in this room with us, feeling frustrated and impatient.

Clearly he and Austin had heard a different account from that mage I hadn't actually killed.

That had been a relief, both because if I was going to hurt someone, I'd like to mean to, and also because they'd gotten valuable information from him before he kicked the bucket. Close call. We needed a better system for this stuff, but we were all relieved with how it had worked out.

"Alpha, if I may?" Austin waited for Kingsley to nod. "You have recorded less than half of the invasions that we know of, and those you have noted were assessments, nothing more. They weren't real attacks. You've given them information and gotten nothing in return."

The air thickened in the room. Kingsley's shifters' eyes narrowed at Austin. They clearly thought he was calling their alpha ineffective. Maybe useless.

The former was true, of course, but it wasn't Kingsley's fault. He didn't know mages like we did. He didn't have eyes on their spies, hidden behind spells and potions. Knowing magic existed was a far cry from knowing what it could do. All he could see was what they'd encountered, a low hum of activity, dangerous but manageable, never getting worse, never giving a real threat. Given he led a pack that wanted peace, that were used to a mostly sedentary life, he'd probably had people look at those numbers and whisper in his ear that the coming threat wouldn't be that bad. That their pack was too solid. That Momar had never taken on anyone like them before. After a while, even a guy like Kingsley would probably start to believe.

We would need to be a wrecking ball to that pleasant fiction.

"And you got this from the fevered mutterings of the badly wounded mage?" Kingsley asked, his skepticism thinly veiled.

"Yes," Austin growled, his gaze not dropping into the submission zone this time. "Under the guise of an invisibility potion, working solo or in pairs, these mages, called runners, have been slinking around this territory for months. They've hidden devices to enhance their magic throughout the territory, along with hookups for military-grade steel that'll lie over the river in its narrowest places to act as bridges. That'll give them a lot more access to your town. I'm sure you identified those setups this morning, though I'm not sure why you hadn't found them before now. They've also laid track for some sort of magical framework that'll help them orchestrate a large…shield or something. I haven't had a chance to talk to our mages about that yet. Tristan wrote that down, in two instances, and neither description was clear to me."

"Twice, huh?" Nessa said to Tristan quietly, standing near him, her eyes narrowed in suspicion. "The mage must've thought you needed to hear it twice to get those notes perfect, maybe."

"Pardon me," Austin said, the rest of the room not paying Nessa's comment any attention, "but they've been lulling you to sleep, alpha, while they set up their weapons in your backyard."

The heaviness in the air intensified with Austin's words, but I didn't dare look Kingsley's way lest I randomly get worked up again and make a show of myself. All the power being thrown around made me feel…aggressive.

Instead I watched Tristan slowly look Nessa's way, his bearing loose and easy and his eyes clear and open, glowing brightly.

"Obviously so," Tristan murmured. "Or why would he have repeated himself, much more slowly the second time, as though he wanted me to get every detail?"

Nessa's eyebrows drew together and her face flushed just a little, three parts anger, one part…something else.

Sebastian had been intensely frustrated that he'd slept through the mage's mutterings, thinking (probably correctly) that what the mage was saying would make more sense to him and Nessa than to Tristan. He'd calmed down after seeing Tristan's notes. They really were very thorough.

Nessa hadn't said a peep about the situation. She'd listened silently to Austin's account of the night, looked at the notes Tristan had handed over, and then spent the rest of the morning seemingly lost in thought. When asked what she was thinking about, she'd shaken her head and bounced back to life.

"I don't like your tone, Austin," Kingsley replied, his gush of magic pulling my focus back to him. "Nor your implication that we've been asleep out here, twiddling our thumbs." He pointed at the projector. "We've cataloged every instance since the patterns began to emerge. We've doubled our defenses and worked day and night to protect our families and our homes. Some of us have been wounded, and we lost a good man, all while battling a force the likes of which we've never faced before. In case you've forgotten, we don't have the ability to see through magical potions. Nor have we found a mage who *somehow* has secret information. But we've been doing this for *months*. So before you come in here with your swagger, thinking you know all, why don't you get on a team for once and work *with* us, not against us?"

Austin's power surged and his gaze heated.

This was less about two leaders trying to compromise and more about two brothers struggling to work out their issues on a public stage. That was all well and good, but it was not the time for this confrontation.

"If you think—"

"We haven't forgotten," I said loudly, moving away from Austin a little and putting out my hands, not wanting to seem like I was solely on his side. "We definitely have not forgotten, alpha. Austin is expressing his frustration badly, not at you or your people, but at the situation. At our—*all* of our—helplessness against this magical tyrant. But we're here to fill in some gaps. Before we captured that mage last night, we didn't know any more than you guys. We've been flying blind—that's the problem. So let's talk about what we know and come up with a plan to find out what we don't. The blame game is a waste of time."

I didn't break my gaze from Kingsley's, but softened it so that it wouldn't seem dominating. Sometimes leadership took an iron will, and sometimes it took the patience and finesse of a kindergarten teacher. The trick was knowing when to use which tactic.

After a moment, Kingsley nodded but didn't comment. Austin nodded as well—a truce. The floor was mine.

"Tristan," I said, "why don't you go over, in all the detail you have, what that mage shared with you? That'll help us all get on the same page. Then, Sebastian, I'd like to hear all you know from your spy network about what Momar might have in store for us. I'd also like to remind everyone here today that Sebastian and Nessa will be tortured and killed if they are caught by the enemy. They usually battle people like Momar from the shadows. Most people battle him that way, and we know why based on what's happened to other packs. Stick your neck out, meet the axe. That's how it works. So before we go discounting our mages because they happen to have the same magic as the enemy, let's instead use their knowledge to help us all stay alive, okay? Let's not lose any more men or women."

Tristan started by recounting the situation in which the mage had died and then waited to see if there were any questions. None were asked, so he took the pages of notes back from Austin and recounted what was there, stopping a couple of times to add things he'd remembered that didn't make it onto paper. After finishing, he returned the notes to Austin and lifted his eyebrows, silently asking for questions.

Kingsley was looking at the projector, though, the slide with the dates of the attacks. Someone else was filling in the time stamps provided by Tristan, some exact and some guesses.

The whole time Nessa stared at Tristan thoughtfully, *suspiciously*, and for the first time I found myself tilting my head at the situation as well. Those were some very detailed notes. I hadn't gotten anything half so detailed when I used the nightmare spell. It was like Tristan had cracked the guy's skull open and looked inside.

Then again, Tristan's subject had already been muttering about things, asking for some sort of deal to get out of his predicament, and that was before the bit with Edgar and Mr. Tom. It made sense that things might go a bit more smoothly without all the mayhem.

I pushed away the niggling feeling that something was amiss to focus on the situation at hand. I would ask Austin for his thoughts later.

Kingsley swore, his whole countenance brimming with anger. He turned to look out the window.

"I'd thought they were testing our defenses in the beginning," he said. "For a while they changed it up enough that it seemed like they were feeling us out. But when the instances stopped evolving, and didn't escalate…"

Austin nodded slowly. "They surely were testing you in the beginning. And then, once they had the lay of the land, they used those instances as distractions."

There was a tone to his voice that hinted at *you should've known that.*

Before Kingsley could react, Sebastian stepped forward, the normal guy dealing with shifters and not the powerful mage with his shiny watch. "Do you know what else you did? You took away their sense of urgency. Austin…Steele. Austin? I'm confused about what I'm supposed to be calling him, but that guy"—he pointed at Austin—"said they'd lulled you to sleep. That's not even remotely true. Sorry al—Austin. Steele."

"Use Austin here," Austin said.

"Thank you. Anyway, Alpha Kingsley, you said you doubled your defenses. You worked long hours. You drove away their distractions and ran around and secured the perimeter, right?"

Kingsley didn't answer right away, probably not liking the "ran around" part.

"Yes," he finally said.

"Right. But you didn't notice their runners. All these many months, you've felt secure in chasing them off, and they've felt secure in studying how you operate. They've snuck around your territory, infiltrated the border towns, listened to your drunk shifters, snuck in and got out again—"

"Is there a point to this?" Kingsley growled.

Sebastian hunched. "Yes. It's that you've changed your entire playbook by bringing us here. They are now operating with a false sense of security. That gives us the upper hand. Jessie, if I may?"

He approached the map and waited for my go-ahead. I nodded.

"Okay. Well." He pulled a bunch of green and red Monopoly houses and hotels from one pocket, and cards and other little items stolen from board games in the other. He bent to place them in a pile at the edge before pausing and glancing up at Kingsley again. "I have an expansive network in the mage world. Much of that network, at this point, works in some way or form for Momar. He owns a lot of real estate, people and places alike, and he's the most notorious mob boss you've ever heard of. From that network, I get bits of information that Nessa and I piece together. There is guesswork, there is some wrong information, and there are plenty of holes. But we're good at what we do because if we weren't, we would die. Just know that this is my best guess, and things can change. Yes?"

Kingsley didn't nod or comment, his arms crossed over his chest.

"Just keep going," I whispered.

"Right. Yeah." Sebastian started placing the pieces around the map. "I know what sort of magical shield they are trying to construct. I've heard of it being attempted before, but no one has ever gotten it to work. They must think they'll have all the time in the world with you, because that's a massive undertaking for a territory this size. It makes me think they'll have other, smaller shields to keep you guys at bay. Then again, they have an absolutely enormous host of mercenaries and their own ground troops. Maybe they think those'll be enough. Broken Sue can attest that it was enough to take down his pack, the mercenaries creating a human wall that the mages could hide behind and fire magic over. It's been done many times before."

He worked around the map as Nessa stepped forward, rolling her shoulders and then her head. She looked like an athlete trying to shake off a bad play. Behind her, Tristan watched her with sparkling eyes.

"You should be asking how we'll disable that shield." I pointed at Kingsley with a disarming smile. "But don't bother. We won't be."

"No way," Sebastian said. "We want them focused on that massive undertaking. We want it sucking away their energy. That only helps us."

"What if it works, and they get it erected?" Kingsley asked.

"He said erected," Sebastian murmured with a smile.

"Dirty boys, these shifters," Nessa quipped, the two working off each other the way they did best. "In order to *erect* the spell, it's necessary to send magic from one mage to the next, each holding a *rod* that connects to the magical currents running through the ground—the spike. Once enough spikes are engaged, it'll take powerful mages to send the collected magic over the intended space and connect with the mages on the other sides. Side to side, over and back. It's seriously work-intensive. Right, Sabby?"

"Work-intensive and complex, and mages don't work well together. There is a chance they could make it happen. They've been practicing in larger and larger areas—yes, I'd heard about this before today. But one little sliver in their network, and the spell will have to be started all over. Nessa may not be a powerful mage, but she can still be enough of a sliver to ruin their day. Jessie and I could blow their spikes out of the ground. So if none of us die, we should be fine."

Sebastian stopped after he'd done a loop of the map, arranging his pieces.

"I am a little worried about the magical enhance-ments that were mentioned," he said, studying his handiwork. "They do exist, but usually not in an outside environment like this. Maybe that's what they plan to bring in over the river, I don't know. I'll do some research, but I'm wondering if it's some backup mechanism of some type." He tsked. "It would've been better if I'd been there with the mage. I might've connected some dots."

"Yes, it would've been better," Nessa said quietly, her eyes flicking toward Tristan.

"Anyway," Sebastian went on, "alpha, I don't want to give you a false sense of security. But this is what I am guessing their positions will be. Roughly."

I stepped closer to the map, finding a sea of board game plastic pieces spread around the board. My heart dropped to my stomach.

"You're sure about those numbers?" Kingsley asked in a subdued tone.

The change must've alerted Sebastian that something was amiss, and he looked up before straightening slowly, glancing around the room.

"That does look like a lot, Sabby—talk 'em through it," Nessa said.

"Oh." Sebastian put his hand out over the map. "It is a lot of people, yes. We've always known it would be. But as I've seen with Austin and Jessie's team, the magical type matters a great deal more than strictly numbers. Bear with me."

He went through all the pieces and what they meant. There would be scores of mercenaries in the first wave—the human wall—followed by the more resilient ground troops, kind of like super mercenaries. We'd dealt with some of them in the past, and they were pretty hardcore. Some would have vehicles, and others would be on foot. After a delay, the mages would show up, likely on vehicles. Ultimately, though, they'd want to be on solid ground to do their magic.

"The mercenaries and ground troops will have magical guns," Sebastian went on, and I noticed a few of Kingsley's shifters taking notes. "Nessa and I brought a couple of examples. We'll make sure you all get to take a look at those. It might be good to practice dodging the beams. Kingsley, you've dealt with them before in Austin's territory, remember? Same type. The ground troops, though…" He grimaced. "I've heard they have some new equipment, although I haven't gotten any details beyond that. I'm afraid we're flying blind there."

He moved around to various clumps of pegs, the "people" from the Game of Life.

"I've *heard* the mages will be working in teams. Now…this might be partly their strategy to get that shield off the ground. Or they might be pairing a couple of potion users with a couple of rapid-fire spell throwers. This strategy also allows the groups to put up small magical domes in case the large shield fails to—"

"Explain this shield to me," Austin said. "The large one. It sounds like it'll extend over the whole town?"

"Shield is a terrible word for it," Sebastian said. "I mean, it *is* a shield, because it's to prevent magic, teeth, and claws from getting at the mages on the other side, but it's essentially locking the town inside. It's a cage, really. A magical cage. That's a better term."

"A much scarier term, though, which is why shield might be better for us to use going forward," Nessa said.

"This is true." Sebastian nodded, looking over his handiwork again. "So the shield is a magical cage. If they were to *erect* it, magic could be fired into it, but not out. People could walk into it, but not out. Once locked inside a spell like that, you're trapped—unless you have enough power to break the spell, which, I'm guessing, at that magnitude, we wouldn't."

"Then what?" I asked, not quite understanding. "With a town this large, with buildings and everything, they wouldn't be able to hit us with spells. And the pack isn't *that* removed from Dick society, so we could call for help."

Sebastian shook his head at me. "The air would be trapped inside with us. Sound. They could drop magical bombs on us from a helicopter without anyone hearing the blasts. Shoot down at us with silencers. Spray down acid. Release poisonous gasses that Momar acquired through the magical black market—or Dick black market—and let it run its course. Drop down fire, somehow flood—"

"Okay, okay," I said, feeling a little sick. "I get it."

"Being trapped like that in a magical battle, no matter how large the circumference of your cage, is death," Sebastian said. "That's why people keep trying to build that massive magical shield."

"But it's not likely to be erected," Austin said.

No one cracked a joke about his choice of words this time. The room was deathly silent.

"No, it's not likely. What *is* likely is they'll manage to create domes," Sebastian said. "Domes are like the cage but smaller, weaker, and easier to break. If they do that, it'll be to shield themselves and keep us off them. Magic will be able to go out but not be shot in at them. Physical attacks would be thwarted unless the creatures attacking have more power. Those domes will keep them stationary, and for us, that's a great thing. It makes them sitting ducks. I've already started potions to eat through that magic. We have creatures powerful enough to claw through it. And, if nothing else works, Jessie and I can magically break into one at a time. Domes are doable. I still need to come up with a few miracles to help us fight the odds, but there's hope."

"He's very good at coming up with miracles, folks, don't worry." Nessa put out her hands as though settling everyone down.

"Yes, call me miracle man." He said it in such a droll way, I couldn't help a smile. "But to get to the mages, possibly in their domes, we'll first have to make it through the mercenaries." Sebastian took a deep breath, pointing at the mercenary tokens. "After that, the ground troops. Those won't be a problem if we can thwart those magical guns. There's a pretty easy potion to reduce their effectiveness, but it hasn't been made because we have a lot to do and Austin—and Kingsley! Alpha, I mean. They need to decide what's the most important use for our time."

"In summary?" Nessa prompted.

"Summary. Right. All told, if we can get around the magical guns, even with two- or three-to-one odds, we'll be able to handle their mercenaries and ground troops. Our problem is the need to do it quickly, because the mages will be firing spells at us the whole time. And if they get close enough, they'll also fire spells at your loved ones. Broken Sue has real-world experience with just such a situation."

"Brochan has dealt with a mage attack where innocents were involved," Austin told Kingsley.

"Correct," Brochan said, his raspy, haunted voice

carrying through the room.

He went into some detail, explaining how they attacked at first light, a wall of mercenaries rushing their borders and into their town. The pack had had no warning, but they'd mobilized quickly, their sentries incredibly effective and their defenses well trained and organized.

His voice faltered when he recounted the enemy kicking in doors and shooting in houses, aiming for innocents.

"We were badly outnumbered," he said, "but we could've handled the mercenaries. Not the mages, though. We were defenseless against their magic. They used the mercenaries to keep our fighters occupied, and then they desecrated our town. They did not even spare the little ones. They spared no one."

The painful memory was a warning for Kingsley, I knew. This wasn't an enemy with a conscience, and certainly not an enemy who fought fair. Broken Sue was rehashing his past so that Kingsley knew *exactly* the sort of demon he was up against.

The room was quiet for a moment when he finished, until that asshole Bruce muttered, "Well...not *all* of you, it seems, right?" His eyes just barely squinted, hinting at a sneer. "No one was spared...but the alpha. I guess you don't hold with the saying that the captain goes down with the ship. In this case, I guess the captain uses the only lifeboat—"

Broken Sue launched forward, power exploding from him as he barreled through the room. Aiming for Bruce. Intending to kill.

CHAPTER 19

JESSIE

"**H**OLY—" I PUT out my hands, but my mind had gone blank of all non-harmful spells.

Bodies flew to the sides, knocked down by Broken Sue's muscular girth. He flung James and some other guy like they were paper sacks stuffed with feathers before grabbing Bruce and landing a solid punch. Amid shouts and movement, Bruce went limp immediately, not conscious for long enough to even fight back.

Austin dove at Broken Sue, arms wide, tackling him to the ground. The two men fell onto some of Kingsley's people, all of them scrambling now, some to get away, Broken Sue to get back at Bruce, and Austin trying to keep the incensed, raging man down.

Tristan raced into the fray, not gentle in how he threw Kingsley's people away to make room. One woman sailed toward the wall, hitting it with a loud thud. Another crashed against the podium holding the projector, knocking everything down.

Austin continued to wrestle with Broken Sue, dodging punches, throwing none of his own. Tristan bent to help immediately, and the two men hoisted a still-fighting Broken Sue up and then manhandled him to the door and out.

I pointed at a still-limp Bruce and rounded on Kingsley. "Get that bastard out of here," I yelled in a magically enhanced voice. "Get that guy out of here and do not bring him into our collective presence again—do *I* make *myself* clear, Kingsley Barazza?"

Kingsley's shoulders bunched. "You forget yourself, Jacinta. I am not Austin. You're exhibiting challenging behavior right now. I'll give you a moment—"

"I know exactly what sort of behavior I'm exhibiting," I said, stepping toward him. "And I damn well know you're not Austin. Neither Austin—nor I—would ever allow that sort of egregious behavior in our presence. You spoke to me about my loose team? At least my team has integrity and our unit has heart. When they take matters into their own hands, they help. They get things done. Your enforcers just seem to threaten and wave their dicks around, even when they haven't got 'em. You better clean up your people, Kingsley, or I will do it for you."

I felt Austin coming toward the room, and I

slammed the door. If Kingsley and I were going to rumble—and I would absolutely do it to prove a point about how they'd just treated Broken Sue, especially since that jackass Bruce was still in the room—I didn't want Austin to feel like he had to defend me, or his brother.

Then I shoved everyone away with my magic, creating a bubble that Kingsley and I could work in.

"Is this what you really want to be doing, Jessie?" he asked, moving around the table, prowling toward me like the tiger he was. "A challenge to an alpha isn't a game. This isn't something you can do over or opt out of once it gets going."

"I took down a phoenix, Kingsley, and I've only grown in power and experience since. This isn't something *you* can do over, and there is not one person in this room who can save you from me. I just locked that man outside. Your move. Get rid of that dickhead Bruce or battle me in front of your people and then watch while I get rid of him for you. I do not compromise when it comes to the wellbeing of my people. Choose. *Now.*"

Austin wiggled the handle outside, pushing at the door. Understanding came through the bonds, followed by frustration. He banged on it now, calling my name.

I cut the outside sound from the bubble. My magic

throbbed within it, and I stared Kingsley down and then took a step forward, knowing that would antagonize him. Knowing he was weighing the situation before engaging.

I was nothing but fire and readiness, confidence and might. He was so much taller and broader than me, thicker in every way, but size didn't mean crap.

"We can't hear them," Kingsley said to me in a low voice. "Can they hear us?"

"No."

He took a step toward me now, closing the distance slowly. "Are you going to take up my brother's mantle and try to kill me in front of all these spectators?"

"This has nothing to do with the past, Kingsley. That clown Bruce didn't slap Austin in the face—he slapped a man who's still struggling with the loss of his family and life as he knew it. A man who rehashed all that pain to help you understand. *That* is the reason I'm ready to attack you in front of all these spectators. But don't worry, I'd stop short of killing you. I'd never take you away from your family over this. I just need to make a statement."

I saw Austin in my peripheral vision, stalking along the exterior of the bubble I'd created. He must've broken through the magic holding the door. His mouth moved, probably calling to me. Maybe trying to talk me down. Then he looked at the air in front of him, testing it with his hands. The shock he got made him step backward, but he immediately flexed and approached it again. He'd handle the pain to get through to me if he needed to. It wouldn't be the first time.

I put out my hand to stop him, back to focusing wholly on Kingsley.

He didn't seem to notice Austin. He moved at an angle now, his eyes on mine, walking like he wanted to circle me, ever the big cat.

I didn't play the game. I stood right where I was, turning a little to lazily keep him in my sights.

"Pretty soon I'm going to get bored, and then I will prod you into action," I told him. "You have precious little time to figure out what you're going to do."

"You don't think your words are prodding me enough?"

"No, because you haven't attacked yet. Quit stalling. Come at me or don't."

"It's not as simple as that."

Annoyance ate through my minimal patience. Tension started to fill my body, and my power throbbed. My beast itched at my skin.

"It needs to be, Kingsley. I shouldn't have to prompt you to act. Have your scars from Austin's challenge, so long ago, clouded your judgment to the point that you welcome the animosity your people are throwing at ours? At him? Your children are watching you, Kingsley. They are learning from you. Is this the sort of behavior you want to teach budding alphas?"

He stopped in place, his posture suddenly rigid. Emotions ran lightning fast over his expression. He stared at me for a long moment, and now I turned to face him fully, my gaze no longer hot, my power starting to ebb. I didn't say another word. I knew I didn't have to. I'd hit him right where it counted. I'd shined a flashlight on where it hurt the most.

Tears sprang to my eyes, because I suddenly understood his pain. The hurt caused by his brother nearly killing him. His regret that his daughter had had to bear witness. The embarrassment, probably, of her having to rescue him. His scars from that time weren't buried as deeply as he tried to pretend. The proof was there in his tight shoulders and tormented gaze. He wasn't like Austin, who raged and fought and wore his heart on his sleeve if you looked hard enough. He was more like his mother, suffering in silence.

They needed to heal. They both did. Together.

Taking the high road, I stepped forward and put out my arm at a ninety-degree angle, almost like I was asking for a high five but with my hand turned. A handshake shifters tended to use to show unity. A peace offering, in this case.

He didn't hesitate. He met my step with one of his own and clapped his hand against mine, stinging my palm, our forearms meeting (mine looking like a child's compared to his), our gazes locked.

"Take down the spell," he said softly, hardly moving his lips.

I nodded when it was done, very little changing, because the room had gone silent.

"You have a lot to learn, Jacinta Ironheart," Kingsley said, loud and clear. "But you'll make an incredible alpha shifter."

He shook my hand before dropping it again and stepping back. "Bruce…" He stopped when he realized the shifter was still out cold. "Is he dead?"

"No." James knelt next to him. "He's breathing. Knocked out."

"I agree with Ironheart. Get him out of here. He's relieved of duty. Let this be a lesson to everyone here. We stand a lot to gain from having Austin Steele and Jessie Ironheart's help. Without them, it's beginning to look like we wouldn't have had a chance. We weren't equipped to handle higher-powered mages. They are our visitors, our allies, and my family. I expect you to treat them as such."

James stood slowly, disbelief and anger kindling in

his eyes. He didn't dare push back on his alpha, though. He must have recognized it was a battle he would easily lose.

"Yes, alpha," he said crisply, then motioned for someone else to deal with Bruce.

Austin hadn't moved from the position he'd been in when the spell went down. His gaze was rooted to me, his emotions still turbulent and aggressive. He hadn't recovered yet.

"Shall we take a minute?" I asked him softly.

He shook his head, glancing at Kingsley. "No. Continue the meeting. I'll be back shortly."

With a stiff back, he about-faced and walked out of the room.

"He's not mad, he's just—"

Kingsley held up his hand. "It's not easy seeing a mate in danger and not being able to help. I get it."

I quirked an eyebrow at the "in danger" part, but let it go. Let him nurse his ego.

"Okay, what's next?" I looked at Sebastian, but it was Edgar who spoke up.

"Jessie, I do believe we haven't talked about the flowers yet."

A crooked smile worked at the glamour on Sebastian's face. "We're done for the moment anyway," he told me. "I'd like some more information on Momar's mage configurations, if I can find it, and we need a better plan for using our potions. We can meet with Austin and Ki—the alpha when we have more information. Please, see to your flowers."

He offered a little bow, and the image of his face wobbled again, probably because he kept laughing.

"Okay." I clasped my hands in my lap, facing Kingsley with a grimace. "So. You know how we just had that thing, and everything worked out swimmingly?" I winced. "This is going to undo all of that. This time I'll probably just jump out the window so you don't have to go through the effort of throwing me out."

"Proceed," Kingsley said.

"I'd really rather not," I murmured, motioning for Edgar and Indigo to step forward. "Firstly…let me walk you through what we're talking about here—"

"Jessie, maybe I'd better?" Edgar offered, slinking much too close to Kingsley.

"Edgar, back away from him, and no, I'll do it."

He was much too honest.

I described what Edgar had done and the two types of flowers he'd created. I also told him about the flower show, quickly interrupted by Ulric, who took over the storytelling. Thank God, because that had been a royal mess, and Ulric was really good at making terrible things not sound so bad.

When we were finished, having eaten up Kingsley's goodwill and his patience, I gave him the really bad news.

"You know how I don't have complete control over my people?" I started.

"Any control, you mean?" he replied.

"Basically, yes. Well…" I cleared my throat. "Edgar was worried that the aggressive flowers—"

"Annihilators," Edgar said.

"That's what he calls…one group of them. Anyway, he worried they were going to…dig themselves a spot into the ground where they were being kept." Partly true. "He wanted to place them out of harm's way. And then, having lost his brain about one hundred years ago or so—"

"I might've," Edgar mused. "It's really hard to notice the smaller details."

"—decided he should plant them."

"All mostly outside the perimeter, though, alpha," Edgar said. "And don't you worry, they are ready for friendship. All it'll—"

"Edgar," I said.

"Sorry, Jessie." He curled in on himself a little. It was like a normal person curling his lips together.

"That's what Cyra was checking out, not the place where the mage was found. She was looking at one of

341

the flowers and stumbled upon…whatever it was."

"I was imprinting on the flower," Cyra said. "That's what we have to do, right, Edgar? Strike up a friend-ship?"

"Correct. You just have to—"

"Stop." Kingsley held up his hand before turning to the window, looking out for a while. "Please stop." After a moment, he barked, "James, clear them out."

"Yes, alpha." James gave me a guarded look before leading Kingsley's shifters from the room.

"Austin," Kingsley said.

"Yes, alpha?" said Austin, who'd returned and stood near the back wall with Tristan and a mostly composed Broken Sue.

"Send all nonessential personnel out."

"Me too?" I asked in a small voice.

"No, Jessie, not you too."

A shiver washed over me as I watched the shifters and Tristan leave. Austin stayed where he was, and my people exchanged looks, suddenly unsure about what was happening. Kingsley's family had stayed, though, so I hoped that meant he wasn't about to murder us.

"Jessie," Kingsley began, still looking out the win-dow. "I consider myself a patient man. A man who is flexible enough to bend so as not to break. It's what has kept me the alpha of this territory. I understand that many aspects of magic will be beyond my ability to comprehend, especially after what I've heard today, and I can make peace with that."

I tried not to wilt, feeling the *but* coming on.

"I have also realized that I am a trusting man," he went on. "I trust that your mage has our best interests at heart, for example. A big stretch, I will admit, but I am putting myself behind that trust totally. I trust my brother. I trust you."

I clenched my fists. Here came the but, and the sticky problem of what to do with a bunch of magical flowers.

"Your crew is wild. They are unpredictable. While most creatures are capable of being both those things, your crew is also incredibly powerful. They can do an exorbitant amount of damage on a whim. With a sneeze, it seems like. By taking a walk." I didn't glance at Cyra. "The thought of having only loose control over those creatures—or no control at all, it seems like—makes me want to cast them out to protect my territory."

My jaw dropped. This had just gotten a whole bunch bigger than a couple of van loads of magical flowers. I looked at Austin nervously, but his expression was resolute. That wasn't a great sign either.

"But," Kingsley continued, "I am putting myself behind that trust totally, as I said." He turned to face me. "You showed me here today that you will put your neck out for your people. That you won't lose yourself in moments of high tension or prioritize your image over what you know is right for your people. I respect that about you. And so..." He paused, probably for a steadying breath he didn't want to advertise. "I will give you leave to manage your people in whatever way you deem fit. If you think magical flowers are the way to go, and they will be safe for my pack, then so be it. You will be held accountable, both for their triumphs and for their failures. I'm sure I don't have to impress upon you how steep the punishment for those failures will be. You seem to have dealt with plenty. Does that sound fair?"

I wiped my clammy hands on my pants, relief flooding me. I wasn't even bent out of shape about that little dig there at the end, given it was true enough.

"Oh thank God," I gushed. "I thought you were going to kick us all out."

"I would really like to," he said, his eyes glittering. He sobered immediately. "I am trusting you with the safety of my pack, Jessie Ironheart. Don't let me down."

"Okay." I nodded, feeling like a little kid again, built up by their parent. "I won't. Don't worry, you mostly won't regret this."

"You can stop talking now," he said, passing by Edgar and heading for the door. "Let's check out this creature your phoenix accidentally-on-purpose killed."

CHAPTER 20

JESSIE

A S WE STEPPED outside, Kingsley's phone chirped. He pulled it out as we made it to the back parking lot, finding the basajaunak gathered around a hump of fur in one of the parking places.

"Blech." Cyra shivered. "I want to burn it all over again."

"Are you expecting anyone besides the third wave of basajaunak?" Kingsley asked Austin, looking up from his phone.

The basajaunak peeled away as we neared them.

"No, why? What is it?" Austin asked.

Kingsley paused near the burned body, looking down on it for a moment before glancing around. "We've seen these creatures before. We've caught and killed two so far."

It looked like a small mountain lion, kinda, with tan fur and a feline body. But white hair covered its shoulders and neck almost like a mane, dipping down like a small beard. Two serpentine tails ran from its hind end, covered in a pattern of blue and green diamonds, thick at the base and thinning out to points. Long canines protruded from its jaw, too big for its mouth and sticking out beside the lips. The feet had three toes each with long black claws, almost like talons.

"They don't exist in any animal encyclopedia we've found," Kingsley said. "We can't find their likeness on the internet. They've all been slightly different, too—same idea but with hooves or a birdlike head. One was as big as a natural wolf, and the other was like a medium-sized dog. We have no idea what it is. We don't have the ability to do blood work here, and the vets in the closest Dick town have organized an anti-shifter club because they think we're the products of screwing animals or something. They don't believe in magic, so their reasoning for us...can get drastic. We couldn't go to them about these things."

"What would they think about me mammy, do ye think?" Niamh asked no one in particular. "She couldn't choose which creature was the right one fer her, so she rode 'em both, and here I am, two animal forms to me name."

"They might not be an abomination," Mr. Tom told her, "but you sure are. An abomination on rational thought and a peaceful existence."

"A bit of a stretch, that—"

"Okay, okay, settle down before Kingsley changes his mind and kicks us all out," I told them.

"No way," Sebastian breathed, pushing through Austin and me and crouching down beside the creature. "No *way*! Nessa, come look at this."

"What is it?" I asked, knowing by his excitement that this had to be something magical.

"Whatcha got?" Nessa knelt beside him. "First impressions—I am very grossed out."

Sebastian poked at the body before lifting a lip to look at the gums. "A few different animals in this, I think." He slid onto his knees toward one of the tails, shoving Nessa out of the way. "A reptile was involved, obviously."

"What is it?" I asked again, scooting closer.

"I've heard rumors." He took out his phone and started snapping pictures. "I mean, we've all heard rumors, haven't we?"

"They haven't heard rumors, Sabby." Nessa sat back on her heels. "Is this really what I think it is?"

"Remember I told you once, Jessie—or did you tell me? Mages once tried to create female gargoyles. They took the DNA of a male gargoyle and a mage, messed around in the lab with magic and genetics, and *voila*:

female gargoyle. Except their magic was no more powerful than that of a standard mage—or less, most times—and they couldn't shift. They also couldn't reproduce."

"No surprise there," Nessa murmured. "Men aren't known for their understanding of female anatomy."

"What does that have to do with this?" Austin asked.

"The Mages' Guild has an interest in creating their own thinking animals," Sebastian answered, "what they think of as shifters. But their creations would be within their control. Magically, I mean."

"Mixing magical human and animal DNA?" I asked, disgusted and showing it. "That's illegal, right? Doing stuff like that?"

"Highly illegal, yes. Obviously," Sebastian said. "But who knows what science is doing without people knowing, you know? Looks like the Guild got a hold of some scientists who wanted to experiment, and here we are. This...creature." He looked up at Kingsley and then Cyra. "Any idea how intelligent it was?"

"It was trying to stalk me, but it kinda...skittered along," Cyra said. "I thought it was just an animal, not a human driving an animal body, like a shifter."

"From what I've gathered, they're the equivalent of very smart dogs," Kingsley said.

"Okay." Sebastian nodded, standing now and looking down at it. "That's a good thing. I wonder if this situation is a test run of some kind? I hadn't heard Momar was dabbling in that sort of experimentation. The whole idea of shifters disgusts him. He'd think this was so much worse, I would think."

"I wonder if he knows they're out here?" Nessa asked Sebastian, her eyes shimmering with cunning. "If he knows that they're now connected with his name?"

"He might be doing the Guild a favor, hoping for a return favor." Sebastian tapped his phone to his lips in thought. "Or we might've stumbled upon a rift in the making."

"I hope it's the latter," Nessa said, looking down at the body. "It would be amazing to have a little something to piss Momar off."

"It would," he replied as a car rolled into the parking lot filled with three older women with excited smiles.

"What's this?" Austin asked as the car parked.

"Additions to your outfit, apparently," Kingsley responded.

"What?" Austin asked as I said, "What?"

"*What?*" Ulric gasped, walking toward the car. "Aunt Florence?"

"Did he just say *Aunt* Florence?" Nathanial asked,

looking around.

"Bro, that guy's family is so left field, I wouldn't doubt it," Jasper said with a smirk.

"What are you doing here?" Ulric asked as three tittering older ladies got out of the car, which was driven by a surly-faced shifter who clearly was not amused by his latest job detail.

"Olly!" The woman who must be Aunt Florence, wearing a flowered dress over her short, stout frame, smiled at him before kissing his cheek. "Is Patty here yet? We have a whole bunch of garhettes on the way."

"What? Why?" Ulric asked, putting out his hands to stop the ladies from heading toward the rest of us. "What are you doing here?"

"Well, you know…" Florence said with a big smile.

"I don't, though," Ulric answered.

"Patty told me you guys were headed for a big battle and that I might never see you again. She said shifter women head into battle right alongside the men—"

"Where they should be," said a willowy woman with tightly curled gray hair.

"—and that she was going to join the ranks in some way. 'Patty,' I says, 'I am so tired of gargoyles thinking we're breakable just because we can't shift and fly. Don't we have the same fighter genes they do?'"

"Yes we do," the willowy woman said.

"And don't we have the ability to heal quickly—"

"Yes," both of the other women said together.

"And aren't we fierce and tough, just like them?" Aunt Florence went on.

"Tougher, if you ask me," said the third woman, short and round with a kind face and balled-up fists. "You don't see me laid up for a week with a stuffy nose, do you? Or crying because I got stabbed. No you do not."

The other women nodded.

"And you know what your mom said?" Aunt Florence asked Ulric. "She said that even non-magical Janes fight. They fight, shifters fight, *mage* women fight—why can't we fight?"

I wrapped my hand around Austin's forearm, needing a little grounding because I remembered having a conversation about this with Patty. She'd been bent out of shape that she'd never gotten to be a guardian, and I sympathized. That had been some time ago. I'd had no idea it would snowball into Ulric's Aunt Florence randomly showing up in Kingsley's territory ready to fight a big battle.

"Okay, but..." Ulric lifted his hands in confusion. "You can't fight, though. All those other women were trained for it. You...weren't. How do you think you can help us?"

"I can cook," the willowy woman said. "I have great knife work. I can cut out someone's gizzard, sure as I'm standing here."

"I'm not afraid of *nothing*," said the kind-faced, clearly very stubborn woman, fists still balled. "Ask me how many guardians I fought off in my day during raids. Ask me."

Nessa beamed at her. "How many—"

"No." Ulric held up his hand to stop her. "Don't encourage this. Aunt Florence, I get that you want to fight, but baby steps. Starting off in a battle like this is madness. What did Uncle Tom say when you left?"

"He said, 'Woman, where is that sandwich you promised me?' That's what he said. Well, you know what I said?" She paused with raised eyebrows. "I said, 'Same place as the last orgasm you gave me. Nonexistent!'"

The women all howled, bumping into each other and holding their stomachs.

"That's such a gargoyle thing to say," Nessa said with a wide smile. "Seriously, I love their culture."

"Anyway, I mentioned all this to my book club," Aunt Florence continued, and I noticed the rest of our people were coming up behind us, rejoining the group after being sent away by Kingsley. "And you know what? They agreed."

"They didn't just agree, though," the willowy woman said, her hands on her hips. "They passed it on."

"Yes, they did!" Aunt Florence nodded. "And lo and behold, a lot of young garhettes felt the same way in their bones. So you know what we said? We said, 'Ladies, let's go make a difference.' And that is exactly what we've come to do, Olly. We're going to make a difference. If we all go down with the ship, so what? At least we are finally *living*!"

Ulric stared at her, utterly at a loss, I was sure.

"Ladies." Tristan walked around the crowd with a smirk and all sorts of swagger, holding out his hands as though greeting friends. "Ladies, hello."

"Oh my..." The willowy woman turned to the others with a disbelieving smile. "It's the former Gimerel lead enforcer!" she whispered in barely contained excitement.

"He's so handsome," the kind-faced woman said, stars in her eyes.

"Have I died and immediately come back younger and better looking?" Aunt Florence whispered to the other two.

"No," Willowy replied.

"Damn," Aunt Florence responded, and Nessa started laughing uncontrollably.

"Ladies, it's so good to see you." Tristan stopped in

front of them, smiling down at them. "I fully support garhettes showing their mettle in battle." The ladies all smiled sheepishly. "How many of you should we expect, do you think?"

"Oh..." Aunt Florence blew out a breath, and the three exchanged looks. "At least fifty, wouldn't you say, Tekkie?"

"It's really hard to say," said the willowy woman, Tekkie. "You know...they're all excited to take up the cause, but there's the matter of getting out here—young people don't have all the money in the world—and there'll be those who get cold feet and all of that. Almost all of our book club is coming, though. That's fifteen right there."

"A good few younger garhettes are talking about coming," the other woman said. "At least twenty. At *least*. I mean...they made their own armor! So they're definitely coming, don't you think?"

"And you know your mom," Aunt Florence told Ulric. "When she finds us here, she'll tell everyone who'll listen, and more will come after that. We might have a good few garhettes show up to help."

"Okay, okay." Ulric put up his hands. "Aunt Florence, I love this idea, and I think it's a good one, long term. But we have precious little time to get everything here organized, with *trained* fighters, and we just can't devote the ma—*people* power to figuring out how...or where, I guess, you could fit. We don't even know how we'll all fit together."

"Nah, listen." Nessa pushed through Ulric and Tristan before putting her hand to her chest. "I fight. I have very little magic, two knives, and I follow around a vampire who always seems to be in the right place at the right time—"

"She's my shadow," Edgar called from somewhere in the back.

"If you have courage and a trigger finger"—Nessa mimed pulling a trigger—"then I can get in a shipment of magical guns. They'll be older, but I know exactly where a good few are stockpiled. I got people who can get them out here—for a cost, obviously, but we've got Jessie Warbucks, so we'll be good. If you want in the action, I can get you in."

"Except it is going to be incredibly dangerous," Ulric said, half begging now. "Aunt Florence, Mom isn't ever actually *in* the action. She's on the periphery."

"Well, that's fine," Aunt Florence replied. "I can shoot a magical gun just fine from the periphery. I don't care."

"No, that's not—"

"A female gargoyle should have female guardians," the kind-faced woman said, her balled fists on her hips now. "That's just logic."

"You know what?" Tristan once again drew their attention, his hands out, now shepherding them back toward the car. "You have some very good points. Very valid points. You've given us a lot to think about. What do you say we go grab something to eat and let the alphas talk it through? Because your ability to fight isn't the only consideration. They'll need to make sure we have room for everyone, and there are some Khaavalor guardians coming in as well." All their eyes lit up. They were clearly not from one of the higher-status cairns. "How'd you…" He glanced around. "How'd you get to the territory, by the way?"

"Oh"—Aunt Florence waved her hand—"we took a bus from the airport, but it would only go as far as… Oh now, what was that town called?"

"Sa… Seh…?" Tekkie screwed up her face in thought.

"Anyway, one of the towns close by," Aunt Florence went on. "There was this cute little café, so we stopped for a cup of coffee and a slice of coffee cake and got to talking to the woman who works there. Lovely person—"

"Danica," Tekkie said.

"Yes, Danica. And wouldn't you know it, she said her nephew was at home doing nothing—playing video games or something—and he could run us out. Well, that was just fine. So he dropped us at the edges—you know, because cairns can be wary of strangers, and I wasn't sure if shifter packs were different—and then we walked in far enough to meet this fine shifter." She pointed at the still-surly driver. "He's a wolf, I guess. He wouldn't show us his other form, though. Anyway, he drove us here."

"Fantastic," Tristan said, taking all of that in without batting an eye. "How about this? Let's get you that bite to eat or maybe just another coffee while the alphas chat, okay? Patty won't arrive for another few hours or so. I'll meet you there with Ulric." He glanced at Kingsley.

"Take them to the Hot Plate," Kingsley told the driver. "Tell them to bill me."

"Fantastic. Here we go, ladies." Tristan corralled them toward the car. "I'll see you in just a minute, okay?"

"He's handsomer than everyone says," one of the women said as they got situated in the car.

"So large and strong, did you see his arms and chest? Phew." Tekkie in the front seat started fanning herself. "I'd think it was a hot flash if I wasn't beyond those."

They cackled as the car pulled away.

I faced Kingsley immediately. "That's not on me.

This is not my fault."

"Ulric is on your team, as is Patty," Austin said with a smirk. "The garhettes are with them, and they are with you. So they are—"

"Tristan's," I said quickly. "They're Tristan's. He handled them so well, and they know and respect him. Tristan is yours, which then makes Aunt Florence..." I pointed at Austin.

"Yours," he replied. "Tristan is a gargoyle."

"This is all fun and games, but can they fight?" Kingsley asked. "Are the magical guns a viable option? Because if they can't, we can stow them in the border towns."

"You probably should anyway," Ulric said, watching the car turn a corner.

"They have the strength, speed, and power of a gargoyle," Tristan said, standing with us again. "Just not the claws and wings."

"They can fight," Dave said, clearly remembering the occasion in which Patty had attacked him after a joke gone wrong. "They can help."

"Many of the younger garhettes have trained in various fighting styles," Tristan said, "trying to convince the cairn leaders to let them take part."

"The magical guns are a viable option," Nessa said, her phone out. "I'd have to pick them up from a...not very reputable character, but it wouldn't be the first time. If those garhettes have courage—and given what we know about Patty, they do—we can station them around the territory and tell them to point and shoot. Worst case, they can guard the innocents. More hands on deck is not a bad thing here. I say we use them."

"But where are we going to put them?" Austin asked.

Kingsley shook his head, staring off in the direction they'd gone, before glancing over his shoulder at seemingly nothing.

"Desperate times," he murmured. "I have room," he said a little more loudly. "So do Mimi and Mom. We can see if anyone will open their homes, and we'll fill up every last hotel or inn. Worst case, we can put the…less chatty garhettes in some of the friendlier border towns. They are more Jane than shifter, so as long as they don't talk too much about why they're here and what we're doing, they should be fine."

"Just when we get the tiniest handle on things, something else comes up and it all goes to hell," I said, running my hand down my face. "First things first. Edgar, come on. We need to sort out those flowers. And I swear to you, if you get me into hot water with those things, I will finally retire you. Do you understand?"

I didn't even listen to his reply, instead walking off

quickly for the car. The faster we got everyone situated and started training, the better. More gargoyles would be coming in, and now potentially a bunch of garhettes. There was no time to waste.

CHAPTER 21

NIAMH

KIDS SQUEALED WITH delight and came running when Niamh walked through the center of town in her "scary unicorn" form, as the kids were calling it. Her golden hooves and mane sparkled in the sun, something that always made the garhettes loudly *ooh* and *ahh*. And there were now plenty of garhettes to do it.

Five days had passed since Aunt Florence had shown up. Patty had reacted exactly as Aunt Florence had said she would—talking to her network and telling them about the stand the garhettes were making in gargoyle society. First it had been the book club and a few friends who'd followed Aunt Florence, and then some younger ones—twenty-somethings—had shown up, followed by the sort of influx that had made Kingsley reevaluate his earlier stance on *the more the merrier.*

Gerard from Khaavalor had only gotten in yesterday with his people because the garhettes in his cairn had revolted against staying behind. He didn't go into specifics, but the ladies had supposedly made life absolutely unlivable for the gargoyles. With Jessie's approval, he'd brought those whom he'd thought would help the most, relieved that their inclusion had mostly appeased those who hadn't made the cut.

The thing was, unlike the gargoyles, who strutted around and played at being Mr. Strong and Mr. Tough and an unholy pain in the arse, the garhettes were mostly a real delight to have around. The ones who'd gotten taken in by families helped earn their keep, cooking and cleaning without being asked, looking after the kids when the parents were tired, and chatting and visiting in that easy, excitable way of theirs. There wasn't one spare room in the territory that wasn't quickly offered to a garhette, the wives deciding without even asking their husbands.

They'd mostly run out of space, though. Any more showing up would have to start camping in the parks, or head into the border towns. Given the latter still had a host of mages hanging around, Kingsley and Austin had come to a crossroads.

Kingsley had grudgingly accepted that there were *probably* mages in those towns, and the presences Austin's people had sensed upon their arrival were *very likely* those mages. Logic.

However, the mages about town hadn't made a move in all this time. They hadn't started fights, they hadn't abducted anyone to question them, and they hadn't bothered the Dicks and Janes. They were a neutral entity, bringing money into the local businesses. As such, Kingsley didn't want to go in, make a bunch of noise, and potentially have the border towns look badly upon the pack. His pack had to continue living within miles of those towns when this was all through, and they needed to keep some sort of truce.

Austin got all that. Hell, Niamh got all that.

But those mages wouldn't stay docile forever. And Jessie didn't want the garhettes—or any of their people—to be in the danger zone. Those mages in the bars could turn on a dime and decide they wanted to take out the enemy. Austin agreed wholeheartedly.

And so, it was back to Plan A. Go into the towns stealth-like, grab the mages, question them, and say nothing to nobody.

Tonight was the night.

Good thing Niamh had never stopped planning for this. She'd spent the last five days bar-hopping, laying the bait. Now it was time to make good on what she'd learned.

First, though, she was taking the emotional temperature of the shifter town, something she did every day. Basically, help Jessie make sure all her people and the gargoyles were coexisting with the shifters. That was why Niamh trotted around in her alicorn form more often than not. At least where there were children. She didn't have to make small talk with the locals, something that never helped her likability anyway, and the kids had a grand ol' time. Easy.

"Ooh, unicorn," a little girl said with a beaming smile, toddling up and hugging Niamh's front leg.

She stood still while the mother jogged over to retrieve her child. Other kids played within the nicer of the magical flowers, this version of Edgar's concoctions more like dogs than flora. The basajaunak probably had something to do with that, working tirelessly with Edgar to make sure the flowers were happy and well adjusted—also staying near them whenever people were around, ensuring there was no danger to the townspeople.

They'd done some job of it. The flowers, a few spread around the square and the rest throughout the town, swayed happily whenever someone petted them or brushed against their leaves. They reached out to stroke the hair of passing children and tickled the fingertips of adults. One flower caught a little boy who'd tripped. It was hard to imagine these things would protect anybody.

But when another one of those mage creatures had come sniffing through town in the dead of night two nights ago, it'd gotten too close to one of the magical flowers and ended up poisoned and ripped to shreds. When it came time to protect their friends, they did their job. Niamh hated to say it, but Edgar had gotten this one right.

Well...with the town flowers, at least.

The flowers on the outskirts were vicious, surly, dangerous things. They'd found one of the mages' creatures, too. There hadn't been much of the thing left when the flower was done. All the townspeople were warned to stay away, and the pack protectors took pains to make friends or avoid them altogether. One of the shifters had veered too close without trying to make friends and nearly lost an arm. Indigo had to be rushed out to heal him before the flower poison did him in.

Those flowers would need to be destroyed when this was all over—there was nothing else for it. Edgar would just have to soldier on.

Niamh brushed against the leaves of an enormous pink sunflower, feeling it tickle the sides of her stomach as another kid ran at her with arms outstretched. A boy this time. He yanked on Niamh's tail and got a swat with it for his efforts.

"Sorry—Tommy, no!" The man pulled the giggling little boy away.

"Unicorn!" the child said, struggling to get back to Niamh.

"We're good here," said the basandere—Dave's mom—walking over from the nearby trees. "The townspeople seem content. Those with families and children, at least." She glanced toward the north. "The ones who spend time in the bars aren't so content."

There'd been a fight or two, almost always between a shifter and a gargoyle, many of them instigated by someone Niamh had put up to it. Unrest after dark was a great means of distraction. It kept the peacekeepers busy so she could get out of town without being noticed. This pack was just too easy to manipulate.

She nodded and issued a soft neigh before cantering into the center of the grass to take flight. She didn't want to accidentally brain some kid.

A short flight later, she was landing on Austin Steele's property. No wonder he'd designed and built his own house in O'Briens. Coming from this one, with its shallow ceilings, cramped backyard, and narrow staircases, he'd probably been desperate for improvements. She shifted and headed for the door.

A few purple muumuus sat in a stack on the front porch for those flying in to speak to the alphas, and

Niamh grabbed one and pulled it on before knocking. This wasn't like Ivy House, where a body could just walk in. Austin Steele was not as easygoing about his personal space as Jessie was.

The door swung open, revealing the man himself wearing track suit bottoms, a plain white T-shirt, and bare feet. The smell of sweat permeated his person and his hair stuck up at odd angles.

"Does Jessie not have a sense of smell?" Niamh walked forward when he stepped out of the way.

"I was just about to take a shower. I need a word. Come with me." He led her through the quiet house and to the basement, where various boxes had been neatly organized with magical descriptions on each, Sebastian's stockpile of potions. He'd been adding to them every day, working harder than probably anyone in the territory, being drugged to sleep and waking up and going at it again.

"Tristan's story about the mage we caught the other day doesn't check out." Austin Steele paused, probably waiting for Niamh to get on the same page. She nodded, and then he explained the state in which he'd found the mage and the discrepancies in the story.

"It sounds like he made a potentially complicated situation very simple," she said, impressed.

"That's why I didn't call him out on it. Kingsley

bought the story without batting an eye."

"And Tristan thinks ye did, too?"

"I made sure he had no reason not to."

"But ye haven't let it go."

He gave her a glance that said she shouldn't have wasted the breath to ask.

"I had a look around," he said, "and caught a whiff of Tristan's scent in a room we don't typically use. Before checking it out, I asked Sebastian for something that would deaden my scent. He took me down here, and…" Austin Steele stepped around a box and lifted the lid. Two potions were missing from the interior. "This makes people invisible," he said, indicating one of the empty spaces and then shifting his finger to another. "And this deadens their sound. They could scream all they wanted and no one would hear."

"Except for the man who isn't affected by magic," Niamh said.

"Correct."

"Did the weird mage get suspicious when he noticed they were missing?"

"No. He's so exhausted all the time that he thought he'd just been confused. Anyway, he gave me a potion to deaden scent, and I checked out the area where I caught Tristan's scent. I found this under the couch."

Austin Steele pulled his phone from his pocket and

showed Niamh a picture of a pack. Inside were various items of a suspicious nature—little glass bottles, rags, rope. He put the phone away and opened a nondescript box on one of the shelves. Inside were a couple of vials, each with a tiny bit of liquid in the bottom.

"I took samples of a few. The bottles weren't marked in any way, so I'm hoping he doesn't notice a bit of the contents gone. Can you find someone to analyze these and maybe figure out what they are? Someone we can trust or blackmail into silence?"

Niamh tsked, feeling a smile grow. "By *jaysus*, Austin Steele. I believe ye've crossed over to the dark side."

"I now appreciate how easy it is to deal with shifters. A show of strength and an ability to lead is basically all you need. Dealing with mages, though, and now dealing with…whatever Tristan actually is… I'm getting an education. In order to effectively protect Jess and my people, I'm going to have to get my hands dirty. I've realized that."

"Fair play to ya. Yeah, I reckon I can find someone to look at this. Not around here, though. This isn't urgent, right? What he did was for the greater good, ultimately. I don't think he's against us."

"No, I don't think he is. He's loyal, he's just…not ready to share his origins, I think." He put the samples he'd collected back. "We can bring them back with us when we leave."

Assuming they'd be leaving this place, sure.

"Did Nessa get a line on those magical guns?" Niamh asked, climbing the stairs after him.

Austin Steele sighed as they entered the main level of the house. "She's had problems getting the supply we need." He walked them into the kitchen, where Nessa had her head in the fridge. "Nessa, what's the latest on the blasters?"

"Hello?" She straightened up, one hand still on the door and the other leaning against the fridge. Her face was slightly drawn and her eyes puffy. She'd been pulling late nights trying to get more information from her network. Her days were spent training the garhettes, teaching them to use knives or the couple of blasters (what they were calling the magical guns to help the garhettes understand that they were more like *pew-pew-pew* than *bang*). "Oh. Hey. Are you guys hungry? I'm starving. I was going to make something easy."

"Here." Austin Steele put his hand on her shoulder and gently nudged her away from the fridge. He reached in, coming back with a fruit tray and some cold cuts. "Why don't you have a snack for now? I'll make something when I'm out of the shower, okay? Take a break. You've been going steady with those garhettes."

She sighed as she lowered onto the cushioned bench

by the windows. "Except you've also been going steady, too, training and trying to get everyone to work together. You and Jessie are pulling double time."

"No, she's pulling double time. As are you. I don't do magic or work with networks in the evening," Austin Steele said, setting the plate of snacks next to her. "You girls are pulling the load. I'm just doing long days. Chill out for a moment. Should we bring Indigo in to help you? Or Jess will be home pretty soon, I think."

"Nah. They've got their hands full. The garhettes keep stabbing each other. They don't seem to realize that you're not supposed to hurt your opponent in training. You simply *pretend* to hurt them. They think that's a half-assed approach. We haven't been able to get through to them. They're exactly as stubborn as the gargoyles, but with less regard for their personal wellbeing."

"They seem to be able to take a magical blast like a gargoyle, though, right?" he asked. "Has Sebastian verified that?"

"What?" Sebastian walked in with a cape pinned into his clothes and rustling around his calves. One of the garhettes had heard the story from the border town, thought it was hilarious, and made him a better version as a practical joke. He'd get some use out of it for their plan tonight.

Niamh heard the front door opening and then the unhurried gait of Tristan, his footfalls light despite his size.

Austin repeated his question as Tristan walked into the room, showered and fresh with a button-up shirt and trendy, snug-fitting trousers.

"Yer not supposed to stand out," Niamh told him.

Tristan glanced her over. "And you thought a muumuu would accomplish that task, did you?"

"I've got a change of clothes, ya muppet. What about ye? Are ye going to spend all night changing in and out of yer posh attire?"

"What's going on?" Nessa asked, pausing with a piece of salami near her lips.

Sebastian ignored Nessa, answering Austin Steele's question about the garhettes.

"Yeah, isn't that wild?" He grabbed a nut from Nessa's plate. "They don't have the thick gargoyle skin, but they can withstand the same blasts of magic. Some of them can withstand even more because they have higher pain tolerance. I asked about that, and they said that if I'd been split in half by delivering a baby, I'd understand. To which I replied that I was fine being left in the dark. They thought that was hilarious. Funny 'cause it's true, I guess."

"No…" Nessa gestured between everyone. "What's

going on here? Are you going somewhere, Sabby?"

"Oh." Sebastian frowned at her. "I thought I told you last night. Yeah, we're going to relieve the towns of their mages." He pointed at Niamh. "The gargoyles are already in position, right?"

"Yeah. We've got Ulric and Nathanial having drinks in Seyanna, Jasper and...that strange cairn leader, I can never remember that clown's name, in St. Stein. We'll meet Phil in Hensford. I figure we can hit those three towns tonight, no problem. They're the closest. Then I need to start casing other towns. I don't have a presence anywhere else yet."

"You've been busy," Tristan told her, leaning against the wall.

"I take my drinking seriously." Niamh nodded at Nessa, whose brows had pinched together. "What's the story with the blasters?"

Nessa shook herself out of her stupor. "I've got thirty nailed down, plus a bid in for twenty more. There's no guarantee they'll all work. That's all I can find on such short notice without people asking too many questions. You're going into the border towns tonight? Why wasn't I told?"

"Because you aren't going," Tristan told her. "You need the rest. We can handle it."

She stared at him for a tense beat before swinging

her gaze to Austin Steele. "Dealing with mages is *my* part to play on this team. Those mages are going to have fail-safes. They'll need to check in periodically or their superiors are going to know something happened to them. I can crack the phone codes and get that information to keep us from being exposed. You know this. Why wasn't I told this was happening tonight?"

Austin braced his hands on the island. "Niamh can work the phones. I was told the fewer the better, and that you weren't needed for this one. I agreed that you'd stand out."

She paused for a beat, her eyelashes fluttering against her cheeks. "You agreed I'd stand out," she murmured. "And what is it about me that would stand out, pray tell? You assume, I suppose, that I'd dress to the nines and show off my tits? You don't think I know when to tone it down to do my job?"

It was Tristan who answered. "You don't have the ability to tone it down. You could be in a muumuu with your hair in a messy bun and literal shit on your face and you'd still be the most striking woman in any of those establishments. People notice you, Natasha. We can't have that for this detail."

"*You* notice me, Tristan," she said in a rush of anger, standing up. "Just you. And what, you think no one is going to notice a god of a man with glowing eyes and a fucking cape?"

"I can blend into walls," he replied calmly. "So no, they won't notice me, even godlike as you think I am."

Her face turned red with indignation and frustration as she turned to Austin Steele again.

"Please reconsider, alpha. I've been doing this all my life. I'm a pro at it. I'm better than Sebastian. Certainly better than Tristan, no matter what sweet nothings he whispers in your ear. I'm more up to date than Niamh. This should be *my* detail."

"Careful about your tone," Austin Steele warned, his power crawling up Niamh's spine uncomfortably. "You don't have the magic Sebastian does, Nessa, and I need you to rest up so you can keep working with the garhettes. Sebastian thinks the mages who might disappear tonight will start the countdown and prompt Momar to act. I understand how much you want to go, but we have to think of the larger picture here."

She huffed out a little laugh, her hands braced on her hips. Tilting her head, she stared at the floor for a moment before looking back up and searing Tristan with a glare. Her eyes shimmered just a little, as though she might cry, before she started off down the hall without another word.

Sebastian stared after her, his shoulders hunched. "She was the one who said that Momar would act fast once his mages started disappearing. There was already that one in the garage, and now there might be more tonight. He'll know something is up." He sighed softly. "I didn't know she'd react like that. I can always put a glamour over her face. Apparently I make very ugly false faces."

"We don't need everyone for everything," Austin Steele said, a little crease between his brows. He hadn't anticipated she'd react like that either. "Let's get tonight underway. Keep your heads down. *Do not* create a situation that will reflect unfavorably on the pack."

"Yes, alpha," they said in unison.

"Let me know if our trap catches a mouse, yes?"

"Yes, alpha," they repeated.

"Good luck."

As they headed for the door, Sebastian still clearly feeling guilty, Niamh fell in next to Tristan.

"Ye don't seem put out by Nessa's reaction," she said. "Or seem to have an ounce of guilt."

"Nope."

"And why is that? Grudge match? Proving you have the louder voice in this pack, or whatever we're calling it now?"

"Neither. She doesn't want to be a monster, and there's no reason she has to be. I'm perfectly fine taking the morally questionable jobs so she can keep her hands clean."

Niamh nodded slowly. Suddenly the situation with the mage in the garage made a lot more sense.

"Noble," she said as they reached the front door. He held it open for her. "But yer doin' it wrong."

"Why is that?"

"She doesn't know whether she's fine bein' a monster, as ye say—I take offense to that, by the way. That must mean I'm a monster, too, since I don't mind any of this one bit. It's natural, like. Kill or be killed."

"If the shoe fits."

"I'll tell ye what wears shoes—donkeys. If I'm a monster, yer a donkey, how's that?"

"Actually, most donkeys have sturdy hooves and don't need shoes. But that's fine. I'll be the ass of the outfit if that makes you feel better."

She huffed. "Well, anyway, Nessa's path in life was chosen for her. She's looking at that white picket fence and nice yard and annoyin' neighbors and thinking that's what her life should've been. Maybe that's what it *would've* been, if she'd been allowed to choose for herself. But her life was forced on her by circumstance, wasn't it, Sebastian?"

"Yes, unfortunately," he said quietly.

"It's the grass is always greener situation," Niamh went on as they reached the front yard. "What she really wants is a decision about where her life goes next. We all do. Yer takin' that away from her. Yer forcing her in the other direction and telling her it's good fer her. Yer using yer position to take away her power, like. With a woman like her, that'll mean yer head, just you wait."

He slowed to a stop in the driveway. "She told me what she wanted in the form of wishful thinking and emotionally breaking down about the life she had. She told me her dreams, and also what she hated. I'm just carrying it out. Is that not a choice? I'm not afraid of her violence if I'm helping her rest a little easier."

"That's not her choosing a life path. That's her struggling with her demons. Different thing." She tsked in annoyance, pulling off her muumuu. "Men are daft. They think they have all the answers. They try to decide what's good for women without bothering to under-stand a woman's wants and needs, and then wonder why the women aren't grateful. A bunch of wankers, if ye ask me. And yes, I'm talking about ye, Tristan, specifically, in case that wasn't clear."

Tristan studied her silently for a long moment be-fore looking back toward the house. "It was plenty clear."

"Too late now, though. We don't have time to change things up." Niamh realized she'd forgotten her satchel and lacked a proper change of clothes. "Here,

Sebastian, run over to the porch there and grab me satchel, would ya? I can't be wearing a muumuu to a Dick bar, like. They'll take all sorts of notice."

"I think it's sweet what you're attempting," Sebastian said to Tristan after he did as Niamh had asked. "She's never had anyone try to look out for her like you're doing. She usually gives more than she receives. But Niamh is right, I guess. I never really thought of it that way, but it makes sense." He held on to the satchel, knowing that he'd be riding on her back and therefore carrying it. "And you *should* be afraid of her violence. Jessie makes Nessa pretty tame. It's easy to feel safe here. But you haven't even seen Nessa's wild side. What she's capable of when she feels threatened. Not even close."

"What's the plan with Edgar, by the way?" Tristan asked after stowing his clothes in the satchel with Niamh's. He clearly wasn't worried about Nessa's wildness. He'd have to find out the hard way. Hopefully. "I thought he was part of this."

"We don't need him for the bars," Niamh said, stepping away a little to shift. "He'd just creep people out. I had Ulric drop him at the warehouse to set things up and then work on his doilies. I didn't give him any specifics. Whatever he comes up with is going to rattle our new mage friends, I have no doubt."

CHAPTER 22

SEBASTIAN

AFTER NIAMH AND Tristan changed behind a closed movie rental store with boards on its windows and a foul-smelling dumpster off to one side, Niamh handed the satchel back to Sebastian and led the way around the corner.

"Just follow my lead tonight," she said, motioning for Tristan to walk beside her, on the side closest to the building. "I've established a different rapport with each bartender and let slip certain details that should help us round up all of the mages. We'll have to be sly, o'course, or it might get back to Kingsley, but if we just keep our heads low, it should be handy enough."

"In four days or whatever it is, you've managed to become friends with all the bartenders in three different towns?" Sebastian asked in disbelief.

"Lads, listen to him," she muttered to herself. Then to him: "These are tiny towns in the middle of nowhere.

There are two or three bars per town at the very most, and the mages seem to only visit the very busiest, which are not that busy. The shifters stopped coming around, too. Mostly, anyway. These bartenders are cryin' out for someone to talk ta. All I needed to do was show up, like."

"Right, but..." Sebastian slowed as they approached the bar they'd visited the day they'd arrived. "You piss people off more often than you make friends."

"Only when I don't need somethin'. Ah, there's Phil." Niamh nodded to a clump of bushes and trees just beyond the bar. Sebastian barely noticed the furry foot sticking out, exactly like someone might expect of a Bigfoot foot.

"How's he going to know if he needs to grab someone?" Tristan asked.

"How'd he get here?" Sebastian wondered aloud.

"He's got a walkie-talkie. Sebastian, run over there and pick up the other one. And he ran, how else? Did ye think he grew wings? I bet ye think that cape will actually help ye to fly, too, do ya? Maybe you should try it when this is all through."

"I feel like we're circling back to my question about you making friends," Sebastian grumbled as he started jogging toward the foot.

"Don't jog, for heaven's sake!" Niamh seethed.

"*Janey mack,* everyone is going to know something's up. See what ye did, Tristan? I blame ye. Instead of the competent one, we get the weird one."

"He's good in a bind," Tristan replied as Sebastian tried to unsuspiciously approach the bush.

"Probably because he gets himself into so many of them. Not like that, fer feck's sake—would ye look at him! He might as well have on Mr. Tom's getup with the way he's slinkin' and slouchin' around. Just act normal and get the thing. Let's go. I've never seen someone so awkward in all my life."

She had a way of talking about Sebastian and to him that made him incredibly nervous. They definitely should've brought Nessa. If she were around, this was about when she'd step in and smooth everything out. Because he could be way more awkward than this.

He tried to act normal, no longer quite certain what that entailed, and peeked behind the bush to find Phil drinking out of a flask and looking through a *Playboy,* of all things.

"Hey, uhhm." Sebastian cleared his throat, and Phil looked up. "I just need the other walkie-talkie."

"Oh." Phil pulled it out from deeper in the bush and handed it over. "Sure thing." He hefted the magazine. "This has some pretty funny jokes."

"Right, yeah. Okay then." Sebastian tried to walk

normally back to Niamh, but her glare was a tad unsettling. "He's reading a *Playboy*," he blurted as he got closer.

"He found that a town over. A bunch of boys were giggling about it. They dropped it when Phil stuck his head out from around a tree to see what they were laughing at." Niamh slipped the walkie into the satchel and slung it over her shoulder. "One of their dads is probably gonna miss it. They don't make those anymore, I don't think. C'mon. We're behind schedule."

She led them into the bar and claimed the seat she'd had the last time, in the corner with an open stool to her right. Sebastian got motioned into the open stool, nearly forgetting to drink down the revealing potion to help him see anyone using an invisibility concoction. He pulled a second out of his pocket and slid it to Niamh as Tristan stood against the wall next to Sebastian in the corner of the bar, quickly blending in with the wall.

The dying sun threw long shadows across the floor as the evening waned into night. The bar was half lined with singles or doubles, none of them wearing the telltale watches, and one booth was occupied in the back. No one bothered to glance up as Sebastian and Niamh sat down.

"Hey." The bartender from the other day—Timmie or something—sauntered down the bar, her gaze on

Niamh. "How goes it?"

"Good, now. Uneventful day." Niamh put her elbows on the bar, holding the little vial in her cupped hand, hidden from the bartender. There would be more in the satchel in case the few vials Sebastian had in his pockets weren't enough.

Timmie glanced at the door with a frown. "Where are the guys?"

"Ah." Niamh rolled her eyes, leaning back a little. "They got in a tiff about something-er-other. They didn't want to see each other at the bar, so neither came. Don't worry, they'll be back out soon enough. This happens all the time. They're as bad as brothers, so they are. And the *stupid* things they fight over." Timmie poured Niamh a whiskey, listening. "One time Ulric caught Jasper wearing his socks. The wrong socks ended up in Jasper's drawer and he wore them. Well, ye should've seen 'em! Yellin' at each other, threatenin' to give the other a box. They're children. Yer better off not troublin' yerself. Didn't I say so the other day? Well now. Here's the proof."

Timmie laughed. "I'm not looking for forever, I'm just looking for a good time. And those boys are a real good time." She winked at Niamh, finally noticing Sebastian. "Who's this?"

"Sure, ye know him. He was here the other day."

Niamh took a sip of her drink. "The gangly gargoyle, remember?"

"Oh yeah," she said, squinting at Sebastian and then glancing at his cape. "That's right. Didn't he come with the female gargoyles? The ones that don't shift?"

"Yes, yeah," Niamh said without missing a beat, quickly building a new story about him. "Yeah, he didn't make the cut as a guardian, but he wouldn't be left behind, so he pleaded with the ladies to bring him. Those female gargoyles are only here to look after their mates and watch the pack kids and what have you. Don't know why they gave in. He's pretty well useless. He can't even run a mop 'round the place, sure he can't."

Sebastian put out his hands in feigned indignation. "Dude, I'm *right here.*"

Niamh acted like she hadn't heard him. "I figured I'd get him out of their hair for a bit by bringing him for a drink. Maybe he'll get in trouble with the big boss for leaving the pack lands and be sent home, huh?"

Timmie laughed, and Sebastian continued to stare in indignation.

"What'll ya have?" Timmie asked him.

He just shook his head. "A ride home, maybe?"

"Bourbon, neat," Niamh answered for him.

The bartender moved away, and still Sebastian

stared at Niamh. "Really?" he finally prodded.

"Everyone knows it, why pretend like we don't?" she replied.

"Unbelievable," he muttered as the bartender served his drink and looked around in confusion.

"Weren't there three of you?" she asked with squinted eyes.

"No?" Niamh glanced over her shoulder. "Why? Did someone walk in behind us?" She hooked a thumb Sebastian's way. "He never notices when danger's around."

"You're going to give me a complex," he grumbled.

"Maybe I got it wrong. So what did you..." Timmie's words drifted away as she watched a skinny guy with a plaid shirt and a shiny gold watch walk in through the door. He stared straight ahead, walking in an equally straight line, until he got to the open stool he wanted. Then he did a ninety-degree turn and sat down. It was more than a little unusual.

"Is he serious with that watch?" Sebastian murmured without thinking.

"*Right?*" Timmie whispered, leaning toward him before sparing Niamh a knowing look. "They're all like that, I swear. Right, Niamh? You must've noticed over the last few days." She looked skyward, shook her head, and slowly made her way to the newcomer.

"That's one of 'em, right?" Niamh asked.

"Obviously, yes," Sebastian whispered, his lips against his glass as though he were about to take a sip. "Lower level and insecure, so he's overcompensating with the watch. He hasn't got the funds or the position to wear a nicer one, though, so he's gone for gaudy. You'll get some scheduling information from him, maybe. His contact, what his contact is hoping to achieve, what he's learned from the shifters here, but you won't get anything the likes of which that runner gave Tristan the other night. But we'll wait and see who else shows up. This guy could be the low-hanging fruit. The one you trip if something scary is chasing you."

Niamh chuckled. "Makes sense."

"You haven't been using the potions to see invisible mages, right?" Sebastian asked before lowering his glass.

Niamh coughed and then threw her head back really quickly, downing the small vial before slipping it into the satchel, the strap resting around her knees.

"No. I've felt them around but didn't want to give anything away by looking right at them."

"Smart." Sebastian tapped his fingers against the bar.

Niamh looked over slowly. "Would ye stop that? When did ye get so annoyin'?"

"We're still in character...right?"

"Is that what this is? Yer bein' annoying to play some sort of part?"

Sebastian lowered his brow at her but stopped the tapping.

She settled in to her drinking as Timmie talked to the new guy.

"Have Jessie and Austin been out since the night she got challenged by those girls?" Sebastian asked, not able to settle down. He wasn't used to working like this, with zero defined plan and now under the guise of a ridiculous story he likely wouldn't remember. They were all flying by the seats of their pants, and he was not good at doing that. If he didn't come up with small talk, he'd look as stressed as he felt.

"No," she replied, seemingly staring at nothing, but he could see her eyes flicking discreetly toward the mage. "They say it is because they are tired, though that's not why."

"I know Jessie isn't fond of beating people up in a jealous rage," he said, watching the bartender serve a few more people as another awkward-looking guy walked in the bar. He was also wearing plaid, though a different color, and oddly fitting jeans. The waist was cinched too tightly and the legs were too short.

Was this some sort of signal meant to communicate something with each other? There was no way these mages could dress so poorly by accident.

This one was wearing another ridiculous watch, too much bling on something that looked like it came from a department store. He might as well scream, "These are fake diamonds and I have no real status!"

"Jessie might not be, but her beast is happy enough fer it," Niamh said, appearing not to notice the newcomer except for her flicking eyes. She sipped her whiskey slowly, giving the bartender no reason to return to them. "That's not it, though. She flexed her power at Kingsley in front of his people. The ignorant ones among them, who already hate that Austin Steele needs to help them, will take that as a slight. It's enough to make a past wound fester, sure as I'm sitting here."

"Except Kingsley told everyone to get along. And they have, as far as I've heard. The trainings have been going well, all things considered, right?"

"Trainings are going fine, yeah. And they are all under the watchful eyes of the various alphas." She adjusted in her seat. "The whole pack knows by now that we have to work together. They need us, want us or not."

"So what's the problem?"

She took a deep breath, leaning forward onto her elbows again. "The problem is that their respect for Kingsley isn't enough to negate their hatred for Austin

Steele, especially now that his non-shifter mate has shown everyone what she's made of. Hell, she got their pack-mate kicked out. She's not the only one making waves, either. Broken Sue's got a lot of power. More than any of Kingsley's enforcers." She shook her head. "The problems from Austin Steele's past have been set on the stove to boil, and he knows it. I don't think he quite knows how to go about it, though, wanting to respect his truce with his brother. It's a dicey situation."

Sebastian opened his mouth to reply. Closed it.

A somewhat shimmery figure slowly walked into the bar, sticking to the middle of the space between the stools and the booths. He wore properly fitting trousers and a black button-up, casual attire for a mage. His watch was plain, decently made, and with a face that subtly glowed in a telling way.

The potion was reacting to a magical tracker hidden within the watch, a way for magical entities to keep track of their people. Maybe that was why the other two had such hideous models—they didn't want to ruin their good watches to magical tracking. The practice tended to corrode the gears and render the piece ineffective, a waste for those without the means to replace them.

"My guess is that it's going to come to a show-down," Niamh went on as Sebastian felt a poke in his ribs.

He jerked toward Niamh, the poke having come from Tristan, and let out a loud and surprised "Hah!"

Several people glanced their way. Niamh shoved Sebastian back to his seat, glowering.

"What in the sweet Jesus are ye at?" she demanded.

"Sorry." He hunched over his drink. "I'm ticklish."

"For God's sake, man, I barely touched ya!" she shouted at him. "The next time I give ya a dig in the ribs, I'll make it hurt. Now what do ye want to drink? I'm dying of thirst!"

He had to hand it to her—she was world class at improvisation.

"I'm good," he mumbled.

"No, yer not *good*. Get it in ya. I didn't agree to be the babysitter of a sober man-child. The more ye drink, the faster ye'll pass out, and the easier it'll be to get rid of ya."

"Is it too late to deny the invitation for a drink?" he asked, and he didn't have to fake any part of that.

"You okay?" Timmie arrived with a grin.

"Two more, please," Niamh said in a huff. "We've got'ta get going. I can't take much more of him."

Timmie laughed and moved off to get the drinks.

"Plan?" Tristan asked softly.

Sebastian coughed in case anyone had heard.

"Would ya…" Niamh jerked her arm away, feigning disgust. "Are ye diseased?"

Or maybe not feigning it.

"Sorry," he said again. "I really am ticklish, though. Just so we're on the same page."

"I could not give a rat's toe," she replied. "But *schure*, I shouldn't be out of pack limits, it's true. Ye don't really count because yer good fer *nathin'*, but the alpha might be fair *pisched* if he realized I was out."

Sebastian was not so good at improvising. He had no idea what direction she was heading with this new conversation. Hell, her accent was currently so thick he could barely decipher what she was saying.

The closest mage inclined his head a little and brought up his watch hand to rest it on the edge of the bar. The fellow farther down leaned back in his chair a little, resting his watch hand on his knee. Niamh kept talking as the bartender wandered over to her, at which point she shifted her conversational attempts to the bartender. Sebastian didn't hear what they said, though, trying to decipher what the mages were relaying.

The invisible mage glanced toward Sebastian's end of the bar. He worried an invisible crumb with his finger, feigning boredom, his face in his hand and his elbow braced on the bar. He looked like a petulant kid, someone not fit to sit at the adult table. It would deflect interest from Sebastian and onto Niamh or literally anyone else. Sebastian had no idea why this posture worked so well, but it was a tried and true method of avoiding interest, especially from other mages.

A moment later, the invisible mage started walking toward them slowly, methodically. Sebastian wondered if he'd been backed up into a few times, or maybe a shifter had felt his presence and grabbed for him. He acted like someone who'd had a few close scrapes.

"Yeah, but I think I'll make them disappear now," Niamh was saying, her words infiltrating Sebastian's focus. "I never much liked those stockings, anyway. They run, ye know. Ye barely scratch 'em and they are all running, all over the place."

"I've never much liked them myself," Timmie said, her expression a little confused. "Oh, by the way." She leaned harder on the bar. "Do you know what I heard?"

"But ye got..." Niamh pointed down the bar. "Drink order. Tell me when ye get back."

Sebastian glanced that way, still following the invisible mage with his peripheral vision.

The invisible man worked around Niamh, pausing as she leaned back. His fellow mage down the bar glanced over, looking at Niamh first and then leaning forward a little and looking beyond her. He could see his friend, obviously, so he would also notice when

Tristan grabbed him and hauled him out. That was unfortunate.

"I don't mind stockings," Sebastian said, trying to make it sound like it was a stray thought.

Timmie paused in turning. Niamh looked at him as though he'd grown two heads.

"What?" he said. "If you need to rob a bank? Stockings. You can *see* right through them, but no one sees your face. Because it…" He straightened so he could hold his hands up. "Scrunches it up, you know? Talk about running. Rob a bank, run like hell, right?"

Timmie started laughing—Sebastian was pretty sure it was *at* him—before finishing her turn and heading down the bar.

"What?" he said to Niamh, who was staring.

"Did yer mammy drop ye on yer head when ye were a wee baby and then kick ye around the floor?"

"That was a valid—"

"I swear to all that is holy, I am going to tell the alpha to kick ye out," she said, then shook her head and took a large sip of her drink. "Ye've got no reason ta be there. Ye and the rest of those lady gargoyles. Sure, they don't even shift! What is the point of all those people if they don't even shift? All they do is make dinner and clean up."

The invisible mage worked around Niamh now,

wanting to hear more about the pack. He moved so ridiculously slowly, plodding along like he wasn't sure how to balance on his own two feet. He wasn't their best and brightest, that was for sure. He was someone they likely saved for low-leveled mage functions, his task to administer poison and hopefully, but doubtfully, get out alive.

In other words, these mages were expendable. They were bait. Momar had clearly wanted to see if the shifters would sniff them out. If the shifters would find the oddly dressed mages, sticking out like sore thumbs, and then maybe progress to noticing the invisible mages so inexpertly hidden that Nessa might as well have made their invisibility potions.

But they hadn't noticed. The shifters had remained oblivious all this time, making Momar think he had the upper hand in stealth.

Meanwhile, in an effort to lure the mage in, Niamh was giving him misinformation that could greatly help Austin and Kingsley. The message was that Kingsley had a lot of people coming in, sure, but they weren't worth anything.

Capturing these mages was the wrong play. Kingsley had had it right all along, and he hadn't even realized it.

"Let's go." Sebastian stood up, staggering back

quickly. The invisible mage froze, and then started back-pedaling. "I've had enough of you picking on me," he told Niamh, lurching toward her to ensure the mage kept moving. "Gargoyles like me might not be all that great in a fight, but we can at least shift, okay? I can shift."

"And what, flap around and get in the way?" Niamh's brows were pulled together as she surveyed him with calculating eyes. She hadn't moved from the chair yet. She wasn't getting his meaning.

"Yeah, fine, whatever. Not like you do much else, lush. I want to go. *Now*. Or I'm telling on you."

Niamh sent a long-suffering look down the bar to Timmie before downing her drink and climbing off her stool. "Yer gonna create an enemy over this one, lad," she said, her movements shooing the invisible mage away.

"You'll keep quiet if you know what's good for you," Sebastian said as she laid some cash on the bar.

"Someone like ye giving me threats?" She huffed. "Might as well put a stocking over yer head."

"That doesn't even make sense."

"Yeah. Exactly. Just copping that now?"

She turned to go, but he hesitated. The invisible mage was looking their way. If Tristan came away from that wall, he'd be visible again, and that mage or one of the others would see his magic. He didn't want that trick getting back to Momar if at all possible. Gargoyles' abilities were mostly unknowns to mages. They needed to keep it that way.

"*Well?*" Niamh asked, motioning at the door. "Get movin' or I'll give ye a kick in the hole."

"I might have to go to the bathroom," Sebastian blurted, really, *really* bad at improvising.

Niamh stared at him for a solid beat, then said in a low voice, "Ye don't know how yer bladder works?" And then, in a much louder voice, "Are ye some sort of *eejit?*"

"I need to go to the bathroom," he said with confidence. "Maybe number two, I don't know."

She seemed to be developing an eye tic. "Well then," she said very slowly, the tension rising, "ye'd better get yer arse to the toilet before ye shite all over yer drawers. Here, let me help ya."

"No, no, I can manage," he said, expecting something awful. He wasn't quite sure whether they were acting anymore.

"It's no trouble, here." She grabbed him by the back of the neck and an upper arm and started marching him through the bar. "Maybe ye'll feel better when I stick yer head in the toilet and flush a few times."

"Uncle!" he shouted, at least remembering to flail as

they went, shooing the invisible mage into the corner. "I've changed my mind! Uncle, *uncle!*"

"What are ye on about, *uncle?*" Niamh got near the back and then threw him. He hit the corner of the hallway leading to the bathrooms and bounced off, ricocheting to the other side and face-planting.

"Oww," he drew out, staggering on toward the bathroom.

"Give me a shot, Tam-tam, would ya? That lad has done me head in. *What are ye looking at?*" Niamh hollered, and a glance back said she was mad-dogging one of the mages and the other two were watching her with wide eyes. At the back of the bar, Tristan slipped out without anyone noticing.

Sebastian peed, because at this point it was probably wise in case she berated him again and he lost control of his bladder, and hurried out.

"I don't like the look of him one bit," Niamh was saying to someone sitting beside her at the top of the bar, pointing around a corner at the closest mage. "What are ye even wearing? Do ye not know how jeans work? Yer as bad as that muppet in the toilet." She leaned harder on the bar, and though Sebastian was behind her and couldn't see her eyes, he'd bet they were bugged out. She did that sometimes to unsettle people when (for some reason) her personality wasn't enough.

"Don't know how to speak?" She huffed and went back to talking to the guy next to her as Tam-tam (where'd he gotten Timmie?) smirked with her hands crossed over her chest. "Doesn't know how to dress, doesn't know how to talk…"

"Ready," Sebastian said in a small voice, hurrying past her.

"What a night," Niamh told Tam-tam as she pushed away from the bar. "What. A. Fecking. Night."

"And it's just getting started," Tam-tam said.

"Don't remind me." Niamh raised her hand as she followed Sebastian for the door. "Sorry for the display. I'll be sure not to bring this gobshite again."

"Bring him! That was the most fun I've had in a while," Tam-tam called as Sebastian made it outside and turned toward Phil.

"Abort," he said, making it to the bush. "Phil—"

"I already told him." Tristan stepped forward from the side of the building, wiping his eyes for some reason. "He's gone. What's the situation?"

Niamh came out next but didn't stop to chat. She pushed Sebastian in front of her and over the grassy knoll to a hole in the fence beyond, dumping them both into an alley.

"Do ye mind telling me what we're doing?" she asked, thankfully not yelling at him anymore.

"We need to call everyone off. Bringing these mages in is the wrong play."

She stopped him with a hand to his shoulder. "Are ye positive? I can still go in and bag those mages. If you made a mistake, it's fixable."

"I'm positive. One hundred percent. You see—"

She waved her hand. "This isn't the place to go over the particulars. If yer sure, let's call them off and get back. We can talk about it with Jessie and Austin Steele."

Tristan put his hands on his hips while biting his lip, his body shaking.

"You okay?" Sebastian asked as Niamh started to strip.

"No," he said with a wheeze, wiping his eyes again. "I think I'm going to have a hernia from holding in laughter. I don't know how I didn't crack in there. I had both hands over my mouth and was shaking against the wall. I almost blew my cover."

Niamh looked skyward while shaking her head. "Easily amused."

"I was not at all amused," Sebastian grumbled, and Tristan slapped his hand over his mouth and turned away again.

Next time, Tristan should be the butt of Niamh's jokes. They'd see how he liked it.

Sebastian's phone vibrated in his pocket, and he pulled it out.

A text from Jessie: *Nessa is MIA. Is she with you guys?*

"Hold up." Sebastian put up his hand. "We need to stop by the warehouse to see if Nessa's there. She's gone from Jessie and Austin Steele's house."

"Now Tristan, how's that? Ye stick yer nose in and see what happens?" Niamh asked. "It's probably for the best anyway. We should check on Edgar. Lord only knows what he's got up to."

CHAPTER 23

NESSA

TRISTAN CUT THROUGH the night like a predator, every movement of his large body graceful and sleek. The shadows slid over his face, accentuating those glowing eyes as he walked up the pathway to the little bungalow he shared with Gerard from the Khaavalor cairn and Gerard's lead enforcer. Kingsley had made the accommodations available, figuring a cairn leader should have more space than a hotel room, and Tristan was worthy to share it.

His shoe scuffed the concrete before he stepped onto the dark porch, looking up at the dead light. Not broken, just a loose bulb. There'd be no signs of tampering—Nessa had made sure of it.

Only the moonlight reached him now, allowing Nessa to see the loose, hardly buttoned shirt and trousers with the belt undone and fly open. It wasn't like him to be so messy in his appearance. Then again, he was clearly home for the night after visiting those bars and taking down those mages. Probably interrogating them as well. Why not? He'd shown he was incredibly competent in getting information. They wouldn't need Nessa so long as Tristan was on the scene.

Frustration and fear ate away at her. She didn't know what she'd do if she became irrelevant. There was no family to cushion her fall. No friends to share in her misery. If they took her purpose *and* Sebastian, she'd have nobody. Nothing.

At the front door, he hesitated a moment before reaching for the doorknob.

She was action.

She launched from her hiding place in the rafters at the corner of the porch, tossing a rope around his neck as she did so. That dark rope had been looped inconspicuously around a rafter board and tied to her belt. It pulled tight as she landed on top of him, jerking him backward. He staggered, immediately starting to grapple instead of reaching for his neck. She'd figured he would react that way.

She slipped a loop of a parachute cord with an arbor knot around his reaching hand, sliding it down to his wrist and pulling tightly, first one hand and then the other. It connected to a series of pulleys above, adding much-needed strength to this rig. She hadn't dealt with someone this large and strong before, but she was a master engineer when it came to this stuff. The adjustments hadn't taken but a little thought.

As he grabbed at her waist, she yanked the ending of the parachute cord with all she had.

The pulleys whined. The taut cord nearly dragged her body from his, but she wrapped her legs around his torso and held on. She had to land on top of him or he'd have the scant few seconds he needed to weasel his way out.

His wrists jerked over his head. One of his shoulders popped as he continued to fall backward, the rope around his neck constricting, swinging his body to the right.

She unhooked her belt and the rope fell away, dropping him nearly toward the destination she'd chosen for him. He fell like a ton of bricks, his wrists held aloft but pulling dangerously at her setup. The knots continued to constrict, though, cutting off his circulation and causing pain.

Not like that would help with someone like him, but every bit counted.

She rode him to the ground like a spider monkey, his size helping her hang on and balance—she had a lot of real estate with which to work. At the last moment she pulled her legs up from around him; the right one banged painfully against the wood of the porch and the other kneed him in the stomach, safe from what he'd fallen on.

The knife was released from the center of her bra in a flash, her shirt loose and low cut to accommodate the weapon. The point waited at his eyeball by the time he settled to the ground.

From beginning to end, the whole situation had taken less than thirty seconds. Now he lay there, struggling to breathe through the rope still around his neck.

"Hello, Natasha," he said with a grunt, his eyes rooted to hers. "What did I fall on?"

"Nails. I hammered them up through the boards."

"Very clever. They hurt."

"Good." She pressed the blade into the skin right below his eye. "You can heal the holes from those nails, but you won't be able to grow another eye, so it would be best if you cooperated, don't you think?"

"It seems so, yes. The others are still looking for you. They're worried about you."

"Not you, though."

His eyes traced her face slowly, like glowing embers in the deep night. "I wasn't worried about you, no," he said softly. "I knew you'd find me. Nice setup you've got here. I feel honored you went through the trouble. Do you travel with pulleys and parachute cord?"

"Parachute cord, yes. You never know when you'll need it."

"Very true. And the pulleys?"

"Hardware store at the edge of town. They have all kinds of neat stuff in that store. There might be a large BDSM undercurrent here, considering how many options they have in stock."

"Or just a bunch of handy people."

"Or that, I guess." She leaned into him a bit, rocking her weight from his stomach to his chest, pushing his back harder into those nails. "What is your game here, Tristan? Why are you trying to cut me out of this team? Are you holding a grudge for some reason, or have you gone back to thinking I'm some sort of sprite who wants to cut out your heart?"

"Not a sprite. A beautiful deathwatch angel with hidden talents she is oblivious of." A devious smile curled his lips. "I like this side of you, little monster. It's a pity, what with your dreams of fluffy clouds and tire swings, that you can't see how beautiful it is. But make no mistake, you will cut out my heart. Or rip it out…and keep it as your own. And I will let you do it gladly, at your leisure."

She showed him her teeth. "You didn't answer my

question." With one hand on his shoulder, she shook him a little. *"Why are you trying to cut me out of this team?"*

The glimmer left his eyes, seriousness taking over. He studied her for a long time, his expression patient, his eyes open all the way down to his soul. Something inside her tightened up before a blast of fear shuttered the feeling.

She leaned toward him a little more. "Answer me," she ground out.

"I'm not. I'm getting my hands dirty so that yours can stay clean."

She frowned at him, surprised by his answer. "What are you talking about?"

"I see your pain, Natasha," he murmured, pulling at the ropes a little, straining his hands to get closer to her. "I see your scars. I can't fix your past, or erase it, but I can smooth out your future so that you have time to heal yourself. I can do for you what you're trying to do for Brochan. I can take over the darkness in your life so you can walk in the light. I'll be the monster of nightmares so you can step out of the shadows. So you can finally pursue the perfect life you seek. It is within my power to give that to you, and it is my pleasure to be of service."

She shook her head, her knife hand starting to

shake. "I don't understand. We're all in this mess. Why me? Why are you singling me out? Because you think I'm pretty?"

"I do think you're pretty. Very. And I think you're fun and funny, ruthless and smart, broken and haunted. You strike me as a woman who's given plenty of handouts but not received any. Well, now it's your turn. I can do all of that for you. If you'll let me."

She shook her head again, a rush of emotion coming to the surface. "I don't believe that. Tell me the real reason."

"Listen, Natasha—I handled this badly. I'm man enough to admit that. I was trying to help, and an insightful woman with a penchant for surliness—"

He cut off for a brief moment as his body started to shake.

"Ow," he said, and then started laughing, jubilant and carefree despite being tied up and stuck to nails with a knife to the eye. "Sorry, the scene at the bar went...very differently than how I'd imagined it going. Niamh and Sebastian—"

His laughter was louder this time, completely unabashed.

"I'm actually glad you weren't there," he said, a tear slipping down his cheek, "because you probably would've had it figured out in minutes, and it was a lot funnier how it went down. I needed the entertainment."

He sobered, and given she didn't really know what he was talking about or what to say, she just held the knife as still as she could.

"I'm not trying to cut you out of your team, Natasha," he said, and she hated how erotic her name sounded coming from his lips. Dark and sexy and so gloriously smooth. "I'm trying to shield you. I remember your tears. Your self-loathing. It haunts me in the same way your past haunts you, whatever happened. I understand the darkness you feel. I understand the things you've been made to do—and the way they stick with you. The way you hate yourself for your willingness to do them over again. I know because I've lived it. I continue to live it. I've made peace with my morally gray life. I thrive in it. But you don't, and it's not in me to ignore your pain. Not when I can help you. But I…now realize…that you need to make that choice for yourself. I can shield or even hide you. Or I can stand by you if you want to hold people at knifepoint or ambush them on their doorsteps. Whatever you need, I can give it. Let me."

Tears ran down her cheeks, and the knife shook so badly that she pulled it away.

"I don't understand," she whispered, that self-loathing he spoke of pooling within her. "Why would you offer that to me? Why *me*?"

He shook his head, his eyes seeming to drink her in. "My reasons are my own."

She blinked, dislodging another tear. "I don't deserve—"

He ripped his hands forward and down, an incredible show of strength. The cord caught, too strong for him to break, but the pulleys couldn't handle the pressure. They pulled from the wood, clanked through the rafters, and fell to the ground, freeing his hands. He unstrung the loosened rope from his neck and discarded it before touching a thumb to her lips and letting the other arm fall around her.

"No more of that," he told her, lifting his head a little, his breath smelling like chocolate. "No more talking about not deserving something good in your life. I don't know what happened in the past, Natasha, but the woman I see now is strong and courageous and caring. You constantly look after Sebastian, you build up Brochan, you guard Jessie's back—"

She shook her head, guilt adding to the turbulent emotions currently drowning her. "You know better than to say I guard her back."

"Throwing her into the fire to help harden her or forcing a situation that will help her achieve her goals *is* guarding her back. You can be good and wicked at the same time, little deathwatch angel. Hell, Jessie is. Her beast wouldn't have it any other way. The same is true of Austin, without question." He grinned, his hold on her tight, his other hand now softly tracing her jaw line. "You can try to kill me one minute and then ride me to completion the next. It adds to the flavor."

She fell into those beautifully glowing eyes and saw no lie. Nothing held back.

"No one is riding anyone anywhere," she whispered, feeling a delicious hum vibrate up from where they touched. Him still lying on the nails with her in his arms. Feeling his heat soak into her. "We're not compatible."

"That's just the fear talking. I can wait."

"You'll wait forever."

His words rode a soft breath, his lips curving. "No, I won't."

She shook her head as she fell into that hum, mixing it with her own, feeling their energy swirl and build, the sensation so unbelievably delicious. She felt suspended, like a single moment had multiplied into many. The air between them shivered with heat. With possibility.

"You could've gotten loose the whole time," she murmured, her head drooping just a bit, her body melting against his. "You allowed me to threaten you with a knife."

K.F. BREENE

"It wouldn't be the first time."

"Did you know I was hiding up there, waiting for you?"

"Of course," he whispered, his aura so tantalizing now that she allowed herself to soak it in. His energy sizzled into her palms and along her flesh, the connection more intense than she'd ever shared with anyone else. Wilder. It felt like it was burning her up and breathing life into her at the same time.

"I can see your essence through a wall," he said, his voice whiskey smooth. "You don't think I'd notice you in the rafters? Especially after I pissed you off and then you went missing. I returned home thinking you'd be waiting for me. I had no idea your attack would be so elaborate, though. I'm impressed. If I'd been completely unsuspecting and couldn't feel your intoxicating presence, you very well might've truly captured me. The knife near the eye was an excellent touch."

Her head drooped just a bit more as she looked at his pillow-soft lips. Felt his hard body humming beneath hers.

His palms ran up her sides, his hands splayed.

"I didn't see the nails," he said, the sound hardly more than his breath. "If I had, I might've tried to land anywhere but on them. I must say, though, the pain mixed with the pleasure of your touch is...stirring. I wouldn't mind exploring these sensations a little more."

"I don't understand you," she finally said, thinking about kissing those lush lips. Bending toward them, she felt a jolt of nervousness climb up through her middle and expand within her stomach. Her core throbbed, and his hardness pushed up against her.

Her senses warned of danger, though, of the monster caressing her skin. This man was mysterious. Cunning. He'd buttoned up that situation in the garage with the enemy mage in such a simple yet thorough way that spoke of expertise. Of many dark deeds. Even Austin was wary of him. Something about this gargoyle didn't scream *genuine*.

He was a guy who would offer a favor but treat it as a debt. Who would keep his secrets but gather those of others. He already had dirt on her. She couldn't allow him to collect any more. Before long, he'd trap her with damning knowledge and blackmail her to serve his purposes—or service him in his bedroom.

Molten heat coursed through her at the last thought. She couldn't help a soft moan escaping her lips as she considered the possibilities.

What was happening to her? Why did that thought seem like it was pulling her apart little by little until all she wanted was to give in to his dominating presence?

She didn't trust him, no, but oh God, she couldn't

deny wanting him. Now more than ever. The problem was, she didn't just want to revel in his incredible body or stare at his handsome face. She didn't just go weak in the knees at the knowledge that no one, not any creature, could get through to her if he was standing in the way.

She craved his danger. His deviousness. The way he looked at her, like he'd drag her down into the abyss and keep her there. Her jailor. Her tormenter.

Her savior.

Because, despite the danger, she could let down her guard with him. She could show her true self, beneath the sunshine and good spirits. Beneath the dirty jokes and genuine laughter. She could show her tears, give in to her memories. Scream at the unfairness of her life.

He didn't judge her. It still seemed unbelievable, but she knew it was true—he didn't judge her for the things she'd done. He understood her, actually, probably in a way no one else did, not even Sebastian. Maybe in a way no one else *could.*

The guy of her nightmares-turned-dreams was impossible to trust and didn't hide his unwillingness to let anyone close. Could her luck get any worse?

She pried herself off him and took a deep breath, her body still humming, her breathing shallow. Damn it, why did he have to be so hot?

Why was she continually attracted to totally unattainable guys?

"Thank you for your offer," she said. "But stay the hell out of my life."

He nodded and then put out his hand.

"What—Oh." She took it and helped him up off the nails, standing with him.

"That offer isn't an all-for-one situation," he said, shaking out his wings and grimacing with the effort. He reached down and tucked himself back into his pants before zipping up, though the bulge was still incredibly pronounced. "When you need something, ask. When you don't want to get your hands dirty, let me know. It'll always be between us. You know I can keep secrets."

She narrowed her eyes at him. "Keep them for a rainy day and then collect on them. Yes, I know."

His smile was devilish. He stepped close, making her breath catch.

His voice was a low, deep hum. "You don't trust me, fine. I assume there are very few you do trust—"

"Do you trust me?" she asked.

His smile held more confidence than he had any right to. "I don't have to trust you. I understand you. I know when you're going to make me a brownie to be nice, like the other day, and when you're going to show up at my lodging and try to cut my nuts off." He looked

K.F. BREENE

down on her for a long, tense beat before nodding. "Fine. Like I said, I'll wait. Eventually you're going to need me, and you're going to learn that I mean what I say."

"What if I just want to use you?" she teased.

In a sudden motion, he grabbed the back of her neck in a firm hold, making her gasp. Slowly he reeled her in, his strength undeniable, his fervor slithering across her flesh. He bent to her, his power wrapping around her, the sweet smell of chocolate on his breath mixing with his intoxicating scent and drying up any protest she might've made.

"Use me anytime," he growled, before yanking her that last little distance and wrapping his lush lips around her bottom lip, sucking it in.

A rush of electricity lit her up. She groaned into his mouth, running her hands up his chest, wishing she still had her knife.

He opened her mouth with his, his hold rough, his tongue swiping through and then swirling with hers. Energy swirled up around them, running between them, vibrating through them. She held the edges of his shirt, delirious with the sensation. High on it.

His hold tightened then, the kiss deepening, his other hand wrapping around her waist and hauling her tightly to him. His hips moved against hers erotically, his tongue mimicking what she wanted other parts of him to do.

Holy crap, he felt so good. He moved against her expertly, the disproportionate sizes of their bodies somehow not making any difference. They fit together passionately, made to explore each other. To take each other, over and over, until they could stand it no more.

Panic flared. *What am I doing?* That was all she needed, a dangerous addiction.

She pulled back, but he held her tightly, his growl warning her to stay put.

A delicious shiver ran down her spine. She liked when romantic interests were dominant, and he would take dominance to a new level.

No! Get out now!

She swished her hips to the side and swung down her hand at the same time. Fist connected with crotch. Tristan's grunt matched his flinch. He didn't pull away quickly, though, merely backing off his kiss. Slowing down the fervor.

She drank it up, falling into it, just about to clutch him again and beg him to take her back to his bedroom.

"Dang it!" She pulled away, and he let her go easily. Clearly he *did* understand her. He knew this time she was serious. Super serious. Must-leave-right-now-or-lose-her-mind sort of serious.

He watched her with those glowing eyes before looking at the space between them. His smile was smug.

"You're only so strong, little angel. You'll crack. It's only a matter of time."

She leveled a finger at him. "Stay out of my life and stay out of my job."

"Yes, ma'am. But I won't stay out of your dreams."

CHAPTER 24

JESSIE

THREE DAYS AFTER Sebastian made the call not to collect the mages in the border towns, I flew above the town with gargoyles spanned out all around me in an intricate flight pattern that Tristan had devised. It was a beautiful thing, perfectly organized with all the various gargoyles swooping and crossing and diving, working off each other's movements. Below, Kingsley's shifters patrolled the town, led by his beta, James.

Our forces had started on the outskirts of town and pushed out to the perimeter, Austin and Kingsley working together to organize their people while the basandere took control of the basajaunak. Although she hadn't come with the goal of leading her people, she'd fallen naturally into the role. We were working together to test strategies for the coming battle.

A battle that we hadn't gotten any word about.

Nessa and Sebastian's network had gone silent.

They hadn't heard anything new for nearly a week now, not even a whisper.

There hadn't been any mages testing the defenses, either. Usually they operated on a sort of loose schedule, showing up every so often. Kingsley said there should've been one by now, a group of two or three. Not the invisible mages, which we hadn't noticed or caught either, but teams poking around and making a racket.

Silence was not golden. Our mages were getting increasingly nervous that Momar was mobilizing. Time was short, but Nessa still had to pick up the shipment of guns, an apparently seedy affair involving dangerous characters who were just as likely to double-cross her as deliver the goods. Arrangements were being made slower than she'd anticipated. The garhettes were doing well with their knife work and hand-to-hand combat, no shortage of aggression and a good dose of speed, but they needed those weapons. Without them, most of them wouldn't be able to stand up against a mercenary, even an unarmed one.

I stilled my thumping heart and focused a little harder, feeling Nathanial touch my foot before soaring above me. I pushed up skyward and then snapped in my wings so he could grab me, flying me fast toward the north end of the perimeter and then quickly maneuvering east, practicing his ability to fly at dizzying speeds with quick changes of direction while holding on to me.

Without warning, he tossed me left and dodged right, simulating what would happen should someone blast a gun or spell directly at us. I swooped down to confront a potential enemy before climbing back up again. He dove below me, and I wasn't sure what that was supposed to simulate. He was trying to do double duty, work with Tristan and equally help me.

Another gargoyle grabbed me, flying me south, and now it seemed like I was a prop. All well and good. Few of the gargoyles were used to carrying one of their own in battle. They needed to learn. Lives might depend on it.

"You're trying too hard," Ivy House told me, the first time she'd spoken to me since we'd left.

"What do you mean?" I replied, opening my eyes as the gargoyle dropped me and swerved away.

Another grabbed me quickly, diving before pulling out gradually and releasing me at exactly the wrong moment.

With a growl I worked to right myself and fly straight, shooting magic at him to let him know he'd screwed up.

"You're trying to get too detailed with the connections," she said. *"That part of your magic isn't supposed to work like the Ivy House connections. It's supposed to*

be a general guide. It needs to connect everyone together, not just connect them to you. You're pulling at strings when you should be pulling at groups and teaming that with magic."

That didn't make much sense to me.

After a moment of being flown south by a big gargoyle without a lot of speed, I told her as much.

"It's easier in battle, but here..."

Strange tingles covered my skin, and I zapped the guy holding me so he'd let go. I pushed him away and lowered so everyone would know I didn't want to be bothered.

The tingles turned into pricks of pain, and then it felt like my hair was standing on end. Within my mind's eye, I sensed a swell of lights and colors moving through me and then over and under me, all around me, merging together. The strings I'd been plucking one by one joined together into a symphony, notes rising and falling above the mass to pull at my attention.

"Do you see?" she asked. *"This is rudimentary, since I've never been able to directly teach the heirs, but it's an idea."*

"It's a very good idea, are you kidding me? You're telling me you could've been helping me all this time, and I've instead been blasting my crew and flailing around?"

"No, I can help you with certain things, like the con-

nections to your team and issues relating to the property, but magic on the whole is your responsibility. I don't do spells; I house the magic. Because I'm a house. See how that works?"

"And you couldn't offer this up before now?" I asked with a *tone*.

"I've learned that when the heirs figure things out for themselves, they have a better grasp on the magic."

"And how has that worked with the past heirs? You know, all the ones who have died early?"

"Again, I just house the magic," she said, now also taking a *tone*. *"I don't pick their terrible mates who try to steal the magic in jealousy or won't take the magic out of cowardice…"*

She was talking about Austin now.

"Thanks," I said, because she had helped me get a handle on this new way of perceiving the gargoyle connections. It was certainly a *lot* better than what I was doing before, but I got what she was saying—I'd need to develop some finesse.

A shock of pain brought me out of my reverie. Another followed it up quickly, stabbing into my side. A third through a wing.

I looked around in confusion and rising panic, taking in the grove of trees in the park at the southeast edge of the town below me. The grassy area beyond it was devoid of people. Patrols mostly passed through here going elsewhere, as this area of town was not heavily populated yet.

Something struck my leg, digging in, and more popped through my wings. Arrows. Someone was shooting arrows at me! *What in the...*

I twirled to look around, but I'd sunk low in the sky, lost in my own world. No one flew nearby, giving me space. Another arrow flew up and pierced me. Pain reverberated through my wings with each pump, and wind passed through instead of keeping me airborne.

There, in the trees, a person—a man—stepped into the clearing and lifted a bow. He let go, and another arrow flew, missing me. A second person—a woman this time—stepped into the space between the trees, and a man walked onto the grass beside her. They had their bows out. More arrows flew.

I swiveled to get out of the way as my altitude lowered. With the air passing through my wings, though, I wasn't effective. More arrows slammed home, sending shooting blasts of agony through me. Thankfully my gargoyle hide was a lot tougher than human skin, and the arrows weren't going anywhere near deep enough to cause serious harm, but it still hurt like the blazes.

Not to mention people were shooting freaking arrows at me! People from the pack. Mages would use magic, number one, and two, our people were all over the territory perimeter. This many enemies couldn't have snuck in unnoticed.

Fury burned in my chest.

Kingsley's people were trying to get even for my getting that moron Bruce kicked out of the top hierarchy. That, or they didn't like that I'd challenged Kingsley and nothing had happened to me. Hell, maybe this was still about Austin and they stupidly thought I was the weakest link.

Whatever their reasoning, they'd made a very grave mistake.

I flapped wildly now, pretending like I was trying to maintain altitude while sinking lower and lower. The arrows kept coming, making me wonder if they were actually trying to kill me.

Below the treetops now, I sent out a blast of magic, a stinging spell that would hopefully give them false confidence. None of them had ever been hit with magic before—maybe they'd think it wasn't that bad and stick around. I sure hoped so.

Another arrow struck deep, fired at close range. My anger spiked. I folded up my wings and hit the ground. Making a show of stumbling and falling, I used that time to rip arrows out of my body and legs, before crawling forward and laboring to my feet, all for show.

James stepped out of the trees, that bastard. He was supposed to be leading the pack in town! His smile was smug and his swagger ridiculous.

Bruce came out, too, along with that woman from the bar last week and a few other shifters, all with bows in hand. All of them were supposed to be participating in training right now.

"Oops," James said, walking toward me in the nude, having clearly shifted for this. "Looks like, for all the magic you have, and the strange light show, you aren't impervious to something as simple as an arrow."

The arrows removed, I shifted into my human form. Blood trickled from my many wounds, already healing.

"And you think you aren't?" I asked, breathing heavily and hobbling toward them a little. I wanted to see their eyes widen when I blasted them back to last century.

"Think you run this pack, huh?" Bruce walked forward, a block of muscle. "Think you and your *boyfriend* call the shots?"

Ah. So they subscribed to the belief that shifters shouldn't mate non-shifters. What idiots.

"What is it you guys want?" I asked, hunching a little, trying not to let my anger send pulses of magical intent. "You think the alpha is going to be cool with your killing me? You think that'll help your pack?"

"We're not gonna kill you," the woman from the bar said, walking forward also. All of them did, moving in to surround me now. "We're just gonna teach you a lesson. You and your boyfriend have been sticking your noses where they don't belong."

"Teach *me* a lesson?" I asked as they fell in all around me. "What about Austin? You're not going to teach him a lesson?"

"Well now, see, that's the great thing about this…" James sneered. "By working you over, we can teach you both a lesson. Plus that beta and the strange gargoyle who seems to like you so much. Get to you, and we send a message to you all."

I huffed out a laugh, my magic building. "You really haven't thought this through. Again, you think Kingsley is going to be cool with your beating me up?"

"Beating you to within an inch of your life, actually, and he won't know. That piece of crap brother of his has all but advertised his resolve to handle this person- ally. This will be our invitation to him. I think he'll take the bait, don't you? Then we can remind this territory what he really is, an unbalanced excuse for a shifter who should've been run out long before he'd been allowed to go wild."

I caught a flash of movement out of the corner of my eye. The awareness of my Ivy House links filtered in slowly, informing me that Edgar waited just within the trees to my right. A little shape flitted in my peripheral vision on the left, skittering behind a trunk. There was a flash of red, like a hat.

Like a gnome's hat...

Horror struck me.

We didn't somehow bring the gnomes with us, did we? They couldn't have burrowed into our supplies before they were loaded into the vans...could they have?

I pushed the thought away. I must've been seeing things.

I sure hoped I'd been seeing things!

Shifter power clouded the air all around me. I stared at James for a long beat. My words came slowly and evenly as I straightened my body, shedding my ruse of uncertainty and pain.

"If your goal is to sacrifice your life to prove that Austin is wild, you won't succeed. Not only will everyone agree he's in the right to retaliate against you, but I won't let him kill you. I won't let him, so you won't be able to make a statement at all."

"How cute, you thinking you have control over that wild thing." James stepped closer, done with talking. "He thinks he's a man of honor. He'll come at us on his own, and there is no way in hell he can take all of us, though with his delusions of grandeur, he'll sure try. And when he challenges us, we'll do what our alpha should've done a long time ago. We'll put him in his place for good."

The guy at my right lurched forward to grab me.

Then a whole lot of things happened at once.

"Hey, Jessie, care to dance?" Nessa bounded from the trees, a knife in each hand, behind the guy stepping forward. He nearly tripped over his feet as he half turned in surprise.

The shifters had been so focused on their little plan that they hadn't paid attention to their surroundings.

"Hello," Edgar said from the other side, puffing into a swarm of insects and heading for the woman on my left.

The man behind me lunged forward, as did the woman next to him.

I turned to meet them, blasting them with magic intended to crumple them to the ground.

Nessa reached the man on my right, jumped up to wrap her legs around his middle, and slung one arm around his chest with the blade facing in. Stabbing with that knife, she sliced across his neck with the other. The movements were so fluid and graceful that it looked like an actual dance they'd rehearsed.

"Don't worry, neither wound will kill him," Nessa

said, sprinting across the circle at a man who'd also frozen in place. "You can be much less careful with shifters. No, Edgar, maim, not put to sleep!"

Edgar looked up from his limp victim with raised eyebrows, red dripping down his chin. He put his hands up, like this was a holdup, and the man dropped to the ground. "I know. The gnomes can do it."

My heart constricted. "Wait… *What?*"

But I didn't have time to ask more about it. James was the last man standing. He looked around wide-eyed at the team he'd assembled, which we'd flattened in no time at all.

"Should've shifted," Nessa told him, wiping her blades on the grass.

"It wouldn't have helped," I said, closing the distance. "I don't fault you for not wanting to give Austin another chance." I put up a wall of magic so he couldn't keep backing away from me. "It can be hard to forgive and harder to forget. Using me to get at Austin, though?" Anger burned in my gut, making my stomach roll. "That's disgusting. You'll get your wish. I won't hide what you've done from him. I will keep him from killing you, but I won't temper his reaction. Good luck. Until then…"

My magic surged, and I pummeled him with spells, the pain seeping down deep and dragging him under.

He gritted his teeth, handling it for a while, but then sank slowly to his knees. A little more power, nothing like I'd throw at his shifter form or a gargoyle, and he shouted obscenities at me and curled up in a little ball.

A gnome dashed out from the trees with a pair of scissors, cackling.

"Damn it," I said, hopping away from it. "Edgar, how did this happen? Tell me Kingsley *also* has a gnome infestation and it wasn't our fault somehow."

Nessa held up her hand to Edgar before filling me in on what Edgar had apparently told Sebastian a few nights ago, something Sebastian had assumed was a sort of fever dream. Clearly it was not.

"Damn it," I repeated. "Kingsley will never forgive me for this. And I wouldn't blame him!"

"Don't worry, Jessie," Edgar said, putting out his hands to back Nessa and me toward the trees. "I know what I'm doing."

"But do you really?" I pushed.

"Almost a little bit, yes."

Three more gnomes rushed from the trees.

"How many did you bring?" I screeched.

"Just a couple besides the one that escaped at the airport. They colonize quickly. But that's good, because magical spells don't bother gnomes, you see. Now, don't kill them," he said, pointing at one of the gnomes, this one with a paring knife it had obviously stolen from someone's outdoor kitchen.

At least, I *hoped* it was from an outdoor kitchen and these little nightmares weren't invading houses now.

It made a sound like "*Grrrraw*" and lifted its knife at Edgar.

"I think we should walk away slowly," he said, motioning for us to keep moving back. "They don't seem to have the rapport for me that I do for them."

"That doesn't even make se—" I stopped myself, rubbing my hand down my face. "We can't leave them to the gnomes. That's not right. We beat them, we've won—we should *all* just walk away now."

"Oh, it'll just be a little chop-chop," Edgar said, not sufficiently alarmed. "Nessa did far more damage than the gnomes will probably do. Besides, they really do deserve it."

Nessa paused. "Should I go slit the rest of their throats? Practice makes perfect."

"No. Oh my—no! Just—" I turned and started walking. Those shifters had started it, that was true. They should've paid more attention to the type of outfit I ran before picking on me.

Besides, whatever those gnomes did would likely be nothing compared to how Austin would react. So...maybe I shouldn't say anything to him at all? After this, I doubted very much those shifters would ever try to attack me again, and if they did, I wasn't worried about their succeeding.

"Why are you guys here, anyway?" I asked as I walked them back toward the town. "I thought you were supposed to be working with the perimeter crew."

"We were," Nessa replied, looking up through the trees. "But they're all really fast, and I couldn't keep up."

"And I don't go anywhere without my shadow," Edgar said.

"So we decided to check on the flowers, and we saw you acting funny in the air. We thought we'd check it out. It wasn't until we got closer that we saw the arrows. You have witnesses if you need them."

"I'm not worried about witnesses," I murmured. "I *am* worried about Kingsley's people. I knew there were problems, obviously, but this is on another level. For all of us, not just Austin."

"I think their positions have gone to their heads," Nessa said. "They've had an established power structure for over a decade. They don't like suddenly being shoved down the line."

I stopped beyond the trees and checked over my body. The puncture marks were nearly gone. My wings should be fine. Time to get back up and finish the day.

"As I was saying." Edgar clasped his hands together

as I struggled to remember which part of the conversation he was referring to. "Magical spells don't affect gnomes—they hide very well, and they can kill if they really want to. I'm pretty sure they can, at any rate. And if not, they can certainly wound. It's only to our benefit if we have an army of small, animated stone creatures to chase after the mages!"

"Are they still stone when they're alive?" Nessa asked with squinted eyes. "They don't look like stone."

"Actually, Shadow, I'm not sure. I'm always too busy getting hacked at and running to pay much attention. Regardless, I think they'll help us, Jessie. I really do."

"Except they also chase after friendlies," I reminded him. "They chase after anything."

"Oh no, I brought only the most loyal of the gnomes," Edgar said.

Only he could say that with a straight face.

I opened my mouth to reply, but really, what was there to say?

Instead, I shifted and took to the air. Kingsley might forgive me for an awful lot, but I didn't think those gnomes would make the list. He'd probably try to retire me over them before this was through, and I couldn't say I'd blame him.

CHAPTER 25

JESSIE

WITH A WEARY sigh, I toweled off my hair and slipped into my PJs. The rest of the training had gone fine. Uneventful for the most part. When everyone broke up for the day, I checked in with Sebastian and started making potions. Now I was expected to go over spell work, but I honestly just needed a night off. Just one night where I could put my feet up, pour a glass of wine, and stare listlessly at the TV before going to bed. I knew we had precious little time, but we'd had precious little time for a while now. We'd been sprinting toward this battle for months, it seemed, and it still hadn't happened. Occasionally a body needed a break.

"Knock on wood," I murmured to myself, clunking my knuckles on my head. With my luck, the cosmos had taken note of that thought and the battle would come tomorrow. We still weren't prepared for that.

K . F .   B R E E N E

Of course, I doubted we'd ever be prepared. We were flying blind and hardly knew what to prepare for.

In the hall, Tristan was just walking out of the study as I was approaching. He glanced my way and paused for me to catch up.

"Where'd you come from?" he asked, continuing with me to the kitchen, where everyone in this house seemed to congregate. I guess that was what happened when you had not one, but two passionate cooks on board.

"The morgue," I said eerily. "What's in the study?"

"I was half thinking of grabbing a book, but the only things in there are old magazines and nonfiction history. Hard to escape reality when you're dragged back to the often horrible deeds of the past."

"True statement. How do you think training went?"

"Fine. I worried that when Gerard got up to speed, he'd try to take over command of your gargoyles. Doesn't seem like that'll be an issue, though. He keeps complimenting me on our flying patterns."

"That's good." I paused, giving him a look. "You could probably be a cairn leader if you wanted to be."

"Not with my background. The second I tried to establish some power of my own, the other leaders would cut my knees out from under me. As you know." He ran his fingers through his loose, unruly curls. "I'm good here. This is the perfect setup for me. Strong leadership to shield me, plenty of challenges to keep me from getting bored, many uses for my skillset, and a very pretty lady sitting in your kitchen, staring at nothing as though something is wrong. How could I ask for more?"

We paused in front of Nessa as Tristan's words died away. She was sitting on the cushioned bench, and although the failing light masked her face, she was doing as Tristan had said—staring at absolutely nothing. I hadn't seen her since I'd gone back into the sky, but at that point she'd seemed in great spirits. Looking at her now, though, it did seem like something was gravely wrong.

"You okay?" I asked, wondering if I should flick on a light.

She inhaled, leaned back, and glanced up at me. "Yes. Just thinking."

"Need a sounding board?" I took the few steps and hit the switch. Light showered her face and outlined the fine lines that must have been caused by stress. "Did the gnomes follow you guys after I left?"

Her smile was faint and Tristan sat down beside her. Until she gave him a hard look, that was. Then he stood, moved down a couple steps, and sat down again.

"An independent buyer consolidated my arms purchase," she said. "In other words, another—unknown—party took over the deals I was doing for the guns."

I furrowed my brow as I walked over to grab a bottle of wine. No spell work tonight. "What does that mean? What are the implications?"

She crossed one leg over the other. "That's the question, isn't it?"

"Walk us through it," Tristan said, his voice subdued, matching Nessa's mood.

She lifted her eyebrows, her gaze losing focus again. "Well, let's see. Someone usually consolidates an arms order like this for a couple of reasons. The two most common are money and information."

"If it is for money?" he said.

"If it is for money, the situation is not much different than I'd already expected. There is always the risk of one party trying to kill the other for the goods or profit. So I'd show up and they'd kill me, take my money, and keep their product. Given I've made this deal under an alias that isn't well known on the circuit and with no real background or records—on purpose—the sellers will be skeptical. They might think I mean to show up, kill them, and take their guns without paying. But I'm paying more than the guns are worth, and not enough to raise any alarm. So yes, I'm thinking this is an informational query."

"And what does—"

A blast of rage ate through the bonds from Austin. It crackled and burned. He was on the move now, headed in my direction and coming fast.

"Crap," I said as my phone vibrated.

"What's up?" Nessa said, pulled out of her reverie.

Text from Broken Sue: *He knows about the attack. Keep him from killing anyone.*

"*Crap.*" I grimaced at the phone and then glowered at Tristan. "How did Broken Sue know about the attack on me today?"

"From me," he said with zero remorse.

I'd sought him out after training, asking him to make sure the gnomes hadn't gone overboard.

"I specifically told you not to tell him, Tristan. I wanted to think about it a little more before I approached him. I gave you that command as an alpha."

"And I respected that command. I didn't breathe a word of it to Austin."

"But you told Broken Sue?"

"Well, first I asked Edgar about it so that I could get the particulars. He spoke mostly gibberish about gnomes, though, so I called his shadow."

"He didn't mention he planned to use the information for evil," Nessa said, her focus back and applied to me.

"Once I had that information, I retrieved Indigo so she could help the downed shifters heal faster. I didn't want to lie to you about their being on the mend. The gnomes had done a number on a couple of them, seemingly trying to emulate what my little monster had done."

"I'm not *your* little monster, and…" Nessa grimaced.

"Yeah." He started to laugh, of all things. "They were having a good time. I don't recommend being left alone with one of them when incapacitated."

I was sure the whole kitchen could hear my teeth grinding. "And so you sought out Broken Sue in hopes he'd tell Austin and absolve you of your promise?"

"Not yet. First I spoke to Niamh so that she could call off her plans to drink in the border towns tonight in favor of getting a seat at the bar Kingsley's beta regularly goes to. When we first got here, she expressed a desire to watch Austin teach those…gobshites, I think was the term she used, a lesson."

A smirk pulled at Nessa's lips as she watched Tristan with obvious delight.

"*Then* I told Brochan," he finished. "Every last detail. Edgar's shadow was incredibly thorough."

"I like to give an accurate account of my travels," she said, playing off Tristan the way she always played off Sebastian.

Austin drew closer, his rage pulsing in time to his quickly beating heart.

I swore.

"Do you know what you've done?" I shouted at Tristan, then swung my glare at Nessa. "He's been waiting for this. He's been building it up in his mind since that idiot Bruce first stepped up to me. He'll be out for blood."

"This is a shifter matter, Jessie," Tristan said, his voice holding compassion. "It would be the same for gargoyles. Those shifters attacked someone he loves. He will first ensure she—you—are okay, and then he will respond in kind. You have to let him."

"As if I'd be able to stop him."

"Would you want to be kept in the dark if someone attacked him?"

My mute stare of angry frustration was answer enough, because yeah, I'd want to end anyone who dared attack Austin like that.

Tristan inclined his head. "Your job now is to make sure he doesn't actually kill anyone."

"Or ruin the bar," Nessa said. "Destruction of property makes business owners unreasonable."

"Valid point," Tristan said as Austin arrived at the front of the house.

His power pulsed outward in waves. I could feel it throbbing as he neared the front door, and then it gushed down the hall toward me. He'd dramatically slowed, though, closing the front door as normal, not slamming it or breaking the door down. Taking measured steps down the hall. Coming around the corner with a smooth stride and loose shoulders, hiding all the tension I could feel tightly coiled in his middle.

"Jess," he said, his growl not doing a great job of hiding his fury. His gaze traveled every inch of my body, as though he could see through my clothes. He pulled me away from the counter and gently laid his hands on my sides. His eyes were so blue, so soft. And in a moment, his voice matched them, his fury stored away so he could treat me with kid gloves. "I heard what happened. Are you okay?"

My lower lip trembled, not because of what had happened—they'd gotten their asses handed to them—but because of what *could* have happened. If I hadn't been able to defend myself, I wouldn't have fared well at all. It was a scary realization.

"I'm okay," I said softly, laying my hands on his chest. "Honestly, Austin, I'm fine. They didn't know what they were getting themselves into. Not to mention Edgar and Nessa were there. They helped me."

He pulled up my shirt to look at my stomach. "Did

the arrows go in far? Does it still hurt?"

His thumb brushed across a pink spot where an arrow had pierced me, the injury healed but for the tiny discoloration. The deeper ones were like that, but the shallower ones were completely gone.

"No. It's fine. It was my gargoyle form—"

"They shot her down," Nessa said. "She looked like a pincushion. You know, in case the guys didn't mention that."

Austin stilled, the rage inside of him flaring. He breathed in through his nose and closed his eyes for a moment.

"I heard," he growled.

"I'm fine, seriously." I showed Nessa my teeth before laying my palm against Austin's cheek. "Honestly, baby. I'm okay."

He pulled me into a tight hug, his hand on the back of my head, his cheek pressed against me. He rocked me slowly, breathing me in.

"I want you to stay in tonight, okay?" he said, his voice rumbling through his chest. "I see you have the wine open. Have a glass. I'm going to go out for a bit, but I'll be back later to—"

"No." I pushed away from him. "Do you think I'm crazy? Austin, this town is holding a grudge against you. I can understand answering their challenge, especially since it's disgusting that they are targeting me to get to you, but you cannot kill them."

"Brochan and a few others will be there to make sure I don't go too far."

"Do you need me?" Tristan asked.

"No. I want to keep this strictly a shifter matter. It'll hit home a little harder that way."

"And I will keep the situation from escalating," I said firmly. "I'll stay out of it, but I can control the crowd without strong-arming them and causing more aggression. I can keep you from going too far without having to drag you off like some dog." I poked him in the chest. "I'm going, Austin. We'll knock that out, maybe have a drink, and then come back here and cuddle on the couch. And if that dickface Momar has any of his people attack me tonight, so help me God, I will go scorched earth on his ass."

CHAPTER 26

NESSA

NESSA COULDN'T HOLD back a lopsided grin as she watched Jessie stomp down the hall and Austin stare after her in dismay. That big, fearsome alpha would not be saying no to her. He was many things to a lot of people, but he was not pushy when it came to Jessie. Not when she'd set her mind to something.

"You did good," Austin told Tristan, bracing his arms on the counter and hanging his head. He took a deep breath before straightening up. "You did real good. You handled that perfectly. Except maybe"—he tilted his head to either side—"telling Niamh."

"She'll have that place primed, everyone in whatever mood is likely to suit you best, sir. She'll be your ace in the hole on this one, I think."

"No." He glanced in the direction of the bedrooms at the other end of the house. "That has always been my mate. I don't want to drag her into this, but…"

"Pardon me for saying, sir, but you dragged her into this the second you decided to bring her to this pack. It was always going to go down like this. I don't know what kind of man you were back in the day, but it certainly rattled some people."

"For a while I was a nightmare incarnate." His arms flexed, but he kept himself from showing emotion. "I was young, though. Stupid. For the five years after that, I did everything I could to turn myself around. I was a model citizen and always submissive to the hierarchy." His whole body flexed now, like he wanted to punch something. "But then I left, and I think it ripped the fiber of the pack."

"Staying would've almost certainly done the same thing, don't you think?" Tristan countered. "Your coming back to help is tearing that fiber in the other direction it seems, right?"

"Damned if you do, damned if you don't," Austin murmured, his body starting to relax.

"You can fix it," Nessa said, crossing one leg over the other. Dealing with their drama was so much more refreshing than making decisions about her own. "Our people and Kingsley's are *mostly* getting along. The shifters in town absolutely *love* the garhettes. The kids like Edgar's weird flowers and how creepy he is, the basajaunak are blending in nicely, and I think most of

Kingsley's people are coming around about the gargoyles. When they realize we helped save them—presuming we do help save them and don't all die in the process—I don't think very many will think of you as a pariah anymore. Everyone loves a victory, but they revere a hero." She paused, her mood dark. "And, you know, if we all die, then who cares anyway, right?"

The room was silent for a moment after she'd finished.

"You good?" Austin asked her.

"I mean…" She shrugged. "Sure, why not. Aren't we all?"

"Okay." Jessie returned wearing jeans and a T-shirt with her hair up in a ponytail. "Let's get this done. I have a couch and cuddling to return to."

Nessa shook her head, watching them leave. "Relationship goals, right there."

Silence crept between her and Tristan, alone now, and the house suddenly seemed very still. Sebastian was out collecting ingredients for some potion or other, and everyone who might stop by was probably at the bar waiting to see how it all went down. Nessa hoped Austin absolutely crushed the crew that had ambushed Jessie. What cowardly, despicable bags of shit.

Soon the creeping thoughts from earlier filtered back in, a thousand scenarios rolling through her head.

The unnamed buyer had changed the plans, setting up the new situation, trying to play her like a pawn as if she were new to this schtick...

"What are the particulars of an informational situation?" Tristan asked. His smooth, deep voice jolted her back to reality. She'd almost forgotten he was there.

"Um..." She sagged against the cushion. Might as well talk it through. There was only so long it could be trapped in her head, circling 'round and 'round. "Okay, well, there are a few possible scenarios, usually pertaining to the identity of the buyer or the current landscape in the mage world." She took a deep breath. "That said, I have a shell of an alias buying a decently sized order of artillery with a time constraint—"

"Meaning a last-minute purchase?"

"Correct. A fake persona—a persona not hiding its fakeness, at that—is purchasing a good few weapons at the last minute and having them delivered for pickup to a Podunk location where Momar just so happens to be gearing up for a full-scale attack on shifters."

Tristan sat back as well, saying nothing for a moment. "Is it possible people might think it is Momar's organization placing the order?"

"Very, *very* unlikely. These are second-rate weapons coming from disreputable people on a type of magical black market. And he wouldn't use an alias. He wouldn't have to. It *is* plausible for a band of mercenaries to place an order like this. If they got a last-minute job, perhaps, like Momar hearing about all the gargoyles and garhettes showing up and adding more low-rung resources to his stockpile."

"Would they use an alias?"

Despite the lead weight forming in her stomach, she couldn't help the grin.

"You catch on very quickly, Tristan…" She frowned, blinking. "I don't even know your last name."

"Do you know anyone's last name?"

"Brochan's, though he doesn't like to talk about it. It reminds him of his lost family. Austin's. Jessie's." She squinted. "No one else. Touché. Anyway, Tristan Shadowmaster—"

"You're the shadow, not me. Isn't that what Edgar calls you?"

"Moving on. To answer your question, it's unlikely they'd use an alias. The person consolidating the order could be someone who's following the situation and wants to know what new players are jumping into the fray. Maybe to catalog who will sell services to Momar, or something like that."

"Is that plausible?"

"In a faraway universe, a distant galaxy, maybe. For us, it's wishful thinking. Not many people would want to check up on Momar in this way, and those who would probably wouldn't be poking around *here*. There are always surprises, but it's not likely."

"So you're thinking it's Momar, and he'll show up to this pickup party."

"Momar himself? Never. He would never sink so low. He would send his people, though." She chewed on her lip, back to imagining scenarios. "I've been going over and over this, and this is what I'm thinking. His people have been watching the area, that we know. They've seen the influx of people coming to this territory. Not just animals. No, people who can hold weapons when fighting. Now there's a last-minute order of weapons, placed in a dark corner of the magical black market by someone who's sophisticated enough to place an order like this and get a decent price despite their obvious need for the goods. That hints at a knowledgeable mage working with the shifters. And *that* is where things get sticky. They've probably been wondering for a while now whether there's someone besides the purple creature with house magic helping the shifters. Someone powerful. This transaction will point to someone who's at least knowledgeable. Power and knowledge usually go hand in hand with mages."

"Can they find you through this alias?"

"Not even their best would be able to, no. Another

hint that it was placed by someone who's been around a while. Someone who knows how the mage system works."

"But you're not powerful. In magic, I mean."

"Sebastian is. All powerful mages have minions. I am said minion. I represent his power. They will be dying to know who's behind this."

"So it's one of Momar's people," Tristan said.

"Almost certainly."

"They hope the power player will show up to collect the guns."

"I'm guessing so. Under no circumstances can he go. It won't just jeopardize our current situation—it'll jeopardize all our plans for the future."

"Elliot Graves's plans."

She jerked her head toward him, studying him now, his easy demeanor, the knowledgeable gleam in his eyes. "Yes," she said slowly. "His alias, yes, as it coincides with Jessie's future plans."

"That you are helping create for her."

A tingling started in her chest, like butterflies on fire, spreading through her body. Her skin crawled, the feeling of danger upon her.

"That her team is helping create," she said, trying to read that strange look in his eyes. "His alias is crafted as a dark dweller. A cunning mastermind. A mage that

K . F . B R E E N E

doesn't directly get his hands dirty. If he pokes his head up, a great many people will line up to chop it off, and mine with him."

"You mean the Captain's more than just a minion. Much more. Someone who pulls strings like a marionette. A super villain in her own right. A great many people would like to get their hands on both of you, I gather."

The air seemed to heat up between them, almost solidifying, sticky and gooey and hinting of great danger now surrounding her. But there was no one here, only Tristan. A clearly knowledgeable Tristan, who'd come from unknown origins with powerful though mysterious magic. Someone that had found his way into the fold and now held power and the ear of the leaders.

Colors seemed to dance between them, light and jubilant and energetic, so opposite to what he was saying. To the feeling of panicked dread lodged inside of her. It didn't make sense. Usually she could count on her sixth sense to steer her in situations like this, but this time her gut and the energy in the room seemed at odds.

"There you go," he said softly, his eyes glowing a burnished orange now. "So you do know how to use it occasionally."

Oh yeah, she used her brain plenty.

"What'd you do with the other set of notes?" she asked, her tone neutral, the way she always handled her work affairs. "You gave one set to Austin, and the other? The one about Elliot Graves and the Captain?"

"Clever girl, though I must say, the hints were borderline obvious." He gave her an assessing look. "You aren't treating me like the dangerous thing you make me out to be."

"But you *are* a dangerous thing."

"Sometimes." He paused, crossing an ankle over his knee. "I put them in a safe place. The mage didn't know enough to incriminate you, if that's what you're worried about. Either of you. Hearsay, mostly, random stories, how you're perceived. Add that to what I know about you, though, and a different story emerges."

Her chest felt tight, as though her breath were trapped inside. As though danger had caught up with her and the plank she'd been walking for years had finally been cut out beneath her.

She wanted to ask what sort of story he'd surmised. If he'd told any of his suspicions to Austin. If he'd seek to ruin her or simply use her.

That blasted energy connecting them had slowed, though, leaving only an erotic feeling. An *aching*.

What was happening to her? What new magic was this that he held?

"Calm yourself, little deathwatch angel," he whispered, putting his hand down on the cushion beside him. The ripples of magic traveled slowly along the fabric, like a throbbing syrup, until it soaked into her side and slithered into her body. She closed her eyes on a moan, lost in whatever sort of magic this was. Sinking into the hypnotic lure of it.

"Is this how you get people to talk, then?" she asked, her words wispy, her hands clutching her legs and her core clenched tight. It took everything in her not to spread her thighs and invite him in. "You mess with their emotions until they start begging to tell you everything?"

"That is how this magic works, I think, yes. But it isn't mine. I use pain and nightmares, as befits my magic and personality."

"Come closer," she whispered, not able to help it, needing this ache to go away. She couldn't think like this, and she *had* to think. She had to figure out this thing with the guns. With the battle. Maybe with her life, if his knowing smirk and obvious confidence meant anything.

"Do you think that is wise?" he asked, that voice like an exfoliation treatment.

"*Please*, Daddy."

The last word had just slipped out. Maybe it was

mental warfare, on herself more than him, but it drew him in like sugar water would a hummingbird. He was in front of her in moments, the possessive dominance of him swirling powerfully around them. Her body was on fire as he leaned between her knees, pushing them wide to accommodate his big body. His lips felt like heaven and tasted like sin, consuming her as his hands made a path up her thighs. One reached between them, cupping her, rubbing firmly. The other slid over her breast, and his thumb rubbed the hard peak.

She clutched him, and then her hands were at his shirt, working his buttons as she groaned into that kiss. That scorching, incredible, consuming kiss.

"No, angel, stop," he said, capturing her hands as they worked down his bare chest and went for his pants. "Stop, Natasha. You're overwhelmed by your magic. You'll hate yourself for this."

"I don't care," she said, pulling free to go for his belt.

"No." He pushed his forehead against hers, breathing heavily, and grabbed her wrists firmly. "*I* care, little one. Stop this. There'll be plenty of time for this another day. Get your mind back on track and finish telling me about this meeting."

"Have you told Austin whatever you've surmised about me?" she asked, pulling back enough to meet his eyes, on fire, drowning in desire.

He pulled his lips to the side, that smirk so devilish. "Amazing. I'm almost compelled to answer. You're strong. You need to get a handle on this facet of your magic, Natasha. It would work so much better that way."

"What magic? What are you talking about, my energy?"

"Yes, your energy, to put it incredibly simply." He held her hands tightly so that she couldn't reach for him. Couldn't continue undressing him and escape into his body for a while. Dive headfirst into this incredible feeling between them that didn't make any sense—stronger than it had ever been with anyone, even though half the time he drove her nuts—but she didn't care to analyze that with the danger mounting around them all. She just needed a distraction right now, and he'd do.

"No," he finally said, answering her question but also responding to their mutual desire in that moment. "And that's all I'll say for now."

My reasons are my own, he'd said outside his quarters. It clearly applied here, too. He just kept collecting those secrets.

Before she could yank her hands away in irritation, he captured her lips again, this kiss long and languid.

Their fervor cooled within it, though, the aching from a moment ago subsiding into the glorious hum of energy and desire and...something else. Something that was growing like a weed. Spreading through her like a plague. Something she didn't want to think about anymore.

"Fine." She shoved him away and stood, needing air. Needing a moment. Needing a freaking lobotomy. "Back to work."

He let out a long, slow, *shaky* breath.

It was her turn to grin. At least she'd had an effect on him.

"Assuming it *is* Momar's people..." he said, finding a seat on the bench again before adjusting himself.

"Okay." She poured herself a glass of water. She needed to refocus here. She shook herself out. Damn him for making her feel this way. "Well, if it's his people, and we show up for those guns, they're not going to leave one person alive to tell the tale. Not like we do. They'll take anyone who might give them information and kill everyone else."

"And their version of getting information?"

"Will make whatever you did to that mage pale by comparison. It won't just be magic or head games, it'll be tools, and by the end, we will beg to be killed. Some of us won't get that luxury, though."

"Someone like you?"

"Specifically someone like me, yes. And if Jessie went, especially someone like her. With Momar, it isn't just death staring us in the face—it's so much worse."

CHAPTER 27

NIAMH

THE RUMBLE MADE the ground tremor. Glasses danced on the bar top. A moment later, the door to the bar exploded into the space, cleanly ripped off its hinges, and slammed into tables, spilling glasses onto the floor and driving people to the ground.

Austin Steele walked in like vengeance incarnate, his rage flooding the four walls of this posh establishment where the pack social elite, such as they were, hung out. *Wrath* had come calling.

His eyes were on fire as he stopped just inside the doorway, the glow from the street highlighting wisps of smoke or fog all around him. Or maybe that was Niamh's imagination, because his rage was such a potent thing, it *should* be visible. His gaze swept the bar, and half the people in there pissed themselves with fright while pretending this was their big moment. They'd drawn together after Indigo patched them up, probably figuring there was power in numbers. They'd reassured themselves they could take Austin Steele as a team, having collectively forgotten that his mate, a dimwitted vampire, and a magic-less mage had beaten them up and left them for garden gnomes just a handful of hours before.

That right there was enough to make you question their intelligence.

Broken Sue walked in behind Austin Steele and branched off to the side, followed by a line of shifters, all of them clearly displaying that they would not help. Trailing at the end was Indigo, her hands stuffed in the pockets of her loose jeans and her glasses pushed high on her nose. They were all there for damage control.

Jessie walked in last, her expression annoyed, of all things, her demeanor impatient.

She glanced at the door, which was lying on a broken table, before glancing around. Then she sent a sparkling bit of magic back to the open doorway, locking them in. Niamh wondered if the shifters knew that. They'd certainly heard about her doing it before when she'd met the two ladies' challenge.

"I hear you went after my mate," Austin Steele said in a growl, his presence seeming larger than life. "Shot arrows into her and dropped her from the sky. The goal? You intended to beat her within an inch of her life...to get at me." He put his arms out wide. "Well, here I am. Invitation accepted."

"You're not welcome—" James started, but Austin Steele was already moving, not bothering to shift to his polar bear form.

He raced across the bar, knocking tables out of the way, and grabbed James by the neck before he could even flinch. Austin Steele hefted the shifter with one hand before swinging him back down and bashing him against the ground. His head gave a sickening *thunk*. Austin Steele lifted him, leaving blood behind before doing it again, following that move up with punch after punch, breaking his face. With a roar, Austin Steele stood with the shifter, lifted him high, and then slammed his middle down across his knee.

"*Jaysus,* Mary, and Joseph," Niamh whispered, sitting in the far corner of the bar so she'd be plenty out of the way but get to see everything.

"He'll need healing before he dies," Austin Steele said, throwing the limp body against the magical wall. "Make the pain last as long as possible. I didn't take as long with him as I really should've."

"Lay him out," Jessie said to the shifters immediately. "All his bones need to be mostly in line for healing. Hurry. He doesn't look too good."

"He deserved it," Indigo said, slouching as she

walked slowly over to him. Niamh agreed wholeheartedly. "Are we sure these guys are worth our energy?
They started it."

Jessie, crouched next to him, said, "Aren't healers
supposed to want to fix everyone?"

"I'm not God," the other woman responded. "God
decides who lives or dies, not me. Healing is a job like
any other. Sometimes I don't want to go to work."

Jessie let out an exasperated sound. "Well, go to
work for Austin's sake, because it'll reflect poorly on
him if he kills any of these people. Plus, we need them
against Momar."

"*Fine,*" Indigo replied sullenly, putting one finger
on the guy's shoulder.

"Well?" Austin Steele said to the pack members,
kicking a table out of the way. It slid across the ground,
knocking over the chairs sitting beside it before smashing against another table by the wall, scattering the
people who were sitting there. "I thought you were
supposed to come at me as a pack? Wasn't that your
plan?"

He spread his arms wide again, walking toward the
shifters who'd backed James, their faces suddenly drawn
and eyes cagey. They held a grudge against Austin
Steele, but they'd clearly forgotten the viciousness by
which he'd earned his reputation. A reputation he'd

doubled down on in O'Briens at the beginning, using his savagery to help the people there. A reputation he was earning again as an alpha of his territory—brutal when it came to protecting those under his leadership.

Now, he was showing these muppets he'd protect his mate against anyone, ever, thinking it was a good idea to go after her.

"You can come to me, or I can go to you," he growled, his face downturned a bit, his eyes otherworldly. Terrifying. "But whatever happens, you aren't leaving this building until you face me."

Three of the more courageous shifters raced forward. They reached him in snarls. Shifters behind them turned into their animals, utter idiots. The last thing they should want was Austin Steele going polar bear. Facing him in his human form, they at least had some kind of a chance.

Austin Steele met all three shifters at the same time, taking a punch while grabbing two throats and bashing the heads that went with them together so hard their skulls cracked.

"Crap," Ulric said, standing behind Niamh in the corner. Jasper and a few of the gargoyles were there, too, the smaller ones whom the shifters wouldn't be wary of. Phil hadn't been allowed in, which had made him very prickly. "They need healing. I'll drag them over. Jasper, help me."

"I'm with Indigo. They made their bed," Jasper said, not budging. "Let 'em rot in it."

"Take 'em over," Niamh said, seeing Jessie stand out of her crouch, her expression troubled. "Otherwise Jessie will pull Austin Steele away, and he's just getting going."

"*Fine,*" Jasper said, mimicking Indigo. Niamh had to admit, the healer's reluctance to help certain people was downright hilarious.

Austin Steele punched the third shifter in the sternum, making him suck in a surprised wheeze and clutch his chest. Then he stomped on the backs of the others before Ulric and Jasper could get to them, the resulting cracks so incredibly brutal, before grabbing the paused shifter by the throat and nuts and lifting him above his head. He threw the man at the emerging wolves, knocking them to the side before he sprinted at them, all fists and rage and power and strength. He worked through that crowd like a falling star, ripping and gouging, tearing and pummeling.

Ulric and Jasper jogged into the fray, not at all concerned that Austin Steele would mistake them for enemies. That fact went a long way to show that this alpha's people weren't afraid of his anger. He was in enough control to know whom to attack and whom to leave alone.

The last three standing ran in a blind panic, trying a side door, screaming at Jessie to let them out. Bruce was one of them.

Austin Steele walked up behind them, blood splattered across his white T-shirt. Niamh reckoned that not an ounce of it was his own. He was breathing heavily but showing no other signs of fatigue. He'd always kept in great shape, but Ivy House had given him the stamina of youth.

The three shifters turned as though the boogeyman were right behind them, their expressions terrified.

"You two." He pointed at a man and woman Niamh didn't know. "I don't know you, and you weren't involved in the attack on my mate. If you apologize for joining this half-assed attempt to dominate me, I'll let you go."

They all apologized, Bruce the loudest, pleading to be left in one piece.

Austin Steele motioned the couple out of the way.

"Not you," he growled at Bruce, taking another step closer. "I remember you from when I was here before. I never understood my brother's decision to elevate you, but then, I've never given someone more than one chance to mess up. The alpha is a lot more patient than I am. I have benefited from that patience. You have not.

You made grave errors, the least of which was going after my mate. While I'd love nothing more than to rip your throat out, I'm not going to."

"Thank you, alpha," Bruce said, falling back against the magic closing in the doorway. "It was all James, I swear it. He was the one leading all of this. What was I going to say, no? He's the beta."

Austin Steele tensed, and anger rose once again through the bonds. Instead of braining the guy like he clearly wanted to do, he took a step back.

"Brochan, have at him."

"What?" Bruce said, his eyes rounding again. "W-wait—"

"Well, *this* is an interesting turn of events," Niamh murmured as Ulric came jogging back.

"*This* isn't going to go well," he said, putting his hand on the edge of the bar.

"Would ye get out of me way? I can't see!" Niamh gave him a shove.

Bruce wiped his sleeve across his nose before straightening a little, watching Broken Sue step away from the rest of the shifters. As he passed Austin Steele, the alpha stopped him with a hand on his shoulder.

"He can be healed if needed; he can be killed if you want; he can be spared if that's your intention," Austin Steele said. "He challenged you at that meeting. This is in your hands."

"And if he is spared?" Broken Sue murmured.

"I'll stow the body bag I brought and act like I expected it."

"Oh crap," Ulric whispered.

"Oh, lads," Niamh whispered just as softly, leaning forward in her seat with what probably looked like a manic grin. "That lad is just about to get a *baytin*."

"*Broken Sue*, is that what they call you?" Bruce said, rolling his head a little, readying for the fight. He probably figured Brochan would be an easier tussle than Austin Steele. And while he was right, he was still on the wrong end of the power scale to be able to save himself. "Broken, I get," the idiot sneered. "Like your old pack. Too proud to ask for help and they all died, huh? And you called yourself an alpha?"

"What the hell is he doing?" Ulric murmured as Jasper hurried to stand to Ulric's other side.

"False bravado," Jasper whispered. "He's trying to build himself up because he's got no way out. He doesn't want to look like a coward while he's secretly pissing his pants. Bet you anything."

"I'm not taking that bet," Ulric said.

Broken Sue rounded a table, not throwing it out of the way like Niamh would've preferred. That would've been more cinematic, at least.

"But *Sue*?" Bruce huffed. "Like a whining little girl?"

"If he doesn't kill him, that comment gives me the right," Niamh said.

"It's been a long time since you were a girl," Jasper said.

"I might look like four hundred, but I feel like a spritely two hundred, and I'll make sure to *bate* your head in after I'm done with that muppet, how's that?"

"You're going to be the one in need of false bravado if you keep talking," Ulric muttered to Jasper.

"Yeah, they call me Sue." Broken Sue stopped in front of the other man, his body loose, his size enormous in comparison. "How do you do?" he growled.

Shivers ran up Niamh's arms as Jasper whispered the Johnny Cash lyrics, *"Now you're gunna die…"*

Broken Sue closed the distance in a couple of steps, his hands down, his power pulsing. Bruce took a swing, then another. Broken Sue leaned back just slightly, letting the first would-be blow barely miss him, and ducked beneath a second. *Then* he engaged.

He hit the other man in the stomach, twice, before stepping back and issuing a clean hit to his face. Next an uppercut. He paused, hands down again, and waited for Bruce to swing and miss before he jabbed, twice, three times, and then hit him with a roundhouse.

"My boy can box," Jasper said, clearly riveted.

"He didn't put his weight behind that last one, though," Ulric said, watching as Broken Sue stood flatfooted in front of the other man, willing Bruce to throw those punches. None of them landed, but still the other man tried.

"Wait for it," Niamh said.

More swings. More misses. Broken Sue jabbed, threw in another uppercut. Bruce bled from multiple areas. One eye started to swell, and his lips were the size of beanbags.

With a last miss, the shifter issued a mangled roar of pain and frustration and launched for Broken Sue.

It was like a switch had been flicked. Gone was the boxer with the perfect technique. In came the street-fighting brawler.

Broken Sue launched himself as well, hitting Bruce midair. His larger body drove the other shifter back, slamming against the magical barrier covering the door, and now his fists pummeled the other man. Into Bruce's ribs they railed, his stomach, his head. Broken Sue was getting out his aggression, clearly. His pain. His past.

He picked up the other man by the shirt and slammed him against the divide. Again. Bruce's head thunked. His arms flailed weakly.

With a roar, Broken Sue dropped the other man and, as he was falling, ripped out his throat.

"Holy—!" Jasper bent forward with his fist over his mouth, his eyes wide, his hand grabbing Ulric's shoulder.

"Ah well, he won't be needing a healer, so," Niamh said, a little giddy from the sheer brutality of this night. It was like the old days when she'd gone drinking with her family and other pucas, and one of them would either start or join a bar fight. They always seemed to end about the same way.

"Note to self, do not challenge Broken Sue," Ulric murmured, sounding winded even though he hadn't done anything.

"You need to make a note about that?" Jasper asked in disbelief.

"A joke isn't funny if you have to explain it."

Broken Sue stood over the other man for a moment, looking down, panting. His hands dripped blood, his shoulders were hunched, and he looked for all the world like the man who'd earned the name Broken and chosen the name Brochan, meaning one and the same.

"Go over there," Niamh said, shoving at Ulric. "He needs a hand out of whatever ditch his mind has fallen into."

But Indigo was already halfway there, drifting as though being pulled, stopping near him and looking up at his face. She didn't say a word, just put her hand over his heart.

He flinched but didn't pull away.

"It hurts," Indigo said, lowering her head a little, looking up at him through her eyelashes. "I can feel how much it hurts. I am sorry for your loss."

Broken Sue's face, always so good at holding a blank expression, crumpled, grief etched deeply in the lines around his eyes and mouth. He took a ragged breath, and then the magic from the door was gone and Jessie was ushering him out of the bar. She always knew how to take care of her people. It was like a sixth sense. Niamh didn't know if it was the gargoyle in her or the person, but she was thankful Jessie had such a gift.

"I just teared up a little," Jasper said heavily. He turned to Ulric and pointed at his left eye. "Look, see? Do you see that tear?"

"Would ye stop bein' a clown?" Niamh shook her head and turned back to her drink, her own shriveled, blackened heart hurting for Broken Sue as well. What a burden to have to carry around. Maybe Indigo could help. She certainly seemed to understand what to do and say to get through to that hard former alpha. Speaking of which, where was Nessa with her sunshine?

"Bittersweet." Ulric took the stool next to Niamh. The former occupant was some chatty wolf shifter who'd clearly legged it at some stage. Niamh hadn't passed any remarks as to when. "What a freaking show. *Phew.* Remind me never to get on Austin Steele's bad side."

"Why would you need a reminder?" Jasper asked, sitting down with them. The whole bar had cleared to the sides. Niamh had been too engrossed to notice or care.

Ulric turned to him. "Is it your goal in life to sound as stupid as humanly possible?"

"Yes. How'm I doing?"

"Very fine indeed, sir." Ulric turned back, looking for the bartender as Niamh's phone vibrated.

Three missed calls. Tristan. He probably wanted to know how the fight had gone.

Since the bar hadn't been set to rights yet and the bartender clearly wasn't sure what to do about the carnage, Niamh figured the *faux pas* of talking on the phone could be tolerated. She tapped Tristan's name and waited for him to pick up as Ulric and Jasper chatted.

"Hey," Tristan answered, and it sounded like he was on the move.

"Ye missed a helluva show, boy."

"I'll look forward to the highlights. I need to talk to you. It's about that weapons pickup. Natasha got some information, and I want to talk through it before I approach the alphas."

From his brusque, no-nonsense tone, Niamh knew it was not good news.

"Where?" she asked.

"A busy bar—loud, preferably, where everyone is too busy talking to listen."

"Sure, sure. Give me twenty. I need to change locations. I'll give ye a holler once I've landed."

She tapped off the phone and pushed off her stool.

"Where are you going?" Ulric asked.

"Away from yer terrible jokes." She walked out of the bar, ignoring the people being healed, working on calming down her adrenaline and getting her game face on.

If Nessa didn't see a clear way forward, it meant that the situation was extremely complex and dangerous.

If Tristan was calling her about it, it meant he wasn't sure the risk was worth the possible reward. Jessie and Austin Steele were allowing that gargoyle-monster to spread his wings and display all his very useful skills, something the cairn he'd previously been in had obviously never needed or allowed. It was just as clear he wasn't yet sure where the line was, probably because it kept moving. It was also clear that he knew Niamh could tell him exactly how hard to push said line.

All this boiled down to one thing: with big risks came great rewards. They just needed the iron tits to reach for them.

CHAPTER 28

JESSIE

"**D**O YOU HEAR what I am telling you?" Nessa asked me, two days after she, Niamh, and Tristan had sat down with Austin and me to go over all the pros and cons of taking this meetup to get the guns. "You can walk away from this. It won't matter at all. We don't absolutely *need* these guns. Sebastian thinks our numbers are good. This is a risk we don't have to take."

"I understand," I said.

They'd gone on to talk about the risks and a ton of stuff that didn't really seem to matter. Because the second I heard who might be behind this situation— likely one of Momar's mages—something had come over me, a sort of confidence that I wouldn't bother trying to understand. Nothing, absolutely nothing, was going to stop me from going to that meetup.

The kicker was, I didn't even know why. I didn't know what I ultimately hoped to accomplish. I just had a feeling that this meeting was incredibly necessary for some reason. My primitive gargoyle instincts told me so.

Also…I was done with Momar calling the shots.

And if it wasn't Momar's people? Well…I'd give them a heartfelt apology and probably coach them through the shock of having seen my wild side.

Now, we were approaching a lonely shack on the outskirts of a run-down town two hours from the pack's territory in vans we'd rented. "We do not want to expose the gargoyles' power to blend in," Nessa said as everyone stepped out of the vans.

The sellers would be going in through the back. We were relegated to the front. The number of people we could bring had been defined, as well as the number of people who'd actually be allowed into the establishment.

We'd brought quite a few more than that defined number. Nessa figured the other side would do the same.

"The gargoyles will walk in with us in a V," she continued as I met Austin at the hood of the first van. "You will not bring in any of your crew except Nathanial, since he's as big as a guardian. The rest will wait outside in case the seller has too many people in the building. If that is the case, it is a violation of the agreement, and we'll know they mean us harm. You'll call in your crew and all hell will break loose."

"I know," I said, having heard all of this before.

"Remember, and this is very important," Nessa said, stopping me from heading to the front door. The gargoyles who'd be going inside with me were already waiting there. More were pressed against the house, ready to step out in case there was trouble. No revealing potion could be used to see them. Still more reinforcements soared high above us, lost to the night. "If they're using an invisibility potion—also against the agreement—and it is powerful, you must pretend *not* to see it. We don't want them to know our revealing potion is more powerful than their invisibility potion. And why is that?"

"Because they'll know we have more power than their most powerful person, presuming their most powerful person made the potion. I know this, Nessa."

"You've heard it before, yes," she replied, "but you never seemed to be listening, and I don't think you realize how pear-shaped this might go. If this is the worst-case scenario, they will be looking to capture. If they can't capture, they will kill. In that case, no one is getting out alive."

"That's not a problem we need to worry about," I responded, my magic throbbing, my confidence at an all-time high. Again, I had no idea why. This just felt so natural for reasons I couldn't explain.

Austin watched me for a long beat before minutely nodding. He'd be waiting outside. Someone would need to rescue me if they got grabby and managed to capture me.

"I got her, brother." Gerard put his hand on Austin's shoulder. "We'll watch out for her."

He'd be leading his guardians and Tristan would be leading ours—a bit overkill, since each would only have three gargoyles to look after, but whatever.

Austin didn't respond, not hiding his frustrated emotions from our bonds. He hated this whole situation. He didn't think the risks were worthwhile and hated the danger I was about to face. But these mages would be more powerful than the others we'd encountered. They might know something valuable.

Basajaunak lingered in the trees, also hidden from revealing potions. Only Dave would go inside, and only then if something went wrong.

Nessa tucked her laptop under her arm. She'd use that to make the money exchange, presuming her contacts actually brought the guns. It was nowhere near as cool as a bag full of money.

"Be tough," she coached as we walked toward the front door. "Don't shy away from being weird. Mages get really cagey when someone is being too weird."

"I'm wearing a purple muumuu and so are all the gargoyles. If my crew enters, Edgar has on a bicycle helmet and Cyra is wearing a sparkly fake wig that she got from a kid's birthday party she wasn't invited to. Niamh is drinking a beer from a can in a koozie that says 'tits' on it."

"Yes. All that is certainly a good start."

We paused outside the front door. I didn't hear a sound from inside. This place *should* be a big room, apparently the interior walls having been mostly knocked down for whatever reason. The details had been listed with the meetup location. There was probably just as much danger of the place falling down around us as being destroyed in a magical shootout. Filtered light bled through the cracks in the wall like lanterns. This place wouldn't have electricity.

"I've never done something like this without Sebastian," she murmured, chewing on her lip as she checked her simple, plain-faced watch with an equally simple brown leather strap. "He always knows what to do if a magical fight kicks off. I'm more of the background girl."

"And they can probably hear us through the door." I put my hand on her shoulder. "Don't worry. I might not be as experienced as him, but I am one hundred times more aggressive. We're going to be okay."

"Why are you so confident about this?"

"I have no idea." I reached for the door as the gargoyles organized themselves around me, Tristan behind me and to my left and Gerard to my right. Nessa stood more or less beside me, shaking herself out as if to dislodge her nervousness.

To hell with it, let's get this done, I thought.

"That's my girl," Ivy House responded.

Wings fluttered as I opened the door, and soft light flickered in the strangely shaped room. A half wall existed to my far right, with another ahead and a third to the left. That one had random boards sticking up out of it and debris at the base. The floor had been swept in the center, where a long, shiny banquet table held an array of guns, with more in crates in the far right corner.

At least they'd brought the weapons.

A man in a pristinely tailored black suit stood behind the table, with one sleeve a tiny bit shorter than the other so as to display the gold and silver watch on his wrist. There was no magical interruption of his image, meaning he hadn't taken any sort of potion. Eight people with similar suits and watches were pushed to the sides of the room, making room for the six invisible guys with distorted bodies and fuzzy faces, their invisibility potions so powerful that the revealing potion Sebastian and I had cooked up barely unmasked them.

That was not great news. It meant they had some serious power in their organization. Either one person had more power than I did, and almost as much as Sebastian and I put together, or they were fluent in working together, something Sebastian had always said was rare with mages.

A ways behind the mages—all guys—and past stubs of walls, another guy waited at the back door, also using the invisibility potion. I couldn't make out his face, but he held himself with arrogant importance and his watch was a lot shinier than the suit guy's. He had to be the highest-powered mage in this outfit, but he was clearly too cowardly to be the front man.

I kicked off my flip-flops before meeting the visible man at the table.

"Put 'er there, bud." I stuck out my hand for a shake.

His brow pinched, and he looked down at my hand in sudden uncertainty. I could do *weird* in my sleep.

"So what've ya got for me?" I tapped one of the guns lying in front of him. "Do these work?"

"Um…" He cleared his throat. "I wanted to explain why we bought out the contract—"

"Nah." I waved it away as I stepped back, sending a

gush of warning through the Ivy House bonds. My crew would know that meant to assemble by the door and wait for my magical signal.

I pulled my muumuu over my head, exposing my body to them, and pretended to get it stuck on my hair.

"She'd never make it as a stripper, am I right?" Nessa chuckled nervously, playing along.

I yanked the rest of it away, feeling the readiness of my crew.

"There now." I gave the lead guy a thumbs-up.

His eyes were rounded in his suddenly pale face.

I gestured to the guys around me, who quickly tossed their muumuus away.

"Perfect specimens, right?" I said, my power pumping. "Now, let's get down to the brass tacks, shall we?" I waggled my finger at him, and then shifted my gaze to the guy at the back. "You brought too many people."

Nathanial, a master at anticipating my movements in battle, darted forward as I started to run. He shoved the table out of the way, and I slammed into the visible guy who'd frozen at my nudity, giving me a clear shot forward. I sent out a peal of magic to bring in my crew and alert the basajaunak and gargoyles around the shanty that there was tomfoolery afoot. If there were any mages outside, they'd grab them. If anyone escaped this room, they'd need to grab them, too.

But no one was going to escape.

I flung my hand forward, erecting a wall to keep that mage at the back from leaving. He might've had some clout, but I didn't think for a second he was the one responsible for the invisibility potion. No one that strong would be endangered in this way.

The invisible mages in my way all startled in one way or other, only one of them quickly pulling up his hands to shoot off a spell. I deflected it just before I shifted, my gargoyle bursting forth in a flurry of claws and teeth. I scraped another guy as the door behind me burst open. Dave's roar drowned out all other sound, followed by screams from three of the mages, two of them invisible. They threw their hands over their heads and cowered.

Their potion didn't deaden sound. That was something. They might have the power, but they didn't have Sebastian's ingenuity. Hopefully there would be more instances of that in our battle.

Another shot of magic came at me from the left. I threw up a shield, my focus on the mage at the back, currently working on the spell I was using to imprison him. My spell wasn't complex—that was the bad news. If he worked at it enough, he'd be able to get through it. I needed to get to him before that.

More roars sounded behind me as the other gargoyles shifted. A mage lifted out of his crouch in front of me, shaking, ready to defend himself.

Too late.

I slammed into him, scoring him with my claws. I dug down deep and then ripped outward, taking flesh and bone with me. His wail of agony ended quickly as his body hit the ground.

One of the other visible mages lifted his hands. Gerard was there in a moment, grabbing him up and biting into his neck. Blood spurted, quickly turning the situation grisly.

More mages started screaming as the gargoyles worked through them, taking the hits of magic if there were any but mostly finding terrified people cowering from monsters.

The head mage continued to pound against my wall of magic. The door behind it opened. They'd clearly kept some mages outside too. Another mage stood behind him, both of them trying to help my target escape. With three of them, that spell would be history in no time.

I put on a burst of speed, but I was slow on the ground in this form, and there were too many people and too much clutter for me to fly.

A large, hairy shape suddenly loomed behind the rescue team. Then two more. Their combined roars

K . F .   B R E E N E

thundered through the space. The rescue team screamed and turned before screaming louder, throwing up their arms to protect themselves.

The basajaunak grabbed the mages, and my target gasped and stepped back, terrified. I was on him a moment later, ripping him away from the door. My punches were clumsy, though. I wasn't really used to fighting this way in this form, and the gouges I accidentally dealt were proof of that.

"Got... 'im," Tristan said, lifting the mage easily and slamming him against my magic. He cracked right through, though, as the spell was grossly weakened from the various mages' efforts to get it down. The mage hit the back wall awkwardly, thunked his head really hard, and then went limp. That would work, too.

Austin appeared at the back door a moment later, pulling it wide and stepping through. He was nude, dirt on his chest and his eyes wild. He'd been chasing mages outside, obviously.

The pandemonium in the room was slowing, bodies on the ground and a couple of mages in little balls in the corner, shrieking and covering their heads. We'd left some alive and dispatched the rest, as per our worst-case scenario playbook.

I shifted to my human form, grabbing a muumuu off the floor at random. "How are we looking?"

"Well..." Nessa stood from the crates by the wall, glancing around. "That was probably the fastest, most effective worse-case scenario I've ever seen in my life. Sebastian has said it a million times, but wow, mages sure are terrified of shifting creatures. Half of them never got one shot off. Not one. The other half were totally ineffective. Did the bigwig at the back do any damage?"

"No. He was too busy trying to get through my spell at the back. The basajaunak showed up shortly after his rescue party, thankfully."

"I didn't get to do anything," Cyra said with a pout, still wearing her disco-style wig. "Hollace shoved me out of the way, and then everyone got in before me."

"Serves you right for trying to cut." Hollace grinned at her. "I got this one." He nudged a downed mage with his foot. "His spell singed my muumuu, though." He pulled the front of the purple cloth wide, revealing the hole and his charred clothes beneath.

"Are you wearing a muumuu over jeans?" Ulric asked as he pulled on a muumuu that was ridiculously too big for him. Judging by the too-tight muumuu on another guardian, they'd swapped.

"Yeah." Hollace dropped the fabric. "I can't really shift in this setting, so I figured the muumuu was just for show."

K.F. BREENE

"Right, but...why not just wear that instead of doubling up on clothes?"

Hollace frowned at him. "It's nippy. The muumuus are too airy."

"I like them," Cyra said, checking the mages on the ground and then picking up a gun. "This is—"

A blast of light shot out, as if it were a weapon from a *Star Wars* movie. It narrowly missed Dave and punched through the wall.

"Someone take that away from her," Jasper shouted, giving her more space.

"Wise." Cyra set it down slowly.

"What's the plan?" Austin said, walking to the middle of the room as the gargoyles started clearing away mages.

"Nessa, you're going to lead a team to...deal with all of this, right?" I asked as everyone regained human shape and muumuus.

"Jasper and Ulric have weapons detail," Nessa said, stepping away from them. "Looks like they're in decent shape. Momar's people weren't interested in those—they were interested in us."

"So it was definitely his people?" Austin asked.

"Without a shadow of a doubt, yes, but let's make super sure." Nessa crossed the room to my knocked-out target and knelt down. She took up his watch, studying

486

the face. "Yeah. A symbol next to the number four. He's the leader of a field crew, obviously, but without a magnifying glass and a blacklight, I can't make out the symbol or if there are any secret identifying factors. We can work all that out later. We'll take him and the two others to the warehouse. Tristan's with me, Sebastian will meet us there, and...Niamh and Edgar should come. Oh, Dave might be helpful."

"What about me, what about me?" Cyra lifted her hand, practically hopping from foot to foot.

"Sure." Nessa shrugged. "You're unpredictable enough. Keep the wig."

"Don't make a big show of it," I told her, having been assured the night before that I wouldn't be needed for any interrogations. The most useful spell I had—the nightmare one—could be done more efficiently by Tristan. "Get the information you need and call it a day. Don't let Cyra and Dave compete for who is better at doing terrible things."

"She is seriously zero fun," Cyra murmured to Hollace.

"Zero," Dave said from across the room, not even pretending to whisper.

"The rest?" Gerard asked, his hair wild and his eyes shining. Gargoyles did love to get their hands dirty.

"We'll handle that," Nessa said with a pointed look

at Niamh.

"Yeah sure," Niamh said, finishing her beer. It looked like she hadn't done much more than step into the space. "There's plenty of land out there for unmarked graves. Or did ye think we should send parts o'them to Momar for a little howdy-do?"

Nessa's brow rose. "I like the way you think—"

"I'm out." I put up a peace sign and turned for the door. While I was fine with doing cringy things in the heat of battle, I wasn't so eager for what came afterward. It was hard to eradicate some of my more Jane sensibilities. Besides, when I got carried away, I became worse than anyone else. It was best just to let the experts handle it.

"Home?" Austin asked as we headed for the door.

"Yeah..." I stalled outside, looking back. "Is no one else coming?"

He put his hand on my shoulder. "I get the feeling they want to see this through. We've been training for a solid couple of weeks now, and people are wound up. These are all battle species, and they just confronted their enemy. Let them relish in their victory."

I couldn't argue with that.

He was quiet on the ride home, unnaturally so. I could sense the tension coiled within him.

"You okay?" I asked softly.

He didn't answer for a long moment. "When you first got involved in magic, I had to play rescue party on more than one occasion. You were taken from me, and I worried I might not get you back."

I felt my brow lifting. "That didn't happen here."

"No, it didn't. We have a lot of assets at our disposal that those mages don't know about. We're also incredibly well prepared and have insider guidance from some of the best in the game. We of course always suspected Elliot Graves—and the Captain—knew their business, but we're getting proof." Another silent beat. "We're fools to think that Momar won't get wise to us, though. Meetings won't always be this easy, especially when the control is all in the hands of the mages—at dinners or banquets, heavily organized meetings, what have you. The basajaunak won't always have trees to blend into, and if given enough opportunity, the mages might develop magic to see gargoyles near buildings. Or they'll learn they can just use a heat map."

I furrowed my brow. "What are you getting at?"

"I can handle many things, Jacinta, but I cannot handle offering you as bait for something like this. Not given the way we know they treat captives. It would destroy me if I lost you. If they took you. This is not a setup I will allow in the future. I will handle any situations like this, or we won't take the risk."

I put my hand on his thigh, counting to ten before I responded. This was his fear talking. I needed to respect his emotional state. But man, I was still geared up for battle. That situation had almost ended before it started, not giving me a chance to release all my adrenaline.

I gave his leg a gentle squeeze. "I had to rescue you once, too, remember? I get how hard it is to be on the outside. But Austin, we're at war, and the enemy plays dirty. There are always going to be risks. All we can do is prepare to the best of our ability. We had a swarm of fliers in the sky. We had basajaunak and gargoyles outside, waiting for something to go wrong. We had *you* out there. We were prepared. I guarantee there was zero actual threat in that room, and even if our revealing potions hadn't worked, our people have trained to feel presences. One day, sure, we might be caught unprepared. But we *do* have insider intel from mages who excel at playing in the shadows, and they're helping us keep as many secrets as we can. Until mages in general know more about us, we have an edge. Other than that, we need to be each other's fail-safe. Asking me to step back from this sort of thing isn't a solution."

He adjusted in his seat, not liking that explanation. "I'm rethinking having you as a co-leader. If you weren't in a leadership role, I wouldn't have to fight with you about this."

"Are we fighting?"

"Yes."

I nodded slowly. "I like your version of fighting. You're very calm about it."

"That's only because you're spinning a lot of logic right now. But take my word for it, I am going to anger-bang you as soon as we get home."

I rested my head on the seatback. "And I'm going to enjoy it out of spite."

CHAPTER 29

AUSTIN

J ESS'S PHONE TRILLED as they neared Kingsley's territory, with Austin slowing to travel through the nearest border town. Her face lit as she looked down at the screen, her eyes still shining and her magic softly pumping through the van.

It felt incredible, that magic, sliding against his heated skin and soaking down into his middle. It tantalized him, promising him more power if he gave in and accepted its counterpart. Promising him a closer connection with her and an enhanced ability to protect her. He didn't feel the dreaded darkness of it anymore, threatening to ruin him. To turn him wilder than he already was. He wasn't sure if that was because he trusted her to pull him back from the verge, just like he'd do for her, or because they'd made peace with themselves.

"Oh my—" She pulled the phone up closer to her

face. "Oh no," she said softly, in a tone reserved for her reactions to Edgar's messes.

"What is it?"

She shook her head, swiping across the screen. "Nessa sent me pictures of Edgar's setup in the warehouse."

"Grotesque?"

"I mean…it depends? He chose a dark corner in the back, it looks like, and then made flowers out of papier-mâché to drape all around it. There's a couple scattered, off-kilter doilies and then…like…a bunch of random decorations propped around the place. But the decorations aren't right." She tilted her head. "Some of them look like heads on spikes. And then there's a canopy of sorts made out of streamers. But he cut and tore the streamers so they kinda look like…entrails." She grimaced. "Something's not right with that vampire."

"Why didn't he clean up when they decided not to grab the mages in town?"

"I don't know. Nessa said the mages are already incredibly nervous. Which is a good thing. They don't like weird, and they walked into…one of Edgar's creations. So… Oh, and the garhette who dropped Sebastian off at the warehouse decided to stay awhile. Get this—she thinks she could win the competition for scariest torturer." Jess shook her head in dismay. "She didn't even bat an eye at them getting ready to extract information. Like...who are these freaking people, you know? I don't understand them. They make an art out of incredible violence."

"Magical beings can be truly vicious, especially when put in situations like this. Where'd she get the car?"

"Borrowed it, stole it, I don't know. Well. I guess the mages don't own the monopoly on being terrible. Give some of these people a green light, and they really run with it."

Austin rolled onto the pack's land, the joy at being home and close to family tainted by his reception over the last couple of weeks. He'd hoped coming back with a mate and a pack, somewhat well adjusted and with a good head on his shoulders, would show people he'd changed. He'd hoped it might prove how much he'd grown and evolved.

Now, he knew it would never happen. He still had some friends here, but even they were once again wary of him.

It wasn't the fact that he'd answered the challenge the other day—that had been his right—but *how* he'd answered it. His wild, vicious, seemingly uncontrolled power set people on edge. They viewed him as a feral animal, one who might seem house-trained...until he killed everyone in sight.

The realization hurt his heart, especially since he knew it would never change here. His perception among these people had been carved into stone years ago.

"You okay?" Jess asked for the second time that night.

"Yeah." But he didn't have a chance to elaborate.

Kingsley's black Range Rover waited in Austin's driveway.

His brother hadn't said much to him in the last few days, since shortly before the attack on Jess. They had worked in unison to train their people, but they'd gone their separate ways after each day's training. Austin knew Kingsley was mulling things over before approaching him. That had always been his way.

This was him approaching.

Kingsley waited in the living room with Aurora, Mac, and Mimi, and all of them quieted down when Austin and Jess entered the room. Kingsley picked up the remote and turned off the TV.

"Hey, guys, how goes it?" Jess asked brightly. "Mimi, it's been a second. I've had to think for myself. It's awful." She put her hands to her hips before remembering she wore a purple muumuu. "Uhm…let me just go…put something decent on."

Austin had on sports sweats and a T-shirt, so he didn't bother changing, instead taking the recliner at the edge of the kinda oblong room. He'd always found the layout of this house a little strange.

"I didn't get an invite to the party," Austin said to break the ice.

"Wait." Aurora lifted a finger and looked at Mimi. "Did she just call you Mimi?"

"I heard that, too. I thought I was hallucinating for a second," Mac said.

Mimi lifted her eyebrows. "So?"

"You let her call you Mimi?" Aurora pushed. "You won't let Mom call you Mimi, and Mom and Dad have been mated forever."

"Your mother and I have an understanding," Mimi said.

"Which is?" Mac asked.

"That we stay out of each other's way and try not to talk to each other. My relationship with Jessie is much different."

Aurora gave Mac a *look*.

"Mom is going to be livid that Auntie Jessie is Grandma Mimi's favorite," he whispered with a grin.

"If you value your life and my sanity, do not tell your mother," Kingsley replied as Jess came back in, a little out of breath from hurrying and dressed in jeans and a T-shirt.

"Sorry. Who wants a drink? Anyone?" Jess asked. "I think we have some snacks, too."

"Yeah, I'll take a beer," Kingsley said.

"Water for me, Jessie." Mimi stood. "Here, I'll help you."

"Kids, go help them." Kingsley gestured them on.

"I think they can handle—"

Aurora knocked Mac on the side of the head. "That means he wants a second alone with Uncle Auzzie, idiot."

"Why are you so violent?" Mac rubbed his head as he stood.

"Because I'm a shifter?"

"That doesn't explain it."

Aurora gave Austin a sideways glance as she passed. Her gaze was calm but with a little sparkle, like back when she was a kid. Inviting, not hostile. The animosity from the other night was entirely absent.

His heart swelled, hopeful. He hadn't had a chance to seek her out, what with everything that had been going on. He also didn't know if she wanted him to. But this gave him hope that maybe he hadn't messed up so badly that he'd lost his buddy forever. He badly wanted to make things right between them. With all of his family.

"Before we get into the other stuff…" Kingsley pulled his ankle from his knee and leaned forward a little. "I want to apologize. I've had my current hierarchy in place for some time, as you remember. They have their issues, but for the most part, they are loyal and they do their jobs."

"I know."

"I knew there was still animosity between them and you. I'm ashamed to say I turned a blind eye to it. But your mate said something that…hit home."

Austin wondered what Jess had said, and when. She hadn't mentioned it.

"I should've cleared this up with them before you came here," Kingsley went on. "Given I didn't, I should've stepped in after your arrival. And I never, *ever* should've given them enough room to attack your mate. Please believe I had no idea they planned to go to such extremes. I thought they might challenge you, but I wasn't worried because I knew you'd be fine. I didn't…"

"I know," Austin told him again. "We talked about this, remember? You gave me leave to handle it."

Kingsley shook his head, leaning back again. "Handle it by answering their challenge."

"I did answer their challenge. Jess and I both did."

Kingsley ran his fingers through his hair, more expressive than he usually was, even with family.

Something had really been troubling him.

"I haven't been much of a big brother," he finally said. "After…our challenge way back when, I shouldn't have left you to find your own way. I didn't shield you from the other members of the pack or from Mom's fears about your becoming like Dad. You were forced to learn how to survive long before you left this pack. I understand why you had to leave like you did. I apologize for the part that I played."

Austin stared at his brother, no idea what to say. Heaviness lodged in his chest, and it felt like he was trying to swallow a golf ball.

"Kingsley, I—"

Kingsley held up his hand. "Let's just leave it at that."

"No," Austin replied. "You're out of your mind if you think I'll let you take blame. You should've thrown me out on my ass after our challenge. Your patience and willingness to teach and guide me even after what I did to you and your family… You went above and beyond. I take full responsibility for everything that happened in the past. You were there for me more than you can possibly comprehend." Now it was his turn to run his fingers through his hair. "You've made me the alpha I am today. I owe you everything."

Kingsley stared at his knees for a while. "I appreciate your saying that."

"*Now* we can leave it at that, because I'm not fond of gushing."

Kingsley smiled a little but sobered quickly. "Mom, though... She—"

"Nah. It's fine. Leave it, seriously." Austin leaned back and got comfortable. "We talked, she and I. She's got her reasons for questioning me, and I understand that. I found my balance, though. I found a mate who pulls me back from the brink."

"Bullshit," Kingsley said softly, shaking his head. "I saw the camera footage from that bar. She didn't pull you anywhere—she just cleaned up after you."

"Well...in that instance...yeah. I would've stayed a little more in control if she hadn't been there, honestly, but she insisted on coming. I felt like I could go a little crazy as long as I didn't outright kill anyone."

"It was your right to kill them, though I'm glad you didn't. Mostly didn't, anyway."

"I know. They are your top people. I gave Brochan license to deal with Bruce as he saw fit, because that waste of a shifter had earned his punishment a couple of times over."

"Yeah." Kingsley leaned forward again. "This is the part where the student outdoes the teacher. I've been thinking a lot about my pack over the last few days. I've been measuring my people against yours in training. I need to make some changes."

"They are loyal to you."

"And that's what blinded me, I think. That and…we aren't usually tested. The pack, I mean. My people. Either we are helping lesser packs by taking down bad leadership, which they handle to the letter, or we're meeting with packs at a similar power level and everyone is on their best behavior because we each need something. I haven't seen much of their true colors."

"Maybe it's just their reaction to me and our history."

"Maybe. But Jessie won't let you skulk away in the middle of the night again, so unless my family falls out with her, we're going to be in each other's lives. I need my people to understand that and be okay with it."

Austin stayed very still, feeling something hard and painful finally releasing inside of him after all these years. Gratitude filled that ragged hole, and a shiver ran through him. He nodded quietly, his emotions nearly overflowing.

"You've lost your grip on hiding your emotions, brother," Kingsley said, shaking his head with a grin. "It's making me a little uncomfortable."

"Your timing, as always, is perfect. I was just realizing on the ride back that I don't fit in with this pack. I haven't for a long time. I'm too wild for this place. Too volatile. I make people nervous. It's...a shock to hear you say all this. I wasn't expecting it."

"You've always made the people here nervous. Always. This is Mimi's pack, after all, and she's mostly levelheaded. Mom too. I'm like them. This is the way it always should've ended up, I think. I hold down the fort here, and you rise to create some crazy freaking situation with all manner of strange creatures. Strong creatures, obviously. Incredibly competent creatures. But...they take some getting used to. And what is the deal with that big gargoyle, anyway? None of the others have absolutely massive monster forms. He's as big as a basajaun."

"I honestly don't know. Jess doesn't want to pry."

"Huh. Creatures and plant life. That senile vampire's flowers caught two more of those enemy doglike things, one of them in the middle of town. It was running after a mom and her teen, so they ducked into the grove of flowers. Planting them was good thinking. The flowers handled it. I had to hear the story twice to believe it."

"Those dog-things are chasing people now?"

"That one did."

"The flowers didn't capture any mages?"

Kingsley's eyes turned sharp. "No. We should've

had an attack by now. Even a mild one. Even a couple of mages showing up to scout. *Something.* Let's go see the others. We need to talk business."

"Yeah, we have some news of an ambush we handled that you'll want to hear."

Mimi and the kids sat on the bench as Jess leaned against the island.

"I told Aurora and Mac that they should come visit the house you designed," Mimi said to Austin. "At least there a body can sit at the island instead of in a strange spectator seat."

"Here, Kingsley." Jess reached into the fridge to grab his beer.

"Something's up," Kingsley told them. "I have a bad feeling. The pattern the mages have followed for the last several months has changed. I heard about your people going into town." His gaze bored into Jessie.

"You gave me leave to govern them. They went into town, assessed the threat, and decided it was best to continue to ignore them. My people didn't disturb anyone or reveal themselves in any way. They made a mockery of themselves and left."

"You had three groups."

"Yes. I heard the other two groups also made mockeries of themselves as soon as they were told not to engage. Gerard got so drunk he flew into a building on his way out of town—he's fine—and Ulric hit on the wrong girl and her girlfriend thumped him a good one. Not a single mage was touched. That's not the reason for a change-up."

"The garhettes, then," Kingsley guessed.

Jess hesitated, glancing at Austin. "Possibly. This could just be their reaction to our catching one of their invisible mages. Or maybe they were banking on things going differently at the weapons deal today."

"How'd that go?" he asked.

Her eyes lit up. "Excellent. They do not perform well in small spaces with large shifting creatures. They'd set up an ambush, and we ensured no one left. Right?" She looked at Austin again.

"No one got out of there, no. Nor will they. Our people are asking some questions of our own as we speak. We should hear from them soon."

Kingsley's gaze dug into Austin now.

"It's not in your territory, Kingsley, nor affiliated with your pack," Austin said. "You need to let us handle the mages."

"You'd stoop to their level?" Kingsley growled.

"Sorry about eavesdropping, but your conversation reminded me of something," Jess said, her voice firm and forceful. "You guys were just talking about those shifters challenging Austin and me. You mentioned,

Kingsley, that it was our right to use excessive force. To kill. Well, those mages challenged us. We are answering that challenge. With a shifter, it's a brutal, gruesome fight to the death. Fine. With mages, it's a magical terror-fest until they tell us what we need to know or one or the other of us dies. Same outcome, different way of going about it."

Kingsley didn't comment, probably because it was impeccable logic.

"The problem we're facing," Jess continued, "is that their magic is powerful. They had an invisibility spell that was almost stronger than Sebastian's potion."

"What does that mean for us?" Kingsley asked.

"We'll need to get through those mercenaries quickly," Austin replied, "and hit the mages before they have time to thin our numbers too much."

"The good news is, they freak out when a growling shifter comes at them," Jess said. "The bad news is that they are likely going to leave a lot of space between the mercenaries and themselves for just that reason."

"At least the weapons seem to be in decent working order," Austin said just as a knock sounded at the front door.

"Hell-*ooo*," came a voice, and he instantly recognized the speaker.

"Oh no," Mimi said, obviously coming to the same

realization.

In a moment, Patty turned the corner into the kitchen. She was wearing red lipstick on a big smile, her blonde curls bouncing.

"Hello, everyone!" She walked a little closer to Jess at the island. "Alpha. Naomi! I haven't seen you around town. You should come out more often. We have some fantastic social events on the Town Green—that's what we're calling the main square. It just gives it a little flare, don't you think? We have chess and checkers, Scrabble, Uno—it's a real good time. Austin Steele! Great to see you again. My gosh, you guys have been so busy! I barely see my little Olly. What do you think about all these garhettes, hmm? They're ready to really stick it to those mages. We'll show those gargoyles just how useful we can be, yes we will. About that, how'd it go with the weapons pickup? I know Nessa was a little worried, bless her soul, but you went ahead with it, so I assume you had a plan. And look! You're back."

She stopped talking, and the silence following her words seemed foreign and almost unbearable. It was weird, the effect she had.

"I was just saying, actually," Austin started slowly, "that we made the pickup and the weapons seem to be in working order. We can get you all training with them tomorrow."

"Oh!" Patty clapped. "Fantastic! That is just great. All the gals will be ecstatic to get to work. The knives are fun, but we'd love to try on a little power, if you know what I mean. Now, the other thing I was going to ask about—"

The front door opened again and heavy treads came swiftly toward the kitchen. Nessa appeared a moment later, her eyes tight and her body movements screaming stress. Sebastian emerged behind her in the same state, with Tristan following, his eyes gleaming and his mannerisms solemn.

This meant bad news.

"Hey," Nessa said, going right for the fridge. "What do we want, dinner or sweets? I'm thinking sweets and a lot of wine. Anyone else?"

"What happened?" Jess asked, grabbing a bottle of wine for her.

"We didn't get much," Sebastian said, plopping down onto the cushions. "Momar has developed some kind of magic to make the mages self-destruct if they're caught. We questioned the lesser mages first, and any magic used on them in an interviewing capacity shorted out their brains. They slumped over, dead. No warning. No lead-up. Just done. Tristan handled the higher-level mage, but even that didn't last long."

"Their boss kills his people if they get captured?"

Mac asked, aghast.

"It's probably nicer than the alternative," Nessa said, pulling out the chocolate torte Austin had made last night. "I'm eating this."

"What's the alternative?" Aurora asked.

Nessa laughed sardonically. "If we sent them back, he'd torture them to find out exactly what secrets they spilled and then kill them for having spilled them. Unless they're valuable magically, and then I'm honestly not sure. He wouldn't want to waste talent."

"He doesn't jeopardize big talent," Sebastian said, leaning back heavily. "He wouldn't put them in a situation where they might get captured."

"This is true," Nessa replied, getting a plate.

"So?" Jess pushed.

"Tell 'em," Nessa murmured.

"The head mage confirmed that Momar's team went dark about a week ago."

"What does that mean?" Kingsley asked.

"It means," Nessa said, pulling out a fork, "that they are mobilizing. Everyone has spies, and any spies who are on the team won't have the ability to relay information."

"Your team is on the inside?" Austin asked.

"That's just it," Nessa replied. "They aren't. I contacted one with encryption on the way back here. His contacts thought they were in Momar's inner circle, but they're still responding to him. He must have tightened up his organization."

"Then what was with that mage and his crew messing around with our weapons order?" Jess asked.

"We don't know for sure," Sebastian said. "He didn't get that far before Momar's spell short-circuited his brain. But he's a field guy. An information acquisition guy, apparently."

"That's what it sounded like he said, anyway," Nessa said, her first slice of torte gone. She reached for the wine. "Stop looking at me like that, Tristan. I stress-eat. Mind your business."

"She's just a little blindsided, that's all," Sebastian said. "She'll bounce back. Anyway, he specializes in information gathering, so it would make sense that he wouldn't be included in the battle. Momar can't drop *all* his operations for this battle."

"And you can trust the mage's assessment that they went dark?" Austin asked.

"Yes," Tristan replied, leaning on the wall. "It's the truth as he knows it."

"It's just nuts that he would know that and not our people," Nessa murmured, stopping to stare out the windows. "Unless they got to our guy."

"I don't think our guy would play turncoat on us.

He wouldn't be that stupid," Sebastian said darkly.

"Doesn't matter," Nessa said, then turned toward Austin. "We need to get everything nailed down, alphas. Everyone needs to know their positions and places like second nature. The attack could come any time, day or night, but it'll likely be very early in the morning. They're coming."

CHAPTER 30

JESSIE

"WELL THEN, THIS is perfect timing," Patty said, beaming at everyone. "When cairns expect a battle, the guardians always push away their stress and anxiety to train and prepare, train and prepare. From what I've heard, all the guardians, no matter the cairn, do this. Given that their stress and anxiety have no outlet, the gargoyles get surly and stubborn and honestly"—she paused to give everyone a poignant look—"somewhat unbearable."

"And that is saying something for a gargoyle," Nessa said. Tristan frowned at her.

"The gargoyles are now approaching that unbearable stage, so…" Patty pulled her purse from her shoulder and set it on the island. Opening it, she took out a few envelopes before starting to pass them out to everyone. "We've planned a luncheon! It'll be in that lovely park where Jessie was attacked. The blood is all gone, I've been told, so we won't scare the children. And anyway, what would they be doing in the trees? The gnomes have nested there—"

"I beg your pardon?" Kingsley asked, pausing in pulling an invitation from the envelope. It looked like no one had told him the bad news yet. I hoped they wouldn't until we'd already left...

"We usually have cold cuts and fruits and finger sandwiches and things like that, but it was brought to our attention that shifters love barbecues." Patty stood at Tristan's side with the envelope held out. When he didn't move to take it, she started to remove it for him. "So we've changed it up to accommodate everyone. The gargoyle sticklers can have their frou-frou sandwiches, the shifters can help each other gnaw on turkey legs or whatever it is they find exciting between pairs, and the basajaunak will have fish and fruit and their special brew that Phil and a few others have been making in somewhat secret."

"What—"

Mimi cut Kingsley off. "This is tomorrow?"

"Of course it's tomorrow!" Patty tsked. "No time like the present. You can train in the morning and then get down and boogey after. Win-win. You'd be surprised how much help we've gotten! It seems the shifters are getting to their breaking point, as well, and all the mates are pitching in to help us."

"And if the battle comes the next day?" I asked, re-membering the state everyone was in after the basajaunak had broken out that brew at a barbecue in their lands.

Patty spread her hands. "There are worse things than fighting hungover."

"Like fighting when still drunk?" Kingsley growled.

"Like not fighting at all." Patty put her fists to her hips. "Alpha, now, you know your people have been working very hard. They are trying to get along with a variety of new creatures, they're doing training they aren't used to, and they're being shown up half the time by gargoyles—"

"I don't know that that's the situation—"

"—and drinking too much in the evenings to com-pensate. There have been more bar fights lately, and the latest ones weren't even organized by Niamh."

"*What's* this now?" Kingsley's accusatory gaze swung to me.

"Our gargoyles fight their best when their heads are on straight," Patty said as though Kingsley weren't scrabbling for a lifejacket in this tsunami of a conversa-tion. "I imagine your shifters do, too. They do not fight well when they are tired, stressed, afraid, and starting to feel cut off and alone... You get my drift. They need a reprieve. They need to remember why they are working so hard. What they are fighting for."

Aurora's brow had lifted, and Mimi was nodding slowly.

"She has a point," Austin told Kingsley. "Not to mention that the enemy has a large force to mobilize, and you haven't heard of anything passing through the border towns. Assuming you have someone to relay information?"

"I do," Kingsley said, his eyes skating over the invitation. "Fine. I…"

His words drifted away as he noticed Patty smiling at him with her fingers clasped in front of her. "Alpha, I do believe you're being rude."

His curious stare hardened.

She pursed her lips, still somewhat smiling, her eyes going first to Aurora and then to Mac.

"Such fine-looking young adults," she said. "Tell me, did you pick them up off the street? Do you not know their names or how to introduce them to new people?"

"Excuse me," Austin said as Kingsley continued to stare. He had spent hardly any time in Patty's presence, and it showed. It might take him a moment to get used to her. "This is my niece Aurora and my nephew Cormac, though he goes by Mac."

"You look just like your daddy," Patty said, zooming in to Mac, taking his cheeks in her hands and squishing them.

"Poor bastard," Nessa said, and winked when Kingsley turned on her with a steely gaze.

"And you, young lady." Patty stepped back and surveyed Aurora, her fists on her hips again. "My goodness, beautiful like a lightning storm, you are. So wild and electric. I love it! Are you going to take over the pack someday?"

"Why does no one ever ask me that?" Mac grumbled.

"Oh my, no." Patty was back in front of him, squeezing his cheeks again. "You're much too nice and kind and uninterested. Aren't you uninterested? You seem so. In the business we've discussed, at least. You're interested in the weird mage, though, right?" She released him so she could tap her finger to the side of her nose. "Aunt Patty notices everything. And why did the family decide to stop by?"

"Dad thought it would be nice if we visited Uncle Auzzie," Mac answered. "We haven't seen him in a while. Except for the other night, but *some of us* didn't act properly."

Patty surveyed Aurora immediately. "Ah, love, that's okay. Of course it is!" She bent to lightly touch

Aurora's cheek, making the young woman freeze. "I heard all about that trouble in the past. You still looked up to him anyway, of course, and then he left." She tsked. "It must've been very hard for you. Good for you for not keeping it bottled inside. Maybe just don't…incite the gargoyle, hmm? We're a prickly breed, all of us. Very unpredictable."

"Don't be alarmed," Nessa said. "This woman has the real estate for the gossip mill."

"Well." Patty straightened up, looking around again. "Good." She drifted toward Tristan, smiling up at him for no particular reason. "And how are you finding things? Quite the change from ordinary cairn life, hmm? Gerard is gleeful about what is going on here. When he's not too drunk to fly, that is. I've heard he was bragging to some of his closer cairn leader friends about all the training and the upcoming battle and all that. His gargoyles positively *revere* him for joining the fray—getting to work with you and two powerful and very advanced alpha shifter leaders…"

She nodded as though to herself before looking everyone over.

A moment later, she leaned into Tristan again, lowering her voice. "I think this convocation idea is a wonderful way of including the gargoyles, don't you? It isn't a *cairn*; it is a collection of various creatures and leaders all working together. Gerard can be a part of this without jeopardizing his cairn." She put her finger in the air. "He's not in Jessie's cairn or Austin's pack—he is part of the whole."

She leaned away again, her brow furrowed.

"No, no," she said, clearly having a conversation with herself. "That explanation is too confusing." Back to Tristan. "But you see what I'm saying, don't you? The convocation is an umbrella, see? Other cairn leaders can be under it, too, but they all keep their current cairn status in the gargoyle world. Because a convocation is a large, formal assembly of people." She tapped his arm. "I looked it up. It isn't gargoyle, it isn't shifter, it isn't mage—it's a meeting of the minds led by a faction of each."

"Oh I like this," Nessa said softly, throwing a grape at Sebastian. "Are you listening? It won't be the shifters taking on the Guild and Momar, it'll be a convocation. Not one species against another, but a group of us trying to establish a sort of governing power for the magical world at large."

Kingsley blew out a breath. "When you go for something, Austin, you really go big."

"Go big or go home," Austin replied.

"Go big. Yes!" Patty poked Tristan this time. "We're onto something. Okay, let's let that stew for now. There is no sense in getting ahead of ourselves. I'll see you all tomorrow. Get some rest." She pointed at everyone in turn. "*No sleep for the wicked* was said by people who did not do a good job at wickedness. Remember that."

"What?" Mac asked as she bustled down the hall.

"You really just need to roll with that woman." Nessa started laughing. "I love her."

Austin's family stayed for a little longer, Kingsley wanting more details about the weapons exchange. Then they left, Kingsley muttering about the need to tell Earnessa about the barbecue. Apparently none of them thought she'd be thrilled to not have planned a pack event herself.

I didn't mention that it was definitely better this way. Otherwise she would've gotten steamrolled by Patty and the other garhettes, and her frustration level would probably have caused her a coronary.

"What are we thinking?" Nessa asked after they'd all said goodbye. Aurora had barely made eye contact with Austin, but Mac and Kingsley had both given me a hug. "Should we make food? I'm hungry and still very stressed. Austin, what do you think? Want to have a small cookoff?"

Austin's hand drifted down to the small of my back. He kissed my temple, and I could tell his heart was full. Kingsley was making a big effort to heal the hurts of the past. To bring Austin closer into the family fold and accept me as one of them. It was touching and sweet and made me feel all gooey inside.

"Are we going to talk about the whole going-dark situation?" Austin asked, pulling open the fridge.

"Whoa, whoa, no way." Nessa slid across the floor, bumping into him and shutting the fridge door. "You can't just decide what we're going to make. And no to your question, too—we're going to ignore it for tonight. Otherwise no one will get any sleep and our wickedness will suffer. Patty said so."

My stomach twisted. I hadn't really let myself process the news with everyone else here. Now, though, the implications increased my heartbeat. The unknown was bearing down on us.

"We're ignoring it!" Nessa pushed me to a cutting board. "We'll get you something to chop. Austin, what are we making?"

"Something with salt," he responded, waiting next to the fridge.

"Har har. The chicken the other night wasn't that bland."

"It was so bland I wondered if you had taste buds."

"God your jokes are terrible," Nessa said, shoving Austin a little farther away so she could get at the fridge.

"You know," Sebastian said, looking off into the

nothing. "You guys were worried Nessa and me would get picked on when we came here. Instead, the alpha, the alpha's mate, the shifter beta, and some of the gargoyles all got picked on. Not us. Not once."

I picked out a knife, grateful for something to occupy my mind, even if it involved cooking. "Maybe on some level, they knew how much we'd need you."

"Or maybe they didn't think we were enough sport," Sebastian murmured, still looking away. "Maybe they are going to be entirely blindsided by what a group of powerful mages can do."

CHAPTER 31
JESSIE

A TEAM OF gargoyles flew in formation around me as I did a last check of the territory. Very few wolves guarded the perimeter. Only a couple of gargoyles sailed in the air at the town's border. The flat land surrounding Kingsley's pack was quiet, the noon sun highlighting all of the territory's rugged features. The river flowed, sparkling, and the mountains, the closest of which would house one of Gerard's gargoyles for the next few hours, loomed. Apparently his ability to see danger coming was uncanny.

No one was coming yet, though. I knew it. I could *feel* it. The enemy was organizing—their preparations methodical and exacting. They were making sure everything was in place, all their weapons working, and all their people rested and ready to go. It would take longer than usual. There was more for them to lose than usual. Because this battle meant a great deal to the

shifters and magical community both. If Kingsley's
territory went down, there'd be no better example of
Momar's might—and it would only be a matter of time
before the rest of the shifter territories followed.

We couldn't lose. If we did, it wouldn't just be
Kingsley's pack and those of us who were helping them
who would suffer. It would be genocide. And after the
shifters were done, Momar's crew would choose
another creature to persecute. And then another.

He already had too much power, this guy. He needed to be taken down.

I dove a little, taking a better look at the river. One
of the flowers moved as we passed, seeming to watch us
despite its lack of eyes. Very creepy. A sparkle of silver
caught my attention, and I circled lower, making sure to
go wide enough for the formation to stay intact. Lower
still, I saw it was another one of those metal hook or
latch things we'd been finding along the river's edge.
They were incredibly hard to remove, driven down deep
and sealed in with some sort of magic. Sebastian or
I would have to crack the spell so a cable attached to a
tow hitch could pull it out. We needed to do a better
sweep of the banks, though. The last sweep had clearly
missed one.

Unless they were still putting them in and we just
hadn't caught anyone…

All was quiet. A bird soared above us. There was nothing else to be done today except go to the barbecue and pretend to relax.

I sent out a peal of magic. *Dismissed.*

Smoke already curled into the air, the barbecue getting started so the food would be hot and ready by go time.

The house was empty when I got there, so I didn't bother putting on my muumuu before heading for the shower. It wasn't until I was slipping on some jeans that Austin walked in, breathing heavily and equally nude.

"Hey," I said as he stopped in front of me to get a kiss. "How'd it go?"

"They're ready." He fell backward onto the bed, his arms out.

"Wait, I thought you said Kingsley's people need more work."

"They do. I was with our people. They're ready. They have the lay of the land, they know all the ways across the river, and they're in excellent shape. They're ready."

"Ah gotcha. I thought you were going out with Kingsley's people this morning."

"Tomorrow—if there's time tomorrow."

He meant if we weren't attacked, and I didn't tell him about my gut feeling. I was no oracle.

"Are you planning on being fashionably late?" I asked when he didn't peel himself off the bed and head toward the shower.

"Yes. Want to make us later? Take those clothes off again and come sit on me."

"You should've been back in time to meet me in the shower. I'm going to go check on Sebastian."

He was in the backyard, sitting on a tree stump with his head in his hands. His various camping stoves were spread out in front of him.

"You okay, buddy?" I asked him, walking up and putting my hand on his shoulder.

He patted my hand before resting his head back into his hands. "I'm okay. I don't want to go to the barbecue."

"You would prefer for Patty to make a special trip to come and get you?"

He sighed. "I'm getting a bad feeling, Jessie." He looked up at me with bloodshot eyes. "We're missing something. Something big. I don't know what it is, though. If they do the small shield-bubble things, we're ready. I have something that should almost certainly work. If they try for the huge shield, we shouldn't have a problem interrupting that. Individual spells? Got it covered. We have a crapload of potions to protect our most vulnerable for a few hours while we get the ground crew out of the way. It should be enough. Numbers? We should have plenty. Maybe more than them if we count the garhettes, and I got word from Nessa a bit ago that all but one of the guns work. Potions for the fliers to use on the mages? Big stockpile. If I look at this logically, we're okay. Better than okay. We just need to show up like you've been training, and we should be fine."

I crouched down beside him, butterflies filling my stomach.

"But…" I said, looking at his camping equipment turned potion kitchen.

"But I cannot shake the feeling that they have something that will turn the tides and we won't be able to combat it."

The butterflies donned razor-tipped wings and slashed through my middle. My own disquiet grew, my chest feeling heavy. Because my gut told me we were both right. Momar's people were taking their sweet time to get ready, and they also thought they had what it took to win.

I stood and patted him again. "Why don't you go get ready? Have a bunch of drinks tonight and sleep."

"I don't work well hungover."

"I can cure you if it's needed."

His head snapped up this time, his gaze finding mine again. He studied me for a long moment, reading me, before nodding. I had no idea what he'd seen.

"If you think of anything…" he told me, leaving it hanging.

What would I possibly think of? I wasn't the brains of this operation.

A knock sounded at the door as I wandered into the kitchen. After a pause with no one entering of their own volition, I headed that way. Broken Sue waited on the other side, dressed casually but looking crisp.

"Hey." I stepped back so he could enter. "How's everyone getting around without cars?"

"The alpha purchased some used vehicles from the border towns. They aren't pretty, but they run."

"Oh." I gestured him in, my brow furrowed. "I hadn't heard."

"You don't need one."

"I suppose not. Does yours play Bruce Springsteen on repeat?"

"No." He walked down the hallway toward the kitchen. "Mariah Carey. We can't seem to get the CD out, and the volume button doesn't work. Another of the cars has a cassette player with the Spice Girls. The alpha clearly has a sense of humor. I never would've guessed."

"He does. He's actually a really cool guy. Austin's in the shower. Do you want something to drink?"

He sat on the bench and leaned back, spreading his arms along the top of the cushion. "No, thanks. Is Nessa around?"

"Doesn't seem to be." I got myself some water and leaned back against the fridge. "Last I—"

The door opened and hurried footsteps came down the hall. Nessa appeared a moment later with her hair thrown up and flyaways all around her face. She carried two paper bags.

"Hello, handsome," she told Broken Sue as he hopped up, reaching for the bags. "No, no, you're fine. I'm already here. Sit down and relax." She set the bags down on the island before turning back to him. "Did you bring six white stallions and a carriage to take me to the ball?"

"I'm here to speak to Alpha Steele...but I can take you to the barbecue after if you want?"

"Yes, I do. Sebastian always manages to get the good back seat, and I have to sit on a spring. Or maybe they both have springs. Hard to tell. Are you going to be here long? I can go get dressed."

"What were you up to?" I asked, moving to peer into the bags.

"Nope." She put her hand out to stop me as Austin walked into the kitchen. "Okay, Mr. Alpha, here's the situation." Nessa pointed at the two bags. "Those are ingredients for a blind cooking contest. The ingredients are exactly the same. You can cook whatever you want—"

"I've seen cooking shows before. I know how they work," Austin said, eyeing the bags with interest. "Who picked out the ingredients, or is this a *cheat to win* scenario for you? Not that it would matter. I am going to absolutely slaughter you."

"Patty did, smarty. I just picked them up." She waved him away. "I've got your number, now. You're a one-trick pony."

"One-trick pony meaning I use salt with every meal?" He grinned.

She narrowed her eyes before pointing a finger at him. "Laugh it up, chuckles. After this is over, *I'll* be the one making fun of *you*."

"Dream on. Hurry up—the barbecue has already started."

"I can take the mages," Broken Sue said. "Sir, before you go, I wanted to bring to your attention that there are several places in the small mountain range to the north where a helicopter could land. Farther out, there are more. They might not be coming through the towns at all; they might fly in and use an off-road vehicle to get here. They could hit us at first light without us getting any advance warning."

Austin grabbed the keys from the counter slowly, his gaze distant. "Yeah, you're probably right, though we'd hear helicopters."

"True," Broken Sue said slowly.

"Still, it's worth covering our bases. I'll talk to Tristan and Gerard about posting a couple of gargoyles high enough to see."

"It won't be any one thing," Nessa said, looking at the plain brown bags. "It'll be several. A helicopter. Campers through town. Horses, who knows. And while they're moving in, there'll be a distraction to provide them cover. Burning buildings, those dog things racing through town, and other atrocious things all of us would prefer not to think of."

Broken Sue and Austin stared at her for a silent beat.

She turned their way and issued a glittering smile. "Not to be Debbie Downer or anything. I think an extra pair of eyes is a very good idea. Now, Austin, we have a problem to solve. There are bound to be items in those bags that need to be kept cool. How are we going to get them into the fridge without you cheating?"

A HALF-HOUR LATER, Austin and I were en route to the barbecue, those razor-tipped butterflies once again fluttering through my stomach. "I want to fly 'round and 'round this territory, not go to a barbecue."

He was quiet for a beat. "I think everyone does. We're all wound up. Patty's right—it's probably a good idea for us all to have a distraction."

I wanted to mention that Sebastian was worried. That I was worried. That Nessa wasn't normally this keyed up. But what would be the point? Worrying more wouldn't change anything. It wouldn't somehow make us all more prepared.

"Kingsley rigged all the music players in the cars," I said instead, watching the town pass from the window.

"Yeah, I heard. He's got an odd sense of humor."

"It was nice of him to get the cars. We hadn't thought about how everyone would get around."

"It was. I was...surprised by what he said last night."

We'd chatted in bed last night for a long time, but he hadn't brought this up. I hadn't pushed.

"He mentioned you said something to him," Austin said.

I thought back. "Yeah, it must've been when we were squaring off in the office. We were in a silent bubble, and I said something about his old wounds not condoning his behavior. I may have also implied he wasn't setting the greatest example for his kids. You know, for not kicking that idiot Bruce out and for letting his team treat you poorly. Though I supposed I shouldn't call him an idiot now that Broken Sue…dealt with it."

He nodded, quiet for a while, looking for a parking place.

"It hadn't occurred to me that he was holding a grudge," Austin finally said, parking a few blocks away. "Not sure why." He got out of the car and came around to my side as I did the same.

"Probably because he didn't act like he did. Not outwardly. It was during that situation that it dawned on me."

"I should have apologized sooner. He's always been so patient with me. So forgiving."

"Well." I toggled my hand. "Mostly, right? But it seems like he's trying to smooth the waters now. He brought the kids over. That's a good sign. Aurora didn't seem pissed."

"She's good at hiding her feelings. She'll be an excellent alpha someday, but she needs room to grow."

I stopped mid-step with sudden horror. "Shoot, should we have brought something?"

He laughed and tugged me along. "No. We're alphas. We bring ourselves."

CHAPTER 32

AUSTIN

A N HOUR INTO the barbecue, Austin stood on the outskirts with Brochan and Kingsley, who were both very familiar with an alpha's role at these things. Flames reached up through the grills all around the park, with meat sizzling and veggies steaming in their tinfoil. Each of the guys held a plastic cup filled with bourbon, a little formal for a barbecue, but Kingsley's people had handed them around. Maybe a peace offering. Maybe they were just being polite.

Organized pits had been prepared for bonfires, although the sun was hours away from setting. The garhettes were clearly planning for this to last a while, and judging by the contests going on with the shifters, gargoyles, and basajaunak, all challenging Niamh to a drinking match, it just might.

"Alphas." The basandere walked up, her hair braided in various areas down her body and her demeanor loose and easy. "I heard that time is officially ticking down."

Kingsley looked to Austin.

"Our mages got word that the enemy is mobilizing. We don't know how long that'll take, though."

She nodded, looking out to the west. "Dave—or is it Missus Smith with outsiders?"

"It's only Missus Smith to outside mages, I believe," Austin clarified, fighting his grin at his brother's suddenly bewildered posture. He still didn't much understand the Ivy House crew.

They'd given Dave two nicknames, one being Dave, and the other provided by Edgar—Missus Smith. It would be used to further knock the mages they met off-kilter, calling a huge, fearsome creature like a basajaun a name like that. Although Dave would've probably done the job as well.

She inclined her head. "My understanding is that the battle could start at any time, so I wanted to take this opportunity to thank you, Alpha Austin, for changing your plans at the last minute to accommodate more of us. We were sick with worry about sending our children into the throes of danger without passable training."

"We're happy to have you, and that's not a platitude," Austin responded.

"And Alpha Kingsley, thank you for hosting us. We have found a nice hum within some of your parks and within the trees along the river. The fish are plentiful and your diligence in ensuring we always have fuel for fires and food to eat has been most gracious. You are as good of a host as any basajaunak could expect and more."

"My pleasure," Kingsley replied. "It's a joy to welcome your people amongst us. There has been no trouble—it's easy to forget that you are a visiting creature and not a longtime resident."

"Well…for some of my people, perhaps." Her gaze swiveled to Phil sitting on the ground behind Niamh, each drinking out of their mugs of the basajaunak's special brew, more intense than most moonshine. "And am I correct in hearing that we are to exert all our efforts in this battle and hold nothing back?"

She was asking if they could kill at will, likely because Jessie was always asking them to hold back and not finish the job.

"Hold absolutely nothing back," Austin replied. "If you can make my mate blanch, all the better."

Her eyes sparkled. "It has been a long time since I have battled like this, and the young ones never have. A part of me is scared. Another part of me is excited. It is a strange feeling."

"Hopefully all goes well," Austin said.

"Yes." She nodded to them before turning away, drifting toward a barbecue setup.

Austin glanced to the right, sensing his mate. She stood with Ulric and Jasper and another gargoyle, her head thrown back in laughter. The sun sparkled on her beautiful face and a warm happiness radiated through the bonds. She reached out to put a hand on Ulric's arm before shaking her head and dropping it again.

"You've really changed," Kingsley said, and Austin realized his brother was watching him closely. "Back in the day, that simple touch would've driven you to madness. You would've killed him without batting an eye."

He was referring to how Austin had been with Destiny, his ex. "Back in the day, my head was twisted and the way she touched other men was a lot more suggestive."

"True."

"I'm still that guy, Kingsley," he said in a low tone, his eyes fixed on Jess. She glanced his way a moment later, catching his gaze and giving him a smile just for him, full of love and longing and joy. "Ask Brochan."

She winked at him before turning back to the guys, a gush of warmth coming through the bonds.

"We're all that guy with someone we love," Brochan

said, and Austin supposed that was true enough. "I can't speak to what you were like in the past, but there has never been a finer alpha—begging your pardon for saying so, Alpha Kingsley. His brutality and viciousness have served him well in the challenges we've faced so far."

"Since we're among equals, even though one of us is currently a beta…" Kingsley paused for a moment. "I'm not facing this coming attack with the bravery I'd expect from myself. Honestly, boys, I'm shitting my pants."

Brochan adjusted his footing—a slight accession to both the humor and vulnerability Kingsley had shown—and Austin nodded.

"Waiting for the unknown is the hardest part," he said. "We've seen hell already, and we've had time to organize. It's better than a couple of situations I've faced with Jess in the past."

Kingsley tensed, and a little liquid sloshed out of his glass.

"What?" Austin asked.

Kingsley's eyes had squinted, his focus acute, on the trees at the other side of the grass. Like he'd seen something. "What did she mean by *gnomes*?"

Jess peeled away from the guys, her gaze finding Austin again. She sauntered toward one of the barbecue pits, her hips swaying. Someone greeted her, and she inclined her head in answer, then spoke to someone else in what was probably a pleasant way. She always sought to make everyone feel at home.

Mr. Tom appeared at her side in a flash, trying to take over her plate. He hadn't gotten to attend to her much during their visit, Austin getting that privilege, and the old butler was trying to make up for it at every given opportunity.

"Gnomes aren't like those dolls at Ivy House, right?" Kingsley pressed.

Jess reached the barbecue with Mr. Tom dogging her steps and stood at the back of the line. Everyone in front of her tried to let her go first, an honor that was customary for an alpha, but she wouldn't hear of it.

"There are no dolls here, no," Austin said, not lying. Truthfully, the gnomes were worse than the dolls, although at least they stayed outside. But Kingsley was already on the verge of shitting his pants—the last thing he needed was news of a possible gnome infestation.

When Jess got to the front, she took a plate and pointed. The shifter at the barbecue placed a steak on her plate, and her glance up said she wanted to share it.

"I gotta go," Austin said immediately.

"Hey," Kingsley said, dragging Austin's focus back for a moment. "If you can tear yourself away from the festivities for a minute, I have a new car to show you.

Brochan, you're welcome too, if you want. You don't seem overly great at small talk with strangers."

Austin watched Jess saunter to a chair Mr. Tom had pulled up for her, away from others. After Mr. Tom had stepped away, she sat, crossing her legs. She slid her finger across the top of the seared part of the meat before sucking it into her mouth.

"Nah," Austin said, eager to get to her. "I'm going to hang around here for a while."

He didn't say *until she wants to go home*. Then again, he clearly didn't have to.

"I was never this bad." Kingsley scoffed. "You might as well bring her. Just so long as she doesn't complain about my cigar and drinking."

She wouldn't care less. Austin would have said so, but he'd already started walking, watching her bite into the meat.

Halfway there, he heard, "Uncle Auzzie?"

He hadn't even seen Aurora approaching. If an enemy wanted to take him down, they just needed to set up Jess at a barbecue as bait.

With considerable effort, he dragged his gaze away from his mate.

Aurora stood with her feet planted and shoulders squared, her chin high but her confidence wavering. She noticed his distraction and followed his earlier gaze, understanding taking the place of determination on her face.

"Yes, Aurora." He cleared his throat, not particularly eager to talk to a family member in this state. "How can I help?"

"I'll let you get back to her in a second, I just…" She cocked her head, clearly building up her courage. "I just wanted to say sorry. About the other night. And also…I realize now it wasn't fair for me to be so angry."

"No, no." He reached out to grab her shoulder but refrained. She wasn't a little kid anymore. She had also seemed to adopt Mimi's stance on physical touch. "Your anger was—is—definitely fair. I should've told you I was leaving. I should've sent you birthday cards. I wasn't in a good headspace and was thinking only of myself, and I'm sorry about that. I should've said it before now. I need to make things up to you. I know that. Please give me that chance. When this is all over, and I have some time to do it right, I *will* make it up to you."

Her eyes were so big and open, so like the kid he'd left behind. The one who'd forgiven him for what he'd nearly done to her daddy, who'd liked to pal around with him, and whom he'd left alone with all the others. He wished things were different right then, and he hadn't been pulled in so many directions with the coming battle that he could've approached her before now. That he could've already started to make amends.

"I see how people treat you here," she said. "Dad says it was worse back in the day. You must've been miserable."

"I deserved it."

"For a while, maybe. Not forever. I just wanted to say…I get why you left. It took me getting older, I think, to realize—or maybe it took me *seeing* it to realize—why you needed to go. I forgive you for leaving like you did. Though…" Her lips twisted at the corners a little bit. "You can make it up to me, sure. How about you owe me one?"

He narrowed his eyes. "Why do I get the feeling that you already know what the *one* thing is going to be…"

She shrugged, about to turn away, but stopped herself. "And your mate is pretty awesome. She's life goals, right there. Except for her being so nice. That seems like too much work."

She shrugged and then put up her hand for a high five, the same way she used to do when she was little. He hit it and then reeled her in for a tight hug.

"I'm sorry, Aurora. Truly."

"I know," she wheezed, and he let her go. She waved her finger in the air. "Not sure I'm into hugs."

"They'll probably grow on you. Jess is a hugger, and

if you're on the fence, she's going to try to tip you over."

"Why…" She took a step away. "Not that it's any of my business, but why do you call her Jess when everyone else calls her Jessie?"

"Because when I first met her, some part of me realized she'd be hanging around, and Jess*ie* reminded me of Auz*zie,* and it hurt my heart to think about it. Now it's just my special thing with her. Only I call her Jess."

Her eyes were big again, emotion rolling behind them. She nodded stiffly and then walked away. Beyond her, a gnome lurked in the branches of one of the trees, eyeing everyone. Yes, no doubt about it, Kingsley was going to be furious.

"Hey, babe, sorry about that," he said when he reached Jess, pulling her to standing so he could sit and direct her onto his lap.

"Everything okay?" She held the plate with the half-eaten steak on it.

"Good. Really good. This situation with Momar sucks, but I'm glad it dragged me back home. I'm glad to be here."

She leaned against him as Nessa skipped by, stopped short, then brought up her phone and snapped the picture.

"I've slacked with your social media, Jessie." She held up the phone. "You look both happy in love and an absolute mess with crap all over your face. I'm not sure yet if I'm going to fix it in Photoshop. Oh, has Kingsley noticed the spies yet?" She jerked her face toward the trees.

"Don't mention it," Austin warned.

She mimed pulling a zipper over her lips. "See ya."

She waved and bounded off again, leaving Austin to soak in the heat of his mate, feed her, and watch the people chat and dance and laugh. They looked so happy in the afternoon sun, mingling as easily as if they'd all grown up with multiple types of creatures around. The garhettes walked among them, dragging people every which way to introduce them to one another. They were essentially forcing everyone to blend, and they had such a *way* about them that no one seemed inclined—or able—to say no.

After another hour or so, when the alcohol was flowing and the gnomes were gaining a bit more courage, dodging out to whack an ankle for seemingly no reason, Austin figured it was time to get Kingsley out of there.

"Ready to go?" he asked Jess, steering her by the small of her back. "I think Kingsley's anxious for an exit. He never hangs out at these things for very long."

After telling Kingsley they'd meet him at the garage, he and Jess walked back to the car. Jess slipped her hand into his.

"I've really enjoyed all this." She shrugged. "The good parts, I mean. There was some bad stuff, but I've enjoyed working together with everyone. I've enjoyed spending time with your family, most of all." In a small voice she finished, "I don't want it to end."

"I know, baby. It won't. We have one more hurdle, and then we can get back to our life."

It wouldn't be a hurdle that showed up, though. It would be a tsunami.

CHAPTER 33

JESSIE

I AWOKE, SUCKING in a breath and sitting up in bed like some sort of mummy restored to life. The night lay still and quiet around me, but my connections were lighting up like a Christmas tree.

"Austin!" I yelled, flinging back the covers and throwing my feet off the side of the mattress. "Let's go, let's go!"

"Jessie," Sebastian yelled from down the hall. I heard his feet thumping before he barged into the room, wild-eyed. "My magical tripwires are going off all over the place. They're here. It must be them."

"I know—"

The loud hum of wings reached us, the gargoyle warning system.

"Let's go," I said to myself as I sent a peal of magic thundering across town. *Attack!*

"Remember our training," Austin called, his voice

relaxed and confident, jogging from the room.

It had been a week since the barbecue. A week of additional training. At the moment, I struggled to remember any of it.

Trying to breathe, I ran after him as Nessa emerged from her bedroom dressed in black with blades strapped to her sides and a gun slung over her back. She'd taken one for herself and proven to be all kinds of aces with it.

"I gotta get dressed!" Sebastian ran back to his room, his nightshirt billowing around his legs.

I didn't bother with a muumuu. It wouldn't last long.

Another peal of magical thunder sounded as I organized the connections in my mind's eye. I'd been practicing, using what Ivy House had taught me to organize my people more smoothly.

Austin grabbed a vial of revealing potion from the counter—we'd kept it there for this very occasion—and guzzled it down. I took it next before grabbing the latest doses of various potions Sebastian and I had finished last night and jogging to get them stowed away in the car. Austin would drive them down to headquarters. The rest were already stored there.

"I'm coming!" Sebastian sprinted down the hall, caught his boot on the corner of a door, and spilled across the ground.

"Take a breath," I told him, lifting him by the upper arm. "Take a breath. Think of Elliot Graves."

He sucked in a breath. "I know. I know. Okay."

Nessa stepped up to him, wrapping her hand around the back of his neck and pulling his forehead to hers. "We got this, Sabby," she told him in soft, urgent tones. "We've survived worse. Far worse. We can do this."

He closed his eyes, still breathing deeply, and nodded.

She let him go and hugged me before grabbing the back of my neck as well. "Do not pull any punches, okay? Give them the worst kind of hell. Hold nothing back."

It was my turn to nod and breathe, feeling the conviction behind her words and her quiet strength burrowing into my body. It almost felt magical in some way, but then she was pulling away and heading through the door, throwing her head back to drink her vial as she did it.

Austin squeezed me into a tight hug a moment later, plastering my body to his. "Above all else, Jacinta Ironheart, you get out of this safely, do you hear me? If we have no hope, you get out."

Yeah, right. Sure.

"Okay," I said, because that was what he needed to hear.

His kiss was bruising, and then he was following Nessa out the door.

"Jessie, I'm scared," Sebastian admitted.

"That's because you haven't had any coffee yet. Let's hope Mr. Tom meets us with some, okay?" I smiled at him.

"He won't. He's mad at you for essentially ignoring him this whole time and allowing Austin to keep him from staying here."

"Mad or not, he won't stop forcing food on me. It'll be fine."

Wings sounded outside, and I pulled Sebastian out with me. The connections were frying my insides now, everyone out of bed, everyone active. I wrestled them together, joining everyone through me. They'd all be able to feel the company as a whole. A unit. Even if they were separated from the pack and isolated, alone, they'd have the comfort of their crew.

Nathanial landed, waiting for me, and a gargoyle called Trace touched down beside him—Sebastian's ride for the moment. I closed the door behind us and half pushed Sebastian toward them. As we got closer, I shifted and rose into the sky, the others with me.

The next peal of magic I sent out said, *I'm coming.*

Sebastian had thought they'd come at dawn. He'd been spot-on, or as good as—the coming sun would start filling the sky soon.

Nathanial swooped in behind me and grabbed my waist before gaining altitude. In a moment, I saw why.

A pale light ran in a huge circle all around the town, glowing even in the water of the river. They'd already begun their efforts to make the large dome. We'd hoped we'd removed enough of their hidden anchors to avoid this, but the mages had been sneaking in for months.

This wasn't like Sebastian had described it, though. There was more to it, the glowing lines on the ground like stored energy they were now harvesting. They'd embellished the spell to make erecting the dome easier and faster, and were already way ahead of us.

It would've been a lot more gratifying if my swear had been coherent.

Nathanial dove, heading for the meetup location. My heart hammered now. I needed to land and shift. Needed to talk to Sebastian. I didn't know by how much this would change things, but I knew it would.

"Jessie." Sebastian stalked up to me as soon as I'd shifted. His determined, steadfast expression was illuminated by the glow from Kingsley's streetlights. That was Sebastian, always at his best in a bad situation.

"How bad?" I asked, a little out of breath from flying and shifting so fast back to back.

His look said it all. "We need to take out their mag-es before they erect that spell."

"How long do we have?"

"Depends on their power level and ability to work together. The color tells us what we're dealing with—"

Another thrum of wings, lower this time. The ene-my had been sighted.

Sebastian started talking faster. "Yellow means it's fragile—"

"It's still at blue, though."

He jerked his head from side to side, his frustration evident.

"The blue is stored magic in the ground. It's like they created temporary ley lines, an incredible feat. It'll fuel them. No, I'm talking about the actual spell. The sheen of the actual dome. So yellow is at its most fragile. Orange is stronger, red is almost there, and blood red... Blood red means we're trapped inside. They can fire at will or toss in Molotov cocktails or drop bombs on the town—whatever. Breaking it at that point would be impossible. Not even Tristan would be able to get through. Do you understand me?"

"Yes. Blood red, we all die."

"They'll have invisibility potions, and given what Nessa described, it'll be damn hard to see them in the dark. Watch for the break in the line. Watch for jets of magic. Home in on them that way."

"Okay. Got it."

He grabbed my upper arms, fully in control of himself now. "We need to take out those mages. Don't worry about anything else. Our job is destroying that spell." He squeezed. "Hurry!"

"Jess." Austin ran up to me, handing off potions to one of the gargoyles. "What's the matter?"

"Your job is still the same."

He didn't waste time asking questions. He kissed me hard and then turned around and started barking orders.

I didn't wait to see how fluid his teams were. I pushed into the sky, Nathanial with me. He'd taken the same potion—the concoction that would both render us invisible and allow us to see other invisible people. Their potions, unless they were made by a mage as powerful and talented as Sebastian, wouldn't be able to do both.

Then again, they'd constructed temporary ley lines, something I'd never even heard of. They were good.

Nathanial grabbed me and put on a burst of speed, getting us high. He'd been there for my conversation with Sebastian and knew what was at stake. Most importantly, we'd worked together for long enough that he almost had a sixth sense when it came to me.

Sebastian rose with Trace and pointed in the opposite direction as me. Divide and conquer.

We flew out over the town. Garhettes jogged or walked briskly through the light cast by the street lamps below us, heading for their posts on the outskirts of town. Shifters raced past them, heading to their positions, ready to synchronize their attacks. They just needed to pinpoint the enemy.

That line glowed, the circle imperfect. Then again, it would have taken an alien with impeccable crop-dusting abilities to pull off a perfect circle. I wondered if that would matter. I bet it probably would, although that could be wishful thinking.

We flew closer through the darkness, nearly pitch black out here. No moon. I had a feeling that was by design. It would help their mages, no question, but it would screw their cavalry. The shifters wouldn't be as affected by the darkness as human eyes. If Sebastian and I managed to do our job, we'd have the upper hand.

Nearer the blue line, I squinted as though that might help me see through the darkness. It didn't.

We angled downward, needing to get closer. And then a softly glimmering yellow sheen filled the air in front of me.

Oh God, so fast?

How had they even gotten out here without being noticed? Our people should've heard engines. We had people in the towns. We should've seen car lights, and they wouldn't have been able to get out here without them.

Dread filled my middle, a painful weight. Momar had tricks. What the hell was in store for us?

Closer to the sheen, I could make out the first shapes on the other side. They stood shoulder to shoulder, their bodies still, no waving extremities working intense magic. They were apparently waiting to see if the trap would work before they ran to confront the enemy. That, or they were waiting for the enemy to come to them.

Request granted.

My peal of magic shot out. *Attack!*

A laser blast of a gun seared the darkness, zipping behind us as we traveled parallel to the blue line. We needed to find the mages, who would be set up on regular points around this circle. It was too hard to see from this far out, though. My eyes played tricks in the darkness, making me think I was seeing the ghostly forms of the soldiers but not quite sure. Pockets of black were interrupted with gray, the yellow sheen strengthening in hue and brightness. They were pulling off the impossible, and they were doing it faster than we could've ever imagined.

My heart sped up as we went, veering closer to the blue line to see the shapes as I watched them for movement. I needed to see mages working.

A blast zipped toward us, then again. Dread pierced me. They could see us, at least a hazy interpretation of us. Another blast, this one from right above. We wouldn't have stealth on our side.

The blue line started to throb now, faint but noticeable. I didn't know what that meant, though. Maybe they were depleting the ley line of its magic. That would be ideal, since they were only at the yellow stage of the spell.

We veered closer, trying to see, risking their guns. The blasts came fast, scraping across my bottom, but more of them missing than hitting. I'd hold back on using magic until I had a real target. A mage target. The darkness was helping us as much as them, maybe more so because our potion was just a bit stronger, but any closer and they'd roast us. There were just so many of them.

Farther along now, Nathaniel first flew upward and then dove down, making us harder to hit. The ground rushed below us. Through my connections, I could feel the others spreading out along the perimeter line, all together. That had been the plan, hit them as a unit. A good plan, ensuring their forces couldn't overwhelm us, but a *slow* plan because the gargoyles had to keep pace with the running shifters and basajaunak. Still, they should be here shortly.

The blue still throbbed. The yellow darkened, heading toward orange.

I had to find those mages! Where the hell were they?

A thought occurred to me. What if they were ducked down near the blue line, and I was only noticing the mercenaries because of their larger stature? Or hell, maybe they were covered in sheets. I had to get closer. Better yet, if I got on the other side of that sheen, I couldn't be trapped within it. I'd have more time.

I tore away from Nathanial and angled up, driving high to cross over. The sheen curved upward, preventing me from getting as high as I would've otherwise flown. Nathanial grabbed me for a boost of speed, and we hit the curve.

Pain screamed across the parts of me that touched the dome. A clear, agonizing barrier, it had a somewhat solid feeling. Nathanial grunted in pain, his skin sizzling. His arms went limp, and I dropped like a stone. My left wing ached from where it had touched the dome, still working but at a cost. Nathanial flapped, lowering in the sky as the blasts from guns cut all around us.

I grabbed him this time, trying to get him farther away, the equivalent of limping through the air. A blast hit my leg. Another got me in the side before I covered us with a magical deflective layer. I struggled to keep going, healing as fast as I could, drifting farther into the darkness.

That barrier reminded me of the time I'd been trapped under a mountain with Dave guarding me. The spell dividing the cave from the outside had been so intense that it had burned off all Austin's and my skin, and I'd blacked out for two days because of the pain. It hadn't been solid, though. That meant this spell would take longer for me to pass through—allowing it to cripple my ability to fly. To stay conscious.

It wasn't just dread that coursed through me this time. It was a primal, mortal fear. I'd need to get through that barrier and take down their mages, but doing so would likely strip me of my wings. I'd be a sitting duck on the other side, open to their attack, unable to effectively defend myself. Essentially, I'd be giving my life to tear down that spell.

CHAPTER 34

JESSIE

I SENT A peal of magic to my crew. *Hurry up!*

I needed cover, and I needed it fast. The yellow sheen had completely given way to orange now, glowing brightly; the blue in the ground was still throbbing, nowhere near blinking out. I dropped to the ground with Nathanial and left him there, heading back up to the barrier and hitting it with magic. Trying to see if my power could break through.

My spell disappeared into the sheen, glowing a little as it spread out, adding to the energy. Crap. That wasn't good. Sebastian hadn't mentioned anything about that.

Another spell, another tactic. Same effect. One more, then I stopped. I couldn't keep adding to their work, and I didn't have the experience to figure out a workaround. Hopefully Sebastian could. He was probably muttering, "Think through it, think it through."

The sky lit with the coming dawn. Specks dotted the open space behind me, the gargoyles flying in. The shifters would be below them. Thunder rolled, Hollace, and a streak of fire headed toward me. Cyra.

She'd cracked one of Sebastian and my defense domes like an egg that one time. Maybe she could help here. Hopefully she didn't just lend them energy.

I thought of the others, Tristan especially. He wouldn't be as affected by the magic. Maybe it wouldn't destroy his wings to break through. He could also withstand mages firing spells at him.

He couldn't withstand the blaster guns, though. We'd tried. Those punched into him like they did any other gargoyle, and if he were left alone on the other side, he'd be overwhelmed.

I swore, the words garbled and unsatisfying. Freaking Momar had come prepared, I'd say that much.

Nathanial met me, following my lead as I flew parallel to the sheen again. More blasts came, these better aimed. Dawn was probably just around the corner. I'd wasted too much time getting the lay of the land. I needed to make a move.

The troops existed in clusters I could now see, shoulder to shoulder in their groups, each group evenly spaced to cover parts of the circle. No one would get through the gaps without heavy fire.

The spell was full orange, continuing to change. Continuing to strengthen. I needed to find those mages! Where the hell were they?

Fire streaked in front of me, the plumage of the phoenix. Gun blasts came as she dipped, spraying fire. It hit the spell, not spreading out. Blackening it a little. That had to be good news. Or, at least, it wasn't *bad* news.

I sent excitement through our bond and gave her a thumbs-up when she turned to look. She tried again, aiming for the same spot. The black increased a little, fading when she let up, but slowly.

Encouraged, I beckoned for her to follow me and continued flying parallel to the dome, looking for those mages. The blasts were strong, but they weren't enough to take us down. At least one thing was going right for us.

Oranges and reds streaked the sky, glowing down on the enemy troops, their guns poised and ready, some of their eyes skyward, some level. The blue throbbed right in front of them, the magic still clearly going strong.

As I passed, guns were lifted quickly, movements smooth and confident. They took aim and fired in a blink, incredibly practiced. The gargoyles and shifters drew closer, running, but they wouldn't be able to get through that barrier. Wouldn't be able to shoot through it, either.

I sent a command to slow them, panicked now as I continued to look for the mages. They had to be here somewhere. *Someone* was working the magic!

Fear ate at me. What if they had a stronger invisibility potion? What if they were there, but I couldn't see them? I wouldn't be able to get close enough to feel them, especially not with the distraction of the gun blasts pinging off my shields.

Onward I went, my blood turning cold. My chest starting to tighten. We couldn't all die here. My life couldn't end like this, in a massacre of my people.

Nathanial squeezed me…and then pointed.

Hunched on the ground next to the ley line was a black tarp, only now visible in the brightening sky. It bowed oddly, covering something. Something that was moving.

What a clever bastard Momar was.

I broke from Nathanial and angled that way immediately, stopping in the air not far from them. The troops to either side finally moved, pushing in around the tarp, looking at me. Cyra joined me and then Hollace, the great bird thrashing air down on me from his mighty wings.

I pointed to the tarp, to the ground next to it forming a red sheen. It slowly radiated upward. This had to happen now.

Cyra blasted the magic with fire before flying at it, ready to try to break it with force and magic. But just before she reached it, she pulled away squawking. Guns flared, going off rapid-fire, hitting my shields on her and deflecting. Those that hit the spell seeped in and made it stronger.

She stayed there for a long moment as Hollace approached an upper part of the dome. Both of them backed off, though, not attempting to go through. Cyra must've thought it would kill her to make the attempt. She'd then be no help to the rest of us.

I tried elemental magic as she rejoined me, the top of my power scale. It acted similar to hers, blackening slightly but not seeping in. Maybe this was a power issue. Lesser power would be consumed by the spell, but higher-powered spells couldn't be commandeered so easily.

Cyra hit it with fire, and I mixed in my magic, the two merging and striking the dome even as the color rapidly changed. We'd been fried at yellow, and red would be nearly impossible to pass.

Come on, come on, I thought as the blackened area formed a patch, the orange-red backing off to just orange.

That was it! We just needed more power.

I turned wildly, seeing the gargoyles in the sky watching, the shifters beneath them. So many beings counting on me. I wasn't powerful enough, though. Not anymore. If I'd known where those mages had been when the spell was yellow, I could've done something. I'd never make it through now, though, not if Cyra couldn't.

But if Sebastian could lend his power and Hollace could figure out how to get his lightning in on the action, then together we might weaken an area enough for me to get through. If I could manage that, I could kill those mages. I'd just have to stay conscious just long enough to do so. That, and hope the spell came down fast enough for my people to provide some cover afterward.

I just had to find Sebastian quickly enough. He could be on the other side of the perimeter.

Roaring to get Cyra and Hollace's attention, I turned to Nathanial to get going. He grabbed me quickly and flew in the direction I was pointing, hopefully understanding my garbled "find Sebastian."

The dome stretched above us, burnished orange. Gargoyles waited, getting out of the way as we flew. Shifters watched us pass. I saw two more tarps, the movement beneath clear. Any one of them would do.

Adrenaline coursed through me, hope and fear mingling. We could do this. We could. If we worked together, we could keep this whole town from being destroyed. But only if we had enough time.

Heart hammering, I searched my connections for Trace, needing to find him fast. Sebastian would probably still be with him.

Nathanial slowed, ripping me out of my reverie, before turning around.

"Wh-*at rrrrr* ouuu do-ngg?" I asked, scrabbling to get free.

"He cccomzz," Nathanial replied, adjusting his hold so I could stretch and look behind.

His wings and body mostly obscured my view, but in flashes I could pick out Tristan's large form, coming fast, holding something. *Sebastian*.

Bless that weird mage. He'd figured out what it would take faster than I had, found the fastest gargoyle in our arsenal, and come to me.

Hope overtook my fear. Adrenaline still coursed through me, and with it, determination. When I dove through, I'd have to stay conscious long enough to claw out middles or rip off heads. I couldn't pass out from pain like I had in that cave. I had to keep shields up for those guns, too, long enough to get the job done. After that, after the trap spell was ruined, I could give in to the pain, come what may.

We raced back toward our first location. I pointed to the tarp I'd noticed, and Nathanial's wings tilted immediately. Cyra and Hollace kept pace. Tristan was still coming. He'd catch us by the time we got there, much faster than Nathanial.

The trap spell started to throb with energy. Tarps lifted, flung away, the mages standing up now as the sun peeked over the mountains. They probably thought they were far enough along in their spell to stop anyone from coming through. That, or they knew the darkness was no longer there to hide them.

Before this battle, we'd only come across male mages. Well, here were all the women.

Working in twos, or threes with one male stuck in, the mages held positions around the circle, working magic in harmony. They were a cohesive team, working together rather than selfishly hoarding power the way Sebastian had said most mages did. Momar had found the team that would elicit the most strength. Their ability to cooperate and share magic was what was powering this spell.

Crap.

Magical gun blasts came at us as soon as we were within range, these people knowing their weapons to a T. The hyper-focused mages didn't so much as glance at us. The nearest group had three. I pushed away from Nathanial and flew toward the next group of two. Less work to do while trying to maintain consciousness.

I looked at Cyra as Tristan moved in to join us. Hollace flew overhead. She squawked, ready. I looked at Sebastian next.

"We need to do this together," he called. "It'll minimize the enemy spell's power. Do it enough and we can make it through without dying. On the other side, one person will need to take out the mages and the others will need to provide cover. We—"

I knew all this. We were wasting time.

I motioned, readying a spell as Cyra shot her fire. I added to it, and Sebastian joined in a moment later. The three bursts of power converged as Hollace moved in closer. His lightning usually went straight down, so he had to find the right angle to get it to hit the spell where the rest of us were.

The color in that one section peeled back to red-orange as the rest of the spell pushed toward blood red. Then to orange. We needed Hollace's boost. But he couldn't get in there just right. He kept missing the mark, not able to add his power to ours. Tristan couldn't help, and I had no idea where to find Nessa, let alone whether her magic would make a difference.

Hope dwindled again as I looked at those mages

working, my energy starting to flag. The guns around them were no longer firing because they knew they weren't getting through my shields. The mercenaries were watching, though, pushed in close to the mages. Waiting. Ready to spring into action at a moment's notice.

The color around our one point of contact continued to deepen. The mages started to slow. We wouldn't get a better shot than this. We couldn't reduce the power of that point any more. If we didn't take action now, we'd run out of energy and we'd all be lost.

The reality of the situation became clear. The person who got through would have to be a magic wielder, because they'd need to continuously hammer that point with magic, even when traveling through the spell. No one else could make it through.

Once that magic user passed the barrier, the point of entry would close and the guns would go active.

One person could make it through, and that one person would have to kill the mages before the soldiers could kill them.

Could kill *me*.

Because no one else could shield themselves from the guns the way I could. Also...there was no way in hell I would let anyone else take this role. It was my duty as heir. I'd signed a blood oath to protect my people, with my life if necessary. Now it was time to put my money where my mouth was. It was time to make the ultimate sacrifice to ensure they stayed safe.

I sent my love through the bonds to Austin, waiting behind me a ways with the others. He'd clearly figured out what was going on and found me. I sent pride and honor (or what I imagined that might feel like) through all of my Ivy House bonds and connections, hoping my team would understand the message of how I felt about them. And then I darted forward.

An anguished roar went up behind me, Austin knowing what all this meant. My heart broke for him. Luckily he'd have plenty of mages and mercenaries to take his vengeance out on, because this was going to work. I would make sure of it. I would not die until my job was done. I would not.

I picked up speed, going high first so that I could angle down. I didn't want to disturb the flow of the magic, plus the spell would burn up my wings. They'd be useless. I'd need to fall on the right spot. A dicey bit of mental physics, but it would work. It would. It had to.

Pushing everything else from my mind—the tortured feelings from my bonds with Austin, the frustration and fear from my various connections, the yelling from Sebastian behind me—I hit my zenith and started down, my eyes on the spot, my momentum ready to carry me through.

Wind whipped by my face. Arms closed around my middle.

"No, Nathanial!" I tried to scream, the words garbled.

With one hand he stuffed my wings between our bodies. With the other he held me tightly, even as I tried to shock him to get him off.

"No, Nathanial," I tried to yell again, his much faster speed barreling us toward the spell now. "*No!*"

Wings stowed, he wrapped the other arm around me tightly, squeezing my smaller frame into his and curling, trying to protect as much of me as possible. Trying to sacrifice himself so I would make it.

Going down with the ship.

"*Noooo!*" I screamed, the spell right there, orange, vicious, ready to burn our flesh from our bodies.

He wouldn't listen. I felt his answering pride and honor through the bond. And then we hit the spell.

CHAPTER 35

JESSIE

P AIN.

No, the word pain wasn't large enough to encompass what my world had plunged into. Torment. Suffering.

The spell slowed us down, like we were blasting through a brick wall. Agony seared across my skin and clawed down to my bones. Anywhere the spell touched roasted away my flesh and fried what was beneath. Blackness encroached, my primal senses wanting to cut off my consciousness from what was happening.

"Stay strong," Ivy House urged me, pumping in my middle. *"Stay lucid."*

Thinking was impossible. My brain couldn't function. A weight from around me fell away, and I struggled to remember what it was. Struggled to remember what I was even doing, why I had to stay awake.

"Fly, damn you," Ivy House said within me, her words echoing around my head, stuck in the sea of this horrible misery. *"Do not let his death be in vain.* Fly!"

His death...

I half felt my lips moving, trying to say that out loud. Feeling points of pressure on my body and not quite sure what those momentary blasts were. Everything just hurt too much. It hurt too much to move. To try to make sense of any of this.

That blackness crept in a bit more, and it felt like I was floating. No, not floating, falling. Air leafed through the black ashes flaking off my body. Not all over, though. The pain wasn't all over. Just certain places. Places the spell hadn't hit...because I'd been protected.

A new sort of agony welled up in me, emotional this time. Lodging in my middle and withering my insides.

Nathanial.

He'd sacrificed himself so I could get this done. So we could save our people. I couldn't let him down. I couldn't let any of them down.

Determination competed with the ongoing torture of my flesh. Anger stole in to block my sorrow. I blinked my eyes and snapped out my wings, everything hazy but seeming to work. My descent slowed as I set my sights on the mages below me, looking up with wide eyes. Gun blasts pummeled me, those points of pressure

I'd felt.

Summoning my magic forth, I put up a defense, deflecting most of the blasts and attempting to heal. It felt like a light bulb with a faulty wire, though, flickering and catching, only to blink out again. It would have to do. I just needed to live long enough to send two mages to the grave.

I tilted my wings and dove at them, struggling to get my hands and feet out, claws up. *Fell.* Their arms worked faster now, their bodies moving. The spell must almost be complete. These were the final moments. The final chance.

I adjusted my course a moment before my vision distorted and I lost feeling in my legs. I still had my arms, though. That was all I needed.

My body slammed into the mages. I dug my claws into them and held on for dear life, taking them to the ground and sliding on top of them. Their screaming reminded me of a dog's squeaky toy, and I started laughing through my dislocated jaw. Or maybe it wasn't dislocated, but it didn't seem to work properly. It didn't matter, though. I didn't need it.

Feet moved around us, bodies bent, guns firing at me from mere feet away. They weren't worried about killing their mages, which meant the mages must've had magical protection from the blasts. Magic wouldn't help them against claws, though.

I scratched and scraped, ignoring their hands trying to push me off or pull me away. Closing my eyes, trying to keep my defensive magic and healing going, I continued to scratch, slowly losing feeling in my arms. Didn't matter. I kept clawing, digging at the soft parts. Feeling the sticky wetness that must've meant I was getting somewhere.

"Hang on," Ivy House said distantly. I could barely hear her through the blackness. *"Hang on. He's coming. Your mate is coming."*

Reality wobbled. My God, I was so tired. The mages had stopped moving, at least. That was probably good. Now, it was just a question of whether it had been enough. If Sebastian had been correct and taking out this one point would bring down the rest. He hadn't been right about some of the other stuff.

The blackness rose around me, and I breathed out a sigh, welcoming its embrace. The ground fell away, and I was once again flying.

✧   ✧   ✧

TRISTAN

SHE WAS NOTHING but pulp. Her body lay broken and blackened from crashing into the spell and burning alive within it. She'd done it, though. She'd broken it. The magic had drained from it quickly, and as soon as it hit orange-yellow, Tristan risked diving through, his aversion to magic helping him at least keep his wings intact. Austin did the same, sprinting at it even as Cyra and Hollace dove forward.

The mercenaries watched the great polar bear with wide eyes. His white coat was singed black and red, but he didn't notice. Tristan was already there, dropping from above them. He didn't attempt to fight. Not yet. There wasn't time. Jessie needed healing immediately. She wasn't quite dead yet. The connection that held them all together was intact, their hub fading fast but still clinging to life.

He didn't bother being gentle, either. Ripping her off the disemboweled and mutilated mages and hugging her close, he pushed hard into the sky. Blasts from guns struck him as he took off before Austin scattered the mercenaries across the ground. The great bear took one moment to watch Tristan carry Jessie away before he was the nightmare this town had thought him. They'd now see what an invaluable asset he had always been.

Tristan also looked forward to showing them what a gargoyle—or mostly gargoyle—could do. Later, though. There were plenty of enemies to go around. First he needed to secure Jessie.

He flew faster than he ever had in his life. Her blood smeared against his chest and fear began to crowd his thoughts. She couldn't die. She was the one who held them all together. She kept that big alpha in check and created a soft, safe space for them all to coexist, even the most dangerous of them. Maybe especially the most dangerous of them.

She'd given him a family. A unit. She trusted him, believed in him, wanted the best for him. Hell, she'd called off the others and looked the other way when it came to his past. It didn't matter to her where he'd come from or what his blood signified—she respected him for the man he was. That meant more to him than anything else in his life, because she was the only person to ever do so. She'd offered him a life as a normal person, something he'd struggled for in his life with the cairn but never achieved.

He'd die for her. But she was the one who was ready to die for him. For all of them.

He couldn't let her make that sacrifice. He wasn't worth it.

Tears filming his eyes, he swooped down at break-neck speed toward the square, where he knew Indigo was waiting along with every able-bodied person who could help with the wounded. She hopped up as he landed, her eyes widening, then ran toward a cot at the side.

"Here," she said, patting the surface. "Here, quick. Oh my God—" She put her hands on Jessie before Tristan had even laid her down. "Oh my God, what happened?"

"She tried to trade her life for all of ours," he said, his words clipped and strangled because of his gargoyle jaw. All these years, and he hadn't yet perfected speech in this form. "Can you help her?"

Indigo shook her head slowly, her hands on Jessie's chest, her gaze drifting down her body. "Not unless she can help herself. She's too far gone. I can keep her at the brink, but she'll have to come back on her own."

His breathing hitched, shallow and painful, emotion threatening to overwhelm him. "She will," he got out, tears coming faster now. "She will. She has to."

And then he was flying, hiding his fear and worry in anger.

The enemy would pay for this. They would rue the day they came up against this convocation.

✧　✧　✧

SEBASTIAN

THE FINAL COLOR bled from the spell, and Sebastian urged his winged chariot forward, trying not to think. If he allowed himself thought, he'd remember the sight of Jessie's ruined body. Of Nathanial's blackened, lifeless form as Jasper scooped him up and hurried back toward the town. If he thought of those things, he wouldn't be able to go on. Because he was the reason they had ended up like that.

He hadn't, in his wildest dreams, thought Momar could ever pull off something of this magnitude. He hadn't predicted his mages would be able to cooperate to such a degree, let alone that they would successfully harness the ley lines. If he'd known, he could've devised better protections. Instead, he'd worked on solutions for smaller-scale magical defenses and offenses, most of them utterly useless in this situation.

He hadn't properly anticipated Momar's abilities. He hadn't armed Jessie with the information she'd needed, and she'd had to use herself to get the job done.

God, please, she had to be okay. *Please.*

The gargoyle who flew him grunted as a gun blast struck his leg. Sebastian should've stopped that too. He was starting to unravel, dammit.

Austin worked below them, taking blasts from guns and magic from the fleeing mages without blinking. He was blackened in places, bleeding in others, and ripping through the enemy like a feral beast. Dave and some of the other basajaunak had joined him, tearing through the enemy with glee. It was more than a little unsettling, and Sebastian was happy he'd ended up on this side of the divide. He'd probably crap himself if he were trying to fight against that. The mages down there certainly were, their groups breaking up, their resolve splintering, many of them turning and running, only to be picked off by the gargoyles chasing them with potions and claws and aggression.

They had been certain their trapping shield would work. They didn't seem to have any backup plans. It was now magic and guns against the shifter army, and the magical wielders were cowards. Because of Jessie's sacrifice, this battle had quickly and effectively tipped in Austin and Kingsley's favor. Jessie had ensured they'd almost certainly win the battle…while she and Nathanial lay dying, one probably already gone.

"Go," Sebastian said, tears stinging his eyes. "Hurry! Fly faster."

He had to keep moving, keep fighting. He couldn't fully unravel, not until the job was done. He owed it to Jessie.

✧ ✧ ✧

NESSA

HER HAIR WAS matted to the side of her head where a

mercenary had clubbed her with his gun. He hadn't noticed the knife in his ribs until he was sinking to his knees. She spun, stowed her knife, pulled her gun over her shoulder, and shot an enemy who had somehow broken through the shifter line. Was he lost? Where the hell did he think he was going?

One of the garhettes chased a running mage who'd also wound up over the line. The enemy had clearly misplaced their sense of direction. Fear could do that to a person. An hour after the spell had come down, the mages who hadn't already run in a blind terror were now trying to retreat. A few had gotten turned around.

The mage turned to shoot magic behind her, missing the garhette entirely and getting shot for her efforts. The mage faltered, staggering, and the garhette was there in an instant, jumping onto her and finishing the job. Those creatures were vicious as hell.

"Shadow," Edgar said, puffing into human form right beside her. He was out of breath and paler than usual, his face drawn and terrified. "Shadow, it's Jessie. Hurry!"

He puffed back into insects and darted in the wrong direction, not out toward the perimeter line where Nessa had assumed the mages would be fighting, but back toward town. Confused, suddenly unsure, she started jogging that way. Gargoyles flew overhead, led by Tristan, east to west. They must've taken out all the enemy on their side and were crossing over to help the crew to the west. That had to be good news.

With a glance over her shoulder to make sure no more enemy had broken through and would shoot her in the back, she started jogging back toward town. She hadn't seen much action, surprisingly. She'd hung back behind the shifters, since they were the more effective fighters, only getting anxious when the spell above and around them got redder and redder. Only being on two feet, though, there wasn't anything she could do. The area was much too big for her to jog around, looking for Sebastian or Jessie, and even if she'd found them, she didn't have the power to help much.

Thankfully they'd handled it, and Nessa had run forward with the weaker shifters, on hand in case anything got through their line. Not much had. Kingsley and Austin had done an excellent job of preparing their people to work together.

She nodded at an older garhette, posted on the sidewalk beyond the last house in town, patiently daring anyone to make it that far. Farther in, she found pack civilians heading in the same direction she was. Still farther, and coldness started to creep into her middle. Near the square, people sat in clusters, holding hands, some crying, some praying.

Nessa ran faster now, dread stealing over the coldness in her chest. In the square, most of the cots had occupants at this point, many of them moving or groaning. That was good—it meant they were alive enough to heal. They'd probably get through this.

A gargoyle landed not far away, holding a bloodied, limp wolf. Two pack women ran to them immediately. The gargoyle paused before pushing back into the air, looking over at a cot on the side. He put his fist to his heart, then took off.

Nessa slowed down to carefully get between the beds without kicking anything on the ground or knocking into a nurse. A guy with an apron, his take on scrubs, noticed her. His face closed down, grim. He pointed in the direction the gargoyle had been looking.

"Oh no," she breathed, weaving between the beds faster now and then stopping dead when she saw her. "Oh my God."

There were no other words.

Actually, she had a few choice ones.

"Why is no one helping her?" Nessa demanded, stopping next to the bed and looking down on the mangled female gargoyle. Blood coated her purply-pink or blackened gargoyle hide, crusted in most places. Several close-range wounds from blasters had been sewn together. One wing was bent at an unnatural angle, and the holes in the webbing hadn't been closed—probably because they weren't bleeding. Tape was wrapped around her head, holding her jaw in place, and more tape held her leg straight. "*Why is no one helping her?*"

"Whoa, whoa." A garhette stepped up to Nessa's side, wrapping her arms around her.

Nessa shrugged her off. "I don't need cuddles. I need answers."

Indigo sat, her hands on Jessie's arm. Blood coated her scrubs and was smeared across her cheek.

"I'm keeping her from dying," she said, her glasses askew. "That is taking all of my power. She has to pull herself back from the brink, and right now, she isn't making the effort. I'm not sure she has anything left to give."

Nessa stared at her, wetness pooling in her eyes, her world suddenly paling.

"She has *plenty* left to give," she ground out, her voice breaking. "*Plenty!* She just needs help. Edgar, come here. We've got work to do."

✧   ✧   ✧

KINGSLEY

OVER THREE HOURS after the battle had begun, the

battlefield lay quiet. The fallen had dotted the land, but all of the friendlies had already been brought in, the enemies placed in groups. If Momar's people wanted to come collect their dead, Kingsley would allow them to do it peacefully. He would not deny them the right to grieve.

So many of his men and women had been lost, yet it was far from the total annihilation that would've happened if they hadn't had Austin and Jessie's help. They'd cleared out all but a portion of the other side. Those who'd run at the first sign of the spell's failure had gotten away. Anyone who had waited long enough to realize the battle was not going their way had been chased down by the basajaunak or gargoyles. Those creatures did not give quarter.

He kept his posture straight and mannerisms stoic, the rock his people would need right now, as he walked through town. He placed his hand on shoulders and took a moment to share grief with any who needed it. Finally, he made it to the square, to the injured warriors who were still hanging on.

This was what he'd been dreading.

He'd heard what happened. He'd seen his brother sprint back toward town as soon as they knew they were assured a victory. He'd looked like a man breaking.

What he found in the square stopped him short,

though.

Gargoyles, shifters, and basajaunak sat in every available space, surrounding the wounded and filling the square. Warriors and civilians alike spilled into the streets and back between shops and buildings. They all held hands, many with eyes closed, softly swaying to a soft hum that rose above them all. Even the flowers had joined in, swaying with the people.

The cots were full with bloodied people, most of them lying still but all looking in the same direction.

"Hey," Kingsley said, stopping by the first cot.

Eunice, a wolf shifter, shook her head, flicking her eyes to him. "I'm focused on the connection, alpha."

Confused, Kingsley nodded and moved on to the next bed, where he was told something similar.

"What connection?" he finally asked after receiving the same answer for the third time.

"The connection with Alpha Ironheart," the wounded shifter said, closing his eyes. "She's still there. She'll feel us. She'll feel our support through the connection."

He threaded his way to Jessie now, finding his brother sitting at her side, bent over her with his eyes closed, tears dripping freely down his cheeks. Kingsley stopped and let out a breath before composing himself again. Given Austin wasn't raging, she must still be alive, but Kingsley had no idea how. Not with that extent of damage to her person. She must've gone through literal hell to get the job done.

The female mage—Nessa—stood at Jessie's feet. She swayed and hummed softly, determination on her face. The rest of Jessie's crew sat just behind her, holding on to one another, even the butler and the puca holding hands with heads bowed, eyes closed.

"If you aren't helping, you need to find somewhere else to be," Nessa said without opening her eyes.

Kingsley looked around for whom she might be talking to, finally catching the healer's gaze. Sitting by Jessie's side, Indigo had her hands on her charred thigh.

"She means you," she said matter-of-factly. "You need to connect, or you need to leave."

"What—" Kingsley stopped when Austin's eyes drifted open, and the ragged sorrow and desperation in them nearly buckled his knees.

Austin looked at Jessie's face, more tears dripping down his cheeks.

"Please, baby," he said, his voice raw. "Please, don't leave me. Don't go where I can't follow. Please come back to me." He bent over again, his voice shaking. "Please," he whispered, over and over. "*Please.*"

It was Nessa's turn to open her eyes, her expression and bearing suddenly hostile.

"You will sit and connect, or you will be removed," she ground out.

Tristan appeared by Kingsley's side, no one caring even an iota about his alpha status. The gargoyle put a hand on his shoulder.

"Those who were in danger of dying have been seen to," he told Kingsley softly. "Indigo left Jessie for long enough to heal them. It's what Jessie would've wanted. No one else needs your attention right now. If you want to help, Nessa is orchestrating the crowd's energy to try to get through to Jessie. Those who are connected to her gargoyle are trying to reach her that way, as well. It would mean a lot to all of us if you stayed, but we know you have duties."

"Of course I'll stay," Kingsley said, not sure what energy thing they were talking about but assuming someone would show him.

The vampire drifted closer, clasping his fingers, his eyes haunted.

"This way, sir." He directed Kingsley to a group of his pack who'd fought bravely on the front line, banged up but otherwise okay. They nodded to him, their eyes tight. None of them greeted him. Many of them closed their eyes after he sat down.

"It helps if you close your eyes," the vampire said, unfortunately sitting beside him. "You'll feel it quickly if you're open to it. I always feel it when my shadow is following me. It's pleasant, and it helps me keep track of her."

Aurora and Mac found him, both sitting down next to him and thankfully prompting the vampire to scoot away a little. Aurora took his hand as Mimi came over, then Earnessa and his mother. Together they bowed their heads, hand in hand.

CHAPTER 36

JESSIE

THE TUG WAS distant, almost unnoticeable. A feeling, kind of. A plea.

"Please, baby," I heard amid a strange rushing sound. "Please."

I struggled to take a deep breath. Decided I didn't really want to because that hurt too much. Floating in the blackness was so much nicer. I just had to thoroughly let go.

"*Please.*"

It was the tone that stopped me. The despair. The *anguish.* The voice expressed the sort of emotional pain that I felt physically through every inch of my body.

I took that breath, fire raging through me. Crap, that hurt like the bejesus. I didn't want any more of that.

But the voice kept begging. Kept pulling at me.

And energy swirled around me, carrying support and well wishes, offering a hand out of the blackness.

That was nice. My connections were also lit up, energy flowing from them, filling me with a rushing sound. If only it didn't hurt so damn much...

I floated for a while longer, that voice still reaching me, the pleas constant. It made my heart hurt. I sensed great loss in it. Loss I didn't want. A connection I didn't want to leave.

Oh man, this was going to suck.

I took another deep breath, and another, trying to ignore the horrible pain that came with it, growing and growing until it was too much for me. I couldn't handle it.

After a break, I tried again. How the hell could the pain still be growing? This couldn't be natural.

I pushed to the surface, hating every minute of it.

The rushing sound increased, so loud now, until it popped. Humming caught my ears then, soft and delicate and all around me, sung by many voices. Then that voice, that plea.

Handling the pain for a moment before I took another break, I forced my eyes open.

Austin.

He held a hand I couldn't feel, bent over me, his tears dropping onto my chest. Sunlight streamed through the blue above me, behind one fluffy cloud. It almost looked like a dragon, that cloud. That was probably a good omen.

I didn't dare move my head to look around. Didn't need to anyway. All I wanted to look at was that face, so handsome. Mine. My mate, staying beside me.

I struggled to say his name, but my jaw wouldn't work. So I garbled instead.

His head snapped up, and I saw clean streaks down his cheeks where the tears had washed away dirt and grime. Hope filled his gaze.

"Oh baby, thank God," he said, his other hand joining his first, though mine was still numb. "Oh thank God. Hold on, Jess. Please hold on. Indigo can help, okay? Just hang on a little longer and Indigo can help you. Keep fighting, baby. Keep fighting for me."

"Yes! She's giving me her lifeline," another voice said, strangely distorted. "She's giving me enough to work with. Hang on, Jessie, I got this, okay? I showed up for work today. I got it."

It was all too confusing. Maybe because it hurt so damn much. I needed a break.

As the darkness welcomed me again, I knew it would be temporary this time. Just a break, and I'd try again.

THE NEXT TIME I awoke was so much better. It didn't hurt nearly as much. The setting was different, though.

Now I was inside, surrounded by smells I recognized. Filtered light came through a window to my right and somewhere beyond my feet. A heavy weight lay across my middle and warmth seeped into the skin on my left.

I fluttered my eyes open, taking stock of my surroundings. Austin's living room.

I lay on a cot with white sheets up to my waist, still in my gargoyle form. The weight was Austin's arm, across my middle. He sat beside the cot and was bent over, sleeping soundly on a sliver of cot at my side. His hair was wild and dirty, his face tear-streaked and grimy, and wounds and muck crawled out of his T-shirt neck and sleeve lines. He hadn't cleaned himself up. He probably hadn't left my side.

"Good afternoon." Nessa stood from the couch, fatigue heavy in her features. She dropped a book to the side. "How are you feeling?"

I opened my mouth, remembering how much my jaw had hurt. It didn't feel so bad anymore, not that I could talk with it. I'd need to shift back to human, but given the pain still radiating around my body, that didn't seem like a great idea.

A tube ran from a needle in my arm to a medical bag on a stand to my right.

"That's to make sure you get plenty of fluids," Nessa said, coming closer. "You lost a lot of blood. Like…a *lot* of blood. Stupid amounts of it. But Indigo says you're out of the woods now. You're going to be okay."

Memories lay strewn around my head. Images. Pain. All I could really remember right now was pain.

"Sleep," Ivy House said. *"Sleep for a while longer until you have the strength to heal. Your mate will guard you."*

I did as she said, closing my eyes once more.

And then opening them again a moment later. Except the light was different this time, and it was Sebastian on the couch instead of Nessa. Someone else stood at my head, and Austin was sitting up in his chair, just as dirty as before. So exhausted looking, like he'd been awake for days.

"Here, sir, you need this." The presence at my head stepped around, and I saw that it was Mr. Tom holding a plate. "You need to keep your strength up so you are nice and healthy when she wakes up."

Austin's eyes were glued to mine, and the look in them made me want to cry. I couldn't explain it with words, but I felt it in my heart.

This time I confronted the pain and shifted, things popping and cracking and creaking, agony lighting me up.

"No, Jess, careful," he said, his voice scratchy, like he'd been screaming. Or crying.

I breathed heavily after the shift was done, things not quite right in my body. My leg felt all messed up, for one, and my arms were tingly in a way that said *danger*. Still, I had magic and energy. I could heal this.

Getting to work, still so tired but no longer in as much pain, I struggled to swallow.

"Oh heavens." Mr. Tom dropped the plate. It crashed on the floor, breaking. "Water. Wait there, miss, I'll get you water. Get out of the way," he yelled at someone. "She needs water!"

Austin's smile was a thing of beauty. "He always did drop everything for you."

The memories pieced themselves together—of what happened, of what we'd done.

"Nathanial?" I asked. It hurt a little to talk. My jaw still wasn't right.

Austin put his hand on my shoulder. "He didn't make it, Jess. He didn't survive getting through that spell."

Emotion welled up and sobs racked my body. "He sacrificed himself so that I would make it." I labored to get it out.

"He's a hero," Austin said as Ulric walked to my right with Jasper in tow.

Ulric put his hand on the cot beside me. "He would've been relieved that you made it," he said, his own eyes swimming in tears. "He would've been happy to know that his sacrifice saved you, and then you were able to save us all."

"He was selfless," Jasper said as Mr. Tom hurried back with a cup and straw. "He's always been selfless. When you're better, Jessie, we'll honor him, okay? But you need to get better."

"And the rest?" I asked, squeezing Austin's hand tightly. "Did we do it? Did we lose anyone else?"

"Just rest now, okay?" Austin patted my hand. "Rest. We won, and Kingsley's people are safe."

WHEN I AWOKE next, it was to darkness. I had a flashback of flying, of desperately seeking those mages, of shadowy figures holding blasters. I jolted, startled, my magic rising.

"*Shh, shhhh.*" A familiar hand smoothed my hair from my face. "It's okay. I'm here."

I could barely make out Austin's face in the darkness. His other hand still held mine. A loud bang sounded from somewhere in the house. A shape rose from the couch.

"I'm here!" Mr. Tom ran into the room in a sleeping gown and a matching hat with a little tassel at the end. "Candles. I'll get candles!"

Flame danced above Cyra's held-out palm, revealing

her on the couch. She beamed at me. "Jessie! It's really good to see you."

"What time is it?" I asked as Mr. Tom came back in with a lit candle, stopping by my feet and looking at me.

"Welcome back, miss. It's just after midnight. How do you feel? You didn't get a chance to drink any water last time—would you like some now?"

"You've been out for six days," Cyra said. "I've been counting because that seems like a really long time for humans, and it was making me nervous."

"Six days?" I asked.

"You had a lot of healing to do." Austin's thumb continued to move over my forehead, not any cleaner than before. He hadn't changed his clothes, either. It was clear he hadn't left my side for long enough to wash off the battle.

My heart ached for him. For what he must've gone through. For how much I loved him.

"You need to look after yourself, baby," I told him, falling into his gaze. He shook his head, but I pushed. "I'm okay now. I feel a lot better. You need to shower and get some sleep, and then we'll get up together, okay? Look after yourself, and before long we can continue our lives."

Tears caught in my lashes. The thought of continuing our lives reminding me of Nathanial, of his last emotions through the bond—pride and honor.

"Okay," Austin said, leaning forward to kiss me softly. "After you fall asleep, I'll go shower, okay?"

"Yes, the miss doesn't want to wake up to a stinky mate," Mr. Tom said, still acting as a candleholder. "I am perfectly capable of sitting beside her, as I've told you multiple times."

I laughed through my tears, hardly feeling the pain at all now, my healing magic up to speed. I squeezed Austin's hand, waited while Mr. Tom literally ran to get me water, spilling candle wax on himself, and then allowed sleep to take me once more. Next time, I'd get up, and we'd do what Nathanial had made possible.

We'd continue living.

EPILOGUE

JESSIE

I T HAD TAKEN two weeks for me to get back to one hundred percent, a helluva long time for a creature who heals quickly and has magical healing abilities. But I'd grown up as a Jane, so I couldn't stop marveling over the fact that I was up and moving. Nor could I forget that one of us was not.

Nathanial's body had been sent home to his family so they could bury him in their family plot in their cairn. Today Kingsley would host his memorial, a tribute to the hero who had saved all our lives. Kingsley had tried to put me in the tribute as well, but I'd respectfully declined his offer. I was only alive because of Nathanial. I wouldn't have made it if he hadn't shielded me and protected my wings. While the fall had broken my limbs, a full-on plummet would've broken my head.

"Are you kidding me?" Nessa yelled from the kitchen.

When I poked my head in, I saw her fuming down at a note. She shook it at me with a furrowed brow.

"Do you see what he does?" She kept shaking it. "He preys on my confidence by giving me notes on my cooking. Just because he won that cookoff last week, he thinks he's Mr. Almighty Chef. Well, screw him, you know? I'll get him next time."

Austin came up behind me, curling his arm around my waist and pulling me back into him. He didn't like to be far apart from me right now. I'd given him a scare that would probably haunt him for a long time. Given how close I'd come, and the reality that he was the one who'd tugged me back from the brink—with an extra push from everyone else—I was happy for the constant PDA.

"You won't," he said, laughing, his hand splayed across my tummy. "You'll try again and you'll get spanked again."

She slammed the note onto the counter. "A score of five to three isn't getting spanked, and anyway, Jessie shouldn't have been allowed to vote. She's biased."

"No, it was just—"

"No, no." She stopped me. "You're biased. I want a redo."

"Anytime." He stepped back and turned, waiting for

me to fall in at his side. "C'mon, let's go. We don't want to be late."

I stalled after opening the door, my jaw dropping open. This was the first time I'd gone out—the first time I'd even looked out the front door. Bouquets of flowers covered the porch, piled up next to the door and rested on the steps. Only a small area had been left uncovered to allow people in and out of the house. More flowers had been arranged beside the walkway, and petals littered the concrete.

"What's all this?" I asked, picking my way through.

"The pack's way of saying thank you," Austin said, following me. "You might not feel entitled to a tribute, but they think you are. They're showing you their gratitude for what you did."

I shook my head, my heart swelling. "I just killed a couple of mages. Nathanial did the rest."

"You have to stop deflecting," he told me softly, walking to the car. "Nathanial played an integral part in taking down that spell, but he didn't do it alone. You nearly died to save this pack. You need to let them honor that."

My hands shook as I sat into the car. "That was my duty," I said when he got in. The mages got into the back. We'd meet everyone else there.

"You were willing to give your life for your duty."

Austin started the car. "Glory Days" started playing its continual loop. "It's one thing to do it in the heat of battle, but it's another to make a calculated decision you knew would likely kill you. Not many people would."

"You would."

"But I didn't have to prove it. You did."

I leaned against the headrest and took his hand when he offered it. We'd lost quite a few people across our various factions. Our numbers had been somewhat evenly matched, but they'd brought plenty of us down with guns and magic before their line broke. Gerard's gargoyles had fared the worst. They'd gone in hot and heavy, too stubborn to think the magic or guns could kill them. Still, they'd also bagged the most enemies. Our people had done the best, having learned their limit the hard way. In the end, though, it had been a victory. The children had been saved, one and all, and the enemy would be in no position for Round Two for some time. Even if they wanted to come back for a reprisal, we'd seriously slashed their numbers.

We arrived at the square, the mood in the car somber. My crew was waiting to the side for us. Each of them touched me as we reached them. That was a new thing they did. I guess they just wanted to assure themselves that I had actually made it back from the brink and wasn't a ghost.

"I never got a chance to thank you," I told Indigo, who hadn't stopped by the house. She'd been busy wandering the town, talking to the grieving. Her healing abilities went beyond piecing together flesh, it turned out. I hugged her, holding on tightly for a moment. "You saved my life."

"Well…" She shrugged. "Not really. I just kept you from drifting farther away. You saved your own life. And my life. All of our lives."

"Do women just not allow themselves to be thanked for saving lives?" Austin asked, looking between us. "Is that some sort of default you're programmed with?"

"I'm sorry about Nathanial," Indigo said, ignoring him. "When he got to me, it was already too late. There was nothing I could do."

"I know. And I heard about you leaving me so you could help the others who needed it. That was the right choice. Thank you for allowing Ulric and Jasper to force you to do it."

"They told you that, did they?" Her eyes narrowed, and she shot the guys a *look*. "I guess they'll find out the hard way what it means when I say, 'Snitches get stitches…'"

Ulric put his hands up. "She was going to find out."

"It's not *her* I'm worried about." She glanced at Austin.

"Point made," Jasper murmured.

Austin directed me on, always touching me, through the crowded street and to the square, standing room only. The crowd parted for us, people bowing to me as we walked by. "Alpha," they said to me respectfully, then repeated the sentiment to Austin.

A little stage had been set up on the grass at the top of the square, and the photos of the fallen were displayed in picture frames stuck into the ground. In the front at the center was Nathanial's picture, and the wound inside of me opened all over again. Tears trickled down my cheeks as I stopped in front of him, putting out my fingers to touch his photo.

"Thank you, Nathaniel, for your sacrifice," I said. "You showed your courage and your honor. Your loyalty. You helped me in a way no one else could. I will miss you at my back, my friend. I will miss you in the house. I will see you again in the afterlife."

I took the tissue Mr. Tom offered and continued on to the next photo, and then the next, giving each of them a silent moment and thanking each for their courage and sacrifice. Afterward, Austin directed me up onto the stage with Kingsley, and we faced all those who'd gathered for the ceremony.

"My brother and his mate came to us in our time of need," Kingsley said in a booming voice. "Knowing what we would face, even though *we* still didn't fully comprehend the danger, they brought their people and helped us train for the worst. When the battle came, a battle unlike anything we ever could've imagined, they stayed by our sides to ensure our victory. They are not simply a pack. They are not simply a gargoyle cairn. They are something different. Something unique. A convocation. In this new, larger organization, I think we can all agree that there are no alphas fitter for their roles than Austin Steele and Jessie Ironheart. It does me proud to see my brother elevate himself to such heights, even if I am a little jealous that he got the lion's share of the ruthlessness in battle."

"The bear's share!" someone shouted to a smattering of laughter.

"Let any of you naysayers be silenced now," Kingsley went on, "because it is my intention to join their convocation. As we saw, we are stronger together. We are unstoppable when united. I will remain your alpha, and we will remain a pack, but we will also be a part of something larger. An organization that will stand up to magical tyrants like the one who tried to destroy us. What say you?"

A loud cheer went up, everyone raising their hands, shouting. I widened my eyes at Austin. I hadn't heard Kingsley would be doing this. He nodded, obviously having talked it over with his brother.

When they quieted down, Kingsley turned and motioned toward Gerard and the basandere waiting on the other side. They climbed the steps and stood beside Kingsley.

"Gerard of the Khaavalor cairn, I thank you for your help. You had no connection to us, but you came to us in a time of need. From now on, you are a pack friend. Should you need us, call, and we will be there."

"Thank you." Gerard wore a crooked grin. "And thanks for having us. Really, I mean it. In that battle, it felt like we were finally doing what we were *made* for. I've never felt so alive as I did when defending this territory. We don't have a fancy term for it, but the feeling is mutual. When you need help, we're your gargoyles. And we, too, will be joining the convocation. It's time we saw more of what exists outside of our lonely mountain."

Gargoyles cheered now, some making *ou-ou-ou* sounds.

"*Her*," Kingsley continued when the noise died down. "Thank you. Your basajaunak are fearless and your leadership something to aspire to. You are a pack friend, and should you need our help, do not hesitate to ask."

The basandere bowed to him before facing the

crowd. "My clan has been isolated for many years, not wanting to partake in the changing world and its troubles. But being part of a larger team has brought energy to us all. We mourn the losses of those we loved. Like the gargoyles, however, we felt the calling of unity. We, too, will be joining the convocation."

Surprise lit up my bonds with Austin, and Kingsley startled. Clearly they hadn't been expecting that.

The basandere asked to get closer to me, and Kingsley stepped out of the way. She took my hand, her eyes solemn. "You have proven that you put your people above yourself. You expect nothing, while giving everything. You are worthy of our loyalty. You are family now."

She bent to put her forehead against mine, and I started crying yet again. When she stepped to the side, Kingsley went on.

"And let's not forget the late additions to our team who showed you don't need wings or fur to fight like a warrior."

Patty and Aunt Florence climbed the steps with wide smiles.

"I don't think we've ever known someone whom an entire territory calls aunt," Kingsley said, gesturing at Aunt Florence. The crowd laughed and cheered. "You ladies stepped into a role that was foreign to you, in a place you'd never been before, with magical creatures with which you were unfamiliar. And despite that, you made lasting friendships, glued everyone together, put on one helluva barbecue, and protected the town from every last enemy, all without batting an eye. You are remarkable, ladies, all of you, and we are proud to have you among us. You are all granted the title of pack friend, and we hope you visit us often."

Patty grabbed Aunt Florence's hand and lifted it into the air, laughing.

After they stepped back, I was gobsmacked to see Edgar climb up the steps, Indigo behind him, her head ducked shyly.

"I never, in all my wildest dreams, thought I'd say this, but thank you, Edgar, for your magical killing flowers. The flowers on the perimeter took down a good many enemies. The flowers in the square provided protection and…companionship is the only way I can express it. Before that, they killed the strange creatures who had been plaguing us. Thank you."

Creatures no one had seen in the battle or since. Sebastian and Nessa were trying to learn more.

Edgar clasped his hands and bowed to the crowd. "Thanks you to been here."

He wasn't the best at public speaking.

"Indigo," Kingsley went on without skipping a beat.

"You saved a great many lives. You worked tirelessly during the battle and have been a saving grace to those hurting in the fallout. I speak for the pack when I say, from the bottom of our hearts, thank you for helping us grieve."

She nodded mutely, hunched, as though physically trying to ward off the attention.

Once they'd all cleared away, Kingsley turned to me, his eyes serious, and enveloped me in a tight hug.

"Thank you," he said softly, rocking me slightly. "If you hadn't saved my brother a year ago and worked to get all these creatures on your team, my pack and my family would've been lost. You've saved us all, and not just by your heroic act in the battle." He pulled back, his eyes shining. "I owe you a debt I doubt I can ever repay."

"Just stay in your brother's life, that's all I ask," I replied, my tears not stopping. "Keep your family together."

He smiled, a rare treat. "I think it's you and Mimi who'll likely do that, but sure, why not."

He faced everyone again, his arm around my shoulders. "There are drinks and refreshments at Hide Park, recently renamed by the garhettes and adopted in tribute. Please, help yourself. Thank you all for coming and honoring those who perished while protecting this town."

"Oh…" I stopped Kingsley as everyone started to exit the stage. "Actually, I take that back. You can repay me by not killing me after you learn how Hide Park got its name."

A line formed between his brows, and I hurried off the stage before he asked questions. Clearly people had been keeping him in the dark about the whole gnome situation. Thank goodness.

"Jessie, a word?"

Sebastian waited a little off to the side, wearing a black suit without any flare or even a watch. Nessa stood beside him, and their faces were closed down in guilt and grief.

"Yeah, what's up?" I asked, meeting them.

"I know you don't want to hear how sorry I am," Sebastian said, and I sucked in a breath. He blamed himself for having missed the mark on predicting how the attack would go down. It was a stupid thing to be upset about. How could he have known? How could any of us have known? "I wanted to thank you for taking us in." He gestured between Nessa and himself. Nessa nodded. "Like everyone, we found an open and receptive family with all of you. I've enjoyed working within Ivy House and enjoyed trying to beat my fear of shifters. But I am unsettled by how much Momar's operations and abilities have changed and grown. He was able to protect secrets that should've been too big to protect. Nessa and I have work to do. A lot of work. We can't risk this happening again. We won't be going back to O'Briens with you."

"What?" I asked, aghast. "Why? You can do your work from there. You don't have to leave."

They both shook their heads.

"We're going to have to go mobile for a while," Nessa said. "Serious shadow mode. We need to make new friends and do new terrible deeds. We can't do that within the safety and comfort of O'Briens. But it'll be fine, okay? We won't be gone forever, and people aren't going to be bothering you for a while. They'll circle you. Let them. I'll reach out with an encrypted line so you can get in touch. If you get any invitations for dinner, let me know and I'll tell you if it's dangerous or not. After this, you're going to be the new big power on campus. When things rev up again, you'll want us to be much better prepared. Until then, take a break. You've earned it."

I hugged Nessa. "Thank you for what you did when I was on the edge. I felt the energy. I think you have a gift."

She shrugged. "No more so than Janes who do healing energy, but I'm glad it worked. Sometimes it does more than others."

I shook my head, just about to launch into a long list of reasons why they wouldn't be leaving, but the look in Sebastian's eyes stopped me. The hurt. The uncertainty. He needed to set himself to rights and get his bearings. I felt that about him. And I needed to support him.

For a little while, at least. There was no way I'd allow him to stay gone for too long.

So I nodded, stopped myself from crying, and hugged him tightly. "Take care of yourself, okay? Don't do anything too terrible. And if you need help, I'm always there. Okay? Don't be gone long."

I watched them disappear into the crowd, feeling like I was losing them, too.

"Today sucks," I said, folding myself into Austin's arms.

"The last two weeks have sucked. Let's go drink some basajaunak brew and try to forget."

"Sounds good." I angled my face up for a kiss. He complied quickly. "I love you," I told him.

"I will love you for eternity."

✧   ✧   ✧

NESSA

NIAMH AND THE rest of the Ivy House crew slowly walked toward the park, apparently not planning to drive. She and Sebastian stopped beside them.

"Okay," Nessa said. "This is it. We're out."

"Wait, right *now*?" Ulric held out his hands like he aimed to hold them back. "No way. Let's go to the park. You can leave when we all leave. There's no rush."

"There's definitely a rush," Sebastian replied. "Momar's people are scattered every which way, and he's got to be pissed. We need to get in there."

Ulric wrapped Nessa into a tight hug, then wrangled Sebastian for one as well.

"This is stupid," Jasper said, hugging her as well. "We never even got to bang. I thought you said you were going to save me a ride?"

"Rain check," Nessa said, pointing at him with a grin.

"That's what you said last time." He pouted.

After saying goodbye to the others, she found Brochan and spread her arms. This time he actually bent to hug her. She breathed him in, feeling their energy kindle but not set fire.

"Stay safe," he said, pulling back.

"Of course. Try not to dwell too much, okay?" She

gave him a wink with a smile.

His eyes didn't sparkle as he beheld her. "Check in with Jessie. Call her if you guys need help. Try not to do anything…that you'll regret."

She took a deep breath. He only wanted the best for her, she knew that, but he didn't seem to understand that regrets were part of the job. They always had been. Regrets beat out death as an outcome, always.

"Okay," she said.

He nodded and turned, not looking back as he walked away. Heart heavy, hating that they had to leave, she headed back toward Sebastian. Halfway there, Tristan stepped out in front of her.

"Leaving without saying goodbye?" he asked, standing too close.

The hum between them sparked to life, which was seriously annoying. She had no idea why he had this effect on her. She didn't want to be attracted to a dangerous creature she couldn't trust, even if he had helped save Jessie's life.

He studied her silently for a moment, his gaze flicking between them. In a moment, he put out his arms. "A hug for an old friend?"

She quirked an eyebrow. "An old friend…or a new enemy?"

"How about an old enemy? It has a better ring to it."

She sighed, did a poor job of hiding her smile, and stepped into him. His hands slid up and down her back and then pulled her in tightly.

"I'll be keeping track of you," he murmured. "If you get into trouble, I'll know. Just wait and I'll be there, okay?"

"You think you'll be able to keep track of me?"

He stepped back, his large hands on her upper arms, his glowing eyes hyper-focused. "Yes. Listen to me: if you need something—anything at all—you contact me, do you understand? You don't brave it alone. You and Sebastian are no longer an island. Call us and we will come, for any reason. Okay?"

The sentiment choked her up, and she dropped all her bravado and all her walls, allowing herself to tear up. She nodded like a child, and he wrapped her into his big body again.

"I know what you are," he murmured, his lips against her ear, "and I like you. A lot. You are a good person with a big heart, Natasha, and I don't want to hear that you've been getting down on yourself, okay? If you can't find the sunshine, just call me. I'll help."

"Stop saying the right things."

"Okay. Fancy a fuck before you go? I didn't make you beg *nearly* enough the other night."

She leaned back and slapped him across the face. He

laughed, letting it happen, before poking her in the chest.

"Take care of your brother," he said.

She put up her hand for a high five, gratified when it landed. "See ya."

He watched her walk away. She felt it.

Nearly to the car they planned to take—the one with the least annoying stuck CD—she ran into Austin's niece, right on time.

"Hey." She stopped in front of the young woman before fishing a key out of her pocket. "Naomi tells me you want to go back with Austin and Jessie but that your dad put his foot down because it's too dangerous."

Aurora looked at her silently, no expression. She could give Brochan a run for his money on that front.

"Well..." Nessa dangled the key between them. "I need a house sitter, and you're twenty-five. How about this—I won't pay you, and in exchange I'll give you all the information you need to get there without anyone telling the alphas until it's too late. I got a line on a basajaun who loves to cause mischief. I'll give you a hint—he's the one in the kilt."

"What does my being twenty-five have anything to do with it?" Aurora asked after a silent beat.

"You're no longer a child. Stop asking your daddy for permission and take charge of your life."

Nessa dropped the key. Aurora's hand darted out and snatched it from the air.

"It's got good soil in the backyard," Nessa said, walking away. "Plant a garden."

"How will I know…which one it is?" Aurora called.

"I've already emailed the particulars. Good luck! Have loud and wild parties!"

Nessa met Sebastian at the car and then slid into the driver's seat.

"Ready?" she asked.

"Very. It's time to remind the magical world what Elliot Graves is really like."

THE END

About the Author

K.F. Breene is a Wall Street Journal, USA Today, Washington Post, Amazon Most Sold Charts and #1 Kindle Store bestselling author of paranormal romance, urban fantasy and fantasy novels. With millions of books sold, when she's not penning stories about magic and what goes bump in the night, she's sipping wine and planning shenanigans. She lives in Northern California with her husband, two children, and out of work treadmill.

Sign up for her newsletter to hear about the latest news and receive free bonus content.

www.kfbreene.com